FOLLOWING
FATE

BOOK TWO OF THE FATE UNRAVELED TRILOGY

M. A. FRICK

ALSO BY M.A. FRICK

The Fate Unraveled Trilogy:
Forcing Fate
Following Fate
Fulfilling Fate
***

The Dragon's Heart:
Between Flames and Deceit
***

Standalones:
The Petulant Princess

To Ali.
You gave me the confidence to fly.

CHAPTER 1

Searing pain engulfed my left side, tearing a groan from my throat. I tried to roll into myself to escape the sensation, but my right hip screamed in protest. I hissed, baring my teeth as my eyes cracked open.

Cold, hard stone dug into my back. Wind howled, but I couldn't see the sky. The burning in my side intensified, and I winced, closing my eyes again.

Where was I?

Careful to only move my neck and head, I braved a glance at my surroundings. There was nothing but darkness to my left, and to my right, moonlight streamed in from an opening in a rock wall. A cave.

The moon's silver glow illuminated a large dragon, guarding the cave's mouth. It lay curled around itself, its gray scales blending with the cave floor. Its face was relaxed in slumber, and it rumbled as its nostrils released a hot puff, sending a hiss of steam into the cold.

I whimpered as another flare of agony cascaded through me. My breaths grew faint. I struggled to keep my eyes open. Part of me fought to hang on, to make sense of this, but the rest of me wanted to escape the torment and let go. Darkness pulled me under.

"Avyanna."

I gasped. Awareness crashed over me. Scalding pain ricocheted across my hip and side. I flinched, but the sudden movement sparked throbbing torment. My eyes squeezed shut, and I clenched my tunic.

"Avyanna. Come to me, little one."

"Jam?" I breathed. My head rolled toward the voice. Any more effort than that, and I was sure I would pass out again.

"We're getting you out of here."

I couldn't see him. Darkness enveloped everything in shadow, and my head felt as if it was split in two. I attempted to shift my leg, then cried out as a fresh wave of agony threatened to tear me apart.

"I can't move."

"Don't," he said. "Tell the dragon we're trying to help. Call it off."

With great care, I faced the sleeping beast. I felt nothing toward it.

"I can't."

"You have to try."

"I can't, Jam. I'm not bonded to it."

Another wave overcame me. I barely registered Jam's heavy sigh as my pain screamed, demanding my attention. My side pulsated, seething as if someone tore into it with teeth and claws. A heaviness settled in my chest, working its way through my body. My hip throbbed, a crushing ache, as if something had broken.

Agony sank into my bones and the world faded away, quieting the pain—and bringing me rest.

"Curse it all, wake up!"

A sharp sting to my cheek jerked me awake. I screamed, reeling as every nerve radiated from the jolt. I grabbed at the hand, but it slipped through my wet fingers. Confusion warred against my anguish. I blinked, attempting to clear the shadowed haze from my vision. Blood soaked my hands.

The cave shook as the dragon roared in outrage. Flames spewed from its maw, lighting the space in a burst of flickering amber.

Zephath crouched beside me, disgust souring his features. "Call it off!" he shouted over the chaos.

The dragon screeched and lashed its tail at something trying to enter the cave.

"I can't," I whispered.

Why did they think the dragon was bonded to me? Because it didn't kill me? Because it snatched me away, tearing my body and discarding it like a kill?

"Yes, you *can!*"

The back of my head tingled. Steep, fiery rage ignited within me as my vision went red. How dare he enter this cave? I was sleeping peacefully, free of this agony! And he woke me to shout at me? To hurt me?

Small rocks shook loose off the walls as the dragon screamed its fury.

"You're bonded! Calm it down!"

A shout echoed the dragon's wrath, and a sense of victory incited my resolve. Whoever tried to get in had been disarmed. It was only fair! They were trying to wake me, trying to hurt me!

"Don't you sense it? Emotions, thoughts that aren't yours? Come on! It's in your head! Calm it down!"

My glare darkened. "You don't know what you're talking about." I bit the words out past my pain.

Outrage danced through me, consuming and feral. If I wasn't so weak, I would have slapped him.

After a shrill cry, the dragon spun, advancing on us. Zephath scurried back, and the beast narrowed its glare. It ignored my feeble body, standing over me as it opened its mouth.

"General!" Zephath screamed, scrambling from the spray of flame.

I peeked up at the dragon's stone-colored underbelly. *Was* I bonded to it? I struggled to scrap together the broken fragments of hours passed. There'd been a flash of light and terrible pain—as if someone cleaved my head open with an ax. It snared me with sharp claws, lifting me from the snow. I fought against it, and its talons gouged my side. I remembered the frigid, agonizing flight, then waking in the cave.

"Stop," I whispered.

Rage. Hatred. Fear.

I recognized those feelings as it chased Zephath to the mouth of the cave and he tumbled out.

Victory. Satisfaction.

General Rafe burst inside, followed by Dane and Xzanth. They rushed the dragon as Jamlin tore in behind.

Irritation. Annoyance.

Rafe dove under the dragon's chest as it charged the new warriors entering its domain. He rolled to a stop a breath away and assessed me before glancing at the beast.

"Can you halt it?" His words rushed as his gaze darted over the scene before him.

I glared up at him. Could he not be nice, even now? I was bleeding on a cave floor, and he couldn't bother to be polite. How irritating.

His fingers dug into my shoulder, giving me a rough shake. Pain pried another scream past my clenched teeth. The dragon whirled on us.

"Stop it!" he bit out.

I whimpered, fighting to take in breaths as I stared into his dark eye. "I can't."

It seemed as if time itself halted. In that moment, urgency and concern radiated across his features. He wouldn't leave me. He would die here, with his men, trying to rescue me.

"Go!"

I blinked as he shouted, not taking his eye off me, and time resumed.

"Go! All of you! Out!" he bellowed, and leapt to his feet, facing the oncoming dragon.

Dane and the others froze in horror, but obeyed and rushed to retreat. The dragon charged, snaking its long neck toward Rafe with its slender tongue extended in a hiss.

Rafe let out a guttural growl and ripped off the cloth concealing his shadow-touched eye. "Be still, beast." His voice carried weight—a sense of command and order. He demanded obedience and would accept nothing less.

With a sharp whine, the dragon stopped short, pulling up its head and slamming it into the ceiling. It sat back on its haunches, tail thrashing.

Betrayal. Hurt. Guilt.

"You will not harm us. You will not touch us." Rafe's silver eye glinted, reflecting moonlight.

He was commanding the dragon.

And the dragon was listening.

Sweat beaded his skin. Tension, thick and quiet, consumed the space as the dragon stilled.

Rage. Irritation. Trickery.

"You will fly with us. You will not attack humans." His voice, though commanding, was strained—as if his strength faltered.

Trapped. Fear. Hatred.

Rafe's shoulders drooped, and he gasped like he just ran a footrace. He dropped to a knee, and I studied him, weary and weak. The dragon seethed and hissed, but made no move to attack. He gave me an exhausted smile and placed a finger on my lips.

"Not a word," he rasped.

I stared, both in horror and realization. His smile fell, and he shifted to sit beside me, locking his eyes on the beast. It flinched and dug its claws into the ground, crumbling the stone beneath it. It curled its lips, baring sharp teeth.

Rafe grunted, fingers gripping his head. The pain in my side screamed in protest as I rested my blood-covered hand on his thigh. When his reluctant gaze pulled to mine, I realized the sacrifice he'd made. He was more exhausted than I'd ever seen. Not just his body, but his mind—depleted and empty.

He looked away, securing the cloth back over his eye. The dragon lurched, darting toward us with a speed defying its size. Its head shot forward, opening its maw, and I flinched away.

Clack!

Its jaw snapped shut in Rafe's face, spit spraying at his shoulder. A deep, rumbling growl choked from the depths of that scaled throat.

"Good dragon," Rafe muttered, standing with a groan.

I scoffed, igniting the burn in my wound. I winced, pressing my hands to the source. It wasn't the first time he controlled a dragon, yet this beast was a far cry from the hatchling he handled at Northwing. I should have been horrified by magic used against Dragon Kind. Yet, as I noted the weary bow of his massive shoulders, and his determination and concern as he looked back at me, I still trusted him.

I always knew he was dangerous. I just never knew how much so.

Rafe adjusted the sword at his hip and crouched next to me. "This is going to hurt."

There wasn't a moment to question his words before he grabbed my arm and hauled me up. I screamed, reeling as though I was being torn in two. He pulled me over his shoulders and stood. I grasped at his fur vest, clenching my fists as tightly as I could. Tears tumbled down my cheeks.

He grunted and shifted me, tearing another cry from my throat. The dragon screeched a deafening roar, shaking the cave walls. He ignored it and trudged out of the opening. I held on to my consciousness long enough to see stars twinkling in the night sky. The hurt grew too much to bear, and all thoughts slipped away. I let myself fall into darkness.

"She won't make it."

"She has to. It will eat us if she doesn't."

"Looks like it will eat us, regardless."

"It's a full day's hard ride back to Northwing. There's no way she could hold on that long."

"Stoke the fire." Rafe's demanding voice drifted into my haze.

Fire? My groggy brain pieced their words together.

Silence reigned, no one daring to speak. Soon, only the hush of people shuffling about and the crackle of flames broke the stillness.

The abyss called to me, and I let myself fall once again.

"Hold her."

I awoke with a start as weight settled on my arms and legs. Opening my eyes, I gaped at the night sky in horror.

"She's awake."

Rafe crouched beside me with a broad knife. The blade glowed red-hot, steaming in the winter air. The dragon behind him whined and scrambled around us, snapping at the men's backs. It shook the ground as it clawed at the snow and blew fire above their heads in short, angry bursts. The men gawked—fearful but determined.

Rafe ignored it. "We have to close the wound."

The dragon snaked its head behind Rafe and unleashed a fierce roar, blowing the fur on his vest, yet he didn't flinch. It snapped and flapped its wings, leaping over the men to the other side, landing behind my head.

Xzanth and Jamlin held my legs to the ground, and Dane and Tegan secured my arms and shoulders. Zephath held my head in his lap. He chewed his lip and looked away.

"No," I breathed, bringing my gaze back to Rafe.

"Be still."

I struggled against their hold. "No!" I bit out.

He moved closer, blade in hand, and I watched in horror as he brought it to my wound. I braved a look, seeing the damage done to my body. The dragon's talon dug deep into my flesh, cleaving it open. Fresh blood seeped from the wound with every breath I took. The marred flesh was as wide as two of my palms, narrowing to the center of my belly.

"We have to close it. You'll never make it to the Healers," he murmured.

Rage. Apprehension. Trapped.

I licked my dry lips. "No!" I forced the word with as much heat as I could manage.

Rafe picked up a thick strap of leather and held it to my mouth. "Bite down."

Help. Assist. Helplessness.

I flinched away from the flash of pain splitting my head. The dragon keened, whining and snapping at the men.

"Wait... Wait!" I gasped against the unrelenting ache. "Let it near me."

The others went still, watching Rafe, whose dark gaze locked on mine.

"You can't control it enough," he said, forming his words with care.

I understood his implication—*he* couldn't control it, not in front of his men. Whatever powers he possessed, they were far too similar to the Shadow Men. His Tennan might not kill him on the spot, but his life would be forfeit.

"Let it come."

I didn't know why or how, but it wanted to help. What it would do, I couldn't guess, but for some unknown reason, I trusted it.

It hissed next to Zephath, spewing spittle over him. His face contorted into a grimace.

It didn't make sense. The dragon showed far too much aggression, yet in my heart I knew it would not harm me.

"Go." Rafe pulled away, burying the blade in the snow. It sizzled and hissed as he rocked back on his heels. "Go!" he repeated.

The men released their hold. Zephath lowered my head—fear consumed every inch of his stark features. They backed a safe distance away, and the dragon paced, watching Rafe with fury. Rafe drew his sword and settled himself near my feet, laying a heavy hand on my ankle. He glared at the great dragon—a silent challenge.

"If you harm her, I'll gut you," he spat.

The dragon hissed, weaving its head a whisper above the snow. It halted to sniff at me, cautiously eyeing Rafe, and with careful steps, edged closer. It stopped, craning its large head above me, red-orange irises burning bright.

Anger. Horror. Loneliness.

It snapped at Rafe, and he shifted his grip on his sword. Snorting, it lowered, brushing its lips against my tattered tunic. It let out a short whine and nipped at the cloth. Flashing its gaze to Rafe, it sat back, as if waiting for something. Rafe leaned close, then slid the tip of his blade through my tunic. I cried out from the pain of being jostled.

The dragon snapped at us again, and Rafe angled his sword at the dragon's maw. It bared its teeth, snarling, but waited for him to finish tearing my tunic. Blood soaked my trousers and chest binding, but the wound was now exposed. Moving back, Rafe lowered his blade and returned his steady grip on my ankle. The men watched on, gripping their weapons, ready for anything.

Concern. Fear. Emptiness.

The dragon slowly lowered its head once again, eyeing Rafe before it dropped its gaze to me. It brushed its lips against my marred, naked skin and my teeth ground together. My pain retreated, my body going numb. Whether from the frigid winter air or blood loss, I didn't know, but I was thankful for the reprieve.

It flicked its forked tongue, and I hissed as it lapped against my bloodied side. Rafe's grip on my leg tightened, but the dragon ignored his tension. Instead, it huffed and settled next to me, resting its head on the snow with its lips pressed against my wound.

I closed my eyes. The heat of its breath felt so welcoming—like the warmth of flames on a wintry day. I was cold. So very, very cold.

A tug within my chest tore a gasp from me—as if a single thread tugged me toward the stars. My body twitched and spasmed. It seemed as though my entire being attached to that one thread wound tight around my heart.

It was pulled taut and yanked. Something gave way, bursting under some unknown pressure. Searing torment smothered all reason. I screamed and thrashed, writhing uncontrollably. My body was on fire, burning from the inside out.

A door opened in my mind, almost as if I viewed myself from outside, detached. Still, my body burned. The dragon must have caused it. I screamed in agony, scraping at my ribs and side, anywhere I could reach. I clawed at my skin, desperate to relieve the burn.

As quickly as it began, it stopped.

I panted and curled into myself. Pulling my knees to my chest, I locked my arms around them and sobbed. My lungs heaved for air. Terrified that pain would come again, I closed myself off from the world.

Breathe. Just breathe.

In and out. In and out.

Time passed, and I came back to myself, aware that I was no longer suffering. I was cold, but the tearing sensation in my side and the crushing ache in my hip were gone. My eyes fluttered open. Rafe crouched in front of me, sword sheathed. Behind him, the Tennan had mixed emotions written on their faces. Horror. Shock. Fear. Gratitude. Relief.

Something hard and warm pressed against my back. I rolled, seeing the dragon's head. It gazed at me with those fiery eyes and reached a paw out to me.

Rafe jerked to his feet and stepped over me, staring the beast down. He clenched the hilt of his blade, and the dragon hissed, shrinking back. It curled into a mountain of scales, watching us from twenty paces away. With a quiet growl, it relinquished me to Rafe.

Relief. Exhaustion. Simmering anger.

I studied the creature, realizing those were not *my* emotions. Those belonged to it. Why did I feel them? Was I truly bonded to it? We shared a connection, but this was unlike any bond I ever read about.

This was something entirely different.

Rafe turned to me, dropping to examine my wounds. His rough hand trailed against my skin. It was healed. No pain emanated from his gentle touch, though I wasn't without flaw.

The scar was nothing like I had ever seen, nothing that should have come from a wound like that. Raised white lines spiraled over my side and curled to my belly. It was an intelligent design, both beautiful and ugly. I placed my hand on top of Rafe's as he traced a thumb over it. Bringing his eye to mine, a pang of loss ached through my chest. I was no longer his.

I was bonded.

CHAPTER 2

I sped back to Northwing with Rafe and Xzanth as my escort. We left the rest of the Tennan behind, Rafe setting a mad pace. The dragon flew anxious circles overhead, drifting in the overcast sky. I was bonded to a dragon and therefore would be transferred to the Dragon Corps to join a Fleet.

It was unspoken, but that didn't change the fact—I was no longer part of Rafe's Tennan.

I rode Thunderbolt hard. My body was tired, but I wasn't in pain. Exhaustion lined Rafe's face, and I wondered how much it took out of him to control the beast. We were mutually silent on the lie that my bond calmed the dragon in the cave.

The secret wasn't mine to tell. He never gave me reason not to trust him. To be honest, I was thankful. There was no way I would've been able to stop it from killing one of my friends, but he did. I didn't know how it worked, but somehow he kept the dragon in check.

It swooped low overhead, and Xzanth's mount snorted nervously. The barracks' horses were accustomed to dragons, being trained to fight alongside them, but this beast was different.

It was Wild.

I peered up, finding its mottled gray and brown underbelly. I noted its tail length and wondered if it was female. Hesitantly, I tried to reach out to it, opening that odd door in my mind.

Screaming, white-hot torment answered. I fell from my saddle, and the dragon echoed my screams above. Pain assaulted me as I crashed to the ground, tumbling into the snow.

"Halt!" Rafe shouted.

Thunderbolt pranced a few paces away, rolling his eyes, as though I was the silliest thing.

Xzanth dismounted, dropping next to me. "Are you well?" he asked.

"Well enough."

I glanced at the dragon coasting in the sky. It drifted, tilting its massive head, then pinned me with an accusing glare.

Xzanth tipped his chin, studying the creature, then rose, extending his hand. I grabbed it. My body complained at the motion of being jerked back to my feet. I would be sore for a few days, thanks to that fall.

Rafe watched the dragon, ignoring me as I mounted. I refused to look at it again and rode hard. The sooner we reached Northwing, the sooner I would find out what was wrong with me—and the dragon. It didn't feel like it belonged to me. I thought when I bonded, it would be *mine*—that we'd be inseparable, like finding a long-lost friend.

Not painful—not as though I was unwelcome in our bond, a hindrance and burden. I was trapped in this with no experience to draw on, no knowledge from my research.

When I studied to become a Chosen, I reviewed every known record about dragons and their Riders. Never had a dragon bonded as an adult—only as hatchlings. Those that refused a Rider disappeared as yearlings. Wild Ones were never spotted after that.

Was that the reason our bond was broken?

The records and training portrayed dragons and their Riders as two halves of a whole. Together, they made Dragon Kind. Were we something else entirely? Did we even have a bond, in the proper sense of the term?

I was terrified to open that door back up. I didn't desire the pain that came with it. Even keeping that mental door shut, the dragon's emotions leaked to my side. I wondered if my thoughts and feelings also filtered over to it.

Heaving a heavy sigh, I tucked myself low against Thunderbolt's neck, his mane whipping at my face. I would get answers when I returned to Northwing. There were a few Riders there. Perhaps they could shed light on the situation.

The tingling at the back of my head increased to an unpleasant pressure.

I only *hoped* they could explain this.

The dragon dove in front of us, crashing into the snow with a clumsy landing. Snaking its head, it let out a hiss. The horses slid and pranced aside. Rafe pulled up short, his hand traveling to his sword hilt. Xzanth sidled up to me and reached for his bow. The dragon's eyes sparked with emotion.

Fear. Rivalry. Jealousy.

I squinted, trying to puzzle it out. We were less than a chime from the barracks, and it grew more volatile as we neared.

"What are you getting from it?" Xzanth asked as his mount danced nervously under him.

"Fear? It doesn't want me to go any further," I replied, words slow with uncertainty.

Rafe pulled on his reins, walking his stallion backward to us, keeping his eyes on the creature. "It doesn't want us to go further?" he asked.

"I don't think so."

It quieted since we stopped. Content to stand there, blocking our path.

"Tell it we're going," Rafe ordered.

I huffed, sending a cloud of fog past my lips. "I can't."

He turned his glare on me and spoke without hesitation. "I wasn't asking."

My lips dipped into a frown, and my grip on the reins tightened. I couldn't control it. And if that pain was what I'd receive as payment—I didn't want to.

Rafe's dark gaze refused to relent, and I let out a sharp curse, dismounting. I tossed the reins to Xzanth and took a few steps before settling on the snow. If I was going to fall, I would at least put myself as close to the ground as possible.

Possession. Anxiety. Anger.

I braced myself and closed my eyes, reaching for the mental door. I opened it. Pain split my head, fevered and searing. My fingers dug into my scalp as a sharp cry wrenched past my teeth. The dragon keened and whined—in pain as well.

"Stop!" I shouted.

The torment kept coming, burrowing under my skin. I lurched forward and vomited, then crumpled to my side, writhing against the onslaught squeezing my head.

Let us pass! I screamed, then slammed the door shut. Whatever that was, I wanted it locked away.

Rafe pulled his stallion up next to me and stared at the dragon. "Mount."

I grimaced, rolling away from my vomit, and wiped my face. He was being hard because he was uncomfortable with the situation. He couldn't risk controlling the creature in front of the others. I had to try.

I snatched the reins from Xzanth and mounted, angry that I was incapable—angry that I settled into the Tennan, only to be taken from it, lumped with a wild dragon with a broken bond.

Rafe led us around the beast with care, studying its every breath. It watched us, head low, with its flaming eyes plastered to me. The pupils were irate, narrow slits. Halfway past, it lurched, lashing out with its tail, swiping fast. The horses bolted out of range, but Thunderbolt leapt, knowing he couldn't move out of its path in time. The dragon's tail flicked upward and struck his belly with full force, throwing us upward.

Air rushed from my lungs on impact. I sprawled, colliding with frigid earth. The dragon whirled just as Rafe shouted something. Thunderbolt's heavy body sped toward me. A huge taloned paw batted him aside, then came down, pinning me to the snow. Its talons spread apart to avoid crushing my limbs. I jerked my head as Thunderbolt crashed to the ground. He screamed in pain, struggling in the snow.

"No!" I shouted, pushing against the thick claws.

Rafe charged, sword drawn. The dragon whipped his way, spewing flame. He dodged to the side, his stallion moving in sync with him.

"Off!" he bellowed, trying to command it.

The cloth concealed his shadow-touched eye, and the dragon paid him no heed. His stallion put on a quick burst of speed, then launched itself over the dragon's paw. Keeping itself close to the ground, it danced out of range. The dragon hissed and pulled its paw back, attention on Rafe, freeing me. I scrambled as black blood dripped onto the snow. The dragon snarled, licking at the slash on its leg where Rafe's blade made contact.

Strong hands hauled me up, and Rafe shoved me in front of him. He held me tight against his chest, and we rode like... well, like a hungry dragon was on our heels.

"Zan! Send for a Rider! Meet us at the gate!" he roared, his stallion galloping through the snow.

Xzanth wheeled his horse and took off, charging toward the barracks.

Rafe crushed against me as we leaned forward over his stallion's neck. My pulse raced, terrified of what the dragon would do next. Would it hurt Rafe? Had he lost control over it?

I didn't see Thunderbolt get up. My heart twisted as yet another tie to Rafe was severed. The sight of him thrashing in the snow haunted the back of my thoughts. No mount could take a blow like that and not break a leg. Sorrow flooded through me, but I pressed it down to be dealt with later.

His stallion ran quick and sure. Northwing's main gate came into view. Rafe jerked the reins in an abrupt stop. The horse dug his heels into the snow, and Rafe pushed me off, jumping after me. He slapped the stallion's rump. After a sharp neigh, it bolted. The dragon dove from the sky, and Rafe planted his feet, angling his weapon.

My limbs ached from the cold as I pulled myself up to stand beside him, unarmed and vulnerable. I was helpless, useless.

I hated it.

Possession. Anger. Fear.

"It wants me!" I yelled over the dragon's roar as it dropped, shaking the earth on impact.

Rafe didn't speak. He positioned himself in front of me, sword raised. Ripping off the cloth covering his eye, he snarled, facing the beast down. The dragon spat and hissed, darting around us as quickly as its size allowed. It snapped at his face, nearly taking off his nose. Even so, he didn't falter.

"You will not damage the city."

The dragon threw its head back and gave a deafening screech of objection. Hatred. Anger. Trapped.

Its tail lashed in irritation and it lowered itself, circling us. Rafe mirrored it, shielding me from the massive beast. He stumbled and dropped to his knees. I grabbed at him, noting his feverish skin, slick with sweat.

"Rafe?" I moved, seeing his sickly gray face. This taxed him beyond his limits. "Rafe, stop." I stepped between him and the dragon, cutting off his gaze, then dropped to my knees as his sword dipped toward the ground.

"It won't hurt you," he breathed.

I nodded and let him sag against me. He was spent. My General risked his life, his reputation, *everything* for me. With a heavy sigh, his full weight collapsed on me and I spun to the side, letting him fall. The dragon advanced, and I ignored it as angry tears burned my cheeks. I reached for his cloth, tying it in place. His eyes were closed, dead to the world.

I forced myself to stand, then turned to the dragon. It sniffed and flicked its tongue, testing the air. It snaked around me to look at Rafe, and I stepped between them.

"He's mine," I growled.

It brought its head up short, squinting. Dismissing me as no threat, it walked to the side, extending a talon to his body. I rushed forward, pushing the massive claw with all my might. The dragon recoiled, not because of the strength behind the movement, but because I shoved it away.

"He's *mine!*" I screamed. I wouldn't let it touch him. It wouldn't harm him. I cracked open the door in my mind and pushed my emotions across with all my might.

Possession. Anger.

I slammed the door shut as the dragon shrieked and pulled back, stumbling in the snow. It righted itself, hissing and baring sharp teeth.

I pried Rafe's sword from his cooling hand and sat beside him. Placing part of my cloak over him, I watched the dragon. It eyed me back with wariness and distrust.

This was unlike anything I ever dreamed.

This was a nightmare.

The beast sensed the approaching Dragon Kind before I did. It scanned the skies, and flicked its forked tongue out, tasting the scents on the wind before rising to stand.

Dragons were reptilian in nature. They might not be fully cold-blooded, but they didn't do well in frigid temperatures. In winter, the dragons that remained at Northwing stayed in the warm caverns beneath the school, or they entered brumation—a type of hibernation for reptiles.

They could rouse themselves, but they were slower and less sharp than in the summer months. This dragon expended a massive amount of energy in the bitter cold and was weakening at a quick rate. I was thankful it was finally winding down. Without Rafe to control it, I didn't know what would prevent it from attacking the convoy headed our way.

At least six horses charged across the snowy landscape. The bright sun peeked from behind the overcast clouds, illuminating them. The dragon shifted with unease, backing away. Its nervous gaze flicked between me and them. It wouldn't leave me, but it didn't like the men.

Fear. Distrust. Possession.

I rose to a crouch, keeping the dragon in my sight. I wouldn't let it get behind me to harm Rafe. As the riders approached, they angled themselves toward me and Rafe. Not the dragon, thankfully.

"Hail!" one called.

I squinted against the sun. Xzanth pulled his horse to a stop, dismounted, and sprinted to Rafe. I stood, keeping an eye on the dragon, and strode toward the men.

"Hail!" I called back with a salute.

A man wearing the crest of a Dragon Rider on his spaulder dismounted. He offered me and the dragon a beaming smile. "What's this?" he said, coming to stand beside me.

The dragon watched him closely, creeping toward us.

"Sir, I–"

"Where have you been hiding it?" he asked, watching the beast with open amusement.

He flung a heavy arm over my shoulder. As soon as he made contact, the dragon lunged. I threw off his touch and darted to the side as it opened its maw, snapping at his arm. He shouted in alarm and jerked back, narrowly avoiding his limb being eaten.

"What's the meaning of this?" he demanded as the dragon positioned itself between us.

The creature was huge, its enormous body pushing me further away from him... and Rafe's prone figure. I grimaced and stepped forward, slamming a fist into its thick hide. It whirled at me.

Confusion. Possession. Protection.

I shoved it, pressing against its broad, muscular thigh, and it blinked, confused. Growling, I walked around it to stand by Rafe. I wasn't leaving him.

The Rider came to stand by me. The others in the convoy eyed the beast, their nerves apparent. It hissed and spat at them, snapping its jaws from time to time.

"I told him we needed more soldiers," Xzanth said with a curse. Concern lined his face.

I fidgeted with my tunic. It was my last one in any kind of decent shape. "I think I'm bonded to it," I muttered.

"Of course you are." The Rider smirked. "Now, where have you been hiding it? Why have you kept it a secret?" He shared a wary glance between me and the beast.

"I haven't been hiding it. We found it three days ago."

"You lie. There've been no dragons sighted without Riders since the treaty," he scoffed.

"She speaks the truth. I was there," Xzanth said, straightening his shoulders.

"It was not a hatchling?"

I bit the inside of my cheek. "No. We met it as is. Full-grown."

"Impossible. How did it bond you?"

I shrugged, and the fierce beast stilled. It laid its mammoth head on the ground, watching us.

"You don't know?"

"No," I muttered.

This man wasn't instilling any sense of reassurance. He seemed as clueless as I.

"It attacked our camp and abducted me. It took me to a nearby cave, where General Rafe found me. From there, we made it this far."

The Rider considered the scene with fresh eyes. "What happened to the General?" he asked, his friendly expression closing off.

"He exhausted himself, forcing it to keep its distance. You can see where he landed a blow on its right foreleg." I pointed to the dragon's injury, where hot blood still dripped into the snow.

"It attempted to attack you?"

"In part, but only as a means to an end. It wants me. It doesn't care about anyone else."

Possession. Anger. Suffering.

"Well, you're its Rider. It wouldn't hurt you."

"But it did."

I pulled my tunic free from my trousers. Lifting it to my chest, I showed the Rider. The soldiers behind him murmured, and he frowned.

"What is that?"

"Its talon split my side, then it healed it somehow. Please, let me assure you, I have no interest in letting it get close enough to repeat that experience."

"It healed you?" the Rider breathed, reaching out toward the scarred design.

The dragon leapt in a sudden move, and we tore apart as its maw snapped in the place where we once stood. It pulled back and craned over us, arching its neck.

I rubbed at my temples. This was all too much. How could I explain this?

It snorted, raising its head to the sky. Flicking its tongue out, it rumbled in warning and kneaded its claws in the snow, bringing dirt and stone to the surface.

"Flinor and Dareth are coming," the Rider explained.

Up ahead, a green dragon darted below the thick clouds. Flinor was a large male, tasked with guarding Northwing in the winter. He was a friendly beast, though, as most, retained a moody demeanor throughout the colder months. Dareth rode on his back, sitting tall in the saddle. His long blonde hair flew behind him like a banner.

The gray dragon lashed its tail—irritated.

Possession. Annoyance. Flee. Fight.

Nervousness skittered through me. "Please, tell them to keep Flinor away." I rushed my words as they dove toward us.

The Rider shook his head. "Perhaps he can shed light on the situation."

"No, you don't–"

The wild dragon let out a trumpeting bellow and jumped with a flap of its massive wings as Flinor dropped from the sky feet first. Flinor pulled up, taken by surprise, but the gray dragon pressed the advantage, stretching its neck and snapping.

I raced toward them, stumbling over frozen clumps of snow. Flinor playfully butted his head against the gray dragon's muzzle, shoving it away.

"No!" I shrieked, arms pumping at my sides as I ran.

The beast lashed its tail and clawed at Flinor's chest. Its talons sank in as it snarled, pulling back. Dareth shouted in warning, placing his hands on his dragon's neck.

"Stop! Back off!" I yelled.

I sped for the gray dragon and slipped under its tail to ram my fist into its leg. My fist, to a creature that size, was as annoying as a fly landing on me. Still, it turned to me, eyes flashing in anger. I belonged to it—and it was staking its claim. The other dragon would not have me.

"Stop! Please!"

I opened the door in my mind and cried out against the onslaught, even as I shoved in the sense of peace and calm. If the dragon was on the other side of that door, I could only hope it understood.

Aggression and possession roared in response.

Defiance. Fury. Loneliness.

I shrank from the emotions, placing a hand on its side and held onto its scales. I pushed back with peace and calm, with fatigue. Slowly, anger faded, and exhaustion answered. It was tired, too.

My knees sank into the snow, and I rested my head against the gray scales of its paw. Its claws were as long as my forearm and easily as thick as my frame. I grimaced and closed the door in my mind. It was tired. That's all I needed to know.

The dragon crouched low and wound its neck around its body to flick its tongue at me. Its eyes conveyed understanding. The creature was far more knowledgeable than perhaps I gave it credit for. Motivated by base instinct, it acted like a mindless beast, but inside, it was intelligent.

Flinor crooned, peering down at us curiously.

"Hail! New Dragon Rider!" Dareth shouted from above. He peeked from around his dragon's neck with a nervous smile.

My gaze dropped to the wounds on Flinor's chest—superficial scratches. A mere warning that he, hopefully, wouldn't take offense to.

"Please don't fight me," I whispered under my breath.

The gray dragon rumbled in reply. Its bright eyes followed me as I approached the Rider and his men. He stood stiffly, watching both me and the dragon.

"It's tired," I said. "Perhaps we can discuss this somewhere more secluded?"

"That would be best," he replied, scanning the nervous soldiers behind him. "Dareth, care to escort them to the canyon?" He cupped his mouth, projecting his voice to the Rider above.

"No, I can't ride," I blurted.

"Then you will ride with us." He frowned, then jerked his chin at the gray beast. "It has to fly."

I heaved a sigh and returned to the grounded dragon. It waited impatiently, flicking its tongue out, testing the air. I knew it wanted to whisk me off somewhere, but right now, it was tired. It was trusting me.

Why?

I hadn't any idea.

I neared its great head and reached out. It bared its teeth in a silent warning, but didn't move. I pulled my hand back and closed my eyes.

"Please follow. Please," I whispered, cracking the door in my mind. Pain whipped at me, tearing through my head. I flinched, but pushed harder. "Please don't hurt anyone. We'll get away soon."

'*Mine!*'

Possession and belonging rang through me as clear as day. I slammed the door, cutting off its emotions before more came through. I ground my teeth against the throb in my head. The beast thought I belonged to it. By definition of the bond, I did.

Blinking against unwelcome tears, I turned away and headed toward the Rider. I refused to look at Rafe's large body tucked into the snow. This should have been my dream come true—I was bonded to a dragon! I finally belonged somewhere, not forcing my way.

The Rider motioned me to one of his soldier's horses and I mounted. Glancing back, I found Xzanth watching me with a disapproving frown.

I wanted to be a Dragon Rider all my life. I thought that was my destiny—until I joined the ranks. Bitter tears rebelled and fell down my cheeks as I turned the horse away from my General.

I never resented a dragon so much in my life.

CHAPTER 3

My fingertips clung to the rocky surface, grasping for purchase in every crevice I could find. I scaled the steep cliff on foot, walking along a narrow path high in the Dragon Canyon—hundreds of paces above the canyon floor. One small misstep would send me plummeting to my death.

The caverns for full-grown dragons were the hardest to reach. Normally the beast carried its Rider to such heights instead of forcing them to traverse the treacherous journey on foot. The lower caverns were smaller, more suited to the younger creatures unable to fly with their Rider.

Flinor gripped the top of the cliff, watching us with interest. The gray dragon had its massive head extended from the cave just ahead, refusing to let me out of its sight. It wouldn't carry me. I dared not even try.

I ground my teeth together and climbed with care. Dareth was waiting for me to enter the cavern, then he planned to follow. If the dragon moved to attack him, he would use Flinor to make a quick escape.

Within ten paces of the opening, the gray dragon stretched its long neck, flicking its tongue. I glared, but ignored it and shuffled forward. Its lips pulled back, nipping at me as I neared. I shoved its maw away. If it wouldn't let me ride, I wanted nothing to do with it at the moment. It snorted in offense and ducked into the cavern. I cleared the path and followed it inside, pausing at the threshold.

The space was massive. The dragon could stand on its hind legs, stretching its neck and still not touch the ceiling. Too large for my comfort. The entire barracks' dining hall could've fit inside. It dwarfed me—and I felt too minuscule, too exposed in the cavern.

The dragon backed into the far corner and curled in on itself, studying me. I looked around at the barren cave, wondering what I was doing here. This was so beyond me. I never thought I would inhabit a place like this. Even when I was First Chosen, I figured I'd be fighting on the front long before my dragon ever reached the size that required a space like this.

"Hail!"

Dareth crept behind me on the path, peeking his head into the cave. I frowned when the gray dragon hissed in warning. Dareth grinned and shooed me further inside.

"Put a little space between us, would you? Your dragon will tear me apart in a fit of jealousy if you don't," he said.

I strode to the wall nearly twenty paces from him and collapsed against it, sinking to the ground. Bringing my knees to my chest, I wrapped my arms around them. He took a step inside, watching the gray dragon with a nervous smile. He rested against the wall beside the entrance and settled on the cold stone floor.

"So, tell me your story, new Rider."

"First off, I'm not a Rider." I smothered the irritation in my voice. I wouldn't dare ride that dragon. That would be a death wish. It lowered its massive head to the floor, and I wondered if I ever would be a 'Rider'.

Taking a deep breath, I launched into the explanation of how we found it and what transpired since. I clarified I couldn't communicate with it, at least not like a Dragon Rider. Rafe's method of intervention, I left unspoken. I needed to leave my emotions out of it and spoke as factually as I could. I didn't want to skew the story by coloring it with my feelings.

"So... it's one of the Wild Ones," he mused.

"Perhaps."

"That's the only answer. There are no dragons beyond the yearlings who disappear. I wonder what brought her to you. She had to have sought you out. That was no mistake." He rubbed his chin thoughtfully.

"She?"

Its tail was tucked against its side. Not distinctively short or overly long, I hadn't been able to guess its gender.

His lips turned up in a sheepish grin. "Aye."

"Are we... well, are we bonded? Truly?"

"No doubt." His assurance came without hesitation.

"Then why can't I speak to her?" I waved toward the beast with a flippant gesture. "Why can't we communicate? It's painful—like I'm dipping my head in a forge every time I reach out."

"Well, think of it this way. She grew up alone and developed separately from you. Hatchlings are reliant on us for communication, and for putting their thoughts together coherently. You're attempting to communicate with a creature that's never needed communication." He scratched at his jaw, shifting against the stone. "If a child had no need to express their wants, desires or feelings to another, would they ever learn to speak? No. She's communicating the best she can by pushing emotions at you. Whether she's aware of her actions, I'm not sure." He shrugged, his gaze darting between us as he spoke.

"As for the pain you experience... I wonder if that's because the bond is new. As you both have minds that have matured separate from one another, the bridge between you is poorly built. Hatchlings are impressionable things. They go wherever their Rider goes, and do whatever they ask. They are reliant on their Rider for how to process thoughts and feelings. Riders guide them through this process.

"Hatchlings are trusting, to a point of fault. Your dragon is not. She's grown in the wild and trusts her instincts—nothing else. You can't expect her *not* to lash out when you try to open the bond or communicate. I wouldn't be surprised if you harmed her when you try. You are the same. Your instincts would be to fight and push against anything that lowers your mental defense."

Flinor's face popped into view, hanging upside down from where he waited at the top of the cliff. The gray dragon raised her head and bared her teeth with a low growl.

Dareth looked at his dragon with an exasperated sigh, and Flinor flicked out his tongue, then disappeared. "Curious beast," he muttered.

"What happens now? She won't let me near anyone."

"You should take a few days. Stay by her side. Let her know you won't leave. Reassure her. She sought you out for some reason. Try to give her what she needs. Give her a reason to trust you. I will talk to the other Riders, perhaps send for the Dragon Lord. I assume he'd say the same and have you train as though she was a hatchling."

My lips pressed tight as I glanced around the cavern. "Am I to sleep here?"

"Aye." Dareth chuckled. "I'll retrieve your pack and a few blankets before nightfall. I would hold off on leaving for a few days. Wait until she's more comfortable with you."

The dragon blinked a fiery eye, giving me a guarded look. I wasn't prey, but I wasn't an ally either. I was just something curious, and apparently from the length of the blink—slightly boring.

He gestured to the cavern's entrance. "Flin is the only one awake. The others are in brumation, so you don't need to worry about unwelcome visitors." He paused. "Is there anything else you'd like to add?"

This was all new to me. There was so much to take in. I was angry, disheartened, and exhausted. I didn't think there was anything else, so I shook my head.

He stood, stretching with a loud groan. The dragon hissed but didn't deign to raise her head at his movement.

"If I may, I would advise you to name her first. That would be a good place to start together," he said, moving to the narrow path just outside. He faced me, giving a silly little wave, then fell backward.

My heart jolted. I knew Flinor wouldn't let him fall, but that was unnerving. When his dragon darted past the mouth of the cave in a steep dive, my fears were put to rest. There was a chirp, and the sound of Dareth's laughter followed.

He was mad.

I sighed, peering at my bonded. How did one communicate with a beast? She *was* a beast, after all. She might be sentient, but she had no way to communicate.

"He said I should name you," I murmured.

Her large eye, the color of autumn leaves, blinked—indifferent to my words.

"I would think you already have a name. I do—I'm not waiting for you to name me. You're an adult. What do you call yourself?"

Her paw shifted, scratching her talons against the stone floor. Other than that, she seemed to have no other input.

"Perhaps you're a skilled hunter?"

Nothing.

"Cunning?"

Nothing.

"How old are you? Perhaps you're unique in some way?"

She blinked.

I closed my eyes and rubbed my temples against a throbbing headache. This was too much. It was like trying to talk to a horse.

Thunderbolt.

My breath snagged. Was he alive? Caught up in the chaos, I never got a chance to ask about him. The last I saw, he was screaming in the snow. Worry rolled over me in waves, hoping against hope that he somehow made it.

Would I be permitted to ride him again if she wouldn't let me?

Fiery anger rose in my chest. "I finally settled, you know?!" Sadness threatened to strangle me, and I fought it off. "I accepted the fact that I wouldn't be a Dragon Rider. Then you came along and ruined everything. I trained for two years to be a soldier. That time is wasted now."

She blinked, watching with no reaction to my rising temper.

"I had–" My voice broke, dropping to a whisper. "I had *Rafe.*" Tears burned my eyes. I was no longer his.

"You took me from him."

I rubbed my face as loneliness sapped my strength. I had finally been *happy.* We could have resolved our differences, tried to make it work. Now, all chances of that were gone. She took it from me. She plucked me up from my comfortable life and tipped it all on end.

"You took everything from me!"

Her head snapped up and she roared. The cave walls amplified the sound, and I pressed my hands against my ears, recoiling.

'*Mine!*'

The single word tore through my mind with blinding pain, chased by the sense of loneliness, anger and possession.

"No! I'm *not yours!* I belong to no one!" My screams shredded my throat—I didn't care if anyone heard. "I made my choice! I was a soldier!"

Her talons tore at the stone floor as she rose and stalked over, snapping her teeth at the air. Furious eyes locked on me.

'*Mine!*'

For once, I was living the life I chose—this beast uprooted everything I'd worked for. "No, I'm not! I am my own!" Seething, I scrambled to my feet.

She thrust her muzzle into my chest, knocking me to the floor. I pulled my arms in front of me as she pinned me with her heavy paw. The heat of her breath warmed my cheek as she snapped her sharp teeth in my face with a *clack!*

'*Mine.*' Her tone was not angry. It was cold and final.

I lowered my arms and glared. The behemoth of a predator didn't scare me one bit.

"Never."

Dareth brought a pack and a few essentials before night fell. Being at the top of the canyon, we had the sun's last warm rays, but winter's chill clung to the air. He mentioned he would look for a tapestry to hang over the opening to help block out the cold. There had been no need for them in recent years, as the larger dragons took up residence in the underground spring caverns, where it was warm. Those in the smaller spaces below hung tapestries to act as a door, but none were large enough to cover this entrance.

I rummaged through the items he brought. Food, blankets, a lidded chamber pot, a waterskin and a tincture for pain. I took a dose of the tincture as I was sure my body would appreciate it on the morrow, then ate the cold meal. It was a simple spread of dried, seasoned meat with hard cheese and stale bread. It was sustenance, however, and I devoured it.

The dragon slumbered in her corner, not even opening an eye when Dareth dropped the items off. I caught her tongue flicking out, but she was either too cold to be bothered, or she no longer deemed him a threat. She hadn't moved after our fight, content to ignore me.

I relieved myself and spread the blankets as far away from her as I could get without putting myself near the frigid air outside. I wouldn't risk getting sick, but I also wanted nothing to do with her at the moment. Tomorrow, I would try again, but for now, we were both simmering.

I didn't quite understand what she had to be angry about. She sought me out, not the other way around. She needed *me* for something, and yet she was angry at me? It almost felt as if she held resentment for bonding with someone so weak.

Burrowing under the blankets, I covered my chilled body. I was soiled and filthy, yet if I slipped away to wash, it would rile her. I flopped to my side, trying to find a comfortable position. If I was too weak for her, she could simply fly off and leave me in peace. At the moment, I'd rather be a failed Rider and return to the Tennan than be stuck with a beast as my bonded.

She rumbled in her sleep, as if sensing my thoughts. My eyes pressed tight, trying to hold back more tears. I would rather be on watch right now, or running the obstacle course. Curse it all, I would rather empty the Tennan's chamber pot.

Everyone thought bonding a dragon was the greatest thing, and perhaps it was.

Any dragon but this one.

The next day was quiet. Dareth stopped by after the eighth chime with more food. I woke feeling ill, and he assured me he would bring more medicine before nightfall. I stayed on my blankets almost the entire day, watching the sleeping dragon. She hadn't awoke for anything. I wondered if she was slipping into brumation, or simply ignoring me.

I wasn't willing to attempt communicating with her again. She could sleep for all I cared.

Pain in my abdomen grew as the day went on, and I couldn't even rise to meet Dareth at the entrance when he came before nightfall. He slipped in, Flinor watching us upside down.

Dareth wiped at my sweat-lined brow, concern edging his features. The gray dragon snarled at his touch, but didn't move.

"Have you been vomiting?" he asked.

I winced. "No."

He adjusted his position so the dragon could see what he was doing, then lifted the blankets, then my tunic. He gasped at the raised white scar on my side and stomach.

"This is where she healed you?"

"Yes." I groaned as a stabbing wave of nausea overcame me, forcing me to curl in on myself.

"The magic should have healed everything," he muttered, chewing his cheek. "I have to fetch a Healer."

The pain was too much. I nodded, unable to speak.

He slipped out, and I drifted into a cycle of bracing against each wave of agony. The dragon stood, flicking out her forked tongue as she neared. Her lips pulled back as if she tasted something sour, then stared down at me with burning eyes.

"Go away," I rasped.

She recoiled as if I struck her, then retreated to her corner, snarling. Whatever she was thinking, I just wanted to be left alone. Once the pain receded, I would handle her. I didn't have the strength to deal with an incompetent beast.

"Hail!"

I attempted to turn toward the mouth of the cave when I heard Dareth, but another stabbing wave crashed upon me. I tried to roll with it, grinding my teeth together.

"Great dragon, this is a Healer. She will help... Go. Quietly and slowly." Dareth's voice dropped as if he spoke to someone else.

The dragon stood, taking a step forward and hissing.

"Dareth?" The feminine voice hesitated.

"Your bonded is ill. She needs help," Dareth said. "Slowly now. Flinor, keep watch."

The dragon's hiss shifted into a deep growl, and I opened my eyes to see her advancing on the two with teeth bared and head snaking low to the ground.

"Stop it, you fool," I gasped. She turned on me with a snarl. "Go back to your corner."

She opened her mouth and let out a defiant roar, objecting. I flinched and curled into myself more tightly. The barrage ended with a hiss, and I cracked my eyes to see her return to the corner, scratching her claws against the stone floor.

A Healer came into view, her features familiar.

"Avyanna. We meet again," Rashel murmured.

She brushed her fingers across my forehead. I tried to give her a small smile, but only managed a grimace. She pulled the blankets back and froze.

"Dareth, leave."

"I don't think that's a good idea, considering–"

"Go back outside." Rashel's tone took on a commanding edge. One that mothers and Healers perfected.

"I really must protest–"

"Protest, and I'll make sure to slip a laxative in your tea for the next month," she snapped.

The dragon growled from her corner, and Dareth retreated, mumbling under his breath. Rashel pulled the blankets off and rolled me onto my back. I ground my teeth and tried to relax.

"Avyanna, when was your last moon cycle?"

I flinched as she pressed on my abdomen. Her gentle touch felt as if she stabbed me with a hot knife. The dragon snarled and spat.

"I don't remember." Pain shot up, and bile burned my throat. Swallowing against the urge to vomit, I tried to lie still.

"Have you lain with a man?"

My eyes shot open and I managed a look of horror. "No, I–"

"When did you last lay with him?"

I let out a hiss and glared. "I've not lain with a man... ever." Not even once. I never had the urge until recently.

"I don't understand," she murmured.

She pulled at my trousers, and I lifted my hips to help, seeing my blood-soaked garment.

"If it's not a miscarriage–"

"It can't be," I gasped. "I was taking tinge berry tea."

She froze, her mouth striking a fierce frown. "Tinge berry tea? And who gave you that?"

"General–" I flinched as the sting pulsated through my stomach.

She bit out a vicious curse and set to working on my clothes. "No Healer in their right mind would ever give anyone that cursed tea. There's a reason a woman's body goes through a cycle with every moon. It is the way we were made, and nature is not to be tampered with."

She removed my trousers and under-breeches, then folded a spare blanket between my legs. "Missing a single dose causes your moon blood to flow with all the vengeance of every missed cycle. That fool had no business–"

"He's not a fool."

"Don't justify his actions, dear. I know how the tea works. It's easy for a man to say it's the best option. Were he in the same position as you, he would think differently."

She gave me a few different tonics, some to help me sleep, others for pain and inflammation. She readied to leave, taking my soiled clothes and blankets with her. The dragon let out a small whine as she left, but I sank into a dark, peaceful rest.

At least once during the night, she roared and snapped. The sleeping tonic was too strong to allow consciousness to fully surface, but I swore I felt someone's large hand lay over my heart.

Drifting back into a dreamless sleep, I wanted to believe it was Rafe.

CHAPTER 4

D areth and Rashel stopped by over the next few days. The worst of the pains passed in three nights. I was embarrassed that Dareth saw the bloodied sheets and rags, but he handled the situation with casual indifference. He didn't pull a face at them, or treat them as though they were diseased.

For that, I was thankful.

Rashel gave me a few tonics to take if the pain returned and made me swear never to drink tinge berry tea again. She explained that it not only withheld my moon cycle, but could potentially render me barren. Having children didn't concern me. Still, I understood that was a heavy ramification. It was a consequence I wasn't willing to risk.

The dragon and I made no progress, mostly ignoring one another throughout the day. I didn't know when I would ever leave this blasted cavern. Now that the thick clouds paused their relentless snowfall, I wanted to be out in the world, drinking in that crisp winter sunshine, not trapped in a stifling cave.

"Why did you seek me out?"

She didn't even crack an eye in interest. It felt as if I spoke another language, one she couldn't be bothered to understand. I received a single word from her, one she learned from me. She hadn't said it until after I claimed Rafe as mine. I must have pushed the sense of possession and defiance, and she discerned the word meant those feelings.

I sat on the cold floor, looking out across the canyon. Birds flitted to and fro, sensing the shift of seasons. Calls of dragonlings drifted up, echoing off the canyon walls. Any occupied caves were out of my line of sight, but from my place, I witnessed the sun rising above the far lip of the canyon. It was a beautiful thing—observing the world awaken every morning.

Resting my back against the cool stone wall, I watched the sunrise. I was strangely empty of anger, though it was still there, buried deep under my apathy. I gathered my feelings at the moment, the joy of watching the birds and the sunrise, and held tightly to them.

My eyes fluttered closed, and I hesitated before reaching for that door, hoping against hope I wouldn't be met with pain. Tugging at it, I took care to be gentle as I slipped those feelings through the door.

'*Content.*' I let go, letting it drift close.

No wave of torment greeted me, no irritation or hatred. No growling or snarling. I heard movement behind me and faced her. She lifted her head, studying me, tasting the air. I had the distinct feeling she was looking for anger from me.

A sad smile lifted my lips, and I turned back to the canyon. The world woke slowly. Each passing chime bringing more and more sounds to our ears.

The dragon crowded the mouth of the cave beside me. She eyed the expanse with curious scrutiny, her steady gaze on the sun. Warmth rushed over me, a burning heat—not unpleasant, but comforting. Within it, I could rest and forget my troubles. A flash of sunlight filled my mind's eye, and I realized she was pushing at me through our bond. Gently, I tugged the door open again.

Warmth. Rest. Tired. Weary.

'*Content.*'

I smiled at her use of the word.

My stomach rumbled, and I placed a hand over my belly. She lowered her muzzle and flicked her tongue curiously. Her giant eyes blazed with an inner fire. Gazing up at her, I gathered memories of eating. Good food, and the taste and flavors that came with it. I tried to capture the feeling of desire, and want, the slight pain in my belly demanding I eat soon. Pushing those through the bond, I voiced a word in my mind.

'*Hungry.*'

She tilted her head, studying the sky once more. Large migratory birds flew above the canyon and she tracked them with eager eyes.

'*Hungry.*' Her voice was low and guttural—rasping along with a slight hiss.

I snorted in amusement. "Go then. Eat. I'll be here," I said, reaching out to pat her foreleg.

She recoiled from my touch, slamming into the side of the entrance. She hissed and bared her teeth as rocks and loose stone rained down on us. I sheltered my head and ducked away from the shower of debris. I'd forgotten she was a Wild dragon, not some bonded hatchling.

She slithered to her corner. Curled in a ball, she watched me with a wary glare, as though I had done something terrible. Whatever fragile understanding we built was shattered. I frowned and went back to watching the day. Odd how such a thing as a dragon—a full-grown one at that—would be so terrified of a human barely five paces tall.

Running a hand through my short hair, I wondered about Rafe. What was he doing? Was he training his men? Was he eager to release me to Ruveel? I hoped he would come see me, but then again, why would he? If I were simply a soldier, he wouldn't.

I brought my knees to my chest and hugged myself. There was something between us, something I was eager to pursue. He was content to let me go, but what about my wants? What if I wasn't content letting him go? He claimed he was too old for me, too wounded—both inside and out. He decided he wasn't good for me. Didn't I get a choice in that? Wasn't I allowed to have a say in what my heart craved?

If he did not *want* me, it would be different. I would cut my losses and move on. However, it was clear the desire was not one-sided. We realized a union between us wasn't permitted, but that didn't stop us from wanting it.

I grabbed a pebble and tossed it out into the canyon.

This wasn't fair. None of it. I tried forcing my way to be a Dragon Rider, and that hadn't worked. I tried forcing my way to be a soldier. That hadn't worked. I fell in... *want*—I dared not say love—for a man. That didn't work out, either.

Why did nothing I strived for work out? What was I meant to do with my life if I kept failing at everything? Now, I was tied to a Wild dragon with a foul temper and a dislike for people. What choice could I make here? How could I push toward what I wanted?

These thoughts felt childish, yet I was almost the age of a lady. I should've been allowed to have a say in the things I did with my life and the direction it took. I thought I had. Then this creature came and shook everything up.

A dragon trumpeted, and I stood, shaking out my stiff limbs. Flinor was on his way. A rasping sound came from within the cave and I glanced over my shoulder to see the dragon thrashing her tail.

"He has his own Rider. Besides, he wouldn't want me, anyway." My voice was bitter. No one wanted me. Why did she?

Flinor hovered with a load of supplies secured in his claws. I shuffled aside, and he landed on the edge of the cliff, leaning in. The gray dragon rose, snarling.

"He's just dropping some things off, then he'll leave." Dareth pulled his legs free from the leather stirrups.

Flinor dropped the goods, then backed out, flapping his wings hard to bring him to the top of the canyon.

"I bring you, your door!" Dareth dipped into a deep bow.

I beamed as he unrolled an enormous piece of heavy cloth—a vivid mottle of red and purple.

"It's beautiful." My fingers trailed the striking abstract design.

"It was the only one we found that would fit," he said, pulling a set of heavy iron brackets out of the crate.

We installed the thick curtain, Flinor using his tail to heft Dareth high enough to push the brackets into pre-drilled holes from the previous inhabitants. The two brackets secured the curtain's long iron bar. Large hooks on either side provided a way to fasten the fabric against the wind, and offer more privacy.

When we finished, Dareth pulled it aside, letting a little light in, and admired our work.

"Splendid!" He raised his chin in satisfaction. "I'm pleased to see it works well!"

"Thank you," I said.

"My pleasure. Anything I can do to help the new Riders." He rounded on me with his hands on his hips. "Speaking of which, the Dragon Lord has ordered that he receive a record of your bonding by your hand."

A frown pulled at my lips, but I nodded my acceptance. I really didn't want any reminders that I would be removed from Rafe's Tennan.

"Also," he continued, "there are quite a few that wish to see you. The Master of Women has specifically requested she be allowed to meet with you. We have not permitted her due to," he glanced at the gray dragon, "certain circumstances."

"Master Elenor?" I was so pleased to hear her name. She was one of the few I wished to see.

"Aye, that's the one. Another—I can't remember her name, but my-my, she has a temper to match that red hair. She's been at the Rider's throats to see you."

"Niehm."

"That's her! Aye, we all find her quite amusing. She slapped Brugeor the other night when he insinuated that as a Rider, you were better than her."

"I could never be as good as her, let alone better." I laughed.

Dareth grinned. "Aye, so she agreed."

I genuinely liked this man. At first, I thought him to be simple. But he was like Rory, always determined to find something good in a situation, never knowing when it was time to be serious. My stomach constricted with sadness, remembering Willhelm and his friends.

"So, how is communication going?" he asked. "Have you named her?"

The smile fell from my face, and a blush heated my cheeks. "I thought we were getting somewhere this morning, but I ruined it."

"Oh?" He prompted with a steadfast smile, leaning against the rock wall.

"We were actually communicating. She knows the words 'mine,' 'content,' and 'hungry.' I thought she was hungry, so I told her she should go hunt. I reached out to touch her, and she lost it."

Dareth grimaced. "Mm-hmm. Remember, she has the same mentality as a wild animal. I don't know what she's seen of humans. You'd think she'd have some memory of us from when she refused the bond.

"When the first Wild dragon came to be, we forced the issue quite a bit—I'm ashamed to say. We thought they just needed the right Rider. The dragonlings were chained and muzzled so all the Chosen could touch them. We were ignorant back then. We didn't realize there were dragons not suited to the bond."

My heart pained at the memory of a little blue hatchling. I couldn't imagine dragonlings chained and muzzled, forced to accept the advances of the Chosen. I blew out a breath, regaining my resolve. "Perhaps she's older than we know. Can Flinor guess at her age?"

"We think she's at least ten winters, though how much beyond that we wouldn't know. I could go through the records and look for a description that matches hers. My only concern is—well, don't let the other Riders know I mentioned this." His voice dropped to a whisper. "I wonder if the Wild Ones have been breeding. Perhaps she's a Wild hatchling."

I frowned, flicking my gaze between him and my bonded.

"Think of it. If she hatched from one of our eggs, she would have at least a year of human interaction. Has she acted as if she remembers humans? A dragon's memories are like a deep well. They go on and on. She should be able to pull from that experience and if she's near ten winters, she would know we mean her no harm."

"If not, then I'm working with a blank slate," I muttered.

Her blazing eye flashed as she watched us. She certainly didn't act as though she had been near humans before. She was bigger and stronger than us, but she had the same fear that came with all wild animals. They feared our intelligence.

Ever since we met, I either pushed her away or struck her to get her attention. I thought nothing of it because any other dragon would've brushed it off. If she was Wild born, that would have been her only experience with human touch.

Guilt welled up within me. If she was Wild born, she wouldn't understand any of this. She'd be following her magical instinct, figuring it out as she went—as new to this as I was. Perhaps my anger blinded me, and I'd been too hard on her.

"That could be a good thing. If she has nothing to remember humans by, you can show her kindness and strength. You were First Chosen two years in a row. You know enough about the bond to guide her through."

"I was expecting to be bonded to a hatchling," I countered. "A little one without its own opinions."

I was still frustrated that life as I knew it was ripped from me, that I was thrown into this mess. However, that didn't excuse my actions. My ire had no place being aimed at her. I could be angry at life, at my destiny, but perhaps she was as innocent as I.

"That might be what you *expected*, but she is what you *have*." He sighed, a faraway look in his eyes. "Magic chooses what it will. In bonding, it's the dragons who reach for the magic. They have little control over it and follow its lead. It led her to you. Magic saw you two fit for each other, however difficult a fit that might be."

He leaned close with a conspiratorial whisper. "Always trust the magic."

"Say that to the Rider that lost his mind, unable to control it." I snorted.

Everyone knew the horror stories of those who drew upon magic and could not contain it. Magic was described as a slippery, tricky thing. It was hard to handle and even harder to focus. If it wound its way out of grasp, it would find its own purpose. Whatever that may be.

Dareth snickered and turned to leave. "Will you need anything before dark?" he asked, stepping onto the slender path outside the cave.

"I think I'll be fine."

He looked up and smiled at what I could only assume was Flinor. "Pity I can't bring hot food. I'm sure you'd welcome it in this cold. Soon, you'll be able to rejoin the rest of normal society. Till the morning!" With that, he dove off the path and into the abyss.

I waited, counting the seconds. One. Two. Three. Four.

"FLIN!"

Flinor trumpeted and zipped by my cave in a streak of green. I smiled at their antics. They were clearly made for each other. Their personalities fit like two pieces in a puzzle. Glancing at the gray dragon, I wondered if we were truly suited for one another. She was curled in the corner, staring at me with her head resting against the stone floor.

She looked... lonely.

The stubborn beast refused to leave me, yet we always ended up lashing out at each other. Why did the magic lead her to me? What did I have that she needed?

I sighed, walking over. I didn't think—I simply sat and rested my back against her shoulder. She tensed and peered down, baring her teeth and flicking out her tongue. She was trying to figure out if she should be mad or welcome my company. Smooth scales the color of granite covered her frame—hard as steel, yet as flexible as cloth. Beneath them moved muscles larger than my entire body. She was a massive, formidable beast.

Her lips twitched to cover her fangs, but she continued to taste the air. Our problem didn't come from the fact that we were two separate beings—we just couldn't communicate. This had to be resolved. I had to teach her somehow.

I was a lousy teacher.

Sighing, I closed my eyes and leaned my head against her. Picturing in my mind a mother holding a baby, I gave a soft tug on the door to our bond. I slid the image through the crack.

'*Mother. Child,*' I whispered through the door.

There was silence... and I waited. Surely she would respond. Either in anger or with an answering image. She wouldn't hold a grudge. Right?

A vision drifted to the forefront of my mind—a clutch of eggs. Dragon eggs. Plants and animal bones formed a nest. Vegetation held the structure in shape, cradling the precious brood. There had to be at least ten in the nest. The image faded even though I tried to hold on to it.

Was she a mother? Did my dragon already raise young? In the wild?

I pictured her, as fierce and defiant as she was, beside the clutch of dragon eggs. With a silent question, I pushed it through and waited.

Another image came in answer. It was as if I looked down at the eggs. In the memory, I reached out a large gray-scaled paw to nudge one.

'*Mother,*' came her rumbling voice.

I smiled in wonder, admiring the image as it faded. My dragon was a mother. She had little dragonlings out there somewhere. There were more dragons in Rinmoth than we thought. That knowledge made the world seem a much bigger place. Tears formed behind my closed eyes as I pushed a picture of my mother to her.

'*My mother.*' I accompanied the image with an essence of love and comfort, trying to convey how I felt about her.

We spent time with one another, trading words and feelings, learning more about each other. I never expected to share this with an adult dragon. I always assumed I would grow with my dragon, but somehow, learning about her life and what she knew offered me a deeper connection. She was her own soul, a separate entity. And I was my own person.

We didn't grow together, but we were brought together.

It was well beyond dark by the time I made it to my bed. I drifted into sleep, realizing she wasn't as bad as I thought. I misjudged her.

Perhaps we could be happy, bonded together.

CHAPTER 5

Vicious snarling tore me from a restless sleep. I jerked upright. Arms locked around me, stronger than steel bands, securing me against a hard chest. The dragon roared in the darkness, close enough to feel the heat of her breath.

"Vy."

Relief flooded me as I stilled. My heart faltered for a moment before it took off at a breakneck pace.

"Rafe?"

He loosened his grip, and I squirmed against him to glimpse his face. The tapestry concealed every trace of moonlight. I couldn't see a thing.

There was the snap of powerful jaws, and the clack of teeth near my head.

"No!" I cried.

She wouldn't hurt him. She wouldn't take him from me. I struggled in vain against Rafe's grip as he held me tight.

"Hold." He grunted, shifting as if he meant to push me behind him.

"No! No, Rafe don't!"

He froze, then his hand trailed across my chest to my neck. "Can you control it?" he whispered in my ear.

Chills ran up my spine even as my body heated. I shivered. "Let me try."

"No *trying*," he growled.

I relaxed against him as the dragon hissed. Laying my head on his shoulder, I looked up, still not seeing anything. "She hasn't killed me yet. I don't think tonight will be any different."

A grunt was all I received in response, but he let his arms drop. I scuttled forward on my hands and knees until I was clear of my belongings. Standing, I felt around wildly. I would never close that blasted curtain again.

Rafe chuckled from behind me.

"What is it?" I whispered.

"She's looking at you like you've lost your mind. A dumb kit, but still hers."

I lowered my arms. A blush heated my cheeks, and I opened my eyes as wide as they would go, searching for any source of light.

He chuckled. "To your right."

"It would have been nice to know you can see in the dark, General," I muttered, grasping to my right.

His amused snort filled the cavern. "Ah, there, in front of you."

I reached, seeking any kind of contact.

"Still looking at you like you've lost your sanity."

"Thank you for the commentary." I huffed. I wasn't truly angry. My heart was happy that he was here.

My left palm landed against warm dragon scales. I sighed in relief and opened the door to our bond to tell her he was safe. Blinding white pain assaulted me. I fell, screaming in agony as the heat of an unseen flame tore through my head.

Hatred. Anger. Death.

I clenched my jaw, tasting blood in my mouth. The dragon let out a deafening roar, and I tried again, struggling to touch her.

"No!" I shouted over the chaos. My hand landed against her, sensing the trembling of her rage. Tremors ran under her skin, but she held still.

Anger. Fear. Hatred.

"No!"

I pushed against the onslaught of pain with images of Rafe helping me, laughing and smiling with me. Of him saving me from Victyr and the others. I shoved my feelings through—safety, friendship and desire. I drove back with everything I had.

"He's *mine!*" I snarled through gritted teeth.

'*Mine!*'

I nodded, tears slipping through my closed eyes. "Yes, but *he's* mine!"

Her confusion rushed over me, and I held tightly to the door. How could I convince her he was safe without making her feel like I was betraying her? She had to know I was hers, but she feared Rafe and thought he would take me from her.

I pushed the picture of two dragons flying the mating dance high above the King's grounds. A scene of the male caring for the female by bringing her food, of him protecting her against others.

"Mine," I said, pressing against her scales.

She threw a picture of dragon eggs at me with a silent question. I choked on my breath.

'*No. No Hatchlings. Love. Care.*' I tried to explain. The pain was fading, leaving me numb.

'*Mate,*' she rasped in my head.

'*Yes.*' I cringed. At least no one could communicate with her besides me.

If it kept her from eating him, I would claim that. After all, I did desire him and she would feel that. A mate would care for and protect their own.

She heaved a shuddering breath but didn't move. She pushed an image at me; Rafe separating her from me with his silver eye naked to her. I felt her terror as he commanded her, binding her with magic and forcing his will on her. I glimpsed another memory, one of a human-like creature with a canine skull for a head—gleaming eyes that matched Rafe's.

She recoiled, slamming the bond shut. I stumbled forward as she backed away. He reminded her of a Shadow Shaman.

A heavy hand found the small of my back and slid up to grip my shoulder. "That was poor control."

"But I did it." I offered him a shaking smile, looking toward his voice.

His touch retreated and a whisper of steel followed his grunted reply. He had drawn his blade. He was willing to face down a dragon for me. My stomach twisted in a nervous knot.

"I want to see you."

"I'm prettier in the dark," he scoffed.

I snorted, reaching in the direction of my bed, feeling along the stone floor. If I could find my bed, I had a candle in my pack. I could light it and–

There was a crack of flint, and a spark flew to my left. Rafe nursed a candle to light. "As amusing as it is to watch you crawl around in the dark," he secured the candle in a holder and settled on my blankets, "I wouldn't want you to crawl off the cliff."

The heavy curtain to the entrance hung a few paces in front of me. I sighed and stood, looking around. The dragon huddled in her corner, watching Rafe with hungry eyes. Her bright orange orbs glanced my way before returning to him, her pupils narrowing into slits.

I gave her a gentle smile and headed over to Rafe. He made himself comfortable, sitting on my blankets with his broad back against the wall and a leg stretched out in front of him. He rested a hand on his bent knee and patted the blanket.

There was something provocative about that movement. I swallowed past the lump in my throat and settled next to him, pulling my knees to my chest. A defensive posture, but I honestly needed all the defense I could get to keep me safe from him. It was an odd sensation. Rafe wouldn't harm me, but those last words we shared the night we kissed... it wasn't a physical hurt I was worried about.

He watched the dragon in the corner, but as he brought his hand to his lap, it brushed against my thigh. Fire flushed through my veins.

"How is the Tennan?" Better to talk of the men I didn't have feelings for.

"Hmm. The same. Jam wanted to come tonight."

"Why didn't he?" I asked. "He snuck under her nose once before."

Rafe's eyes darted to mine, and he gave me a small, knowing smirk.

Heat stung my cheeks, and I buried my face in my arms, averting my gaze to the dragon. I thought he'd given up on us. His playfulness hinted that maybe he hadn't.

"How goes it with the beast?"

"We're learning," I replied. "She's scared of you."

"Is it my large sword?" he teased, patting the sheathed weapon by his side.

I snorted. "It's your eye."

"So, she fears control."

"I don't think it's simply control. She's willing to be led, guided. But I think she's encountered a Shadow in the past." A shred of terror bit at the back of my mind. "She fears it, her loss of will. So she fears you."

All mirth drained from his features as he faced me. "Did she kill them?"

"I don't know. The memory slipped out as if she didn't mean to share it with me."

He grunted, returning his attention to her. She knew he could control her with his eye and whatever magic lay behind it. He pulled the cloth covering from under his tunic and leaned forward to secure it in place. I reached out, laying a hand on his arm. The contact burned my skin in the most pleasant way, but I pulled against him.

"Don't. I don't want you to hide from me—from us," I whispered.

He looked between me and the dragon, battling something inside himself. It surprised me he'd offer to put it on at all. Normally, when he found out something bothered someone, he kept pushing.

"No one should be reminded of that horror," he rasped.

I shifted to my knees, blocking his view of the dragon. I cupped his jaw, enjoying the soft scratch of stubble against my palm. He closed his eyes at my touch and took a shuddering breath.

"You only remind me of good things," I said. "Face away from her if you must, but don't hide from me. Ever."

When his eyes fluttered open, his silver iris shimmered in the candlelight. "Such a demanding creature."

Whatever he battled in his mind, he tucked it securely behind a wall. He turned his head, nipping at my hand, and I dropped it. I stared at him, my gaze traveling to his lips. One would think they would be thin and firm on such a man, but they were full and–

"You keep looking at me like that and I'll leave now." The deep rumble in his voice reminded me he was as much moved with desire as I was.

I shuffled back, pressing myself against the stone wall, then wrapped my arms around my legs.

"Good girl."

I scoffed, snapping a glare his way. "I'm not a good girl."

"Mmm... but you are. Which is why I'm protesting your move to Ruveel."

My mouth fell open. "You're what? Why?"

"Shocked I have a conscience?" He picked a knot of lint from my blanket. "Ruveel would ruin you."

"How can you object to it? Will I get to stay in the Tennan?" I asked, hope flaring in my chest.

"No."

My heart sank. All this time, logic pointed out the impossibility, but I hadn't wanted to believe or accept it. I wanted to stay with the men I fit in with.

"But look at her, she's full-grown," he continued. "Your bond isn't the same as the others. Ruveel will force you into classes with the dragonlings. I can imagine how well that will go. When she eats one of them, or a Rider, they'll send her to the front. If her reaction to me is anything to go by, she would snatch you up and fly off with you before she's forced there."

"What will happen to me then?" I asked.

"I'm going to push for you to travel with Darrak."

"Darrak?" I echoed. "The King's bounty hunter?"

"He's the only one I trust to take down that beast of yours if she snaps."

"That's comforting."

He chuckled. "You need time away. Being stuck in a cave is no good for either of you. You should be under the sky. You need to explore together and give yourselves a chance to grow. Not to become one, but to intertwine."

"You're a modern poet, Rafe. I had no idea."

I gave him a bored look. He threw his head back and laughed. I smiled, but a pang of betrayal ached despite the truth to his words.

"You would send me away?" I asked quietly.

His laughter died, and he turned to me. That look told me all I needed to know about my General. With his eyes, he assured me that if there was a way, he would move the skies and earth to keep me close.

He reached over, gripping my chin. "I'm not sending you away. I couldn't do that." He cleared his throat. "I'm too selfish."

I let out a breathless laugh as his hand fell from my face, instantly missing its warmth.

"Darrak reports to the King once a month," he said. "He'd be required to report on you as well. If you do well, work out some kind of relationship with your dragon, you might make it to the front on your own terms."

"But not as part of your Tennan."

"No." A muscle worked in his jaw. "Not as my Tennan."

Rafe stayed well into the night. We kept our distance from each other but discussed everything. He'd known Darrak for many years, and recognized him when he joined the ranks. He wasn't careless enough to reveal who he was and treated him as he did anyone else. Though Darrak and I spent time together during our training, Rafe knew him far better. He trusted him and even admitted that he was more skilled in combat than himself. Rafe used brute force, whereas Darrak used cunning as well.

Rafe wanted to see me off with Darrak not only because he could defend me, but also because he trusted Darrak's guidance. He believed, through Darrak's care, my training could continue.

He didn't have an inkling of trust for Ruveel. I attempted to press the issue and find out why, though my efforts failed. Rafe said I couldn't trust him and left it at that.

Rafe's words before the dragon bonded me rang through my mind. 'It won't happen again.' He seemed to hold fast to that, making no move to initiate anything intimate, but was still possessive enough not to want me near the Dragon Lord.

As for Thunderbolt, Rafe told me the pigou's injuries would prevent him from ever riding into war. After he healed, he would be retired and sold to a farmer to make use of him as a workhorse. I had to be thankful Thunderbolt was still alive. Most horses, if they broke a leg or were mortally wounded, were put out of their misery and fed to the civilians. He was given a second chance. He had been a wonderful little horse, giving me the confidence to shoot from horseback when I had none.

We discussed the Tennan, and the antics of Tegan and Jam. We talked of their future and how he would continue their training, readying them for the front. A twinge of jealousy reared its ugly head. I was coming to accept the bond between me and the dragon, but I still longed to go back to how things were.

He rose to his feet, muscles rolling his heavy weight. I watched in awe of his sheer strength. He was as powerful as a bear, but as graceful as a fox... in movement only. His brash words still left much to be desired.

"Sleep, Vy," he said, adjusting the scabbard fastened to his hip.

"Stay."

Shadows danced across his glower. "No."

"Please." I didn't want to beg, but I didn't want him to leave. I understood nothing could happen. Still, I craved his comfort, the solidarity of his body next to mine.

He stretched, the bones in his spine popping. That movement alone warmed my skin. There was something mature about it. Whether it be his age or masculinity, just watching him move sent my heart racing.

He dropped to a crouch. I was on my knees, but the difference in height still put me shorter than him. He cupped my chin and pulled my face up. I put every ounce of desire and loneliness into my gaze.

"You are not a child. You do not beg."

I bit my lip. His gaze dropped to my mouth before darting up to my eyes.

"I cannot stay," he said. "Jamlin is waiting."

My eyes fluttered closed, and I nodded, pulling back. He gripped my jaw and held firm against my attempt. I forced my gaze to meet his, noting the burn of determination settle over his features.

"I'll return the night after next."

Relief swept through me. He would not abandon me now. He was coming back. I fought a grin. He wasn't leaving me... yet.

"Farewell," I whispered.

He let go and stood. Tying the cloth over his eye, he looked at the dragon in the corner. She huffed and flicked out her tongue, but didn't move. He started for the mouth of the cave, his form fading to a shadow as he slipped further and further from the weak candlelight.

"Dream of me," I breathed.

I wanted to slap myself. What a ridiculous, love-struck thing to say. Foolish and childish.

He snorted. When the heavy curtain shifted the slightest bit, I knew he was gone. I blew out the candle and pushed it to the side, curling in my blankets. Placing my head where he had sat, I took in the faint scent of the forest, of evergreens and earth, of *him*.

He would be back.

With a smile on my face, I drifted into a deep sleep.

CHAPTER 6

T he next morn I gathered my things to bathe. I smelled foul. If Rafe
was coming the next evening, I didn't want to reek like carrion. Dareth
brought most of my things, except for my weapons. I assumed Rafe still had
those.

I didn't have a spare tunic. The one I wore was my last in any semblance of
order, but I had clean trousers and under-breeches. I hefted my items and sat
against the dragon. Her eyes narrowed in an intense but curious expression. I
sent her an image of me bathing in a spring. The sensation of being clean and
fresh. She shivered against me, emanating a sense of eagerness.

'*Bathe. Clean,*' I said.

She sent me an image of herself diving into a deep lake. She swam in the
depths, hunting for large fish. It seemed she was hungry as well.

'*Hungry?*' I asked.

'*Hungry. Food.*' Her mental voice was firm. '*Bathe.*'

I smiled, waiting for Dareth to arrive. My moon cycle ended this morn, and
I was eager to be clean. I wondered if the dragon would like the springs. All the
others did. Bathing in an icy lake was one thing, bathing in a warm spring was
another.

I tried communicating with her again, trading words to pass the time.
'*Avyanna,*' I said, picturing myself.

'*Avyanna,*' she agreed.

I pushed an image of her through the bond with a question.

'*Dragon,*' she stated.

I laughed against her, and she flicked her tongue out, trying to comprehend
why I was amused.

I tried again. '*Name. Avyanna. Human.*'

'*Name. Dragon.*'

I pursed my lips, thinking of another way to ask. Perhaps if I guessed at names, she would pick one. '*Ainth?*'

I felt her confusion in response.

'*Ferah?*'

Strong dislike.

'*Elizzah?*'

She snorted, baring her teeth. I laughed again and kept trying. We tested out names for nearly a chime, till Flinor flew past our cave. I made no progress. It was possible she had her own name for herself, but I simply didn't know how to ask.

"Oi!" Dareth hailed.

Flinor perched on the edge of the cliff, leaning inside. I had tied the curtain back, so he knew he was welcome. The dragon bared her teeth but didn't snarl or hiss.

"Good morn, Dareth," I called, pushing to stand. The dragon must have sensed something was different, for she stood as well.

"Ah, finally ready to venture out?" he asked, noting my belongings tucked under my arm.

"I was hoping to bathe this morning."

"Wonderful! I'll try to keep the mob away," he said with a wink. He beamed, glancing up at my dragon. "You look brighter this morn!"

I smiled, taking that as praise. I hoped she was a bit more established and wouldn't lash out.

'*People are not food,*' I said.

'*Hungry,*' she replied.

I scoffed, looking at her. She tilted her head and watched me with bright eyes.

"It looks like you're communicating better," Dareth commented as I made my way toward the cliff.

"Aye, we worked on it all day yesterday. She understands a few simple words. She's hungry." I swallowed past the lump in my throat as I eyed the narrow, winding path.

"She still will not allow you to ride?" he asked.

"I wouldn't dare." I held onto the cliffside, careful of my footing.

Starting my descent, I clenched my jaw. It would take me a full chime to get down this treacherous route, let alone the time to climb back up. Would she allow me a whole day free from the cave?

"I'll fly ahead and send for a meal for her," Dareth called. "I'll meet you at the springs!"

Flinor clawed at the edge of the cliff, sending rocks and stones skittering down. He threw himself backward off the ledge, head over tail, launching himself into the middle of the canyon. Dareth laughed maniacally as Flinor streaked through the air, flying like a mad yearling.

Amusement had me shaking my head, and I edged my way down. The gray dragon keened low behind me. I stopped and pushed the sense of yearning and desire, along with the satisfaction after a warm bath.

'*I need to bathe.*'

'*Avyanna. Dragon. Mine.*' She was lonely.

Scared.

'*Come.*' I sent an image of her flying through the canyon beside me.

She hissed, and I turned as she stepped onto the path, long neck stretched toward me.

'*No. Fly.*' I barely fit on this passage. She couldn't hope to.

She threw her sense of abandonment at me. '*Hungry. Bathe.*'

'*Come! Fly!*'

I started once more, watching my footing. She would have to follow to find out. Her teeth clacked just behind, and I whirled to see her maw a handspan away.

'*Stop!*'

She growled and stepped further onto the ledge, trying to nip at me again. I hurried out of her reach, stumbling as fast as I could.

"This is foolish!" I muttered. I jogged down a path that I could barely fit two feet on the same step. One misstep, and I would fall to my death.

Her roar echoed through the canyon, followed by the flap of her mighty wings. I didn't glance back, focusing on putting one foot in front of the other as she flew alongside me. The path steepened with each step—I couldn't stop my momentum.

A thin layer of pebbles and sand had my feet sliding from beneath me. I clutched the rock wall, digging my nails into stone to slow myself. The rough surface scraped against my palm as I fell to my side. I scrambled and dropped my belongings, clutching at the small weeds that grew in the cracks.

The dragon screeched, and her shadow blocked out the sun. She thudded against the cliff, sinking her talons into the stone. Something slammed against me and a sharp sting whipped across my back. I cried out as I was lifted by my tunic. My skin felt like it was being flayed open. The rocks gave way beneath me, and I thrashed wildly against the pain.

The pressure on my tunic released, and I dropped like a stone. Wind whipped at me as I reached for the cliffside that was streaking past me. I had to catch myself. If I hit the rocks, I would die. Something snatched me around my waist and shoulder. My momentum jerked to a halt, and I clutched the thick talons as if my life depended on it.

The dragon hovered in place, flapping her wings hard, then peered down at me. Blood stained her lips, and a slow, hot trickle slipped from my back. She held me loosely but securely. She would not drop me, but I remembered the last time she whisked me away without thinking of my thin skin.

'*Down. Bathe.*' I pleaded with her. I wasn't giving up. If anything, I needed a bath more now, simply to see the damage done to my back.

She pushed an image of the cave, and beat her wings harder, rising.

'*Food.*' I threw images of cows and horses. She faltered in her flight and craned her head down at me again.

'*You're hungry. Food.*'

Her blazing eyes searched mine before she huffed and dropped in altitude. It was mere breaths before we hit the ground, and I stumbled as she released me. She swept her tail against the dirt floor in agitation, sending anxious glances to the top of the canyon.

'*Easy. You're safe.*'

She replied with annoyance, hunger and the urge to hasten.

My clothes were filthy and torn. My chest binding hung on by threads. She must have ripped through my tunic when she caught me. My back stung, and I ignored the prick of tears building behind my eyes.

"Avyanna!" Dareth shouted.

Flinor came to a stop a safe distance from us. He extended his neck, sniffing at me and flicking out his tongue. The gray dragon hissed and crowded in above me.

"What happened? I heard her roar and flight."

"Lost my footing," I muttered, holding out my empty hands. "I dropped my things."

He peered up the cliffside, where over a hundred paces above, my trousers hung against the stone. He let out an abrupt laugh, Flinor trilling along with him. I gave them a flat look, waiting for them to realize I could have been hurt.

"Aye! You did! Come, come, I've secured two boars for your dragon, and Rashel to accompany you to the spring."

I started his way. The gray dragon snaked her head at Flinor, flicking her tongue out with a hiss.

'*It's fine. They're friends.*'

She wasn't convinced he wouldn't try to take me away. His green scales sparkled with the first rays of sun as he turned, walking in front of us. He lazily swung his tail, and she lunged forward, snapping at it. Flinor tucked it up against his side and crooned over his shoulder. She snarled, but followed. I smiled at their antics, trying to ignore the sting in my back.

We made good time, reaching the entrance to the springs quickly. My back grew stiffer as the minutes passed, and I wondered how bad it was. It didn't seem like muscles were torn, but the blood that dampened my waistline had me worried.

Rashel stood at the entrance—a massive cave worn into the side of the canyon. The interconnecting caverns and springs within were expansive, large enough for a dragon three times the size of my gray. Beside the Healer was a young boy and an older man with a cart. Within it lay two dispatched boars.

Dareth waved me on. "Tell your dragon the boars are for her," he said.

She was already drooling, walking over me. I looked up at her underbelly as she moved, at least a pace, if not more, in clearance above my head. She lifted her hind leg high, careful not to hit me, then prowled for the food, hissing and snarling at everyone.

"Tell them to get away!" I yelled.

They glanced around, shifting on their feet.

"Get away!" I shouted at the lad with the older man.

They scattered as she launched at the boars, snaring one in her bulky mouth. She turned on Flinor, who was too close, then snorted and spat, thrashing her tail. He backed away with his head lowered in submission, giving her space.

Dareth focused on Flinor, making sure he was clear of her before he turned in his saddle to look at me. "Your back! What happened?" His mouth fell open, horrified.

I shrugged, instantly regretting the movement as my wound burned. "I fell."

"You and all your misadventures," Rashel cursed, clutching her Healer's satchel at her side. "You're worse than a child."

I frowned as the beast swallowed the first boar and snatched the other in her mouth.

"Hurry along, before she settles to eat outside!" Dareth urged.

Rashel led the way, and we plunged into the dim-lit caverns. The gray dragon followed, snarling around the boar. When we reached the main opening, her eyes flashed, taking in the sights of the steaming pools. With hurried steps, Rashel led us deeper into the cave system. She slowed as we entered an immense private cavern with two springs. The water flowed together, but an outcropping of brick and mortar carved the smaller of the two. The spring itself was so large that the dragon could easily lie in it, stretched from nose to tail.

I sighed as the familiar steamy balm of the springs greeted me. I could almost feel the grime dripping off, simply from the humidity.

"Strip." Rashel planted her hands on her hips.

"Yes, *milady*," I drawled.

"You get more and more defiant with every passing day," she muttered as I disrobed, then rolled her eyes with a sigh. "Where is the girl that sat and listened? The girl everyone claimed to be so sweet, saying she'd never make it as a soldier?"

The dragon settled off to the side, and I attempted to pull my tunic over my head, hissing in pain.

Rashel walked up behind me. "Stop. Let me see." She cursed and picked at the scraps of fabric stuck to my back. I flinched as she tugged the frayed cloth from my wound.

"Hands up as high as you can."

I obeyed, lifting my arms. My skin stretched taut across my shoulder blades. She lifted my tunic over my head and threw it aside.

"How did this happen? I've left you for two days!"

"I fell." My chin jutted toward the beast, crunching boar bones in the corner. "She caught me."

"By shearing off your skin? This will leave a nasty scar."

"She didn't mean to. I don't mind a scar."

My thoughts shifted to Rafe. Would he mind it? I brushed that thought away. He had enough scars of his own, he wouldn't mind any on me. He wasn't that shallow.

"I should stay in your cave. You need a Healer to travel as your personal companion." She pressed against my shoulder, urging me to the pool.

If she did, Rafe wouldn't come see me. I shoved away the panic of that thought. She wasn't serious.

He would come.

A moan slipped past my lips as I stepped into the water. It warmed me completely, soaking into my muscles. Waist-deep, I rested my forearms and chin on the pool's edge.

Rashel looked down at me with her arms crossed. "Don't move. I'm going to get you some proper soap. Perhaps there's a lady under all that dirt." She spun on her heel and walked off the way we came.

I turned my attention to the gray dragon. She was content to watch me with her fiery eyes, gnawing on the boar's leg.

'You should bathe.'

She didn't even bat an eye. 'Hungry,' she replied.

I smiled. She was a simple creature. She had priorities. I couldn't really blame her. She hadn't eaten in days, at least.

Dragons normally ate once a week, depending on their size and activity. In the summer months, they ate more. Younger beasts needed far more to meet the demands of their rapid growth. Adults could eat a deer a week, or a cow every two.

Keeping up with the feed was the most expensive part of Dragon Riders. The beasts sometimes flew off for a day to find their own food, then returned to digest it. Few preferred the hunt, but it relieved stress on the livestock.

She savored the boar. The first one had been a frantic attempt to get sustenance in her belly. With no other dragons around, she took her time with the
second.

She was finishing up when Rashel returned with an armful of clothes and
supplies. After setting the items aside, she eyed the dragon as she brought me
the soap and a rag.

"Wash up, then I'll tend to your back."

I pushed off the edge, taking the soap. My back protested, but I continued
with a grimace.

"Is she as wild as Dareth says?" Her voice carried no wonder, or fear, just
simple curiosity.

"You saw how she acted when she saw the boar," I muttered, washing away
days of dirt and grime.

"She's caused quite a stir," she mused. "People are heading this way for a
morning bath, knowing you're here."

I frowned, sinking below the surface. Holding my breath and scrubbing at
my hair, I wondered how she would act. I didn't want anyone gawking over me
or staring at her like she was some kind of exhibit.

As I surfaced, I caught her slinking toward the larger spring. She sniffed at it
and flicked her tongue out, tasting it. Craning her head up, she batted at it with
her massive paw. She snapped at the water, and I laughed as she whipped her
head in my direction.

'*Get in. Warm. Soothing,*' I said.

She bared her teeth in an unrecognizable expression, then turned back to
the spring. Stepping in with one paw, she trilled and slid her chin just over
the surface. Dipping her head under, she pulled up. Water dripped from her
stone-colored scales.

'*All the way,*' I urged.

Dragons loved the springs. They hated cold water, but warm water was
paradise to them. I understood her reluctance, considering she had only ever
known cold water.

She placed another paw in the spring and took her time advancing. I finished
washing and retreated to the pool ledge where Rashel waited.

"Bend over," she ordered.

I leaned forward, bowing my back. The softened skin stretched, and I
grimaced, waiting. She rummaged through her satchel, then her cool hands
slathered ointment onto my cuts. I flinched at her touch but held still.

"She simply took the skin. There's no muscle or tendon damage."

I nodded and watched the dragon swim through the water, trying to distract
myself. She looked at me, almost playfully, then submerged as much of her body

as she could. Little bubbles surfaced from where her head would be. There she rested.

"Out," Rashel snipped. "I'll wrap it with your chest binding."

I pulled myself out, already missing the warmth on my aching limbs. She reached for the items she'd brought and plucked a clean cloth from the pile

I eyed the clothes. "Where's my uniform?" I demanded.

She turned, eyebrows lowered in a deep frown that challenged mine. "This *is* your uniform," she said, motioning to the garments.

A green dress, simple in its design, but better made than I could normally afford. On top of it lay the single spaulder that the Dragon Riders wore. On its shoulder was the patch engraved into the leather, depicting a dragon in flight over a field of wheat, with spears rising from below.

"That's not mine." My nose wrinkled with distaste.

"True." She pointed to my tattered, bloody tunic and trousers. "Those are yours. This, I retrieved from the Dragon Rider's supplies."

"I'm not a Dragon Rider." My voice remained firm. I wasn't. I was still part of Rafe's Tennan—something I would cling to for as long as I could.

She stepped toward me and offered me the chest binding. I took it, and she pressed the clean cloth to my back.

"You are." She held the cloth in place as I wound the binding around my chest.

"I am not. I've yet to be transferred. General Rafe has not released me."

She stilled as I tied the binding, then moved in front of me. "How would you know that?"

"I know my General. He wouldn't release me so eagerly." I lifted my chin, determined to hide the lie.

She squinted, disbelieving. "This is what you have to wear. You will wear it."

"Please get me something else."

"No."

I glared. She was as stubborn as a hatchling.

"You will wear this, as you now have a dragon, and will train with the Riders." She waved me off. "Your General will transfer you."

My teeth ground together. I couldn't tell her Rafe wouldn't do so without a fight, but I also didn't want to wear the spaulder. I wouldn't mark myself as a Dragon Rider. It felt like a betrayal to Rafe and the Tennan.

The dragon's head resurfaced, and she snorted, spraying water out of her nostrils.

"I will wear the dress. Not the spaulder," I relented, pulling on the clean under-breeches.

"Curse your stubbornness," she muttered.

"Curse your own," I growled, then snatched the green dress.

Careful not to aggravate my wounds further, I pulled the fabric over my head. I frowned. It felt different. Not foreign, but uncomfortable. I'd grown accustomed to the feel of trousers about my legs. They were preferable to the sensation of nakedness from a dress. I tugged on the fabric, trying to make it more comfortable.

"Here." Rashel held out the armored spaulder. When I made no move to grab it, she rolled her eyes. "Take it, you fool. Keep it for now, even if you don't wear it."

I glared, but took it nonetheless. Perhaps I could hide it in the cave. I was well aware I acted this way because I didn't want to cut my ties with Rafe. The strap of leather didn't really matter—he did.

The dragon stepped out of the spring and bared her teeth as she stretched. Fed and clean, she turned her giant head toward me.

'*Tired,*' she rumbled. Through the bond, she pushed exhaustion, sleepiness and the desire for warmth and rest.

An idea formed in my mind. She would want to bask on the top of the canyon.

If I could keep her calm enough to show her.

CHAPTER 7

My hands pushed against the dragon's foreleg as she snarled and hissed. Too many gathered around the spring's entrance. Even one would have been too much for her. Dragonlings, too young to enter brumation or to make the flight to Southwing, cowered behind their Riders.

"People! For love of the sun, move back!" Dareth yelled.

Flinor let out a booming roar, trying to deter the crowd, but most simply laughed at him. They were too curious to be intimidated. They were ignorant of the violence she could wreak.

I pushed calming feelings toward her, but with every passing moment, my anxiety rose. How would I get her out of here? I didn't want her hurting anyone, but I understood her fear and anger.

She snapped her teeth, and I spun as a young man danced out of reach with a laugh. His bonded dragonling lingered behind him, flicking its tongue. It tasted the danger she posed, but apparently the Rider ignored it. No one had seen an adult dragon lash out at a human. It simply wasn't done. Dragons were respectful creatures, knowing they were far larger and more powerful than us. They treated us with care, almost as if we were babes.

She coiled in tight and stomped her feet. Snaking her head out with a bellowing roar, her body shook from the force of the cry. The crowd gawked at her display, but took a few steps back.

'*Fly.*' I sent an image of her soaring with me down to the canyon floor. '*Fly with me.*'

She hissed, lips twitching with her snarl.

'*Fly high,*' I urged, staring into her fiery eyes.

In one swift move, she snatched me and pushed down with her wings. Her talons were sharp, but not so much that I would carelessly cut myself on them again. The tips of her talons were another story. Her weight and size made rising in place a slow matter, and the Riders below urged their young dragons to take flight with her. They flicked their tongues out, tasting her irritation and anger, then shrunk away.

Flinor watched us go but didn't rise to join. She built up speed and flew through the canyon. She aimed for our cave, but I pushed at the door to our bond, prompting her higher. I pressed the sensation of crisp sun and fresh winter air, of peace and rest. After a grunt, she changed her course a fraction, bringing us to the clifftop.

She landed roughly on the top of the canyon, releasing me. She whirled and spat, searching for anyone who dared crowd her. I backed away, giving her space, and waited as she calmed, realizing no one followed.

My dress billowed around me, whipping in the stiff wind. Spring was still a long way out, but the break in snowfall couldn't be missed. Up here, the sunshine glistened across the layer of white—a blinding, iridescent shimmer. Winter could be beautiful, too. The sun's rays offered a touch of warmth as the bitter wind nipped at my skin. I rubbed my arms as she settled, peering up at the bright, cloudless sky.

I waited until she laid down completely before joining her. Pressing my back against her, I winced in pain but tried to convey safety and contentment. She flicked her tongue out, still feeling vulnerable. My breath billowed in gray puffs as I peered over the frigid landscape, watching the world as it went about its day.

The Dragon Canyon was more or less a gorge cleaved between two mountains—a giant seam that ran between what was once a small mountain, but now separated them in two. It had been around since the beginning of records. No one discovered what event caused such a formation.

Miners hollowed out many of the caves, though some occurred naturally. It was the perfect place to put up a fort to train Dragon Kind, as it suited both dragons and humans equally. To the west, the King's Lake glittered, its shores gleamed white with a layer of ice. Beyond, the great Sky Trees grew, though I couldn't see them from this distance.

The barracks lay to the southwest, and the Dragon Kind quarters were separate from both the barracks and school grounds by being placed in the canyon. Dragon Kind's training took place to the south, directly east of the school.

Everything was gathered together tightly, yet distinctly separated.

The irritated dragon huffed a breath and dropped her head to the ground. She closed her eyes, savoring the sun, and I smiled. She was still wary of her surroundings but relaxed enough to bask. I tugged open the door to our bond, bracing for pain, but relief dismissed my fear when none came.

Her serenity rushed over me. Satiated hunger. Cleanliness. Calm.

A purr rumbled from her, and I beamed. She was finally happy. I laid my head against her and talked to her. She wouldn't learn fast enough by me teaching her simple phrases here and there. Dragons could rifle through their Rider's thoughts. That's how they learned to communicate with words so quickly.

My mind was closed and guarded, something I didn't know how to remedy. Not to mention, I wasn't sure if I *wanted* that. If I let her in, and she saw something she feared, she could very well take it out on my fragile mind. If I couldn't let her in, I would have to talk my thoughts out with her. She would have to learn from my speech and feelings.

We sat on the lip of the canyon while I rambled about anything and everything. I told her about my family, about the school and the people there. All about Niehm, Elenor and Willhelm. I explained all I learned about dragons and their Riders.

Much of what I told her about dragons, she responded to with amusement. I sensed her confusion and mirth, as if much of it was silly. I pressed on, explaining details of fighting and what we understood of magic. When I mentioned magic, she hummed, and her body seemed to vibrate with excitement. She didn't understand the word, but the feelings and knowledge I pushed through the bond she grasped.

'*Do you know magic?*' I asked, holding my side with the intricate scar.

She replied with a memory of her hunting a deer.

'*Is hunting magical to you?*' I pressed, confused.

She opened a bright orange eye without moving her head. The sunlight drove her pupil to a slit as she examined me. She related an image of herself basking in the sunlight.

Still puzzled, I nudged my silent question across to her.

She sighed and dropped a scene of her mating with another dragon. It was a great blue beast, and they flew high above the clouds.

Want. Desire. Instinct.

I pulled away from the vision and emotions, embarrassed at being exposed to something far too private. Everyone witnessed the mating dance in the sky. I had not, however, experienced their feelings.

She lifted her head and craned over me, pushing another image. She was basking in the sun when movement caught her eye—a young doe at the edge of the woods. She rose and gave chase, not hungry but out of instinct to track prey.

She visualized me lying in the snow. I was bleeding, my lifeblood staining the ground crimson. Rafe stood over me. She pushed that familiar instinct, the need to do something.

'*It's instinct,*' I mused. Filtering the feeling, I sent her a blinking eye, a flinch from a bang, jerking away from a tickle.

She approved of my assessment and settled once again. So for her, magic was instinctual. She didn't consciously reach for it. We assumed that's what happened with hatchlings. They grasped magic by instinct, but it was trained into them as they grew.

Even older Riders were careful and very limited with their magic. It was still a feared thing. Some Riders flourished without the knowledge or ability of how to reach for it at all—as if they were unable to find the door.

Could I grasp magic? Was it beyond a mental barrier like the bond was? Perhaps if I reached to the dragon's side of the bond, I could grasp magic through her. Or was it something I had to go through myself? I would learn soon enough.

I sighed, leaning against her scales, the warmth soothing my aching back.

My grin faded, thinking of the classes we would be put in. The other Dragon Kind would be around my age, but all the dragons would be hatchlings. The surly dragon did not need to find out what she preferred to eat, or how to fly. She wouldn't have to learn how to breathe fire. She was an adult. The wild taught her those things. She would be an outcast, and therefore, I would be as well.

We spent that day on the canyon's crest, trying to communicate and simply *being* with each other. She wasn't as violent when I was the only one around.

My back stiffened as the chimes passed, and the scab grew tight and painful. As darkness fell, she flew with me in her paw to our cave. She retreated to her corner, not scrambling like she normally did. I smiled, realizing she was more relaxed around me now. We shared a measure of trust.

The next day was more of the same. After another bath and having my wounds tended by Rashel, the dragon and I basked in the wintry sun.

My mind kept traveling back to Rafe, and the fact he was coming to see me tonight. I was nervous and anxious. I buried the Dragon Rider spaulder deep in my pack. It felt childish to hide such a thing, but I didn't want him to think I wasn't loyal to the Tennan. I was out of the uniforms and even Dareth thought it was absurd that I requested a new one.

So today, I wore a soft dress, the darkest blue. I blushed when I asked Rashel for a night shift. She nodded and took it in stride, not thinking anything of it. It was, after all, what women slept in. Though not soldiers. I hadn't slept in something so feminine in months.

And I knew exactly why I wanted it.

I bounced my head against the dragon's warm scales. Nothing could happen. Not only was I still his soldier, but I was not taking the tinge berry tea. There were other teas to help prevent pregnancy, but if I asked for them, everyone would know why.

Rafe and I couldn't be together—that didn't mean I didn't enjoy playing with fire. He pushed me away before the dragon bonded me, and I meant to remedy that. There was something addictive and powerful about driving him to his limit, testing to see how mad I could make him. I knew he desired me, yet I also knew he was strong enough of a man to resist it... to a point. If his resolve ever broke, I wasn't sure I could stop him.

Or if I would want to.

'*Mate,*' the dragon rumbled, tasting my thoughts.

I stiffened, getting a sudden dose of reality, and a stark reminder that my mind was not mine alone anymore. If I wasn't careful, feelings and emotions would drift across our bond. She couldn't reach out to my mind, and I couldn't reach into hers, but we shared more now. After almost two weeks, we were finally coming to understand one another.

Yet, this felt too private.

It was one thing to call Rafe my mate when I was defending him, trying to keep her from eating him. To have someone know my feelings, my innermost secrets—I wasn't ready for that.

'*No, not really.*' I didn't want her to think I had lied... but how could I explain this to her?

She envisioned me with a babe in my arms.

'*No!*' I shrieked, pulling back.

She recoiled, and her head shot up, peering down at me. Her gaze was wary, but curious. She visualized Rafe and me the other night. I studied the sight of us through her eyes. He rested against the wall, stretched out and relaxed. I sat beside him, knees up to my chest. I was talking with him and gesturing with my hand. We looked... happy. Content. The warm candlelight danced over us, glinting in his shadow-touched eye. He smirked at something I said, and I buried my face in my lap.

I couldn't help but smile at the mental picture. It meant everything to me. I wanted to remember that moment forever and never let it go. No matter what happened. That scene was the essence of *us*. It was a secret moment, stolen away from society and the judgment we would get from others.

'*Friend.*' I corrected. I thought about sending the feelings that arose from that image, but decided against it. If I did, she would notice I might... love him.

I didn't, of course. Did I? Love was a silly thing that other women experienced. We simply got along well. We liked each other—desired each other. He was a powerful man, and he saw something in me he admired.

Was that love? Did I know enough of my own heart to know I loved him? A blush crept up my cheeks as I remembered the night the dragon found us. I had thought I loved him—but was that love or want?

I wasn't foolish enough to demand he be my life mate. That dedication... We already traveled down that road. And he made it clear he didn't want children. I didn't want to think about lifelong dedication or children.

I just wanted to be happy *with* him.

Was that too much to ask?

"My, my. Don't you look like a proper lady."

My lips curled against the blanket I had bunched up as a pillow. The dragon hissed in the background but was content to stay in her corner... or so I thought, judging from the distance of her warning.

I scoffed, sitting up to light a candle. Pain laced across my back, and I winced.

"Stop."

"Rafe, let me light a candle," I whispered, reaching for my pack.

Heavy hands dropped on my shoulders, holding me in place. "Be still. You're bleeding." His rough voice rumbled in my ear.

I shivered against the chill of the night air and his proximity. "It's fine," I breathed.

He pulled the back of my night shift lower. His fingers stopped just under my shoulder blade, tracing the edge of the cloth pressed to the wound.

"How did this happen?" he rasped.

"It's fine, really." I started to turn, but his hands moved back on my shoulders, holding me in place.

"Tell me."

His voice gave no room for argument, and I sighed. Sometimes he was so stubborn. I liked him regardless.

"The dragon tried to catch me when I fell."

"What? With her teeth?" he asked, his tone sarcastic.

"Well... yes."

There was a moment of disbelieving silence, followed by a grunt. When his touch retreated, my breath caught. I pulled the night shift back in place and clutched the front lacing shut. Scouring the dark, I tried to catch any movement, any hint of shadow. The dragon shifted in her corner, but it didn't sound like she was coming any closer.

I heard the scrape of flint, then a spark lit a small candle. The soft glow illuminated Rafe's face as he set it in a holder. It also illuminated his deep frown. Setting the candle in place, he looked between me and the dragon. He turned away, then rummaged through my things. I watched, intrigued, as he went through my pack and other belongings, his agitation increasing.

An amused smile lifted the corner of my mouth. "What are you looking for?"

"A blasted clean cloth," he grumbled.

"Rashel has been caring for it in the mornings."

He froze, staring into my pack as if it held all the answers. Sitting back on his haunches, he eyed me warily. "That thrice-cursed Healer?" he spat.

"She's made an impression on you as well, I see."

"Been trying to get at me since I've been here." He tapped his shadow-touched eye before he glanced back at the pack, his gaze lingering on it.

"I'm sure you've merely piqued her Healer's curiosity." I leaned forward to pat his thigh. More of the scab gave way, and I winced.

His eyes flashed to mine, and he settled on his heels, watching me. Something simmered across his features, and it wasn't friendly. I squinted, wondering what upset him.

"Ruveel is coming for you."

A chill washed over me, and I clutched my night shift tight. "When?"

"The soonest opportunity." Meager candlelight flickered in his glare.

The dragon hissed and shifted her weight. I frowned, reining my emotions in. She didn't need to sense my fear.

"Will he transfer me?"

"Perhaps."

I exhaled, then held my breath, studying him. What had come over him? He was closed off, his mental wall erected. His playfulness, the easygoing Rafe I enjoyed teasing, hid away.

"Will you still push for me to travel with Darrak?" I asked, testing the waters. Please don't surrender me without a fight.

He stood with a quiet grunt, forcing his weight upright. Looking down at me, he held himself stiffly. "Seems like you'd rather be tied to him."

I tilted my head as my lips parted. When had I ever insinuated I would rather be with the Dragon Lord? My impression of him was slick and slippery, sly and cunning. I didn't trust him.

The blasted spaulder.

I scrambled to rise despite the pain in my back. "No, Rafe–"

"Don't bother." Anger danced in those dark eyes, his brows furrowed deeply.

I stood tall and met his gaze. My state of undress didn't worry me nearly as much as him pushing me away.

"Don't tell me not to bother. You don't understand."

"I don't need to," he quipped, his glare searing my skin. "You're a woman now. You made your choice."

"I did," I snapped, reaching for his tunic.

My fingers curled, fisting the fabric, but he didn't pull away. Somehow, that meager motion made me seem all the more pathetic compared to his bulk.

"I chose you," I hissed through my clenched teeth.

He jerked, shoving off my hold. "Looks like it," he bit out, then looked me up and down with a foul twist of his lips.

He noted my dresses, my night shift, my spaulder—the garb of a Dragon Rider, not a soldier. He thought my dress indicated my choice?

"Rafe, I didn't have any clothes. These are what I was given. Unless you expect me to run around in a pair of simple trousers and my chest binding?" An edge crept into my voice. He had no reason to lash out at me. Did he think I betrayed him?

His eyes flitted down to my chest, barely covered by the night shift, before returning to my face. "And if I get you a proper uniform?"

"I would wear it." I lifted my chin. "You are my General. I am still part of your Tennan. Dragon or no, I'm still yours."

The beast in the corner snarled. I didn't care if she understood fragments of the conversation or not. I belonged to him first.

He eyed me, and something flickered in the darkness of his gaze. He rushed me, and I backed up a step, slamming into the wall. His chest crushed against me, and he hauled my chin up. My back stung and complained, but I didn't jerk away.

"They won't accept you," he hissed.

"I know."

"Ruveel would spread your legs, use you, then toss you to the Shadows as fodder." His voice was heavy with emotion.

"I know."

I heard rumors here and there concerning the Dragon Lord. All the women swooned over him. He left a foul taste in my mouth, and though I only met him once, I knew his kind. Is that why Rafe was angry? Was he jealous?

His temper and viciousness gave way like frost under the sun's glare. It melted away as he searched my eyes. He grunted and braced his hands on the stone above my head. Resting his temple on his bicep, he stared down at me.

"There are choices you have to make for yourself."

I blinked at his words. This was not the Rafe I was used to. He told me what I should and shouldn't do—he didn't give me choices. The one time he had was when he offered the chance to join his Tennan.

"I..." He trailed off, and his gaze softened.

I knew what he wanted to say, but wouldn't. My hand cupped his cheek, then trailed to his jaw. Slipping a thumb over his lips, I gave him a shy smile. "I'm yours, Rafe."

"You have finer options."

"I'm not aware of them."

"Obviously." He barked a harsh laugh. "If you were, you wouldn't say such foolish nonsense."

I frowned and struck his chest in jest. "I've never felt like this toward anyone before."

"Like what?" He straightened his head, arching a brow.

Heat crept up my cheeks. It felt as if I played with fire whenever I was near him. When he let his guard down, when he allowed me to see who he really was, it was like bathing myself in flame, immune to its burn.

"Like I'm on fire." I breathed the words, airy and light.

My palms slipped down his chest, and I hooked my fingers through his belt, giving a gentle tug. His eyes burned with desire, but he remained firm. He didn't allow me to pull him closer, instead having the resolve and strength of a pillar.

"And when did you start feeling this way?" Unspoken emotion thickened his voice.

"I don't recall," I whispered, sliding my touch under his tunic.

His breath came out in a hiss, and I wondered just how far he would let me push him tonight. How far before he'd put a stop to our game... or be consumed?

"Was it, perhaps, when you spied on me bathing?" he asked with a smirk.

"I did not!" I choked on a laugh. My fingers stilled over the hard ridges of muscle that lined his stomach.

"Tell me," he said, ducking closer, "did you like what you saw?"

"I only saw your back." My breaths grew shallow as I swallowed past the lump in my throat. My hands trembled, and I wondered if he noticed.

His arms shook with restraint, but he stayed strong. He didn't touch me or let me bring him closer. His words from our last argument slithered in the back of my mind. 'It won't happen again.'

"Did you find the scars abhorrent?" His gaze sank to my lips, pulling my attention to the present. He watched my mouth, waiting for an answer.

I changed tactics and leaned against the stone, ignoring the protest of my wounds. "Actually," My head tipped as I dropped my hands, offering him a complete view of my submission, "I found them attractive."

"Mmm?" His gaze traveled down my body, hands clenched into fists against the wall.

"They tell me you're strong." I arched my back. Euphoria rushed beneath my skin. "They tell me you're mature. A man, not some boy."

"You want a man?" His voice was rough and deep as his eyes flicked up to mine.

My heart raced. "Yes," I whispered, the word a breathy sigh. My blood pulsed in my ears. Every cell screamed for his touch. I never felt so alive.

"Take him."

My mind stalled. I stared at him in a blank daze, failing to process what he said.

With a curse, he tore from my space, walking a few paces away. I gasped and deflated as the night's cold sapped the heat that built up between us. I clenched my fists, cursing my hesitation.

With his back to me, he dropped into a crouch, biting out a string of curses. He bowed his head, knitting his fingers at the nape of his neck.

I took a cautious step closer. "Rafe?"

"Don't, Vy." He viciously rubbed the thick muscles on his neck. "Give me a moment."

I retreated the single step I'd taken. Secretly, I was thrilled. Not that he was in some kind of pain, but that I had such an effect on him. I drove him to his knees. My teeth sank into my lip, fighting off my smile. I shouldn't have been amused by his struggle.

With a forced exhale, he rose to his feet. He adjusted his trousers, which I had disheveled, before turning to me. His daring smirk stole the air from my lungs.

"You know what you do," he said.

I blushed and averted my gaze to my toes. "Aye," my arms wrapped across my chest, brushing off the chill, "I think I do."

"You're a rabbit playing with a wolf, girl."

I sneaked a look up at him. "Will it eat me?"

He threw his head back with a laugh. Mirth and desire danced in his gaze. "You want it to, don't you?"

"If I did?"

"I would tell you to be careful, little rabbit." He stepped closer, reaching out to grip my chin. "One day it just might."

My lips parted, and my heart skipped a beat. Sparks flitted low in my belly, threatening to start another fire.

"I'll get you your weapons tomorrow. You need to keep practicing," he said, pulling away.

My body leaned toward him of its own accord as he turned. I stumbled and pulled myself upright. "Will you practice with me?"

His deep chuckle answered. "Sleep, Avyanna," he ordered, and a shadow shifted in the dark. The curtain whispered as it drifted closed behind him.

I grinned like a schoolgirl and returned to my pile of blankets. My body tingled, both light and alive—empty and longing. He was addictive, this General of mine. My head screamed that it was foolish. As principled as he was, even he would snap if I kept pushing. My passion was young and immature. If I kept taunting him, teasing him, his desire would break free.

I let out a strangled squeal and wiggled against the blankets, the sting in my back not giving me pause. Yes, it was dangerous... but it brought me so much joy. The dragon snorted, then pushed an image of dragons flying the mating dance in the sky, then a nest of eggs. She clearly didn't see the point in him running off without making babies. I blew out the candle and closed my eyes.

She didn't understand the finer points of seduction.

As if I did.

CHAPTER 8

We spent the next day much like the others, drinking in the winter sun on the lip of the canyon—enjoying the break in snowfall while it lasted. I rambled off names to her, trying to find one that fit. I liked Tea'mar, but she didn't respond to it. Every one I pushed at her, she brushed away.

I leaned against her, enjoying her presence. I was getting used to her... if only a little. Her company reminded me of the Tennan. If perhaps they didn't speak, except in emotions and simple words. I'd grown close to several of them—Jamlin and Xzanth especially, considering I was to be with them at any given moment. Rafe hadn't done that to monitor me, but rather to give me as much training as possible in so little time. He had me tailing veterans to pick up on the simplest things they did. Like how Jam always seemed relaxed but was constantly checking his surroundings. Or how Xzanth would stop and listen when he heard something in the distance and not move until he placed it.

The dragon was more or less my team, or part of it. I still wanted to be in the Tennan, and she would never replace that, but with her, I wasn't as lonely as when I was a simple soldier.

What I was now, I had no idea.

I wouldn't be part of the Tennan. Now that I bonded with a dragon, I was no longer a soldier. I doubted I would be a proper Dragon Rider no matter the number of classes I attended. If Rafe got his way and I traveled with Darrak... well, that was also unheard of. Dragon Riders didn't wander the King's Land. They patrolled the borders of Regent and fought on the frontlines. Ge'org, Ruveel's bonded, traversed to and from the palace, but to have a dragon flying about as they pleased was unheard of.

I tilted my head, eyes closed, to soak up the rays of sunshine. The dragon pushed thoughts against me. She let feelings of being cornered and surrounded trickle through. She sent an image of her in the cave, of her facing off the crowd at the springs, of her at the top of the cliff.

Bound. Trapped. Tied down.

She envisioned herself flying through the Sky Trees—enormous trees I'd never set sight on, but saw through her eyes. She made a nest in their branches. They were so thick she was like a bird among them.

She sent scenes of her hunting, mating, and basking in the heat of summer—slumbering in her nest in the winter.

Freedom. Liberty.

'*You are not trapped,*' I said, frowning.

Was she truly free? She was bound to me. She couldn't live as she normally would. I was an anchor, and she wanted to fly, to do as she pleased, not be restrained by a simple human and their obligations.

I wondered if other dragons felt the same, though I couldn't recall such a thing ever being mentioned. They held so much of their Rider's sense of dedication since hatching. I doubted they ever craved true freedom to do as they would. My dragon was different. She lived a life where she could do as she pleased, eat what she wanted, live how she desired...

Until she found me.

She shifted, then dipped her massive head toward me. Her flaming eye pinned me in place as she snorted.

Loneliness. Desire. Emptiness.

She recalled the night she found me, when she plowed into me with her great muzzle. Feelings drifted across our bond. It was hard to place them with singular words. She felt scared, yet safe. Angry, but relieved. Vulnerable, yet powerful. It was as if the bond weakened her, but also provided the answer to her loneliness.

'*Did you seek me out because you were lonely?*' I asked.

I knew she wouldn't understand, and honestly, it seemed far-fetched. Why would a dragon, one who thrived in the wild, desire company? Were dragons social creatures? From what I gleaned from her, they were solitary. Aside from her chosen mate, she never sent images of another dragon.

She'd clearly been looking for me, but why? What drove her, after so many years alone, to seek me out?

She pulled up to face the sun and closed her eyes in peace.

I frowned. Could she be the reason I was refused twice? Because the dragonlings knew I was a better fit for another? Was magic sentient enough to know I was destined to be bonded to this dragon specifically?

Magic was viewed as a tool, not a living thing. Surely, it had no intent or purpose of its own. It was wild. When someone loosed it without purpose, it seemed aimless, as though it found something to do, then did it. Much like a spark without guidance might engulf a forest, not warm a hearth.

She whipped her head, cutting my thoughts short as she stood. My back complained at the sudden shift. I rose with her, giving her space as she spun, tail lashing. I didn't want to be caught unaware by one of those limbs. She snarled over the precipice, peering down at something. The thunder of wings sounded from below, getting closer. Dareth didn't visit at this time. Perhaps it was another Rider whose dragon woke early from brumation.

My question was answered when a small blue beast peeked over the edge, rising warily, keeping a safe distance. It was young, barely big enough to carry its Rider. If they were fourth years, they'd be sent to the front on Recruitment Day.

The Rider's hair whipped around her as her dragon ascended to the cliff. It rose on its hind legs and fanned its wings as it landed, making itself appear larger.

I eyed it nervously as the gray dragon hissed and snapped at it with teeth as long as the young dragon's head. Perhaps it wanted to sunbathe as well.

'*Calm. It's friendly,*' I assured her.

Annoyance. Irritation. Anger.

'*Child.*' She snarled.

I smiled. Here she was, a mother herself, yet apparently, didn't take kindly to little ones.

"Hail!" the Rider called.

I moved from behind the angry wall of scales and saluted the new Rider. "Hail!"

I shaded my eyes from the sun as she dismounted. The blue put on a grand show, flapping her wings. The Rider gave her a reassuring pat before looking back at me. I headed her way, ignoring the larger dragon's snort of distaste.

"You must be the new Rider," she said, giving us a curt nod.

I met her between the dragons. "Aye. In a way, I guess."

"Shouldn't you be on the front?"

My smile fell. "We were just bonded a few weeks ago." I spoke with caution. Her eyes were warm, but her words were sharp.

"With a dragon that size, you're worth more there than here."

"It's not that simple," I started. "We can't communicate well."

"As well as any other Rider, I'd assume."

"You'd assume incorrectly." I pulled myself up to my full height, still shorter than her, but the motion lent me confidence. "We cannot communicate in words."

"Belany and I don't use words. We simply know what each other is thinking," she said, nodding to her dragon.

"Aye, and that would work with a dragon you bonded with as a hatchling." I tried to keep the venom from my voice, but failed.

Annoyance tightened my chest. I didn't like what her tone insinuated, as if she thought herself better than me. I didn't need to justify myself to this Rider or her dragon.

"If you're not going to the front, are you attending classes?" she asked. She flashed her teeth in a wide grin.

Perhaps this was just her personality. We wouldn't mesh well. Regardless, I was in no mood for an interrogation.

"We would like to bask in peace, if you will," I bit out, then turned back to my dragon, who stood with her teeth bared in a snarl.

"Oh, don't let me interrupt. You've only been lazing around for days, not attending classes or training. Eating your fill and sleeping the week away as if there wasn't a war going on."

I froze in my tracks. Anger flared, and I ground my teeth against my reply. She couldn't understand the difficulty that came with trying to communicate with a Wild One.

"What's your name, Rider?"

"Cyane."

With a quick nod, I returned to my dragon's side. "I'll be sure to avoid you, Cyane. I advise you to do the same."

My dragon was not ready to give up her basking spot, so I started down the thin trail of the cliffside alone. I was running, absolutely, but I didn't want to fight. I would have enough of that if Ruveel put me in the Dragon Rider classes.

Eventually, I would have to stand up for myself. If I was put in a situation with people who didn't know me, or understand my circumstances, I would have to show them how to treat me—something I learned too late in the barracks.

I didn't grasp enough of my bond with the dragon to push back the accusations or comments from other Riders, but I definitely had the upper-hand when it came to fighting. A few challenges, and I would establish my place among them. Riders didn't train heavily in hand-to-hand combat. They focused on air tactics. They could train with weapons, spear and bow were encouraged, but it wasn't a priority.

The bond was the priority.

Even if a Rider had poor skill in calling magic, they were still a foe to be feared because of their dragon's fire-breathing capabilities. They were our greatest weapons on the front, regardless of magical talent.

I slipped and caught myself. Loose stones skittered off the path, and a muffled curse sounded from below. Clutching the cliffside, I peered down to see who I just showered with stones.

"Hail!"

Collins' head shot up beyond the sheer rock face. "Hail, Avyanna!" He smiled before ducking away as more debris fell. "Oi, where's your cave?"

There was a cloth-covered spear strapped to his back, and my mood improved threefold. I pointed. "The large one, there, with the curtain."

He followed my finger, then adjusted his course, continuing to climb.

A shadow passed overhead and the gray dragon peered down at me, her tongue flicking out in question.

'*A friend,*' I said, assuring her.

She leapt off the cliff and coasted to our cave as I ducked inside. She landed on the ledge, tail thrashing as she balanced herself.

Collins cried out, and I ran past her to lean over the edge. His thin frame clung to the solid rock wall with his fingers in the smallest cracks.

"Do you want a hand?" I called.

"And forfeit his bet?"

I spun to face a man with tidy facial hair and a long lanky frame. His blue eyes sparkled with mischief. He leaned against the stone wall outside our cave. He looked for all the world as if he'd been there the whole time, though I just walked past. How had he slipped there so silently?

"Hail Blain!" I had never been so excited to see the man.

He held my crossbow over his shoulder and arched an eyebrow at me.

"Hail, girl."

Collins grunted, throwing an arm over the side of the landing. "Could've given me a warning, Avyanna."

"I didn't know she'd follow." I shrugged as he hauled his body over.

Blain pushed off the wall, handing me my crossbow. "So it's a she," he said.

The dragon hissed behind me and bared her teeth, but made no move to eat them.

"Aye."

"She have a name?" Collins asked, untying my spear from his back.

I sighed, hugging the crossbow to my chest. I really wanted to call her something, but I was running out of ideas. "Not yet. Nothing sticks."

Collins eyed her with keen interest and handed me the spear. A smile spread over my face as its familiar weight hit my hand.

"May I?" he asked, motioning to her.

I frowned, not knowing what he was up to. I didn't want him to get hurt. "She's volatile, but she'll give you fair warning before she snaps."

The dragon eyed him, but let her lips fall over her teeth. The tips of her fangs still hung out, but most were hidden from view. Her irises burned like a furnace as she watched his every move.

"You know, I've always liked dragons," he whispered.

He crept toward her while Blain and I observed—awestruck. My focus darted between her and him, waiting for the telltale snap of heavy jaws, or roar of insult. He hummed a low tune, an eerie lullaby, as he placed one foot in front of the other. His eyes lowered, glancing up now and then, but avoiding her gaze. He dropped into a crouch, not close enough to touch her, but he lifted his palm in silent question.

She eyed him, waiting for him to spring up and attack—or some other sudden, unwelcome movement. I held my breath, but he remained still. Blain didn't speak, watching as Collins worked on her.

She heaved a weary sigh, and I felt something slip across the bond, as if she was humoring the antics of a hatchling. She lowered her head to sniff at his hand. Flicking her tongue out, she tasted for danger and intent. Finding nothing amiss, she lipped his small hand. Snorting, she butted it away and sat back. He gave a breathless laugh and rose.

"That boy has magic," Blain muttered. "I'd be willing to wager."

"You'd lose that bet as well." Collins turned to us with the biggest grin on his face and a spring in his step.

Blain tossed him a coin—I presumed for the bet on whether Collins could scale the canyon cliffs. The boy had an uncanny ability for climbing, as was proven by him scaling flat stone walls with a spear tied to his back.

"Tizmet."

An odd sensation resonated inside. Something across the bond registered and rang true.

"What was that?" I asked, trying to understand the feeling.

"Tizmet." He shrugged, flashing a shy smile. "She seems like a Tizmet."

'*Tizmet.*' The dragon purred. She blinked lazily. Acceptance and pleasure buzzed into the bond.

I pushed an image of herself. '*Tizmet?*'

'*Dragon. Tizmet,*' she replied in agreement.

"Apparently, you've just named her," I murmured.

Collins had a silly grin on his face, clearly thrilled that she liked his name. I was put-out, however, that she chose a name from him and not me. Perhaps that was simply his way with animals.

"'Tis a good name. It's one I know," Blain said, looking deep in thought. He leveled his gaze at Collins. "Dane told you, didn't he?"

Collins shrugged out a nod, and Blain rolled his eyes, heaving a sigh. I waited for him to elaborate.

"It's a bedtime tale from my homeland," he explained.

None of us, except perhaps Rafe, knew where Blain and Dane hailed from. They kept that a closely guarded secret.

"I'd like to hear it," I urged.

Collins settled on the cliff's edge, letting his feet dangle. Blain sank against the wall near the entrance, watching the dragon, Tizmet, with calm interest. I set my crossbow down and sat beside him, laying my spear over my lap.

"It's an old tale, one forgotten by many. A *love* story."

He winked at me, and I smirked.

"There once was a girl named Tizmet. She was fair-haired, with locks like spun gold. Her eyes were the bluest of blue, the color of a cloudless summer sky. A simple weaver's daughter, she was not one of any rank. She fell for the cobbler's son, and they were well and truly in love, promised to be given to each other the following season.

"It's said the lord of the land was traveling through, collecting his taxes when he spied the young maiden. Being smitten by her beauty, he stole her from her village. Both families fought for her return, but the lord would not be swayed. Thinking that after he lay with her, she would accept his advances, he took her by force, against her will."

My smile dropped into a frown, but I did not interrupt. This would not be tolerated in Regent, the King wouldn't stand for it, lord or not.

"Still, he found she would not surrender her true love. The weaver and cobbler roused the surrounding villages in an attack on the lord's grounds. When he saw his people had risen against him, he decided to be rid of her to unburden himself the inconvenience of fighting."

His gaze snapped to my short hair, and I gave it a nervous tug.

"He put out her eyes and cut her hair. Blind and humiliated, he offered her to the masses. Expecting the villagers to put down their arms, he retreated to his fortress and locked himself inside. They were outraged at what he'd done, and set fire to his home. Consumed by their rage, they didn't see Tizmet stumble, in her blindness, back to the fortress.

"As the fire took, the villagers barred the doors and windows from the outside. All the while, the cobbler's son searched for his love. The fire ate at the fortress, devouring wood, cloth and life. It tore through the lord's home, his screams barely audible over the roar of flames.

"Tizmet was seen at the top of his fortress, trying to escape. The cobbler's son screamed for her, but she was already alight with flame. Her body ignited, but she was silent. No cries opened her mouth, though tears slipped from her cheeks. Walking to the edge of the fortress, she fell, a flaming pillar streaking through the sky. The cobbler's son caught her, catching fire, and burned with her."

Blain stopped, and I gaped at him, horrified. His eyes unfocused, and he stared off into the distance.

"Then?" I prompted.

He blinked. "Well, I'd like to say the villagers learned to never get so caught up in their revenge that they destroy what they sought to protect, but... perhaps you can fill in your own happy ending." He shrugged.

"That's horrible. A bedtime tale? That's what your people tell their children at night?"

Blain's eyes flashed. He whirled on me with a malice I had never seen. Tizmet rumbled in the corner as tension prickled like static.

A shadow consumed his face—the look of one who'd witnessed true horror. "There are far worse things for children to hear." He blinked, and as quickly as it came, all hostility disappeared.

I sat back, unnerved by his actions.

"It was probably something about the fire flying through the sky," he mused. "Or perhaps the stolen freedom that caused him to peg her with that name."

I glared at Collins' hunched form on the cliff. "It's a terrible name, Collins!"

"Aye! But it fits her!" he called over his shoulder.

Blain chuckled and tilted his head, watching Tizmet again. "One would wonder how you will meet your end," he murmured under his breath. "Will you also perish in fire?"

The way his darkened stare leveled on her caused my heart to falter. His tone made it almost sound prophetic, as though he were damning us.

"Blain?"

He turned to me again, his eyes unseeing and far away. His mouth curved in a small, sorrowful smile, as if he pitied me.

I stared, not knowing what to make of his antics. He'd always been odd, as well as his brother, but he never acted like this before. What did he mean by it? Where did he hail from that was so terrible?

"Oi, Blain."

Collins nudged him with a boot and Blain blinked again—that far away look waned.

"So the General said you're to train every day." Blain rose to his feet and brushed off his trousers. "Just because you're labeled a Dragon Rider now doesn't mean you get to be lazy."

"I would expect no less." As I stood, I pulled the cloth off my spear and admired the weapon. A dark leather sheath concealed the blade, but the weight was still familiar.

Blain grimaced, looking around. "Aye, and you should get some furnishings. This place looks less homey than a tent on the frontlines."

It *was* barren, and I was sick of sleeping on a hard stone floor, but I wasn't willing to risk the trek along those winding, minuscule paths with any furniture. "If you'd like to haul a cot or table up that path, you let me know," I replied dryly.

Normally, the dragons carried their Rider's belongings up to the larger caves. Mirth drifted across the bond. The idea of dragons carrying such trivial things amused her. I gave her a flat stare, and she snorted.

"Would the other Riders not lend their dragons to the cause?" he asked.

I frowned. The idea of asking someone like Cyane for help made my skin crawl. "I wouldn't ask favors of them. Not if I can help it."

"Wise choice." He nodded, approving of my answer. "We'll be off then."

"Wait," I started.

They paused at the entrance, both raising a curious brow.

"I—can you tell the men–"

"Aye, kitten." Blain offered a knowing smile. "I'll tell them."

With that, they made their leave.

I heaved a sigh, heavy with emotion. When would I see them next? How long had it been since I'd seen Willhelm, Niehm or Elenor? When would I see the Tennan again?

Frowning, I unfastened the sheath and tossed it aside. Moving to the middle of the cave, I stepped into position, spear in front of me. Tizmet watched with mild curiosity.

Dragon Rider or not, I would be ready for anything.

CHAPTER 9

T izmet hissed, and I shot up, wincing against the pain in my back. I scanned the darkness for whatever spooked her.

'*What is it?*'

'*Mate.*'

'*Rafe?*'

A heavy weight dropped on me, pinning me down. Tizmet snarled, and her claws scratched against the stone floor. I shoved against the intruder and whipped out my push dagger.

"Who are you?!" I growled, holding it fast.

They batted my dagger away and clasped my wrists above my head. Their huge frame settled along my body, and I struggled, even as my back screamed in agony.

"Never hold back," a familiar voice hissed in my ear.

There was a roar above us, and the weight on me shifted.

"Tizmet! No!"

The clack of dragon's teeth snapped nearby. He released me and rolled off. I sat up, flailing around for him.

"Rafe?" What was going on?

There was a hiss and a spark as he lit a candle. Placing it in the holder, he studied me darkly. The cloth covering concealed his shadow-touched eye, but the other glittered with rage.

"When someone's attacking you," his mouth twisted in anger, "at night, while you're sleeping—you don't hold back."

"But I knew it was you."

"Did you?" he growled.

Tizmet towered above him, teeth bared and tongue flicking out.

"She told me."

"Did she call me by name? Did she recognize me?"

"I don't–"

"Well, find out!" He snarled. "Was it my size? My scent? What was it?"

I recoiled away from him. "She just–"

"How did you know?!"

"She said 'mate' and I knew it was you!" I snapped back, leaning toward him. "Now, what is your problem?!"

He rested on his heels, and a muscle twitched in his jaw.

"Why are you so angry?" I softened my tone, trying to understand his rage.

Something riled him. I hadn't done anything. Tizmet realized it was him when he entered. That's why she didn't bite him in two. She didn't react till he attacked me and she sensed my fear.

"Ruveel arrives tomorrow."

"Are you concerned he'll attack me in the dead of night? In my own cave?" I pried. Surely, he wouldn't.

"Wouldn't surprise me. He's done worse."

I jerked my head back and studied him. Being a female soldier was one thing, but being a female Rider? Standards were already set. Male and female Riders treated one another with equal respect. There were lines that were not crossed and unspoken rules they obeyed. The idea that a Rider might sneak in was absurd. Dragon Lord or no.

"Do you think Tizmet would let him?" I asked. She curled over us with hatred burning in her eyes. "Does she look like the type to stand by while someone attacks me?"

"Ge'org is bigger. He's fought creatures far more evil than another dragon."

"And Tizmet is wild. She hasn't been coddled since hatching as he has. Don't underestimate her."

Rafe deflated, finally lowering his wall. He bowed his head and rubbed under the cloth over his eye wearily. I scooted to the side and patted my blanket. He sighed and dropped his weight beside me, resting his large form against the wall.

"Tell your dragon all is well."

'*It's all right,*' I assured her.

She snarled and sent an image of him grappling with me in the dark.

'*We were playing.*'

She snorted and lay down directly in front of us. Her massive head came to rest in front of Rafe's outstretched leg. She let out a low growl and bared her teeth. He stretched out and tapped her tooth with his boot. Her fangs were longer than the entire length of his foot. She snapped at him.

"Don't antagonize her." I warned him.

He smirked at her, and I realized as long as I could keep her from eating him, he would tease her as much as he did me.

With a sigh, he rested his head against the stone wall, closing his eye. He looked worn. Tired. Spread thin.

"You paint Ruveel like a monster," I murmured.

He needed rest, but I had to pry into this more. If I was to be forced under Ruveel's command, I had to understand what I was getting into. I didn't want to be near a Dragon Lord who might abuse his power. I struggled to believe the King would allow someone to be in authority, no matter how well-versed they were in combat, if they didn't at least obey the laws.

His eye snapped open, his gaze locked on the ceiling. "You don't know him like I do."

"I don't." I concurred. They fought on the front together. Aside from our limited encounters, I only knew him by reputation.

"He's a skilled warrior." Rafe blew out a breath. "A wicked thing on that fire-breathing beast of his."

Compliments weren't quite what I expected.

He paused, and I waited for him to sort out his thoughts. When we talked like this, it took a few moments for him to establish his words.

"He's in authority because he's good at what he does. But he's also cunning—like a snake."

Now *that* I was expecting.

"When he sets his mind on something, he'll use any means to get it." Rafe's gaze snapped to mine. "I don't want you near him."

"Why?"

I needed to hear him say it. As his stare lingered, I expected anger and rage but only saw weariness.

"Because you're good."

I squinted, puzzled. I was good? Did he truly think after the years he'd known me, I was still a 'good girl'?

"He'll take you and twist you to his will. You're trusting, Vy. To a fault."

"I don't think–"

"You are. You're naïve—foolishly so. It comes with your age."

"I'm not a child." I scowled.

He scoffed, and I would have been angry, but exhaustion simmered in that dark gaze. This was his truth. He was drained and didn't care to play games. Regardless of how I disagreed, he was baring himself to me. I grit my teeth and settled on a frown.

"No, you're not a child," he said. "But you're not quite a lady yet."

"Rafe, I am."

"Soon to be in age, but you lack maturity."

"How so?" I bit out.

He closed his eye and rested his head again. "You've only been off the King's grounds once."

"What does that have to do with maturity?"

"Vy," his tone warned at his limited patience, "you've never been under your own orders. You've never thought for yourself. You've always had someone to tell you what to do."

"I object. No one told me to join the army."

"Oh, ho! One time, and how did that turn out?"

Embarrassment burned my cheeks. "Well, I ended up with you."

"You're rash. You don't think things through. Not to mention the fact that you can't keep your hands to yourself–"

"That's not one-sided and you know it."

"If I hadn't made the Tennan, where would you be? On your own. You need to do that more. Make more mistakes."

"You think I should make more mistakes?" I repeated, not bothering to hide my confusion.

"And live with the consequences." His smile was bitter as he peered over at Tizmet. "You have to grow up. That's part of why I want you with Darrak."

"Let me get this right. You want me to grow up, mature, away from you? With Darrak?"

"Aye."

I shifted closer and placed a hand on his naked shoulder and another on his chest. "Why send me away? Don't you want us to be together?"

"You don't realize what you're asking."

Hurt dulled his features, and I reached up to pull the cloth from his eye. His hand caught mine, holding it still.

"I told you it won't happen again. Not while you're so inexperienced. If you want me when you're done with Darrak, you can have me."

"I want you now," I said, frowning. "Time with Darrak won't change that."

"You say that, but there's no guarantee you'll feel the same a year from now."

My heart shattered. A year? Without him? I swallowed against the sudden fear burning my throat.

"Vy, use your head. For once, stop following your heart." He pressed his hand over my chest. His thumb teased the lace, but his eye stayed on mine. "I'm older than you, by far. I've been your General. You need to be around others, see if there's a better fit for you someplace else."

I opened my mouth to object, to argue, but he cut off anything I might have said.

"Thrice-curse it all. I want you, Vy." His gaze softened as his mouth pressed into a hard line. "You know I want you, you little wench."

I grinned and stared at the ground as he continued.

"I'm not ready to give myself to someone who hasn't matured enough. I'm set in my ways, Vy. I won't change. I am who I am. You, however, you might. Maybe there's a better fit for you elsewhere."

"You wish for me to flirt with other men?" I choked, arching a brow.

"Dragon's dung, no. But if you do, you do. You might find you get along with another." He paused for a breath, dark gaze holding mine. "I'd have to kill him, though."

My lips curved. "I won't. I want *you*, Rafe. No one else."

A weary smile formed on his face. "You'll have time to reflect on that." He stood and patted Tizmet's muzzle, the top of which reached his ribs. "I won't be visiting at night anymore."

"Why?"

"Ruveel's dog can sniff me out anywhere," he said.

When he started for the entrance, I grabbed his hand. "Wait."

He stopped, glancing at our hands, then back to me in question.

"Stay with me."

"I can't," he rasped. No desire burned in his eyes. He was too tired.

"It's your last night with me. Stay. I won't push you, I give you my word."

"What if I push you?" His tone carried an edge.

"I—I won't let you."

"You sound so confident." He deadpanned.

"Rafe, I might be naïve, but I know as well as you that we cannot be together. Not like that," I said, pursing my lips. "Stay with me—just tonight. Sleep with me. Let me be close to you just this once."

He stared at me, and I recognized the burning behind his tired gaze—that this was a terrible idea, of all the things that could go wrong, of how many lines we'd be crossing.

He sighed and pulled his hand from mine. "I'm going to regret this."

I beamed, settling back on my blankets. Tizmet lifted her head, keeping her eyes on him. He started working on the buttons to his tunic, glancing around the cave.

"Chamber pot?"

"There," I said, pointing to the far corner.

He disappeared into the shadows and I laid down, trying to make enough room for him. It would be a tight fit, but we could manage.

Tizmet craned her head to watch Rafe, and pushed the image of dragons mating in the sky, followed by a silent question.

'*No,*' I replied, a blush heating my cheeks. I sent her a picture of me and the Tennan in our beds. '*We're just sleeping.*'

She huffed and watched with wary eyes as Rafe returned, adjusting his trousers. He loosened his belt and shrugged out of his tunic. My heart skipped a beat as I openly admired him. He was a beast of a man—thick and muscled from his neck and shoulders to where his abs disappeared beneath his waistband. He wasn't the thin type of muscular, like most women fawned over, but rather a mature, developed man. Power lurked behind every dip and curve.

"We're *sleeping*." He groaned as he dropped next to me.

I grinned like a schoolgirl and pulled the blanket up to my chin. "Yes, sir."

Tizmet eyed him and nestled near us. She didn't trust him enough to retreat to her corner.

He stretched and blew out the candle, throwing us into darkness. When his body pressed against mine, he grunted. "Vy, half my arse is on the floor."

I giggled and scooted against the wall as far as I could, ignoring the sting in my back. He shifted on the thin pile of blankets, his shoulder nudging up against my chest. He kicked at the blanket, tugging on it. I let go, but fought for it to cover my feet.

"How you fit in this little thing–" he muttered, trailing off.

"It's not like I actually expected you to stay," I said, smiling.

My elbows and hands tucked in between his arm and my chest. I would not taunt him. Not tonight. My General was tired, and trusting me.

"I shouldn't be."

"But you are."

He grunted in response. He shifted again, pulling at the blanket. I laughed and tugged it back.

"Stop, I'm barely covered," he said.

"Aye, and I prefer to stay warm."

"This is why life mates leave each other." He moaned.

"Over blankets?" I couldn't contain my barked laughter.

"It's the little things," he replied dryly. "Sleep, Vy."

I sighed and curled into him, laying my forehead against his shoulder. Moving my toes against his trousers, I toyed with the top of his boots.

"You don't normally sleep with your boots and trousers on," I mused.

"I don't normally sleep in your bed."

"But boots?"

He groaned and shifted, pulling his arm up. "Vy, I'm *tired*. You're young and–"

"Fine, fine. Please don't go on with the old man tirade. Sleep."

His deep chuckle rumbled against me, and I smiled in the darkness. He dropped his arms again, and I curled against him.

One night. We would allow ourselves a single night. We could sleep together, have a moment of intimacy that was secreted away. No one else had to know. Nothing had to happen. I simply wanted to be close to him.

He claimed I needed to grow, mature, make sure it was him I wanted. The notion was ridiculous. Nothing could change how I felt. My heart ached at the idea of being apart.

Pushing those thoughts from my mind, I inhaled the scent of Rafe. Leather, wood smoke, the smell of a man. Not the stink of odor, but the smell that came with long hours of hard work. It was manly and comforting.

Tonight I had him. Tonight would be enough.

A masculine moan woke me. My eyes shot open as I tried to place where I was.

"Easy." His rough voice calmed me.

Rafe gripped my leg above my knee where it lay over his hips. His thumb moved in lazy circles, rubbing the sensitive skin.

"Good morn, Rafe," I whispered, relaxing against him.

I had thrown myself halfway over his body in the night. My right leg was over his, my chest was pressed against his side. His strong arm curved around my back, holding me firmly against him.

"Morn." His voice was groggy.

I smiled and buried my face against his chest.

"What?"

"I love your morning voice," I said, then traced my nails over his side and across his abs.

He hissed and gripped my leg tighter. "We're *not* doing anything."

"Not a thing," I assured, nipping at his bare skin. It was euphoric, waking up next to him. Would it be like this every morning if we ended up together?

He grunted and rolled, pinning me underneath him. The ache in my back was a distant memory as fire ignited inside.

"Don't push me, Vy."

"I'm not pushing."

My legs wrapped around his waist and tugged him closer. He let out another quiet grunt as my core pressed against his hips, but held himself stiffly above me.

"Men don't wake up in the mood for cuddles," he whispered.

"What do you wake up in the mood for?" I taunted.

I knew I shouldn't. We agreed not to, but I couldn't help it. I really couldn't. For all Rafe's talk last night about making mistakes and dealing with the consequences, I *wanted* to make this mistake.

With all my heart, I wanted to make it.

"Vy–"

"Rafe. I'm going to kiss you."

He froze, and every muscle above me stiffened with tension. My hands trailed up his chest, to his jaw. He didn't move—didn't say a word. For a moment, I wondered if he was scared, fearful of what would happen, what we might unleash when we opened that door.

I held his face, feeling the cloth still wrapped around his head, then gave it a gentle tug. "Just this once," I whispered.

I tugged again, but he remained stubbornly still. His arms trembled with the effort of keeping himself above me. My thumb brushed across his lips, and he opened his mouth to nip at my fingertip. At that moment, I knew I had him.

"Just this once."

He dropped his weight, and my body screamed with victory. I gripped him tight as his mouth sought mine with the fury of the ages. I answered his onslaught, mirroring his hunger.

My every nerve sang and burned with need. I squirmed against the length of him, and he traced his tongue along the seam of my lips. I thought I might combust as I opened my mouth to him, allowing him to deepen the kiss.

Kissing Rafe was like sparring. There was no tenderness, no ease or gentleness about it. He pillaged my mouth, and I moaned in willing surrender. He pulled back with a groan and buried his face in my neck. His hand crept down my side in a trail of fire, fingers squeezing my hip. I bucked against him, needing him, craving to feel every inch of him. When he thrust his hips into me, his teeth grazed along my throat, searing my skin–

"Oi, break it up, lovebirds."

Rafe's head snapped up with a snarl as Tizmet let out a deafening roar. I froze, panting, trying to make sense of what was happening.

"Dragon Lord Prissy-Pants is here," Jam called.

Rafe bit out a curse and scrambled off me. He rummaged in the dark, rushing around. What was going on again? My brain was in a haze, completely shocked by the heat and emotion of the moment.

Then Rafe was gone.

No more whispered curses. No more jostled, hurried movements. Nothing.

Tizmet hissed and paced, clearly sensing my unrest and Rafe's urgency. I stood, wrapping a blanket around my shoulders, and walked over to the cave's tapestry.

The morning was fresh, dawn barely lit the sky. Rafe and Jamlin were nowhere to be seen. A great bellow rattled the loose stones at my feet, and the dragons in the canyon roared in answer. A large red dragon, Ge'org, flew above us. He pulled up short, settling on the ledge of an opposing cave.

Ruveel slipped from his dragon's back and set about removing the packs and saddle. I let the curtain close, leaving a crack to study him. He secured his pack, then removed the large saddle and dragged his things inside.

Ge'org turned and faced the canyon, shaking out his mammoth head. He opened his mouth and roared his dominance. The command echoed off stone. He was the alpha here, and he knew it. Craning up, he blew a plume of flame in the air and snapped his jaws.

Dropping his gaze, he stared at me from across the canyon.

As if he knew Rafe had been here.

CHAPTER 10

I retreated to my cave after my morning bath. Tizmet sensed my reluctance to sunbathe and followed me. She stayed near the opening with her head on the ledge, dozing, and I spent the next few chimes practicing with my spear.

I wasn't hurt that Rafe hadn't said goodbye. He couldn't be caught here, not like that. It was against the law for any in the army to lie together, though I doubted that law was written with female soldiers in mind. Female Riders were allowed to take life mates, though it was rare they ever did. If I was transferred to the Riders, or if I was sent with Darrak, I would be free of my status as a soldier and could take whomever I chose.

Yet, Rafe wouldn't be happy with me just being transferred.

Growling, I spun with my spear, slicing through imaginary opponents. Keeping my feet moving, I swung the blade high and followed with a thrust of the blunt end. Tucking the shaft close to me for protection, I danced through every move I knew.

I wasn't angry at Rafe for leaving like he did—I was frustrated that he wasn't content with who I was right now.

No, that wasn't right. I stopped and braced my feet, slamming the dull end of the spear into the stone. I panted with exertion, pausing to sort my thoughts.

He *was* content. He believed I would change. I wouldn't, but he thought I might. He wished to give me time away from him to grow, but I knew what I wanted.

I made my choice.

Tizmet's bright eye flashed as she studied me. She rested, at peace, but sensed my turmoil.

'*I don't know what's going to happen,*' I said.

She might not communicate, but she could listen. The more I talked to her, the easier it would be for her to pick up on words.

'We might be placed under Ruveel or sent to roam with a friend... I don't want either. I want to stay with Rafe.'

Wiping the sweat from my brow, I sheathed the spear. I placed it with my things and headed to the entrance. Tizmet picked up her massive head and eyed something outside the cave. I frowned and stood near her foreleg.

It was nearing midday, and the Dragon Lord had finally decided to join us.

Ge'org glided above, and his Rider gave a salute. It would've been appropriate to have Tizmet retreat inside for him to land, but she wasn't so easy to order around. I saluted back and watched as Flinor flew Dareth close enough to call to the Dragon Lord. Flinor was less than half the size of Ge'org. He was large compared to the other dragons at Northwing, but no match for the beast that was the Terror of the Battlefield.

Ge'org dropped, diving to hover in front of our cave. Tizmet scrambled to her feet, and I dodged to the side. She bristled and roared at the great red dragon. Her tongue flicked out past bared teeth.

"Hail, Avyanna. Call your dragon off!" Ruveel ordered.

I squinted at him, a small thing on his dragon's broad back. His black and red riding leathers went well with Ge'org's bright scales.

"I'm afraid I can't," I shouted.

Ge'org seemed bored with Tizmet's antics, not being riled in the slightest. He was the biggest and scariest, and he knew it.

Tizmet roared again, shaking her head. She lunged to the edge of the cliff, sinking her talons into the stone, and stretched out her long neck to snap at his hovering form. He dodged with little effort and snorted at her.

'I will have to speak with him.' My reluctance slipped through the bond. *'I don't want to, either.'*

'No mate,' she said, pushing feelings of irritation and annoyance.

It only confirmed what I thought. Wild raised dragons were solitary creatures—like wildcats. They probably met to mate, then went to their respective territories. Tizmet was not in the mood to breed and therefore wanted nothing to do with this new male. Why she tolerated Flinor and not Ge'org confused me, though.

'No mating,' I assured her. *'Talking. Feel free to bite them if either tries to mate us,'* I added for good measure.

I started on the path that led to the top of the cliff. She screeched behind me as Ge'org flew to the top.

'Come,' I urged, not turning back as I climbed.

She would follow eventually—as soon as she realized where I headed. Her instant dislike for Ge'org meant she would not let me wander off near him.

I kept climbing and soon heard the answering flap of wings as she left the cave. She flew, circling above me. I scaled the thin path, gripping the stone wall. Before long, my head peeked over the lip of the canyon.

The Dragon Lord leaned against Ge'org, arms crossed over his chest. When I emerged from the canyon, he pushed off to salute me.

"Looks like you're mine now."

Anger swelled within me as Tizmet dove between us in a rough landing. When she snapped at him, Ge'org sidestepped closer to his Rider.

'*Mine!*' she roared across the bond.

It was obvious Ge'org didn't know how to respond to Tizmet's behavior, and Ruveel remained unconcerned. If the roles were reversed, Tizmet would have already attacked.

'*I'm your bonded.*' I coaxed her back to me. She crept closer, inch by inch, snarling and hissing the whole time.

"Begging your pardon, Dragon Lord, but I'm not yours."

He tilted his head and offered me a bemused smile, crinkling the edges of his blue eyes. Soot marked his cheekbones to counter the sun's glare. Wind tousled his dark hair and his leathers fit snug to his frame.

"You're bonded to that beast, are you not?" He jerked his chin toward Tizmet.

"Aye, Tizmet is my bonded." I corrected. She was a beast, but mine, and no one else could use that term in a derogatory way toward her.

"Then you're mine, Dragon Rider."

I had the sinking feeling he was simply trying to spite Rafe by calling me his own. Clearly, he hadn't forgotten about me.

"I'm not." My voice remained steady, despite my irritation. "I answer to General Rafe, sir. I'm still part of his Tennan."

He sneered and sauntered closer. Tizmet snarled and snapped at the air above him, but he pressed on unfazed.

'*Mine!*' she roared in my head.

I flinched away from the strength of her emotion and sent her all the calm I could muster. Ruveel stopped in front of me and took his time, looking me up and down.

"I like what you've done with your hair." His tone was deep and soft as velvet. It made all the girls swoon, I was sure. "Gives you an edgy look."

Tizmet's outrage soared to new heights. She knew I didn't want her hurting these people, but she was scared and angry—and her patience was gone.

"Sir, I warn you–"

He scoffed. "You warn me?" He reached out as if to poke me in the chest.

That was the last straw.

Tizmet snapped.

A giant stone-colored muzzle shrouded Ruveel's head and chest. Tizmet moved as quick as a flash, whipping toward the canyon and released the Dragon Lord into the air.

Ge'org roared and lunged. Barreling into Tizmet, he launched after his Rider. They both disappeared over the edge and I stared at Tizmet in both horror and awe. I couldn't help the small breathless laugh that escaped my lips.

She just threw the Dragon Lord off a cliff.

No other dragon would've dared such a thing, but she didn't know any better. A man called me *his*, ignored her warnings, and reached out to touch me. I should've been thankful she didn't bite him in half.

Ge'org flew straight up from the canyon, a wall of red scales as he darted past. Ruveel was laughing as his dragon landed, talons digging into the ground. He skidded to a stop and opened his maw, revealing teeth longer than Tizmet's. His deep roar of outrage shook the earth. She faced him, stepped closer, and let out an answering bellow, head and neck shaking with the force of it.

Ruveel slipped from his saddle to the ground. He fingered the holes that Tizmet's teeth made in his armor and barked another laugh.

"Call her off!" he ordered, glancing up.

I crossed my arms over my chest. My green dress billowed around me, thrashing about, as my anger did in my head. "It's not that easy."

Ruveel studied Tizmet and spread his arms wide, his dragon looming over him protectively. "I mean no harm, dragon."

I gave him a bored look as Tizmet hissed and snaked her head in his direction. "She doesn't communicate with words, Dragon Lord. She's wild raised."

His gaze sharpened as he squinted against the sun, taking her in. His eyes traveled from her massive maw, down her spine, to her tail. He tilted his head and glanced back at Ge'org curiously.

"It's as if you bonded a hatchling," he stated.

"No, it's as if I bonded an adult dragon with her own opinion of arrogant, overreaching men," I snapped. "I assure you, I have little control over her actions."

"Is she a danger to the other Riders?" he asked, crossing his arms to mimic my pose.

"Not unless they ignore her warnings."

I gripped my dress sleeves. She wasn't a danger—as long as they gave her the respect and space she deserved. She wouldn't attack anyone without fair warning.

His attention returned to me. His smile was rank with charm, and I wanted to slap it off his face.

"Well, then. The King will want to see you. If you refuse to join the Dragon Corps, he'll seal your transfer."

"I choose to stay under General Rafe's command." My chin dipped in agreement. I would never willingly leave him.

"I knew there was something between you two. You sharing a bed with that cold-hearted bastard?"

Resentment ignited inside. He still only saw me as a barracks' whore, nothing else. To him, I was a mere bedmate, not a soldier.

Tizmet moved with my rage when I did not. She lunged, snapping at Ruveel, and dodging when Ge'org bit at the air near her face. Craning high, her chest expanded with a deep breath, intending to roast him.

'*Stop.*'

She whipped back to me, seething in not only her anger but mine as well. I pulled back my rage and hatred and tucked it away. The Dragon Lord watched the dragons' antics with amusement on his face.

"I am no whore to keep beds warm at night. I am a *soldier*, Dragon Lord. Whether footman or Rider, I will always be a soldier first. The warmth of my bed is no concern to you."

"Ah, but doesn't article three state that no soldiers are to lie together? Being a Dragon Rider, you could be far more liberal with whom you take to bed," he replied with a cocky grin.

"If there is nothing else you wish to discuss, I'll be returning to my cave."

I turned my back to him. Tizmet would do no such thing. She would offer these males no weakness of hers, but I wanted to insult them with my dismissal. He only thought of me as a female—as if my only purpose was to be bred like a horse. My snarl curled my lip as I walked down the path. I was worth more than that and deserved to be treated better. I was a soldier as much as him—a weapon. Albeit a different one than he was used to. Rafe recognized this. I was weak because of my gender, but I was also unique.

I was powerful in my own way.

"We head out tomorrow by dragon. Be ready!" Ruveel called after me.

I smiled at my boots as I stomped down the thin, winding path. I would not be traveling by dragonback. Tizmet was appalled by the idea of a human riding her like some beast of burden. I would travel instead, by horse.

With Rafe.

CHAPTER 11

The next morning, I resumed my routine. We headed to the springs to bathe, and back to our cave, avoiding the basking spot. Tizmet was uneasy, and I didn't blame her. She sensed we would move on soon, leaving the only safe spot since we bonded.

I packed my things, taking only what I would need on the road. The only things left were a few blankets and oddities. It wasn't as if I had much to begin with. I hefted my spear and crossbow and walked to the ledge to wait.

My nose crinkled as I caught sight of a woman creeping down the path from his cave, her hair tousled and clothes in disarray. Disgust rolled through me, thinking of the way he looked at me the day before.

Moments passed before Ge'org's massive form emerged from his cave. He was saddled and packed, Ruveel at his side. The Dragon Lord saluted me across the way, and I begrudgingly returned the gesture. Whether he was my General or not, he was my superior and I had to show deference.

He climbed on Ge'org and waited... eyes on me. I arched a brow, though I was sure at this distance he couldn't see the details of my face. Did he expect me to just hop on a Wild Dragon and demand her to fly me about?

Tizmet snarled next to me, actively trying to ignore the large red beast.

'*He has a bit of an ego,*' I agreed.

She snorted in reply and I watched as the male took to the air. Ge'org made the short flight to the cliff above our cave and landed heavily.

"Soldier, where's your saddle?" Ruveel shouted, as his dragon leaned over the edge to peer down at us.

"Begging your pardon, Dragon Lord, but I won't be needing one."

"Riding without? You'll regret that."

I looked down at my lap and rolled my eyes. The man still hadn't caught on.

"I won't be riding dragonback, your Lordship."

Loose stones skittered off the cliff path. I checked my smile, keeping my face neutral as Rafe made his way up with Blain close behind.

"Back off, Ru. She's with me."

Yes. I was. My heart jumped in my chest and I dropped my gaze to my hands as I stood. He came for me. He, at least, wasn't going to send me off to deal with Ruveel and face the King on my own.

After a moment's pause, the Dragon Lord shouted his response. "That's absurd, Rafe, and you know it."

"Take your oversized lizard and greet the King," Rafe jeered.

I brushed my dress off and found Rafe's dark gaze on me. I saluted him, but let my eyes tell my true feelings. Blain leaned around him to tilt his head at me, and I schooled my face once again.

"General Rafe."

"Soldier." He grunted, peering inside my cave.

Tizmet flicked her tongue out but didn't lunge at him. Perhaps she was warming up to him. Rafe nodded to my things and hefted my crossbow. Turning around, he headed down the path with Blain between us.

"Rafe, let her fly." Ruveel's tone was level, not whining, but almost patient, as if he were speaking to a child. "If the King hears of this–"

"Then tell him. She's part of my Tennan. Back off," Rafe said, not bothering to look up.

The Dragon Lord's dramatic sigh echoed over the stone walls, followed by the heavy flap of wings. Tizmet hissed and bared her teeth at the world. She would be in a foul mood today, being forced outside her cave.

'Come. There's no way around it.'

She didn't want to leave, but to have any chance at freedom, she had to come with me. Traveling with Darrak wasn't my first choice, but it was the only opportunity I would have to really get to know her. Cooped up in a cave, or fighting with other dragons and Riders wouldn't let us work on our relationship.

She snapped her jaws as if sensing my thoughts and craned her head. With her neck stretched high, she searched the sky for Ge'org, and deeming him far enough away, took flight. Stones scattered as she launched from the ledge, throwing her great weight into the canyon. She moved slower than the dragons I was used to seeing. Even so, she climbed the air remarkably fast for a creature her size.

"Soldier!"

I jumped at Rafe's barked command and hurried along as she circled in the sky above. She kept her eye on me, not letting me out of sight.

I was growing accustomed to traversing the steep winding trails, but holding a spear made it cumbersome. I was thankful Rafe carried the crossbow. Laden with my pack and both my weapons, I wouldn't have had a hope of making it down alive.

Reaching the bottom, a pang of hurt stabbed my heart. Three horses were readied for riding, Thunderbolt not among them. I reminded myself he was good and well—set to live his life on a quiet farm somewhere.

Rafe strapped my crossbow onto the smallest, a little black mare. She snorted but held still, letting him adjust her saddle. As I strapped my spear down, Rafe's arm brushed against mine. Sparks flew across my skin, and my face warmed. With Rafe, there were no accidents. His touch was no mere coincidence. He wanted me to know he cared, in his own way.

I bit down on my lip, refusing to smile, and let my elbow brush against his in silent reply. He stepped away, mounting his horse. I threw my pack over the horse's back and tied it into place as Tizmet circled low.

"Can she give some space while we get out of Northwing?" Rafe asked, glancing up.

"I'm afraid not," I replied, struggling to mount the mare. Despite her size, my short stature did nothing to help me mount. "She'll stick close. She might trust you and Blain, but she holds no regard for others."

Rafe's dark eye met mine in understanding. Nodding, he urged his stallion on. My mare stepped in behind him, with Blain taking up the rear.

We wound our way through the canyon and to the Dragon Rider training area. I smiled to myself as we passed the storage cave Rafe once pulled me into. It felt like so long ago—over two years. He saved me from my foolishness when I tried to force the bond with a hatchling that refused me. He protected me, even back then. I shivered, replaying the scene in my head. His lips against my neck, body crushing mine, his hand on my face, blocking it from the stranger's gaze. He made it appear as though we were simply another set of lovers caught in the night's embrace.

Bittersweet joy swelled in my chest, knowing that at least for now, I had my General. We couldn't and wouldn't cross certain lines, but I was beginning to understand the game that lovers played. Cat and mouse—quick looks, and secret touches.

Rafe knew he had my heart, and I hated the idea of him pushing me away. If I hadn't known the feelings between us were mutual, I would have given up and moved on. I would have been crushed—but I would have gone on with my life.

That he promised to wait gave me hope. He said if I still wanted him when I came back from training with Darrak—if I trained with Darrak—he would be there. He would wait for me.

That made the pain that twisted in my heart more bearable. Sending me away wasn't his first choice—it was the best option at the moment. Yet, it could be a blessing in disguise. If I were to join the Dragon Corps, I would be free to choose him. Though I doubted Ruveel would let me anywhere near him. He would probably place me on the complete opposite side of the frontlines, or even order me to guard the homelands to keep us apart.

If I proved myself with Darrak and garnered a reputation with the King, I might have more of a say in where I was stationed. Perhaps I could rejoin Rafe's Tennan. After all, a dragon roaming the homelands was unheard of. As with everything in my life thus far, I had been a first. Why not ditch the Dragon Corps and join a Tennan with a footman's General?

I would be with Rafe, no matter what I had to do. No matter how long it took. I would be with him.

I watched his broad shoulders as he rode. He moved with his horse with as much ease on horseback as on foot.

"Oi. Wipe that look off your face or someone will notice."

I frowned at Blain's harsh whisper, but dragged my gaze away from Rafe to the scenes about me. Here I was, swooning like some love-struck schoolgirl. As if I was nothing more than a child with a crush. I was better than that. I could keep a level head.

The dragonlings wrestling about were all three years or younger. They would be sent to the front by their fourth year. These young ones were destined for war while Tizmet and I were safe to explore our bond. I took a deep breath to calm my nerves.

Tizmet dove directly above me and pulled up short, launching herself back into the sky. She sensed my unease. We would be useless on the front in the condition we were in. There was no way we could help if she wouldn't even let me ride her. We had to familiarize ourselves with each other before we could fight alongside one another.

I lifted my chin and rode tall behind General Rafe. I needed to take this journey one step at a time. The first step was simple—get to King's Wall and find out what was to be done with me. I wondered if I would be permitted to be in his presence. I had never seen the King before, only knowing him from stories. This was only a single step in my journey. It wouldn't be so terrible.

Tizmet was angry, not at Rafe and Blain, but at a rather large red male. I sighed as she snarled in the darkness.

We made camp off the main road, Rafe arguing with Ruveel that Tizmet would never allow me out of her sight to sleep at the inn. I let him argue for me, knowing the truth concerning the situation. The Dragon Lord had not flown ahead, but kept his distance from Tizmet while flying above.

Ge'org taunted her, and would inch his tail closer while we all tried to sleep. She snapped and growled in return, and at this point, I just wanted her to bite it clean off.

'*Tizmet. Calm.*' I pushed through our bond.

She huffed and scooted her massive body closer to me. I had already kicked my blankets off. She shared her heat and blocked the wind. The ground was still chilled from winter, but it wasn't unbearable.

'*You're doing well. Next time, feel free to bite his tail off.*'

She hadn't snapped at anyone other than Ge'org and hadn't roasted anyone yet. Being locked away with her for a few weeks at least helped us reach an understanding. She realized I wouldn't leave her, and I learned she wouldn't attack anyone—without good reason.

Blain and Rafe slept next to the fire, and Ruveel lay near his dragon. With the great beasts, we had no need to keep watch. Their senses were far beyond our own, and we could trust them to alert us to predators in the night—if there were any who'd dare the wrath of a dragon.

I smiled to myself, closing my eyes and rolling onto my side. I wouldn't have Rafe for long. Simply being in camp with him was enough for now. I longed to sneak off with him in the woods and play our games, but I also wasn't so foolish to think the others wouldn't notice.

'*Mate?*' Tizmet questioned.

'*Not tonight.*'

'*Soon,*' she urged, letting a sense of impatience cross over to me.

I laughed lightly at her emotion. She didn't understand that I wouldn't be rid of him once we 'mated.' If anything, that would seal our future.

'*Not likely,*' I replied, ears burning as I thought about it.

Frazzled, I pulled a blanket up over my face. I was not some young girl to be flustered by such things. I was a woman, and this was not the time or the place to be pondering such actions.

"Sleep."

I bit my lip at Rafe's rumbled order. His voice was thick with fatigue. I tugged the blanket down to look across the fire. He was lying on his back, arm thrown over his face.

I wondered, not for the first time, about his duties. He trained his Tennan and provided for them. There had to be other duties that he was required to do. Being a General was not simply a title with no responsibilities. There had to be paperwork involved with every movement of him and his men.

I settled against Tizmet's warm scales. Here I was, thinking thoughts about a simpler life with him, and he was probably over there thinking about a mountain of parchment to sort out when he returned to the barracks.

Tizmet lurched beside me, and I yelped as the movement shoved me aside. Ge'org snarled in reply, and Ruveel hissed a curse.

"By the moon, Ge'org! Keep your scales to yourself!"

I smiled as Tizmet settled next to me, a sense of satisfaction spilling over from her.

'*Got him?*' I asked.

She sent me the image of her talon sinking into his tail, drawing blood.

Settling back around me, she huffed. She curled and twisted, cutting off my view of everyone else. I tentatively ran a hand over her smooth scales and she shivered beneath my touch.

'*Sleep?*' I pressed.

'*Sleep.*'

We headed east along the main road, Rafe pulling looks from civilians. They pointed and whispered amongst each other, all wondering why the Shadowslayer was this deep in Regent. A few noted my dress and hair in horror. The Dragon Lord and Ge'org soared above, not attracting as much attention, but Tizmet flew low, making people gawk skyward in annoyance.

As we rode through Wolf Rind, a large town between Northwing and the King's Wall, she caused quite a stir. She flitted over buildings, drawing gasps and shouts of outrage as debris blew about the vendors in the market. Angry mothers glared as they sheltered their children from the wind caused by her wings.

'*Higher,*' I urged.

The amount of strangers around me stressed her. She was too terrified to lose me. She didn't know these people—didn't know if one of them would be like Rafe and try to take me away from her.

I worried as she made another low sweep. A small flock of sheep in the road scattered at her proximity, the shepherd glaring up at her.

My lips formed a line. "General—"

Rafe glanced over his shoulder, leveling his dark gaze on me. The glower alone told me no. We were not speeding up, rushing out of this town. I bit my tongue and nodded, looking back at my hands.

Tizmet was as large as the inns here. The children raised at Northwing had respect and gratitude for the dragons. These people knew they were their protectors, but they didn't deal with them on a regular basis. They would see Ge'org flying in the distance at times, but I doubted they ever saw a dragon up close.

Tizmet remedied that.

That night, the Dragon Lord deigned to press on rather than camp with us. I was secretly thrilled, knowing I might get a stolen moment away with Rafe.

He acted ever the General though and dismissed my efforts to help set up camp beyond my bed.

I caught Blain looking between us and I deflated, realizing Rafe wouldn't let down his guard in front of anyone. He was probably sore over Jamlin finding us. Jam could keep a secret, but only if he wanted to. Otherwise, all the Tennan would know me and Rafe were sneaking around.

"She'll keep watch tonight?" Blain asked, nodding to Tizmet.

"Aye. She might doze, but nothing will sneak up on her. Sun above knows she'd wake us all with her bellowing."

He smiled, aware of last night's antics. "Didn't take too well to the red dragon, eh?"

"Not at all. Ge'org kept taunting her." I shoveled bites of stew, letting it chase off winter's chill.

Rafe sat apart from us, staring off into the distance.

"Is she close to her heat?" Blain asked.

"No, dragons won't go into heat unless they're completely at ease."

"Ah, that explains things."

"That's why the breeding program at Southwing isn't going as intended. The King thought a more temperate zone would be a better place for the dragons to breed year round. Yet, the south comes with its own problems."

"The sand nomads," Blain said, nodding his understanding.

"Not only them, but now the Shadow Men know there are dragons there. The sand storms, the oppressive summer heat, the nomads, and now the Shadows. We might have a cold season here, but the Shadows would have to make it through our forces to the west or through the homelands to the south to get to us. The dragons here are more peaceful."

"Think the reason the clutches have been failing is the immaturity of the dragons laying them?"

"Perhaps. They're developed enough to lay a clutch, but you have to think of their size. Tizmet had at least one clutch out there."

Blain looked up in surprise.

"She laid at least ten eggs, if not more," I said. "There are dragons out there that have never known a human."

"Interesting," he mused. He rinsed his bowl and returned it to his pack. "Do you know where she laid them? Her clutch?"

"The Sky Trees, I'm fairly certain."

The dragon in question leaned low over me, flicking her tongue out in question.

'Aye, I'm talking about you. Your babies.'

I sent the image she had shown me of her clutch. She lowered her head to the ground, blinking slowly. Sadness, emptiness emanated from her as she groaned.

'They hatched? Your young?' I envisioned hatchlings on Hatching Day.

She closed the door to our bond, making me frown. She never showed me her young. Surely her eggs had been viable. From what I saw, they looked as if they were.

"The Sky Trees run along the western border. There's a good many of them, plenty for a dragon of her size to hide among."

"There was another dragon, a blue male at least."

"Curious, that—"

"Blain." Rafe's bark interrupted us.

Blain offered an apologetic smile before walking over to crouch beside him. They spoke in hushed tones and I leaned against Tizmet. I watched the two in the fading light of the sun, over the crackle of our small campfire. Rafe was somber, Blain listening intently.

'Tomorrow we should arrive at the palace, as long as things go according to plan.'

Tizmet huffed and closed her eyes, unconcerned.

'There will be many people. Ge'org and the Dragon Lord. Don't fight.' I tried to stress peace to her.

She cracked open an eye to give me a bored look.

'I wonder if I'll meet the King... or if only Rafe and Ruveel will. I wonder if it will be like Northwing.'

She closed her eye, content to leave me with my thoughts.

The night waned on, Rafe turning in before Blain. I watched with hooded eyes as he loosened his tunic and unfastened his belt. He climbed into his blankets, and they shifted as he settled in.

He heaved a heavy sigh that shook his body and rolled his head to look at me. My gaze flicked to Blain, who had his back to us, peering out into the night. Glancing at Rafe, I gave him a small smile. He blinked and faced the sky.

Beaming, I settled into my blankets to sleep.

The next day was more of the same. The way grew more crowded as smaller roads and paths converged. Tizmet flew low, and travelers stared, wondering at her. I rode behind Rafe at a brisk walk.

We entered the city of King's Wall as the sun set. We made good time, not breaking for lunch, but rather eating dried meat and cheese from our packs.

I gripped my reins tighter as we rode through the press. Rafe looked over his shoulder once to make sure I stayed close. I offered him a tight-lipped smile. I was out of sorts here. There was so much to see. Vendors and stalls lined the outer market, patrons scattered throughout. Crowds bustled through the road, parting for our horses. I felt Tizmet's anxiety, even though she remained silent in the darkening sky.

The buildings were crammed together and towered high. People called to each other, creating a loud cacophony of sounds. Horses and donkeys were tied to posts where people bartered wares and children played in the streets.

I shared her anxiousness. Being in an unfamiliar crowded place brought me back to when we traveled to Hamsforth, the small village outside Northwing. King's Wall was much—much larger than that small town. This was a full thriving city, and the crowds were almost oppressive. I was thankful Rafe led the way, as I had no idea where I was going.

It revealed my naivete that I didn't know how to get to the palace. This man, who had been stationed at the frontlines since he was seventeen winters, could read the road better than me. I glanced up, searching for any sign of the King's home, but saw none.

'*Calm,*' I urged Tizmet again as she passed directly above.

Heads craned to the dimly lit sky, wondering why a dragon flew so low. Those same heads turned to watch us pass, and I felt barren without my uniform. To them, I was a lady with shorn hair escorted by Blain and Rafe. I gritted my teeth, wishing for a uniform. At least it would have marked me as his.

As full dark fell, we pressed through the brightly lit streets. People shuffled here and there, laughing and joyous. There was something different about them.

The civilians in Northwing were all victims of the war in one way or another. They were either refugees, or their parents or providers had been slain by the Shadows. We all suffered loss.

These people seemed to have no such losses. They danced in the streets as musicians performed. Vendors sold hot food, ready to eat. Games of chance were played in the alleys. These people were happy—untouched by the war.

My thoughts were interrupted by a dragon's bellow. I lifted my gaze and my lips fell open in wonder. These buildings were finely crafted with details and engravings on every scrap piece of wood. Beyond the decadent architecture, a fortress rose above the city. It wasn't so much a palace built with luxury and glory in mind, rather a defensible stronghold. It was four times the height of any structures nearby, but more than that, an open area surrounded it as far as I could see.

Tizmet bristled in the courtyard, burning eyes seeking mine.

'*Calm,*' I assured her, riding behind Rafe.

He led us through the less crowded enclosure. Civilians walked here and there, but most were uniformed soldiers. They traveled to and from giant iron gates that blocked off the palace from the dozens of interconnecting city roads.

People stared at Tizmet, awestruck. Many walked far too close for her comfort. She lost her composure and bared her teeth at a woman that held her hand out as if to touch her.

'*Don't eat anyone,*' I said in jest.

She replied with a feeling of disgust. Apparently, humans weren't very palatable. I didn't want to think too long about how she knew that.

She curled her tail and neck tightly around herself, trying to make herself smaller. I let out a breathy laugh that a dragon as large as she would bother an attempt.

Tizmet's eyes were on us as Rafe led the way to the gates. The great iron spikes bore fine points at the top, and were almost as tall as Tizmet, being impossible for anyone to scale.

Rafe greeted the four guards. "General Rafe, with two of his Tennan."

"You're expected, General Rafe Shadowslayer," one replied, giving a formal salute.

I noted the glances they snuck my way—an oddity, traveling with the great Shadowslayer. I self-consciously ran a hand through my short hair, tousled by the ride.

Two guards opened the gate and let us pass through. An outbuilding off to the side housed four more guards and a small boy. He was dressed in a black uniform, and I dipped my chin, peering at him. When he spotted us, he jumped off his chair, rushing to meet us.

"Runner Jakob, at your service, sir!" he called with a salute.

Rafe frowned at him, but kept his comments to himself. "Show us to the stables, boy."

"Yes, sir!" The boy turned on his heel and marched down the path. He marched better than most of the soldiers—a sharp lad.

We passed the grand entrance—massive stairs leading to immense doors, also well-guarded. I took in the sights as we rounded the palace. The huge structure loomed on our right, blocking the sky with its towering walls. Tall trees lined the perimeter, barren of leaves, still dormant from winter. The space was mostly clear, allowing dragons to move about as they would. Distance muffled the city's scents and noises, but the dull roar lingered through the courtyard.

Tizmet huffed and flew over the iron fence, landing roughly in the area inside the palace grounds. I smiled at her. She lashed her tail, irritated we left her on the far side.

'*Most dragons would be flying right now,*' I told her gently.

She snorted and sent me an image of her soaring high—me, Rafe, and Blain nothing more than specks below.

Jakob tried to hide his glances at her. As I expected, any dragon other than Ge'org would cause a stir this deep in Regent.

The stables were built into the side of the palace, protected against the elements. I followed Rafe's lead, dismounting as a man came out with another boy.

This boy looked far less put together, and I deemed him a stableboy. Not one of official rank.

"We'll take your horses General–"

"We'll see to our own." Rafe cut him off.

My legs shook under the strain of my weight after being on horseback all day. Rafe led his stallion past the two, Blain and I following close behind. I gave them an apologetic smile. The stableboy's brown eyes were as wide as saucers. The Stable Master gave me a quick disapproving look, and I frowned back at him.

Tizmet whined, but lowered her head to the ground, watching me walk into the stables. I sent her a push of assurance and kept going.

I led my mare into a stall beside Rafe's as he set to remove the stallion's tack. The stableboy brought me brushes, fresh water and hay for my mare. I traded him my tack and set to brushing her down. Jakob remained in the aisle, standing at attention, awaiting his next order. Blain took the stall next to mine, and the only sounds were our soft murmurs to our mounts and the shuffling of bedding them down.

"Jakob, see Blain to the door," Rafe growled as he emerged from his stallion's stall.

Jakob saluted and turned on his heel, leaving. Blain followed, not even sparing us a glance as I picked out the hooves of my mare.

Rafe glared at the stableboy till his fidgeting gave way to him running down the aisle and out of sight.

"Don't scare the little ones, General," I murmured.

His dark eye settled on my face, and I tilted my head. I let the mare's foreleg drop, then stood. Ignoring my barb, he took the pick from me and lifted the mare's rear leg.

"You've been walking her with a pebble in her shoe," he said, working at her hoof.

"I have *not*, sir." I would have noticed if she picked up a stone—I wasn't that incompetent. When I peered over his shoulder, his hushed tone drew me in.

"Be careful."

I froze, watching him work. "Of what?" I breathed.

Outside, Tizmet snarled, sensing my sudden spike of anxiety.

"Everything." He dropped the mare's hoof and patted her rump. She snorted and turned to him, but he ignored her, focusing on me out of the corner of his eye.

"That's ominous," I whispered.

"You're different, Vy. Don't let them change you."

With that, he handed me the pick and left. I blinked, confused, as he walked down the aisle and out of sight.

What exactly was I in for?

CHAPTER 12

T izmet hissed her displeasure when I disappeared through the side entrance doors—doors far too small for her. The walk to my room was a short hike down a hall and up a few flights of stairs. Her relief flooded over the bond when I entered.

A maid poured hot water into a basin as another servant escorted me inside. Tendrils of steam had me shedding my clothes faster than I cared to admit. She stood off to the side as I slid into the tub, sighing in delight.

The massive space had an open balcony, in which Tizmet could land to join me. The room was twice as big as our cave, its ceiling almost as tall as two houses stacked atop one another, and wide enough for her to pace comfortably. Furs and rugs decorated the stone floor, something I wasn't accustomed to. At one end was the tub, shielded by a privacy screen. Opposite the balcony was a bed—the largest I'd ever seen. I was beyond thrilled that I could sleep on it.

Tizmet settled in the middle of the room, curled up and exhausted. I scrubbed at my skin with a sweet-smelling soap, a far cry from the harsh soaps in Northwing. The maid in the corner kept her eyes down and waited for me to finish.

"My name is Avyanna, by the way," I offered, then dipped below the surface. Rising, I pushed water from my face and scrubbed at my hair. "I apologize for not introducing myself earlier. I was desperate to be clean."

"Yes, milady," she murmured.

"May I have the blanket?" I didn't like the deference she showed me. It was awkward and uncomfortable.

She handed it over, keeping her eyes down. I stepped out and wrapped it around my shoulders.

"Would you like me to..." she struggled for words, "do something with your hair, milady?" She wrung her hands, as if I would bite.

"It's fairly easy to care for. I braid this bit." I pulled at the longer strands at the nape of my neck. "Not to worry, I can manage."

"Yes, milady. I'll just be turning down the bed for you, then."

My stomach rumbled in protest. I hadn't eaten anything, but I suffered through worse. I reached for the clean under-breeches and night shift set out for me. Dropping the blanket, I dressed quickly, catching the maid as her eyes snagged on my side.

"Begging your pardon!" She busied herself with pulling the blankets back on the massive bed.

"No need." I smiled. "Did my scar unsettle you?"

Her gaze crept to mine, then to my side as her hands kept working.

"It wasn't anything major—a simple misunderstanding," I said when she didn't respond. I tugged the night shift up so she could get a better look.

Tizmet snorted, sensing my blatant lie.

Her jaw dropped as she took in the white welts that circled over my old wound. "It's beautiful," she breathed.

Frowning, I looked down at it and traced a finger over the raised lines. It was a stark reminder of who I was and what I was becoming. Perhaps one day, I would find it beautiful, but for now, it was more of a burden.

"It hurt worse than it looks." I jested, walking to the bed.

She snapped out of the spell and rushed to the balcony to close the heavy curtain that hung over the opening. I climbed onto the plush, downy blankets, stifling a moan as she collected the two lanterns on the far wall.

"Is there anything milady will be needing?" she asked in a hushed voice.

"This is wonderful, thank you." I sighed, sinking into whatever material the mattress was made of. I couldn't remember the last time I slept on a proper mattress, not a cot.

"Well, um... If I may—"

Her stuttering drew my attention, and I propped myself up on an elbow. "Yes?"

"If you need assistance tonight—as in after... Well, if you need help cleaning up, simply ring the bell." She motioned to a small bell on the bedside table.

"Cleaning up?" I asked, scanning the room. What would there possibly be to clean up? If Tizmet defecated here, I'd clean it up myself.

"After you—after your services."

Realization dawned, and I rushed to my knees. "No, no, no," I growled. "What *services*?"

She shrank away from me, edging toward the door. The blush that crept up her face only confirmed my assumption.

"Your services—as you would, milady!" she blurted.

I hissed a curse, and she flinched as if the words stung her. My teeth sank into my tongue, ashamed that such remarks came so freely. I'd been around Rafe for too long.

"Let me be clear—look at me," I ground out.

Her eyes met mine, wide and frightened. My irritation twisted knots in my stomach, but I didn't want to take it out on her.

"I am a soldier—a member of General Rafe's Tennan. I am no barracks' whore. Do not misunderstand me. I'm not here to *service* anyone."

"Yes, yes, milady!" She whimpered, shoulders hunched.

"I mean it. Spread the word. I'm here at the Dragon Lord's request."

Her eyes flashed in understanding, and I slapped a palm to my forehead.

"No. At his request for a *transfer* from General Rafe. Not at his request to... keep his bed warm," I spat out.

"Yes, milady," she said, creeping closer to the door. "If you need me though–"

"I won't!" I shouted, and she made a run for it. She curtsied and ducked out, letting the door close softly behind her.

'*They all think I'm here as a whore!*' I complained, falling back onto the bed.

Tizmet picked up her head, her flaming eyes flashing in the night. '*Mate?*'

'*No! I'm not mating anyone!*' I sensed her shifting and cringed, hoping she didn't take that as anger.

'*No mate?*' she asked, pushing an image of Rafe and me lying together in the cave. Her anger and hunger spilled out, and she envisioned Rafe alone, followed by her eating a deer.

'*No, you cannot eat him.*' I laughed to myself.

She huffed and settled back in the darkness. I smiled, thoughts once again on Rafe. I fell asleep quickly, hanging onto memories of him as I drifted into dreams.

I woke to the sound of clanging. My body shot upright in bed as my brain tried to catch up with where I was and what I was seeing.

Tizmet rested on the floor where the furs and rugs had been pulled away. She gnawed on a large bone of some creature she already devoured. She peeked up from her meal and tilted her head, fiery eyes dancing.

'*Calm,*' she told me.

I cracked a smile at her attempt to ease my nerves. Another clang sounded to my left, and I jumped, skittering across the bed. A heavyset maid, well into her years, glared at me over a tray laden with food.

I frowned at the intensity of her glower and righted my night shift. "Good... morn?"

My greeting did not diminish her anger, and she didn't speak a word—only tried to murder me with her glare.

"May I help you?" I trailed off, not knowing what she expected of me.

"That's my job, milady. If ye would be so kind as to lie back down, I'll be passing yer first meal," she snapped.

I grimaced at her tone and sat back. She slammed the tray in front of me and I eyed her, my nervousness outweighing my hunger.

"I apologize," I muttered. I couldn't figure out if she was simply ill-tempered or if I caused some offense.

"Don't bother apologizing to me, milady. Will ye be needing any tea this morning?" she asked, returning to a cart laden with foods and drinks.

"Erm, water will be fine."

"Aye, water it is then. I'll tell ye, take no ale while ye'r with child. Advice from my grandmother."

"Pardon?" I choked out.

"Ye are with child, are ye not? Not my place to be asking who the father is, though everyone would like to know."

"Wha–? I'm *not* with child. What in all of Rinmoth would make you think that?" I looked down at my belly, flat and muscled. I didn't have an ounce of fat on me besides on my chest and rear, thanks to all my training.

"Ye will not be taking the after morning tea then, miss?" She turned slowly, almost menacingly. "Ye want to carry a child without a life mate?"

"I beg your pardon, but I can do without any tea—or first meal, for that matter—if you and your attitude come with it. I'm not with child. And I did not take a bed mate last night, I–"

"Then who brought those?" She pointed a meaty finger at a pile of clothes neatly folded on the table beside me.

I opened my mouth, then closed it, at a loss for words. There was a letter on top.

"I'm—I'm not sure." I managed.

"None of my business who ye take to yer bed, milady. I'd only ask that ye not lie to the young maids who are only trying to help. They don't know how to properly care for a–"

"If you call me a whore, it will be the last thing you say."

My patience shattered. I grabbed the knife meant for carving whatever meat was on my tray and slid my feet to the floor. The maid paled as I stood, gripping the dull blade with all my might.

"I am no whore. You needn't care for me as one. In fact, I need no care. *Begone.*"

She huffed as if I inconvenienced her, but hurried out the door with her little cart of food.

I screamed through clenched teeth and threw the knife to the ground. Rage shook my limbs. Why would no one accept me for who I was? Why did people always assume the worst?

I blew out a breath, attempting to calm the anger heating my skin. '*Who was it?*' I asked, reaching for the note.

'*Mate.*' She gnawed on her bone, disinterested now that the argument was over.

'*Rafe?*'

The parchment read, 'Wear it.' That seemed like something he would write.

'*Mate.*' Apparently, to her, Rafe needed no other title.

I placed it aside and couldn't help the smile that lit my face. It was a uniform, crisp and new. The tunic seemed too small. It would be a tight fit, but the detailed patch on the sleeve had my heart singing. A black embroidered dragon leading a golden lion with crossed swords behind.

His Tennan patch.

Beneath was a pair of dark trousers, which looked like they would fit marginally better. I jerked off my night shift, eager to put it on. After securing the trousers with my belt, I fastened the bandit breaker in place. Binding my chest as tightly as I could, I pulled on the tunic.

My happiness warred with unease as I struggled to fasten the lacing. It was low enough that if anyone taller stood beside me, they could peer down my tunic. The waist fit fine, snug enough that it wouldn't hinder my movements. If Rafe ordered this, I couldn't imagine him telling the seamstress to allow extra room in the bust.

My fingers traced along the Tennan patch as I bit my lip. I would wear this today, but it would come with even more accusations. One option was to compromise the integrity of the lacing and pull it taut and uncomfortably tight, or make sure no men stood over me.

I could deal with the precautionary measures.

'*Do I look like a soldier?*' I asked, threading the long hair at the nape of my neck into a simple braid.

Tizmet froze, her eyes locking onto mine for a moment. '*Human.*' She affirmed, then went back to crunching the bone.

I smiled, sitting down to eat. The tray was laden with fruits, breads, meats and odd little pastries bedecked with flowers. I tried to puzzle out what it all was and ate what I recognized.

Belly full, I sorted my belongings and stepped into my boots.

'*What now?*' I mused, sitting on the edge of the bed.

The curtains had been opened for the morning sun and I wondered why Tizmet hadn't alarmed me when the servants came in. I knew why I hadn't woken. The bed was so glorious it wouldn't release me from sleep.

'*Food. Hungry,*' Tizmet answered my unspoken question.

'*They bring you food and you ignore their threat?*' I scoffed, then made my way to the balcony.

Tizmet crunched the last of the bone as I passed. She stretched out like a cat with her haunches in the air and yawned, showing off her long white fangs. Resettling herself, she laid down and slept.

At the balcony, I leaned over the railing. From this point, I could see much of King's Wall, as well as part of the courtyard. To the side, there was a garden. It was alive with workers, prepping the winter soil for spring.

Would I be stuck in this room until my transfer was settled? I wrinkled my nose, hoping Rafe would get his way. I was willing to wager Ruveel would put me with the other Riders who bonded hatchlings. It would be both miserable and humiliating—for me and Tizmet.

We weren't ready to fight on the front, that was for sure, but we also weren't children. Not that all Riders were young, there were a few First Chosen who were middle-aged. Yet, they bonded a hatchling, not a full-grown dragon. If I was lumped in with the first years–

A knock interrupted my thoughts, and I turned toward the sound. Tizmet lifted her head and pulled her lips back, baring her teeth.

'*Friend or foe?*' I asked, crossing the room.

She pushed confusion at me, and I shook my head, reaching for the handle.

The door swung open before I could answer, and I backed up a step. The man at the threshold was tall with a lean build and a nasty-looking face. He wasn't ugly, and he might have been handsome... had he not been sneering.

"Begging your pardon for my interruption, milady."

His voice dripped with sarcasm, and I had the strongest urge to punch him. What would be my penance for laying hands on a King's Servant? It might be worth it.

"Get on with it." If he wanted to treat me with disrespect, I could give it straight back.

"Your Majesty, the King, requires your presence."

My stomach revolted, and Tizmet scrambled to stand, sensing my unease.

"Oi, where?"

It needed to be an open area that Tizmet could get to. If I disappeared into the bowels of the palace, she would tear it down stone by stone to get to me.

"That need not matter, milady," he replied, lifting his chin. His eyes flicked to my chest, and a wave of disgust rolled over me.

"To be fair, it does. I am bonded to a Wild Dragon. If you prefer to keep the roof over your head, I'll be meeting him outside or in my room."

"In your *room*? You dare insinuate the *King* enter your chambers?!" His shock was palpable.

I ground my teeth, gripping my bandit breaker. I wouldn't take his head off, I wouldn't. Tizmet pushed an image of the servant, then one of her devouring a deer. She would eat him if I let her.

"I'm insinuating that the King needs to meet with me in an open area. One that she," I gestured to Tizmet, "can access."

"His Majesty has already considered this. Come." He lifted his insulted nose higher and took off.

I shrugged, watching him go. My arms crossed over my chest, and I leaned against the door frame just as I imagined Rafe would.

"Milady!" The manservant bristled when he realized I had not followed. He stalked back to me.

"See that hall? She can't fit down it," I said in a bored tone. Tizmet snarled behind me.

"I am aware, but she can fly–"

"Where I go, she goes. Send General Rafe or Blain for further instructions." I huffed, righting myself, then slammed the door in his face.

Where did these servants get the idea that they could order me about? I was not only a soldier, but a Rider. That had to carry some weight if nothing else did. I ducked under Tizmet's head, who was still glaring at the door, then plopped on the bed. I would wait until someone else came to get me.

Someone I could trust.

I was jarred awake by someone kicking my boot. My eyes shot open, and I blinked at the stark-white ceiling. Stretching out languidly on the bed that was softer than any fur, I looked down. Rafe stood at the footboard with his arms crossed, smirking. I froze, then beamed in response before glancing at the door. It was cracked open with the same manservant peeking through the slit.

"We have an audience, General," I whispered, sure the servant couldn't hear us.

"You do. Up, Avyanna." He nudged my boot with his knee again.

"Yes, sir." I smirked and pushed myself upright.

His gaze traveled to my chest and lingered. I grinned and dipped my head to his line of sight to let him know I caught him staring. He shifted his feet, but arched a brow in a silent dare.

"It fits," he rumbled.

"Barely. Please tell the next seamstress she's making this for a woman."

When I stood, he didn't back up to give me space. Towering over me, fire burned through his features.

"Aye, perhaps I will." He spoke so low, his voice broke. He turned abruptly, heading toward the door. "Come."

Tizmet rose, flicking out her tongue.

'*Trust him,*' I urged.

She bared her teeth, but stayed where she was.

I followed Rafe as he shoved past the servant without a glance. He led me down the stairs and hall, then outside.

Tizmet's bellow echoed behind us.

'*Calm. I'm here,*' I assured her as I broke free of the palace and the sun kissed my cheeks.

She roared and leapt from the balcony, crashing in front of me. Rafe eyed her as if she was a puppy he was entertaining, and walked around her mammoth form. I trailed my hand along her scales as I passed. Her muscles shivered under my touch, but I pressed on, keeping at Rafe's heels.

We ended up in the gardens where the workers milled about. The sweet fragrance of spring hid in the winter chill. It was on its way. I took a deep breath, wanting to savor that smell, remember it.

Rafe stopped, crossing his arms. I looked between him and what garnered his glare—the palace entrance. Tizmet shifted behind me anxiously. The workers offered polite but confused smiles, puzzled as to why we were here.

The doors burst open, and everyone turned as six guards dressed in blue and gold marched out. There were frantic but hushed orders and the gardeners scattered like flies. Behind the guards, dressed in blue and gold, strode a man with a crown.

The King.

I dipped to my lowest curtsy, staring at the ground.

A hand jerked me up, and I bolted upright as Rafe scowled at me. Perhaps I was not supposed to bow as a soldier. No one told me what to do! Tizmet let out a low keen as my fear spread to her.

"Greetings, Avyanna of Gareth."

The King was an old man, with no color in his white beard and short hair. He was adorned in white, from his robe to his freshly pressed pants and tunic. All of which were embroidered with the lightest gold thread, finely detailed with flowers and sunbeams.

"Hail, Your Majesty." I grimaced as my voice squeaked and I dropped my gaze to the stone path.

"Shadowslayer, I see she has more manners than you," the King said softly, almost as if he found it amusing.

Rafe didn't reply, instead offering a grunt of acknowledgement.

"Dear one, come sit."

The King took a seat on a bench near a bed of golden-yellow flowers—late winter blooms. He smiled and patted the space next to him. Panicked, I glanced at Rafe, who offered me a raised brow and a bored look. Scrambling, I moved to sit beside the King.

"Blade." A guard stepped into my path.

I freed my bandit breaker and placed it in his waiting palm. He moved aside, holding it gingerly as I took my seat. I perched on the edge, not quite knowing what was proper.

Tizmet growled, head craned above us.

'For love of the sun, don't eat the King!' I begged her.

She snorted and flicked her tongue, tasting the air.

"She is yours?" the King murmured. He admired her with an expression of both amusement and wonder.

"We're bonded, your Majesty," I stammered.

"Is that not the same?"

He had the clearest blue eyes—like glass. Not cold, but clear as a fresh stream. His face was old and wizened, but retained the sharp angles of his youth. His thin lips were curled into a small smile.

"In our case, no." I rubbed the back of my neck, trying to explain. "She is not mine, as much as the flowers are not yours."

"Do they not belong to me?" he asked with a smile.

"Not truly. You may hire servants to care for them, or even plant the seed, but who is to say they're yours? They grow under their own power, they perish under their own power." I tugged on my sleeve, fighting back against my nerves. "Tizmet has grown without my influence. She is not mine entirely. I suppose through the bond we're connected, yet she is independent."

The King's smile grew, and he peered at Rafe. "You have chosen a good one here."

Rafe merely squinted in reply, and I offered him a tight-lipped smile. I didn't want to ruin his work if he'd managed to sway the King. He gave nothing away. I wished I knew what I was supposed to say.

"I do so love a midday story. Tell me yours." The King leaned back on the bench. He was relaxed, yet his posture and demeanor screamed royalty.

"What would you like to know?"
"Everything."

CHAPTER 13

Therefore, I told the King everything.

At first I gauged his responses, wondering if the brief details of my childhood bored him. He listened to all I had to say, nodding here and there when I faltered, encouraging me to go on. I left out the details of mine and Rafe's relationship, as well as his ability to control the dragons. That was a secret I swore I'd take to my grave. I told him of my time in the school, the barracks and as part of Rafe's Tennan. I tried to keep it as emotionless as possible, simply giving him my story from the beginning.

"And here we are," I said.

While I spoke, Tizmet settled on the ground just beyond the gardens to bask in the midday sun. Her eyes flashed as she took everything in.

"That's quite the story, soldier." The King ran his slender fingers through his beard.

I smiled at his use of the word, instead of lady. After all, I was a woman, but I was not a lady by proper terms.

He continued, "My Dragon Lord seeks your transfer. I have to admit, I was curious to meet you. A wild dragon!" His gaze slipped to Tizmet, and I dipped my head in respect.

"However," he went on, "my Shadowslayer has requested you stay within his Tennan."

My eyes shifted to Rafe, who looked to all the world, as if he was bored to tears.

"Tell me, what would you have me do?"

The King was letting me choose? It shocked me he would even ask. I always held the King in high regard, same as anyone else in Regent, yet this was a kindness I didn't expect.

"I would like to stay in the Tennan, as well." My voice cracked as I spoke.

"The Dragon Lord has requested that you take the classes of a Rider. Would you not rather attend them to deepen your bond?" He tilted his head, studying me.

"I would not, my King." I chose my words carefully, clasping my hands together. "Those classes teach hatchlings and new Riders. Not a soldier with a full-grown dragon. It would be–"

"Embarrassing?" the King offered.

"Humiliating. Can you imagine us in a class that encourages her to fly? Or one that discusses what she would rather eat, and the benefits? She knows these things."

"But do you know how to use magic, soldier? If it could help you communicate with her, would it not be worth the humiliation?"

As I looked at Tizmet again, I sighed. It wasn't just for her sake that I was against the classes. I didn't want to deal with the other Riders. I established myself in the barracks, then in the Tennan. Establishing myself in another group was daunting. I didn't want to waste time when I could use it to learn how to fight at the front with Rafe.

When I didn't answer, he spoke again. "I will grant you this boon: Return to Northwing. Train with the Riders until the moon wanes and is born anew. If you are still so adamantly against this, we will revisit the issue." He rose to his feet.

I was both relieved that the conversation was over and disheartened that I would at least have to attend the classes for two weeks.

"Thank you, Your Majesty." I bowed as I stood.

"You're quite welcome, new Rider." He turned to Rafe. "Shadowslayer, you are returning?"

"Before darkness falls," he ground out.

"Leave in the morning. I should like you and your team to join me for last meal. Accommodations will be made for the dragon," he said, gesturing to Tizmet.

The guard returned my bandit breaker, then stepped into formation. I watched the King retreat into the palace, surrounded by his guards in gold and blue.

"Feeding you to the wolves," Rafe grumbled. He glared at the door as it closed behind the last guard.

"Good thing I have my own wolf," I breathed, walking toward him and sheathing my blade.

Gardeners trickled in, resuming their work.

Rafe grunted and turned to walk back around the palace. Tizmet stood with a yawn, showing off rows of teeth, then followed behind us.

'*Tired?*' I asked.

She snorted and pushed a feeling of boredom at me.

Ge'org roared in the distance, and Tizmet searched the sky.

'*I think he'd be willing to offer you some excitement.*'

She looked down at me and bared her fangs in response. I laughed, drawing a side eye from Rafe.

"Tizmet is bored. I told her Ge'org wouldn't mind company."

"She'll see him soon enough," he replied darkly.

When we reached the entrance, I tilted my head skyward. '*Up. Fly. I'll be right there.*'

She flicked out her tongue, watching me disappear into the hall. Rafe hurried me to my room, and Tizmet was pacing on the balcony by the time I entered. Rafe leaned against the door frame and smiled.

"Come in?" I asked.

"Not a chance."

His eyes traveled up and down my body and I smirked, pushing out a hip.

"Enjoying the view, General?"

"Taking in my soldier one last time," he said, pushing off the door. His demeanor was weary, and I wondered what he was thinking.

"You will not attend tonight? If you're not there, I won't go."

It was the truth. Unless I was forced, I would not attend. I refused to be thrown into a situation where I didn't understand the culture or people, left to flounder like a fish.

"Do not entertain the idea of refusing the King," he said, turning away. "Wear green."

Confused, I watched him go. Wear green? I glanced down at my uniform. It was standard issue. I couldn't change the colors as I wished. Closing the door, I turned to Tizmet, who curled in on herself for a nap. That seemed like a fine idea. Might as well take advantage of that luxury while I had it.

I barely settled on the blankets before a team of women bustled inside. I shot upright in bed, gripping my bandit breaker. If they were all here to call me a whore, I would cut someone. Tizmet flicked her tongue, testing the air for danger.

"Oi!" I called.

A stern woman, who reminded me of Elenor, eyed me up and down. Maids behind her bustled about the room, placing a three-sided mirror, almost as tall as I was, near the bath. Others brought in carts with buckets of steaming water and supplies.

"My lady, Avyanna of Gareth, I am Joan, a lady's maid. I'll be readying you for tonight."

There was no way I'd spend any more time with pretentious gossipmongers. "Begging your pardon, but I can ready myself," I shot back, moving off the bed.

"Begging your pardon," she mocked with an eyebrow raised, "but you cannot."

"I am fully capable of–"

"My Lady," an edge of authority sharpened her tone, "I was given this task by the King, and I will obey. I am to ready you for the evening meal, and from the look of things, I have quite the task at hand. Rider or not, I have authority here, and you will respect that."

More maids piled in, bearing rolls of fabric.

Knots of irritation twisted in my stomach. "What will this entail?"

"Dressing you as a proper lady," Joan said, lifting her chin.

"I am no such thing. I am a soldier."

"Return to your game tomorrow. Tonight, the King has requested you appear as *Lady* Avyanna of Gareth, not Avyanna of the Shadowslayer's Tennan."

I grit my teeth and glared. I could always change into my uniform after they left. "Aye then, let's get on with it."

When I had agreed, I had no idea how long it would take. After all, last meal was a few chimes away. I thought I had plenty of time to get through this nonsense, then slip back into my uniform.

Oh, how I was mistaken. The maids bathed me—scrubbing every inch and lathering me in a thick, sweet-smelling cream. Then came the seamstress, and I was in awe of her skill. She worked efficiently, holding up bolts of fabric to my face, judging colors. Torn between the green and blue, I broke my silence, choosing the green.

She eyed me as if it was inappropriate to voice my opinion on such things. Nevertheless, she sent for pre-made garments of that cloth. What arrived was a pile of gowns of varying styles, all sized to fit. It surprised me to find I still enjoyed trying on dresses. It was a natural feminine chore, and I enjoyed every moment of it.

Chimes flew by as the seamstress settled on a style. Simple, compared to the others. It was a deep forest-green, matching my eyes. Bright gold thread edged the trim, akin to the gilded fringes in Tizmet's eyes.

The decadent fabric clung to my chest and slim waist, flaring out at the hips. It was soft—like water on my skin. The neckline dipped, but was not so low that my cleavage showed. My hair seemed at odds with the gown's femininity, and I frowned at myself as they selected matching slippers.

"There's not much to do for it." Joan tsked, noticing my observation.

I shrugged it off. "It's who I am."

The seamstress brought a green and gold scarf and draped it over my head, tying it in place. "This will work," she said with a crisp, satisfied nod.

I grimaced, waiting until she stepped away to yank it off. "I'm not hiding it."

Joan bristled. "You will do as–"

"No. This I will refuse," I said, tossing the fine fabric.

As I studied my reflection, it took a moment for me to recognize the woman staring back at me. She was feminine, but strong. She carried a sense of power, yet softness.

I was pleased.

Joan's sharp eyes assessed me from head to toe, searching for anything out of place. She clapped her hands, dismissing the women, and they bustled out, taking all the supplies with them. I wondered where the small army was headed now.

"You will be collected in less than a quarter of a chime," she said.

I reached for my push dagger, lying on top of my uniform.

"No blades are permitted in the King's presence," she added, arching a brow.

"I never leave without it."

"You will be searched."

I smiled and slipped the dagger under my chest binding. "Let them try."

Joan scowled and dropped to a curtsy, then hurried out.

Tizmet eyed me drowsily, and I gave her a spin.

'*Pretty?*' I asked.

She snorted and lifted her head, puzzled by my question. I laughed at her and admired my dress in the mirror they left behind.

Moments passed before a knock sounded. After a deep calming breath, I opened it, ready to tell off a manservant.

"Oi, aren't you a sight for sore eyes." Blain gave me an easy smile, looking me up and down.

"Blain." I grinned, dipping into a curtsy.

He was dressed in fine clothes as well. He wore colors of black and gold with his Tennan patch sewn into the shoulder of his sleeve.

"You got to wear your patch?" I frowned. "The lady's maid wouldn't let me."

"You look stunning, regardless. Besides, with that hair, everyone will notice you." His eyes danced over my short, white locks.

"Let me change to my uniform. I'll only be a moment." Anxiety strummed through me, and I retreated a step.

"Not so fast!" Blain snatched my hand and pulled me back to him. "I would pay a great deal to get our General's face sketched when he sees you."

The grin that spread over my features couldn't be helped. I bit my cheek trying to hide it, then ducked my head.

"You've never attended such an event?" he asked.

"No. It's not as if I had the opportunity, being raised at Northwing."

"Follow my lead, then. Hold my arm, like this."

He wound my arm under his and placed my palm on his sleeve. The position brought us close, and it warmed my cheeks. Such proximity to a man felt inappropriate. Not that I thought much of it while in uniform, but while I was dressed as a proper lady, it seemed more... unnerving.

"Convey to your dragon that we'll be taking the outside route." Blain nodded at the gray beast.

'*Fly around,*' I told her, giving her a mental shove toward the balcony. Her lips pulled back, but she obeyed.

As we rushed along, a servant bustled by, giving us a passing glance, but said nothing. I wondered if I would be the star of tonight's rumors. I shuddered at what stories the staff would concoct.

"Are you well?" Blain asked as we stepped into the fading sunlight.

My smile wavered, and I doubted it was convincing. "Aye, a bit nervous is all."

Tizmet landed behind, casting us into shadow.

"Nothing is expected of you. We are but simple soldiers, after all." He winked. "Their only thought is that we will be vulgar and crude. You can only exceed their expectations."

"Exceed their expectations in rudeness. I can do that," I scoffed.

Blain snorted, and we drifted into companionable silence. We walked along the back of the palace, through the gardens. Tizmet sniffed the air, showing more of her teeth.

'*Male.*' She sent a sense of disgust.

'*Ge'org?*'

'*Dragon,*' she agreed.

I took a deep breath and let it out. Rafe said I would deal with the Dragon Lord tonight. Surely he would be cocky and arrogant, gloating about my chance to train with his Riders.

"Almost there," Blain assured me, giving my hand a pat. He moved with ease and confidence, as if he'd been raised in this lifestyle. Perhaps wherever he and Dane hailed from, they were part of the court.

My skin turned cold and clammy as the sounds of laughter and music drifted to our ears. We rounded a corner of the palace wall, revealing a portion that looked nothing like the wing that held my room. A great open mezzanine bared a space that could swallow the whole school dorm. The opening was at least twice as large as my room, if not more. It dwarfed even Tizmet.

Blain led me up the extravagant, white-stoned staircase to the crest. I hiked up the hem of my skirt as I ascended. Tizmet took a jumping flight to the top. There, two guards stood at attention. One held out his arm, stopping us when we neared.

"Blades?" he demanded, staring straight ahead.

"I'm a soldier. Of course I carry one," Blain replied, pulling a small knife from the sheath on his belt. He handed it over and peered at me expectantly.

"None." I lied.

The guard snapped his gaze to me, and I arched an eyebrow. "I'm a lady. Care to challenge that?"

After a brief pause, he resumed his stiffened position, letting us pass. "The squire will announce you," he said.

Blain chuckled, leaning close to whisper in my ear. "Always offer them at least one blade. They'll never think to check you for more."

I smiled as the squire's scrutinizing gaze shifted from Tizmet, then landed on us.

"My lady, Avyanna of Gareth?" He inquired.

"And his Lordship, Blain of Rafe Shadowslayer," Blain added, winking at me. He took Rafe's name, which deepened his secrecy.

The squire cleared his throat, then his booming voice projected our introductions. "Announcing Lady Avyanna of Gareth, and his Lordship, Blain of the Shadowslayer."

People of all ages and sizes stared as we made our way down the stairs. The sun set behind us and bathed the crowd with auburn light. The mezzanine lowered to a large banquet hall, brimming with men and women, all adorned in their finest attire. At the far wall, the King sat on a throne, talking with a couple dressed in vibrant purple.

Encircling the expansive space were iron braziers, filled to the brim with bright red coals and crackling flames to chase off the night's chill. Tables were placed throughout, laden with food, and servants carried trays of sweets and drinks.

I inwardly cringed as a group of women gasped, eyes on my hair.

"Ignore them." Blain spoke through his smile and nodded a greeting to a few men.

I lifted my chin and took in the multitude. Tizmet gave a fierce growl, and I turned to see the squire shooing her aside. She snapped at his hand and flicked out her tongue. He jerked back, face pinched with consternation as the crowd murmured at her antics.

'Don't eat anyone.'

She roared, and I ignored her with a smile, lifting my eyes.

Rafe was here.

My heart swelled, and I tried my best to school my features. He leaned against a pillar along the wall, and my pulse raced as I admired him. The formal, steel-plate eye patch replaced his cloth covering. His apparel was far more proper than his usual wear, though I had to look away to choke back my laughter. He wore black, loose-fitting pants. His dark tunic had ruffles at the collar... and one sleeve. He'd torn it off. His muscular arm hung out, bearing his dragon tattoo. His glower dared anyone to give him a second look.

As I peeked up at him again, his gaze heated my skin despite the great distance between us. My cheeks flushed, and I stared down at my dress as Blain led me along. I inclined my head as courtiers greeted me, or rather greeted Blain, then me in turn. People here seemed to know *of* Blain, all treating him with familiar pleasantries and easy smiles. I was sure they also knew of me as well. They simply believed the worst, as the servants did.

We moved through the swarm and tried to look interested in the conversations Blain engaged in. My eyes kept wandering to the dark shadow in the corner where Rafe glowered.

"Announcing Dragon Lord Ruveel of Bernard."

The crowd turned as one, Blain swinging me with him. All eyes watched as Ruveel sauntered down the stairs. Ge'org landed behind him, blocking the dying sunlight. Tizmet hissed and snapped when he swung his tail too close to her.

The women, both those with men and without, ogled with longing. His blood-red attire bore black accents and fit him well. The Dragon Rider insignia was embroidered on his chest, and he wore it with pride. He was the Dragon Lord, and he owned it. His gaze singled me out, and he grinned, angling his path toward me and Blain.

Blain shifted uncomfortably and pulled away from the group he mingled with, tugging me along with him.

Women and men tried to stop the Dragon Lord, but he ignored them, eyes locked on me.

A voice from beside me sent a shiver up my spine, the depth delicious and warm. "She's mine."

Rafe approached, dismissing Blain with a jerk of his chin. He bowed and stepped away, melding into the crowd.

"I am." My breath hitched in my throat as Rafe offered me the crook of his arm. I accepted the gesture, heat flushing through me as his skin brushed mine.

His dark gaze fell, and he frowned. I smirked, returning my attention to the Dragon Lord.

"Lady Avyanna!" he called, holding out a palm.

I stared at it, confused, as Rafe practically vibrated with tension beside me.

"You're supposed to give me your hand." Ruveel winked

I glowered, but placed my palm on his. He bent low and brushed his lips against my knuckles. Some foreign emotion I couldn't place danced through his eyes. I jerked my hand away as if it was on fire and gripped my dress.

Ruveel straightened, and his gaze flashed to my General. "What a terrible sight. Did you perhaps meet a rabid bear on the way here?"

Rafe didn't grace him with a response, his glare dark and unfaltering.

"Ever the conversationalist. Speaking of conversation," Ruveel's blue eyes flitted back to mine, and a victorious smile tugged at the corners of his mouth, "I hear you'll be joining the Dragon Legion."

"No." I lifted my chin. "I'll be there until the moon is born anew."

My instincts urged me to step closer to Rafe, but I held my ground. Having my hand on his arm lent me strength, but I needed to learn to face this man on my own.

Tizmet scuffled with Ge'org on the mezzanine, and the crowd gasped and murmured. Ruveel ignored them and tidied his jacket.

"Adjusting yourself to our ways will be time well spent."

"I think you forget, I trained to be a Dragon Rider until I joined the army." I huffed, my attention drawing to the dragons. Tizmet could hold her own against Ge'org. I needed to fight my own battles.

"Yes! And you've spent the last two years training as a simple soldier. You'll need... realignment." His gaze traveled down my body with a satisfied glint. "It seems as though you're already well on your way."

Anger flushed my cheeks. "I will not–"

Music strummed louder, cutting off my retort. My glare settled in the corner where musicians played on stringed instruments.

"Ah, I shall have this dance." The Dragon Lord bowed low, offering me his hand.

The gesture was a snake, ready to strike. My lips pressed tight, conveying my refusal.

"What, don't know a proper dance? I shall show you." He sneered.

"I need air." My growl was unladylike, but I couldn't bring myself to care. I tore myself from Rafe, and held my chin high, ignoring bystanders' stares and murmurs.

I retreated up the stairs, where the great red dragon pestered Tizmet—pretending to ignore her while purposefully sliding his tail into her space. This was normal dragon antics, though it was never seen between adults. I doubted these

people had ever seen two dragons at once, let alone two as massive as Tizmet and
Ge'org.

My fingers squeezed the railing, and I took a deep breath. My skin was
uncomfortably hot and the slight breeze kissed it with coolness. The horizon
burned a vivid orange hue from behind the buildings of King's Wall in the
distance. The dragons quieted, and the crowd carried on with their merri-
ment—chatting, dancing and feasting. I couldn't help but feel sickened by the
extravagance, thinking of the small portions back at Northwing, about all the
winter nights refugees went hungry when there wasn't enough.

Someone joined my side, and his familiar presence calmed me, anchored me.

"He's living up to your descriptions, General." I sighed.

Rafe leaned against the rail, glaring at the party below.

Tizmet pushed an image of her fighting another dragon, sinking her teeth
into green scales, blood gushing around her maw.

'*If he crowds you, feel free to attack him,*' I said, not hiding my irritation.

At least she would be excused for taking her anger out on him. She was a Wild
One. I was dressed up like a doll. Despite Blain's words before, I felt as though
I would embarrass Rafe or the Tennan if I didn't act according to what people
expected.

"It's improper to deny a man a dance without good reason," Rafe rumbled.

I turned to meet his dark gaze. "I had good reason. He treated me like the
scum of a pond. Is that not enough?"

He smirked in answer, then pushed off the railing. "Come."

He started toward the guards at the stairs leading to the courtyard. He
stopped and glanced back at me—a silent question. I gripped my dress and
walked as calmly as I could. I would not rush and embarrass myself.

As we made our way down the stairs, Tizmet roared, then jumped from the
mezzanine. Her presence was comforting.

"What of Blain?" I asked, glancing over my shoulder.

Rafe led me along a simple cobblestone path. "He knows the game." He
shrugged.

We distanced ourselves from the commotion, disappearing into the night.
We crossed the gardens and paused near the palace doors that led to my room.
Rafe regarded Tizmet, who in turn flicked her tongue, testing the air, meeting
his intense gaze.

"Go. Sleep," he told her.

I scoffed, watching as she snorted and reared up her head, glaring. She
snapped her jaws, as if ridding herself of a terrible taste.

"Tell her to sleep." This time, he aimed his words at me.

I arched a brow at Tizmet. "She won't leave me." I shrugged.

"Tell her to watch from the skies."

'*Fly.*' I shared an image, urging her to the skies. '*Sleep, or fly.*'

She snarled and lowered her head, bringing one giant, flaming eye to his face. '*Mate. Protect?*' she asked.

I smiled at her use of words. '*He will protect me.*' I pushed my sense of trust for Rafe through the bond—indisputable and complete.

She snorted and bit at the air directly in front of his face. He didn't even flinch as the giant teeth snapped together.

'*Mate,*' she said again, flapping her massive wings.

She pulled away and pushed an image of us sleeping together. I laughed as she followed it up with an image of dragons mating. Clearly, she wanted me to mate and be rid of him. She took to the sky, climbing slowly.

Rafe grunted and turned his back on her rising form to squint at me. "Hungry?"

CHAPTER 14

T izmet flew high in the night sky, invisible against the darkness. I followed
   Rafe into the courtyard, then through a gate in the iron fence. The guards
noted his tattoo and gave us a brisk nod in passing.

We entered the city, sticking to smaller roads rather than the main ones.
Positioned at his elbow, I took in the night, enjoying the sights and pleasant
walk. Winter's chill lingered in the air and I pressed closer to Rafe, maintaining
an appropriate distance.

Few squinted and frowned as we passed, but most ignored us, content to
go on their merry way. Rafe wound further into the city until we reached an
area enclosed by buildings—a dead end. There, a small crowd gathered, having
a grand time tucked away from the rest of the city.

Two musicians in the far corner dueled on their stringed instruments, playing
as if they were on fire. People twirled in the center, oblivious to everything else.
My smile grew as Rafe stepped aside to speak with a food vendor nearby.

Not everyone danced, some perched on crates, chairs or even on the dirt
street, admiring the display, clapping in time. The savory scent of spiced meat
and hot bread wafted through the air, creating the illusion of a festival.

"Vy–"

Rafe's deep voice snagged my attention. He held a piece of meat shoved
between two pieces of bread. Reddish brown sauce oozed from the edges.

"You eat street food, but not–"

"And someone at Northwing was smuggling info to the Shadows." Rafe
deadpanned. "I'll eat what I deem safe, Vy."

"Well, thank you," I said, taking it with tentative fingers and shaking my head.
"What is it?" I asked, sampling a small bite.

"Street food."

An explosion of flavor embraced my palate, and my eyes widened as a pleasant burn warmed my mouth.

"It's hot!" I licked some juices from my fingers as I followed Rafe to a bench.

He sat, raising a brow in question. "Can't handle it?" he taunted.

"I never said that." I took my place beside him and sniffled, taking another bite.

Truth be told, I never had something so spicy. I ate it as quickly as I could. The sweet, but intense, mixture of spices heated my belly. We ate in silence, enjoying the scene.

This was better, by far, than the King's last meal.

"Will we be missed?" I asked, watching as two girls danced, laughing as they swung each other about.

"Perhaps." Rafe shrugged. "I never linger at such events."

"Have you attended many?"

"Here and there. Less than one a year." He sighed, and I turned to study him. His face was weary, as if a heavy weight settled on his shoulders. "I'm requested every winter, during the respite. I try to find my way out of it."

"Commander Dewal mentioned something about a winter's respite. What causes it?" I asked, propping my chin on my hands.

"They're after the dragons, not us. In the winter months, dragons retreat behind our lines, too slow and cold for battle. The Shadows back off, not willing to fight us without the chance of taking a dragon."

"Why don't you press the advantage, then?"

"Because," a bitter edge drenched his tone with malice, "without the fire-breathing beasts, we cannot defeat them."

I frowned, returning my attention to the crowd. They reveled as if they had not a care in the world—as if there weren't men dying on the front.

After a moment, I dipped my chin, lowering my voice. "Do you resent them?"

Rafe shook his head, a small smile tugging at the corner of his lips. "No. They *should* dance. It's not their job to fight, it's mine."

I fought against the craving to touch his face. His anguish and exhaustion were obvious.

"I fight—my men fight—so they can keep dancing."

I smiled in understanding. He found joy in their happiness because he played a part in it. Protecting the homelands kept them safe. He fought so they could enjoy their freedoms and not be pulled into war more than what they already were.

Men, women and children swirled and laughed, not necessarily in a reel or together, but independently—simply for the joy of it. I wondered if they all knew one other, or if they were strangers. No one seemed to pay attention to me and Rafe, content to enjoy the evening.

My foot tapped along with the beat. The tune was familiar—one played at festivals back home.

"Go," Rafe said.

I raised a brow, puzzled by his order.

He gestured toward the throng. "Dance. Enjoy the night."

The smallest tug of responsibility whispered inside. It wouldn't be appropriate. A soldier wouldn't dare. I pushed myself up and smoothed out the dress that marked me as a lady, not a soldier, then met the others in the clearing.

As a child, I joined many celebrations such as this during the Solstices. I knew the commoners' dance—a style in which mistakes didn't exist, only good humor and freedom. My feet moved, and I clapped my hands with the music, body flowing where the melody bid it. I might not know a fancy routine fit for the King's palace, but I knew this.

I tripped on my dress and bent down to tie the skirt up to my knee. To free my legs, I knotted it in the corner, as was the custom. Rafe's dark eye glittered as I stood, his gaze on me.

I danced for myself. My feet sped along and I looped my arm with strangers. I threw my head back and giggled as I spun with a girl. She stumbled into a young lad. They laughed, then fell into step with one another.

My lungs burned for air, and I glanced at the musicians, wondering how long they would keep up. Both were grinning at each other, daring the other to be the first to stop. I let out a breathless laugh and spun to face Rafe, feet keeping the steps.

He sat with his arms draped across the backrest. His stare followed me, burning with desire, and I faltered. Suddenly, I was no longer dancing for myself. With my gaze locked on his, I danced for him. My cheeks ached with my smile as I moved with the pulsing rhythm, feet pounding a steady cadence. I twirled again and when my gaze found his, the smallest grin turned his lips.

I laughed freely, swaying my hips as I ambled toward him, beckoning him with my outreached hand. Mirth slipped across his features, but he shook his head, shooing me away.

The music finally cut short, and I gasped, collapsing beside him. My body pressed against his, but I didn't care. I laughed between panting breaths, admiring the musicians as their instruments hung from limp arms. They panted, then nodded to one another. I applauded with the crowd as they gave us all a bow.

Sitting back, I curled into Rafe. His arm dropped around me and I smiled up at him, feeling truly free. Free to do as I would, not bound by the restrictions of society or laws of the army—or Dragon Riders.

"Won't they notice?" I breathed.

He hummed, his hold crushing me closer. "Don't cause a scene."

I snickered and wiggled against him, content to be in his arms.

Tizmet circled lazily in the air as a young couple brought a cart of pitchers and mugs down the lane. They worked the crowd, offering drinks to everyone, trading coin for refreshment.

The lad approached. "Ale, my lord?"

"Aye." Rafe offered a coin from a pocket.

After handing over the drinks, the boy moved on. Rafe pulled his arm from my side to hand me a mug.

I shook my head. "I don't drink."

He took a sip of his with a brow arched in question.

"My spirits are high enough from dancing. I don't need more." I had never been one to drink alcohol and I wouldn't start now. Especially now. Especially because of who I was with.

"Wise of you, to know your limits," he murmured, watching the others drift in their small groups of friends.

I pressed my thigh against his. "Do you know yours?"

"I'm well acquainted with them." His attention dropped to where we touched.

"Tell me, what's your weakness, General?" I gave him a sly grin.

He peered at me over the rim of his mug before tossing the ale back in a long gulp. Setting it aside, his gaze flared. "One would say I've a weak spot for a stubborn slip of a girl."

"Woman." I corrected, leaning back.

His eyes roved down my body, and he started on the second ale. "So you say."

"Wouldn't you say?" I taunted, arching my back in the slightest of movements, welcoming his attention.

"Aye," he rasped, voice heavy with desire. "Aye, I would."

I grinned, pleased with his response.

"Oi, where did you get that work done?"

We both looked up as a young man approached, pointing at Rafe's bare shoulder.

"Reminds me of a military patch!" he added, admiring the design.

Rafe's eye found mine, and he gave me a sad smile. "Game's up, woman."

I sighed as we stood together. He ignored the man and placed the mugs on the cart. Tizmet flew lower, her wing beats stirring the night air as we returned to the palace.

Our stolen moment was up.

The Dragon Lord and his red beast plagued the ride back to Northwing. Ge'org's presence had Tizmet on edge—just as I was put off by Ruveel. I ignored him as much as possible and wore simple dresses instead of my uniform. The last thing I needed was to taunt him, drawing unwanted exchanges.

By the time we arrived at the school, Tizmet reached her limit with Ge'org. She drew blood more than once, and rather than learning his lesson, he pushed her harder.

As we settled into our cave, I silently mourned the loss of the bed in the King's palace. Only moments passed before Ruveel decided to stop by. Ge'org landed on the ledge, and Tizmet rushed him. He flapped his wings, trying to balance his mass as she opened her maw and let loose a jet of dragon fire. I threw an arm up, shielding my face.

As the roar of flame died down, I heard two things—her snarling and Ruveel laughing. Ge'org had apparently dropped out of the path of her flame, but clung to the canyon wall.

Ruveel called from below. "Oi, Avyanna!"

"Yes, sir?" I hissed through clenched teeth.

"Spring's coming early. We're returning to the front," he shouted. "I'll be back before the moon wanes to check on your progress."

I rolled my eyes and adjusted my blankets. "Yes, sir," I droned.

"Oh, and Avyanna?" His head popped up from the ledge. "Don't disappoint me."

Tizmet's rumbling growl almost drowned out his words, but I heard him well enough. I frowned and gave him a quick salute. After the clatter of rocks skittering down the canyon, a massive wall of red scales flew past our cave.

Tizmet snorted and flicked her tongue out.

It would be a long couple of weeks.

I bit my lip, struggling to keep my emotions in check.

"Try again, Avyanna."

I leveled my blank stare at Master Semora. She tasked me with getting Tizmet to the other side of the creek. The dragonlings were all waiting, and their Riders snickered. Tizmet lounged in the sun next to me, disinterested.

'*Fly to the others,*' I asked for the third time.

She didn't even crack open an eye, but rather flicked her tongue, conveying her annoyance.

I resisted the impulse to roll my eyes. "It's no use. There's no purpose."

"The purpose is to work with your dragon, and form a relationship with them." Master Semora crossed her arms.

I gritted my teeth as the dragonlings played on the far side. They scampered about—all of them the size of Tizmet's paw.

'*Please, Tizmet. Just walk over there.*'

The Riders behind me murmured, chuckling amongst themselves. My nerves were beyond frayed, but I refused to take my irritation out on her. I was angry at them for not understanding—angry at myself for putting myself in this situation.

I attempted ordering her. '*Go!*'

Tizmet's eye flashed open, and she turned on me, snapping her teeth in my face. I flinched away, and the Riders broke into a fit of laughter. Tizmet curled her massive lip into a snarl and settled on the ground.

"That's enough." Master Semora sighed and dismissed me with a flick of her wrist. "Now, let the young ones play. Let's discuss communication."

My glare darkened, but I kept a tight leash on my emotions as I joined the rest of the class. Tizmet snarled behind me as Egor laughed in my face. My hand twitched with the urge to punch him, and somehow I restrained that urge and turned away.

"She won't even flap her wings? How are you ever going to ride her?" he jeered. More laughter followed the question.

I closed my eyes, taking a deep breath.

"Hag will be grounded for life—her dragon walking instead of flying."

Tears pricked as the old nickname cut to my heart. These were young men and women I grew up with. I was supposed to be training a hatchling to fly like they were. Instead, they ridiculed me once again. Perhaps they were right. Maybe I would grow old and be alone, despite my efforts.

A rough shove slammed into my back, and I stumbled a step. Powerful jaws snapped behind me—which only spurred more snickers.

They were children in adult bodies.

I was better than this. Turning on my heel, I shot a glare at Egor that had the senseless grin slipping from his face.

"Touch me again and I'll break your hand." My lip curled in a snarl as I blinked away the threat of tears.

He scoffed and shrugged, turning to his friends. My chest ached knowing they couldn't physically hurt me, but their words were barbs in my heart.

I pressed the heels of my palms into my eyes. Why couldn't I have bonded to a normal hatchling?

Another day. Another class. Another humiliation.

"Avyanna, where is your dragon going?"

Tizmet flew off with a cow. The other dragonlings were drooling and watching their Riders, anticipating their meal. We were supposed to be holding our dragons in check, exercising their trust in us.

Tizmet simply seized the largest carcass and flew off toward the canyon.

I rubbed at the nape of my neck. "Our cave?"

Giggles erupted around me, and my glare did nothing to quiet them.

"Call her back," Master Zaya ordered, frowning.

"She won't come."

There was no point in aggravating Tizmet further. We spent the last three days training, and she was sick of it already. Her patience was gone. She wanted nothing to do with being ordered about like a festival pony. If there wasn't a good reason for something, she wouldn't do it.

Once upon a time, I would have shied away from any conflict. Back then, I gave the Masters every ounce of respect. But they were forcing me and Tizmet into their neat little mold. We weren't like the others. We couldn't be taught like them. Tizmet was an adult, and this training geared toward molding the dragonlings would not work with her.

Master Zaya steeled her spine. "Try."

"No."

Something ominous flashed over her features. "Are you defying me?"

"I won't call her back. She's clearly hungry and doesn't trust the little vultures," I said, shrugging my shoulders.

"This will be reported."

I nodded with a sigh. I knew it would.

It was a long trek to our cave, and most Riders were already bathing, being closer to the springs. It had been a rough day after Tizmet left. I couldn't participate in the next two classes without a dragon.

Loose stones clattered from above, then Flinor snorted and flicked his tongue out.

"Hail!" Dareth called. His long blonde hair fell across his face as he leaned over his dragon's back.

"Hail," I ground out.

He bared his teeth in a playful wince. "Oi, it must be going as poorly as they say."

Flinor jumped to the ledge of our cave. Tizmet hissed from inside, but didn't lash out. As I climbed the path, a horrid stench slammed into my face. I pinched my nose, fighting a gag. When I entered the cave, I stopped in my tracks.

'*No way.*'

"You're jesting."

A steaming pile of dragon dung lay in the far corner of the cave, with a dead cow in the opposite. Tizmet growled as if we interrupted her slumber.

"Not exactly house trained, is she?" Dareth laughed.

'*There's a pit for that!*'

She snorted and bared her teeth in reply.

"What am I supposed to do with that?!"

"I suppose you'd shovel it out." Dareth flashed an amused smile. "Perhaps the handlers can clean it up after it's out of your cave."

"Fantastic." I groaned.

"Look at it this way. Either she couldn't hold it in any longer, or she felt at ease enough with you to relieve herself."

My palms dragged down my cheeks. "I don't think there's *any* way to look at it that would make it better."

I spent the next two chimes shoveling her waste from the corner and tossing it into the canyon as far as I could. Part of me hoped one of my fellow Riders would pass by so I could splatter them with dragon dung. Chances of that were slim, as we were tucked well into the furthest part of the canyon—but one could hope.

Dareth and Flinor brought clawfuls of sod and dirt. I shoveled it on top of the residue. It at least made the smell tolerable. Tizmet watched me with disinterest as I worked.

I groaned once it was done and wiped my brow. It was warm now. Like Ruveel said, spring came early this year, and in full force. Hauling dragon dung was hard work.

"I really did only come to check on you," Dareth said in a placating voice. "They say you're doing poorly in classes."

"Aye, well, they didn't formulate lesson plans with adult dragons in mind." I shuffled through my pack for fresh clothes.

"Perhaps. But they will help you if you try–"

"I *am* trying," I snapped, then kicked my pack. Regret reddened my cheeks as my boots smeared dung onto the canvas. "They're not—*she's* not!"

Tizmet growled, sensing my anger, and I stormed out of the cave. I knew my quick retreat was immature, childish, but I was done with the day. I'd been the laughingstock of the Riders. The Master planned to report my insubordination, and my dragon wouldn't listen to me. The chest-high pile of dung topped it all off.

I was done.

Angry tears blurred my vision as I traversed the slim path. Dareth didn't deserve to take the brunt of my rage, but I simply couldn't face another Rider right now.

I headed to the springs alone, Tizmet content to give me space.

The following days were more of the same. The newest addition was the dead cow rotting in the corner of our cave. Tizmet refused to eat it or *do* something about it. When Flinor tried to remove it, she snarled, lashing out at him.

Even with Dareth visiting every few days, I grew more and more lonely. Rafe and the Tennan stayed away, respecting the fact that I was now an honorary Dragon Rider. I still refused to wear the spaulder, but wasn't brave enough to outright anger the Masters by wearing my uniform.

I missed Rafe. Willhelm, Niehm and Elenor had yet to visit me. I missed my friends—people who I could be myself around. This was torture for both me and Tizmet, trying to make us do things in ways we weren't comfortable with. I was an outcast again. I missed belonging somewhere.

Tizmet and I had a rocky relationship, but we understood each other, to an extent. The classes had us pushing each other's boundaries, and we weren't ready for that.

Every morning I laid in bed wondering if that was the day she would finally bite me in two. I began to wonder if we would even *survive* until the waning moon.

CHAPTER 15

T he cow was gone.

I stretched in my blankets. Though the weather was warming, the nights were still cool, and I had left my curtain open to air the cave out. The stench from Tizmet's rotting cow was overwhelming.

That she devoured it was a good omen.

'Finally got hungry?' I asked.

I didn't expect a response. She grew more distant as the days passed, with me making ridiculous demands of her.

'Good. Fire.' Tizmet sat curled in her corner, bright eyes flared wide.

I sat up and squinted at her. *'Good fire?'* I repeated.

She snorted and pushed an image of her breathing fire at Ge'org.

'Rotting cows are good for fire?' I pressed.

She blinked lazily, watching the cave's entrance. Apparently, the conversation was over.

That was all the communication I received from her that morning. I went along with my day attending my classes. She followed me here and there, only when I traveled beyond her sight. As long as she could see me, she was content to ignore me. Unless, of course, she retired to the cave. Usually, when she retreated like that meant I pushed her too hard and she wanted space.

"Therefore, the scales are tough, but not impenetrable," Master Caen was saying.

"So, a sword could cut them?" a Rider asked.

I leaned back on my hands and tilted my head toward the sun. It warmed my cheeks, and I blew my overgrown bangs out of my eyes.

"If wielded with the right force and swung at the correct angle, yes," Master Caen answered. "Though it's not likely your dragons will ever face a sword. You'll be in the sky, after all."

Master Caen was Master of the Dragon Handlers. He knew almost everything there was to know about dragons—at least anatomically.

"What about their fire? Where does it come from?" I asked.

Silence greeted me. I learned quickly not to ask questions. I was met with ridicule or demands for me to order Tizmet around like a tool. In this case, my curiosity won over my hesitations.

"Well, that's another lesson, but I'll oblige. We have a few moments extra," the Master replied thoughtfully. "Their fire results from two actions. Those of you whose dragons will *allow* it, look inside their mouths."

Many of the Riders were brave enough to place their heads inside their dragon's maw. I huffed and looked back at the sky. Tizmet would never allow me such an action.

"Please note the vent under their tongue. Through that vent, they can spew a chemical much like our oil that ignites with a spark and carries a flame. That chemical, also known as dragon oil, is extremely volatile.

"Now please look at the roofs of their mouths. Beyond the ridges of the palate, toward the back of their throats. Do you see the lumps that appear as stones? Bernadette, Liam and Gregory, your dragons do not have them yet. That is where the spark comes from.

"You'll note that your dragonlings, with the exception of those I have just mentioned, have had a tendency to eat stone. They scavenge types of flint and iron, ingesting them. Those lumps are made of the stone and minerals they consume. We are still puzzling out if they ingest anything else with purpose.

"When dragons breathe fire, they inhale through their nostrils and open their maw. Lifting their tongue to upbraid the lump of flint and iron, they spray their oil in a forceful jet. The spark from their stones—the lumps, ignite the oil and there you have dragon fire."

Riders murmured about with their dragons and I tilted my head, studying Tizmet.

"Please note, it will be taught later, but your dragon has a limited supply of oil. It is to be rationed on the battlefield. Once they are depleted, you will return to rest and your dragon will replenish its stores."

"What makes the oil?" I asked.

"Food. Or so it seems. When dragons return from their tour of the frontlines, they are always hungry, and without eating, their stores remain empty."

"Anything special that makes more? Or a more potent variety?"

"Full of questions today, aren't you Rider Avyanna?"

I brought my gaze to the Master, who smiled at me with tenderness.

"Why do you ask?" He inquired.

"No reason."

"Her dragon let a cow rot in her cave. I bet that has something to do with it." Someone spoke up.

"I heard it stank up the whole northern end of the canyon."

"Disgusting!"

I squared my shoulders and schooled my features, shielding the others from my glare. Of course they would know, and of course they would act like petty children and taunt me with it.

"Aye, she said 'Good fire.' I figured it meant something." I shrugged, still refusing to look at any of them.

Master Caen leaned closer, clearly interested. "What exactly did she tell you?"

"Exactly that. Good. Fire."

"Even Dovah speaks better than that," Rider Liam scoffed. His dragon was less than a year old. The others tittered and laughed like the children they were.

"She insinuated that the cow, in its state of decomposition, would benefit her fire?" Master Caen ignored the class.

"In her own way, I guess."

A faraway expression took over his gaze, and he ran a hand through his dark hair. "Perhaps—well, we've always trained our dragons to eat to replenish... were a Wild One needing to... What if it's a mold that causes–" He trailed off, rubbing his chin.

"Are we free, Master Caen?" a Rider called from behind me.

"Oh, yes, yes. Class dismissed. Avyanna, a word?"

As I pushed to my feet, I sighed and brushed out my dress. The last thing I wanted was to linger and discuss anything. I preferred to retreat to my cave, away from everyone.

The Riders all walked off, dragonlings in tow, as I made my way to the small table where Master Caen set his parchments—drawings and samples of scales. He stared at a detailed sketch of a dragon's scale, but his eyes were distant.

"I would like to know more about this discussion with your dragon," he said, looking up with a smile.

"There isn't more to tell. She's ignoring me."

It wasn't a secret she stopped listening to me. Everyone knew I couldn't get her to do anything. Any effort to do so resulted in her lashing out.

"Tell me everything then."

So I did. He took notes with a quill and ink, jotting things down. Not that there was much to share. He asked the oddest questions, like if she relieved herself before or after she brought the cow in, or if I noticed any mold growing on the carcass. I told him I did my very best to ignore the decomposing animal and noticed nothing special about it.

"Well, if she does anything of the like again, please notify me immediately."
He sighed and adjusted his papers.

I nodded and turned on my heel to walk away.

"Also," he called. "Rumor has it the Dragon Lord is due tomorrow to check
on your progress. I'm afraid I cannot praise your efforts." The sympathy in his
tone was genuine.

"Aye, tell him the truth. It's all anyone deserves." I shrugged before taking my
leave.

If Ruveel wanted to know how being forced into his classes was going, he had
the right to know.

The next morning I held in my surprise as I spotted Niehm and Elenor. They
were the perfect image of dignified ladies as I descended. Niehm had no sword,
and my mouth twisted in a sardonic smile. She wore it in the barracks, but felt
no need to wear it among Dragon Riders.

"Praise the sun, she resembles a woman!" Niehm cried when she spotted me.

I couldn't help the grin that spread across my face. She wore a brilliant green
dress that made her eyes shine. Elenor looked up at me with a graceful smile,
ever the proper lady.

"Avyanna." She greeted.

I held myself back from hugging them, refusing to let on just how much
I missed them. Niehm, however, had no such reservations and grabbed me,
pulling me against her.

Tears pricked at my eyes. "Oi, I can't breathe!"

"Stop being a babe." Niehm rebuked.

Elenor appraised me with a pleasant glint in her demeanor. "Not quite the
young lady I remember. You've grown."

I hadn't seen her since before I joined the Tennan. She was always wrapped
up in her duties, and I was off training somewhere.

"Aye, but I haven't grown *up*." I filled out in womanly proportions, though
I retained my muscle. I wasn't as lean as I was before.

"Blossoming into a fine young woman, regardless," she replied.

Her startling blue eyes, I once thought were so cold, sparkled with warmth.
In a way, I understood she viewed me as a mother would. Every girl raised at
Northwing was her family, and she took care of us all.

"Thank you," I said, returning her smile. "What brings you here?"

"The Dragon Lord."

"The cursed whoremonger."

I choked on a laugh as they replied at the same time.

"Really Niehm? Cursed whoremonger?" I snickered.

"Yes, if you knew—"

"Which she does not need to know." Elenor cut her short. "You are aware he arrived last night?"

"No, I—"

Tizmet chose that moment to sound her outrage. I whirled, searching the canyon, but it wound to my right, and I couldn't see her outside of my cave.

'*Tizmet?*' I took hesitant steps deeper in the middle to see if I could catch sight of her.

Ge'org trumpeted, and I saw him bank hard in the canyon's curve, then streak toward me. I blinked in confusion, then spotted Tizmet coming around the bend behind him. She had her mouth open and the spark of flame lit her maw.

'*No!*' I shouted across the bond, pushing at her!

Her eyes darted to me and she clamped her mouth shut for a moment, killing the spark. She pumped her wings hard, chasing the red male, and her mouth opened again, revealing rows of sharp teeth as she let out a deafening roar. Ge'org flew over our heads and Tizmet streaked past, ignoring me and my friends.

"Is she in season?" Niehm asked, watching as they rose in the sky.

"No. He keeps taunting her. She's had a rough few weeks. She'll take none of it from him."

"They say dragons reflect their Riders," Niehm mused.

"I can verify that's true, at least with that pair." I sighed.

Tizmet let out a burst of flame, and Ge'org pulled his tail to his body as he flew from her.

"That is beside the point," Elenor stated, returning her attention to me. "We are here because the Dragon Lord is here."

"Who was seen strutting like a cock through the women's—"

"It is not your concern where he was strutting." Elenor's brows lowered into a scowl.

"He does strut, though." I nodded my agreement.

"Avyanna, Niehm—enough." Elenor shook her head, smiling, regardless of her reprimand. "He has requested I prepare you as a proper Rider for your presentation to the King."

"You'll have your work cut out for you," I shot back. "I'm not a proper Rider."

"I agree. Though he requested, it would be out of my bounds to dress you as a Rider. As Master of Women, however, I will make you a proper lady."

I squinted, waiting for Niehm to speak up and say it was a jest. Instead, she simply stared, pleased with Elenor's words.

"I'm not–"

"I am well aware of what you are not, Avyanna." Elenor straightened to her full height. "I am also aware of what you are—a woman of nineteen-winters. You are to act like a lady, and resemble one, as well."

My breath rushed out in a huff. "I'm not a lady," I bit out.

In a way, wearing dresses and a Dragon Rider spaulder pushed me further away from Rafe and the Tennan.

"Avyanna of Gareth, being a lady is your choice. You are, however, without a doubt a woman. With womanhood comes responsibilities."

"Like what?" I scoffed.

"For one, resembling a woman." Niehm shrugged.

"Being a woman is not a dreadful duty. It's powerful. Embrace it," Elenor added, still staring down her nose at me, but her words were soft.

"I'm not against looking like one. I didn't want to cut my hair, and I wasn't thrilled about wearing trousers." Irritation tightened my throat. "I just—I'm a soldier."

I stared at the boots peeking out from under the hem of my dress. They seemed as out of place as I felt. I didn't resent my gender—I loved the way I felt around Rafe. It was more... I didn't want to be bound by it. If I wanted to learn to fight, I shouldn't be told no, simply because I was a woman.

"Some battles are not fought on the front," Niehm said with a smile.

Elenor sent a sharp look her way, as if there was more to that saying that would remain silent. Niehm looked sheepishly at Master Elenor and I snickered at their antics. I had a rough few weeks. There was no reason for me to take it out on them. They were my friends, after all.

"Well, well. Miss Avyanna of Gareth."

My stomach dropped, and Niehm peered beyond me with her lips parted in horror. Anger flashed in Elenor's eyes, and she lifted her chin, leveling her piercing gaze.

I stiffly saluted as I turned to face the Dragon Lord.

He walked down the path that led to the opposite side of the canyon, making his way toward us. His dark hair was tousled, the soot lines on his cheek smudged, and he was clad only in simple trousers and boots. His body was lean, but strong. Where Rafe was thick with powerful muscles, Ruveel was wiry but defined. It was as if he had been carved out of marble. His shoulders tapered to a small waist, with a trail of hair disappearing into his trousers.

"Dragon Lord, I must object to your state of undress." Elenor's voice whipped from behind me.

He gave her a condescending smile and lowered his blue eyes to me. "I'm in the presence of a Rider. They've seen me in far less." His voice was low and husky with sleep, and he ran a hand through his hair.

My scowl deepened and wondered why he came down.

"I am no Rider," Niehm growled from behind me. "I also have to object to your lack of clothing. As a Master, as a woman—I request you clothe yourself."

"Oi! Didn't think I was that hard on the eyes." He chuckled, glancing up at the sky.

"Positively dreadful, I'm afraid." Niehm cracked, and I had to bite my lip to keep from smiling.

"I just came down to have our newest Rider call off her dragon. Ge'org can't even land."

I followed his gaze, squinting past the sun. Tizmet chased Ge'org like a crossbow bolt. She darted through the air, singeing him with flame, stretching out her claws whenever he slowed.

'*Tizmet, leave him.*'

She roared through the bond, and I winced, holding my head as her rage and anger slammed into me. She pressed an image of Ge'org entering her cave, even as she snarled in warning.

"Your blasted dragon." I groaned, rubbing my temples against the sudden pain.

"My dragon?" Ruveel's tone dropped its sweetness, taking on an edge.

I glared and stepped up to him, not caring that I was almost a pace shorter than him. "Your dragon tried to enter our cave."

"And?"

"It's our cave," I growled. "It's *her* cave. No one goes in without her permission."

It was her territory—the only sanctuary she was allowed in this place. The only safe spot since she bonded me. Her guard was up everywhere else.

"Call her off, Rider. That's an order." He glared, glacial eyes seething.

I offended him.

"I can't. She won't listen to me. She might have before, but after your Dragon Kind classes, you destroyed what little relationship I had with her." I bared my teeth, then faced Elenor and Niehm, dismissing him. "She's your problem now."

CHAPTER 16

E lenor and Niehm made me look as presentable as possible. They packed me with finer dresses than the simple work shifts I was used to. Niehm tried to show me how to braid the side of my hair so that I could at least pass as a proper lady from the front—if not the back. We said our goodbyes, and I was glad we did so in private. Tears were shed, and I didn't want to appear weak in front of the Tennan or the Dragon Lord.

All stress and burdens of the past weeks melted away when Rafe rode toward me. He led the black mare I'd ridden before. His stallion snorted, and he had his characteristic look of indifference on his face. I allowed myself the smallest of smiles, but dropped my gaze to my feet.

Zephath was riding with us this time, with Dane in tow. The change puzzled me, but with Rafe, there was always a reason behind it. Tizmet flew high, coasting in circles as Ge'org nursed his wounds a hundred paces away. The Dragon Lord cursed as he fastened his saddle, frowning at the deep bite marks in Ge'org's tail.

I noted with some satisfaction that even though Ge'org was bigger and more experienced in war, Tizmet was faster—cunning and lithe. She grew in the wild, and it had not always been kind to her. She had her fair share of scars. Nothing too large—nicks and puncture wounds here and there.

"Mount up," Rafe growled.

I did my best to mount in a ladylike manner. All five paces of my height did not lend me any grace. Once astride, I nodded a greeting to the others. "Zeph. Dane."

"Rider Avyanna."

I frowned at Zephath's use of the title.

"Not a Rider, yet," I said, then refocused on Rafe. "General".

"Avyanna," he rumbled without emotion, eyes tracking Tizmet above.

My chin dipped, hiding my smile. I didn't care that he refused to acknowledge me in public. I knew our secrets.

"Head out!"

Ruveel climbed up Ge'org's leg and settled on his withers in the saddle. Rafe spurred his stallion on as the Dragon Lord strapped his legs into the stirrups. That was the only thing keeping a Rider from being thrown if their dragon decided to do an aerial roll.

Not that Tizmet would ever let me put a saddle on her.

After a quick breath, I urged my mare after the others, bringing up the rear. Heading out, I hoped the King would free me of these dreaded classes. I would take any other assignment. Anything other than the classes.

The ride to the palace was the same as before. Ruveel spent one night with us, then flew ahead. I doubted camping bothered him. After all, there were no inns on the frontlines. He acted as though it was inconvenient, as if he wasn't cut out for it. I couldn't help but wonder how tough he was under his soft exterior. One didn't rise to the rank of Dragon Lord without strength and courage. His personality put me off, and I knew enough of his reputation to recognize it wasn't entirely an act. He was, as Niehm would say, a whoremonger.

We reached the palace in three days, arriving the morning of the new moon. The trip had been quiet. Dane was mute unless Rafe spoke with him. Zephath steadfastly ignored me, testier than I remembered. Rafe was... well, I caught him staring now and then, but otherwise, he only acknowledged me when necessary.

Riding through King's Wall, Zephath pulled the hood of his cloak up. I frowned, but didn't mention it. It was peculiar behavior. The day was bright and hot. Perhaps his pale skin was burning. I lifted my hand, studying my complexion. It had taken on a warm hue, courtesy of my hours spent in the sun.

When we arrived at the palace, we followed the same routine as before, with one minor exception.

Tizmet.

Her mood was far more volatile and angry. When we camped, she refused to let me sleep near the others, but abandoned me in the middle of the night to take off flying. She refused to let me enter the stables or retreat out of her sight. Anyone who got too close to me was met with a snarl. Anything I tried to push at her from the bond, she blocked out completely. She was on edge and I couldn't calm her.

After I handed my mare off to a stableboy, I stood in the courtyard glaring at her. I was just as frustrated as she was, but it wasn't like I hurt her. I hadn't left her. She acted as though I betrayed her trust. I didn't know how I could have, or how to fix it.

Her orange eyes narrowed to slits as she flicked out her tongue, tasting my anger.

'*That's right. I'm mad at you,*' I growled across the bond.

She peeled back her lips, baring sharp fangs.

I shook my head and sighed, turning away. It was no use. This dragon held a grudge far better than any human.

"Come. The King has set aside quarters for you," our runner said, giving Tizmet a wide berth.

I nodded and followed Rafe and the others. They escorted me to my room first, Tizmet roaring her discontent as I disappeared through the doors.

When the boy gaped over his shoulder, horrified, I shrugged.

"She'll get over it," I said.

He stumbled over his feet, rushing me to my room. Once inside, Tizmet seethed in the center of the room, smoke trailing from her nostrils. She was extremely upset to have ignited her flame in her mouth.

'*Thinking about torching the place?*' I asked in a bored tone. '*Ge'org might have to put you in your place.*'

Her rage boiled over and she snaked her massive head closer, roaring in my face. I arched a brow as the door slammed shut behind me. When she was done, I wiped a glob of dragon spit off my cheek.

'*Got that off your chest?*' I walked over to sit on the bed.

She made no reply, just sat and snarled quietly, not taking her eyes off me.

I had to admit, after the classes, we had gone from ignoring each other to antagonizing each other. She knew what would make me mad, and I knew what would anger her. Two weeks of Dragon Kind training destroyed everything we established when we first bonded.

The King sent word that I would join him for the evening meal again. I stared at the servant, who relayed the message in disbelief.

"He has been briefed by the Dragon Lord and the Shadowslayer," the manservant said, avoiding Tizmet, who hissed and spat in the center of the room.

I sighed, resigning myself to the evening. "He must want to cause a scene."

The army of maids once again bombarded me, scrubbing and cleaning every inch. They cared for me and dressed me as a fine lady. All the while, Tizmet was a simmering pile of fury in the middle of the room.

The beautification horde released me with a chime to spare. I spun in the mirror they left, the soft blue gown swirling about my feet. With nothing else to do, I sat and tried to replicate the braid Niehm had shown me, attempting to put some effort into my short hair. I managed something that looked presentable, if lacking the finesse that Niehm managed, then rose to greet the knocking at my door.

Zephath stood before me, his formal attire dashing as ever. It fit him perfectly. He wore red and gold, and his sandy blonde hair was combed to perfection. He looked every bit the young nobleman.

Except his eyes.

They reeled in turmoil, even as his face maintained an emotionless mask. I frowned, wondering what upset him.

"Zeph." I greeted.

I glanced at the manservant behind him, and unease rolled through me. His stoic demeanor lacked expression, though his eyes squinted in disapproval.

"Rider Avyanna."

My lip twitched in a grimace at Zeph's choice of words.

"I've been sent to fetch you for the evening meal," he said.

I peered over my shoulder at Tizmet, who had her giant maw open, hissing deep in her throat.

"We'll have to be quick. She's in a foul mood."

"Well enough." Zeph's gaze darted to her and back to me. "She's not the only one."

I took a deep breath and let it out with a sigh as he offered his arm. I took it, and we dashed out the door.

Tizmet raged.

Zephath glanced behind us as her roar echoed down the halls. The manservant chuckled and muttered something under his breath.

I stumbled as Zeph halted midstep. The pure hatred burning over his features stopped the question sitting on the tip of my tongue. His rage was an all-consuming fire, eating him up from the inside. His unfocused gaze turned to the manservant.

"Pardon?" His question was deathly quiet between Tizmet's roars.

The manservant sneered, oblivious to the danger the palace was in as Tizmet bellowed. "Nothing, my lord."

"Repeat your words." Zeph's tone was cold and distant, yet rang with a nobleman's authority.

"I was simply pondering that you two are a perfect pair."

Zeph pulled his arm from mine to give his complete attention to the servant. His eyes flashed with hurt and ire. "How so?"

Zephath and I were close in age. Perhaps that was why the servant thought what he did. I grit my teeth as Tizmet screamed again, muffled by the stone walls.

"Just that both the whores are attending the King's evening meal arm in arm."

I flinched back as if the insult struck me. He was the first to call me such, so far. Tension radiated from Zeph, his body tense like a bow strung tight.

The servant continued, "I'll be planning your after care, Lord Zephath of Othilies."

Zeph snapped under invisible pressure and launched himself at the man. He pulled a blade and pinned the servant to the wall, bracing the knife at his throat.

"I no longer belong to Othilies," he hissed.

The sound of claws tearing stone shook the walls. I bit my lip, knowing this moment was important to Zephath, but Tizmet would bring down the palace if I didn't leave soon.

"Once a son, always a son. Once a whore always–"

Zeph dragged the blade across his jaw. His eyes widened with fear, then narrowed with hatred.

"Pack your bags tonight, scum." Zeph seethed. "You'll be relieved of your position and blacklisted."

"You can't–"

His attempt to choke out words cut short as Zeph pressed the blade harder. My impatience had my fists clenching at my sides. We didn't have time for whatever this was.

"Once a son, always a son?" Zephath mocked, shoving the servant aside. Though he was shorter than the man by a hand, Zeph trained with the Tennan—he was all wiry muscle. "Begone!" he shouted.

The servant stumbled down the hall, holding his bloody jaw.

"Zeph!" I whined through gritted teeth.

He spun on me and I snatched his clammy hand, then dragged him down the passage that led to the courtyard. We burst outside as the sun set and surveyed the carnage.

Tizmet pulled at a large stone in the wall—three already lay broken at her feet. She whipped her head in our direction and let out an outraged shriek, teeth flashing. Guards surrounded her, all with hands on their weapons, though no one had drawn. They were not accustomed to dragon attacks. They never met one who was not an ally.

"At ease," Zephath ordered as he sheathed his blade in his boot. He straightened as a guard approached.

"Oi, is the dragon well?" he asked, looking between us and Tizmet.

She slammed to the earth in a rough landing and locked her burning glare on me. The setting sun painted her scales in shades of orange and red, making her eyes spark and glow.

He looped my arm through his once more. "She's well enough. Stand down," he ordered again.

"Yes, my lord." The guard rubbed the nape of his neck. "We'll be sending a clean-up crew immediately."

"See to it. We'll be on our way."

Zephath hurried along the path, and Tizmet held her body rigid, muscles strung taut, but moved her head with us, tracking me with angry eyes. A growl rumbled from her throat as she lifted her lips to reveal rows of sharp teeth.

Zeph ignored her completely and walked along the path, paying no attention to the guards or the broken stones around us. I sighed and followed, trying to appear as normal as possible. As if we were simply out for a stroll, with a giant dragon stalking us.

"What was all that about?" I whispered as we distanced ourselves from the carnage.

"Your dragon threw a tantrum."

I gave his arm a gentle tug. "You know what I'm talking about."

"You won't repeat it if you know what's good for you." He spoke low and sent a sharp glare my way.

"It's none of my business." I shrugged, letting it go.

Zephath wasn't the kind that took well to prying. The more one tried to get an answer from him, the more he lashed out.

He nodded as if that was the end of it, then led me down the path. The sun dipped lower, and I held onto his arm, listening to the crunch of Tizmet's steps behind us. Her anger slipped over the bond, hot and frenzied.

This was going to be a difficult night.

We made it to the same mezzanine from before. Ge'org already sat at the top, relaxed, watching the crowd. He lifted his head when Tizmet arrived. They hissed and snarled at each other like a pair of barn cats.

Tizmet watched from the mezzanine as I descended the stairs to the dining hall. She attempted to curl away from Ge'org, who crowded her, while also avoiding the squire.

Steeling my nerves, I scanned the crowd, searching for a certain General. I wanted nothing more than an evening alone with Rafe. Even if Tizmet was there, she tolerated his presence. I wanted to escape the stress of the whole situation. Tizmet's unease only amplified my own.

I spotted a shadow near a far wall, black against the white and gilded surface. All anxiety lifted from my shoulders as I met that dark gaze across the distance. His heavy arms were crossed over his chest, and he leaned against the wall, unconcerned with the guests or the King. My heart yearned for him—to be close to him. Yet Zeph led me to the dais opposite of the dragons.

The King sat on a padded throne, speaking with a woman dressed in a fine red gown. As we approached, Ruveel spotted us from a group of nobles. He started toward the King, noting our path.

Great. As if I didn't have enough to handle.

Zeph dropped in a bow, pulling me with him. Following his lead, I curtsied and held it until the King acknowledged us.

"Ah, young Zephath and Avyanna!" The King's voice was light and merry, as if he didn't have a care in the world.

"Your Highness," Zeph replied, straightening.

Ruveel stood next to the King, frowning. He wasn't looking at me, however, but behind me. Tizmet and Ge'org snarled and hissed over the din of the crowd. My polite smile slipped. I'd never seen him concerned over anything.

"Well, Avyanna. I've heard some interesting tales," the King said, looking down at me with a smile.

I faltered, though if he was smiling, surely that meant well for me.

"Tell me, how have you taken to your training?" he asked.

"Your Majesty, I must be honest. Tizmet has responded poorly. They're not–"

"My King." Ruveel interjected, then diverted his attention to me. "Control her."

I scowled, and Tizmet's screech echoed across the room. Turning, I spotted her gripping the stairs leading to the dining hall. She was trying to enter the room. She froze, lifting her head to eye me. Anger and terror swirled in those fiery depths.

The hall was filled to the brim with people and tables piled with food. There was no way.

'*No,*' I ordered.

Her pupils narrowed to slits, and she snarled, flicking out her tongue.

"Do not let her enter."

I spun to the Dragon Lord and leveled a glare at him. I couldn't stop her from tearing the palace apart and he wanted me to keep her from crossing a dining hall?

'*Go,*' I told her, then turned back to the King.

I noted his frown as his gaze lifted to Tizmet. "Your Majesty, I—"

A muffled scream cut me off, and I whirled. She was creeping down the stairs, with Ge'org looking intrigued by her antics. Her eyes were still locked on me and me alone.

I screamed through clenched teeth and hiked my dress up to my knees. Curse all this proper lady nonsense. Sprinting across the hall, the crowd parted in horror. Tizmet raised her head and stopped, watching me approach.

'*Go!*' I pushed at her through the bond, trying to force her back.

She stretched her neck and opened her mouth. Her outraged scream shook the tables and shattered fine goblets. Her forked tongue danced between her teeth, and I hoped against hope that she wouldn't burn the place down.

When I reached her, I stopped and glared, craning my head. She looked directly down at me, hissing. I growled right back, then hiked my dress up further to climb the stairs. The marble staircase was crushed beneath her paws and I wondered just what kind of expense we racked up with all this damage. I would be in service to the King my whole life trying to repay this.

The sounds of her talons crushing the marble were obscenely loud in the now-silent hall as she followed. Not even the musicians dared to play.

I made my way to the center of the mezzanine and spun to face her. I frowned, noting the squire's podium was awfully close to her—too close for comfort in her enraged state of mind. He needed to clear out. I opened my mouth to say as much.

At the same moment, he lifted his hand to shield himself from her presence as her foreleg neared his podium.

She moved in a flash. I had no time to stop her or warn him. A bone chilling scream rent the air, and I gaped in absolute terror.

Blood dripped from Tizmet's teeth as she turned back to me. The squire wailed, holding his stump of an arm, ending at his elbow. I took a faltering step forward as he collapsed to the ground. Terrified screams erupted from the citizens below, and I stared at Tizmet in horror.

'*What have you done!?*'

This couldn't be happening.

This. Couldn't. Be. Happening.

Ruveel raced up the stairs, fury consuming his features. I had never seen him so livid, and I shrank away from him. Ge'org let out a rasping growl, a sound I never heard a dragon make.

'*What have you done?!*' I screamed, letting terror and rage color my emotions.

She snapped her head up and reared back on her hind legs, wings spread, and shrieked. Her whole body trembled with the force of it. I clamped my hands over my ears.

'*You terrible beast!*'

Her front paws crashed down, cracking the stone. There was commotion beside the squire and I could only hope someone sent for a Healer.

Tizmet's head came rushing toward me, and I danced out of the path.

'*You would push me away?!*' I demanded, balling my hands into fists.

I gripped my dress in outrage, furious with this creature. She stole everything from me. It was her fault we were even in this situation. She hurt a fellow human, a fragile being that stood no chance against her strength.

She snarled, and Ge'org loomed behind her. He roared, and it was not the playful or taunting howls of before. It was the dominating blast of a war beast. Ruveel would use Ge'org to put her in her place.

She whirled to face him and I cursed, dodging her feet, then rushed to place myself between them.

'*No! No you don't!*' I crowded her.

She never took her stare off of Ge'org. A deft and massive claw shoved me to the side. The impact ripped the air from my lungs. I collapsed, my head smacking against the stone. I yelped in pain and curled around myself, terrified she would finally finish me off. My eyes blinked and fluttered, wondering why everything went dark and silent.

A rough hand grabbed my arm as my blurred vision returned with a ringing in my ears. Rafe looked down at me.

"Up."

The ringing in my ears muffled his order. He yanked on my arm. I blinked again, trying to right myself, and saw Tizmet's open maw behind him.

"No!" I choked out.

"Ignore her." He hauled me to my feet.

I stumbled against him as her glowing eyes tracked us. Mouth open, she seemed ready to burn us to a crisp, but somehow restrained herself. Rafe pulled me along with him, Tizmet's maw never more than a few paces behind. He dragged me to the stairs. The two guards positioned there watched Tizmet nervously.

"Move!" Rafe barked, and they parted without a second glance.

I scrambled to keep my feet under me as we stormed down the stairs, but he carried most of my weight.

Tizmet growled and leapt to the dirt as our feet touched the earth. She hissed, and Rafe glanced at her, jerking me beside him. I stumbled and would have fallen to the ground, but he held me upright. Cursing, he doubled over and pulled my chest against his back. I cried out as he stood, jerking my arms in front of him.

My General was giving me a piggyback ride.

A hysterical laugh wound its way out of my throat as I wrapped my legs around his waist. He rushed into the courtyard, taking me away from the terrible scene that had not only ruined my reputation, but the reputation of all Dragon Kind.

CHAPTER 17

At the entrance, the two servants we passed froze in shock, then scrambled away in fear when Tizmet's roars followed us. Rafe jogged through the corridor and into my room, kicking the door shut behind him.

Tizmet clawed the railing, and the stone balcony crumbled under her rage. Rafe stalked toward her, his dark gaze locked on hers in a predatory way. She hissed and spat, weaving her head a breath above the floor, claws digging into the stone as she clung to the edge.

Rafe lowered me to the ground and knelt beside me, never taking his eye off her. She brought her muzzle directly in front of him and peeled her lips back, revealing rows of teeth. Her lips quivered with barely leashed rage. My stomach twisted violently. Scraps of flesh and blood were wedged in her front teeth—the only remnants of the squire's arm.

Rafe's hand crept toward his patch, and Tizmet shot upright, jaws opening in yet another deafening scream.

I gripped his arm. "No."

He stilled under my hold, dropping his gaze from the dragon for the first time. That glare had no softness to it. He was not playing games. His King had been in danger. There was a man-eater in Regent, and he was a General. It was his job to protect—not to coddle creatures who harmed his people.

"Please. Not yet." I turned toward Tizmet.

My eyes stung as my vision blurred again. Not from hitting my head this time—but from unshed tears. This dragon had taken everything from me. I blamed her for no hatchlings choosing me in the first place. I didn't know how magic worked, but I knew in my heart that because she was out there—no other dragonling would bond with me. My years as First Chosen failed because of her.

She had been the reason I was stripped of the Tennan, of Rafe. Because of her, I was torn away from my only friends.

She made me a laughingstock during training. She had humiliated me in front of a crowd because she was sore over how I treated her. And tonight, she had irrevocably damaged the reputation of Dragon Riders by being the first dragon to attack a human since the Treaty—with no reason to do so.

Because of her, they would ostracize me even more. Because of her, society would view Dragon Riders in a new light.

"Go away."

Tears burned hot trails down my cheeks, and my head pounded. My body ached from being thrown. She hurt me too many times. She lowered her head to peer at me with a snarl.

"Go *away*," I repeated through clenched teeth.

I blinked back tears to meet her fiery gaze. I was done. Done with her antics—done with treating a beast like a sentient human and expecting her to act like one. I was fed up with being attached to her. The tears kept coming, and I gave up trying to clear my eyes.

"*Go away!*"

I screamed and pushed against the bond with all the strength I could muster. A sound tore out of her mouth, somewhere between a scream and a roar. I yanked my shoe off and chucked it at her. She adjusted her grip on the balcony and wailed her outrage.

My lips pulled back in an answering snarl. "I *hate* you."

She pushed off the railing with a wail, flapping her wings hard, then launched skyward. She disappeared into the night. My legs gave out beneath me. I crumbled to the floor, sobbing.

I was so angry, so hurt. Nothing was going the way it was supposed to. A large part of me wanted to blame the Dragon Lord for Tizmet and me falling apart—but was it really his fault? We were doomed from the start. What I needed from her, she could not give. What she demanded from me, I couldn't comprehend. We were not meant for each other.

Rafe shifted beside me, and his strong arms pulled me to his chest. He was my General. We were in the palace. He shouldn't have been holding me. I couldn't care less. He was the one person here I trusted. The one person who, though he couldn't show it, cared for me. He protected me when no one else did.

Curling against him, he held me tight as I cried.

I woke alone on the cold floor, a blanket wrapped around me. Something tugged inside my chest. I sat up, scanning the dark room. Rafe was gone, as I expected he would be, but what had woken me then?

A sharp pain stabbed my head and my heart felt as if it ripped from my chest. Gasping, I doubled over, grasping my chest, trying to relieve the pain. I stared blindly at the stone floor—the sensation receding.

What was that?!

A quiet roar sounded in the distance and I peered into the moonless night, unable to decipher the hour.

Was that Tizmet?

Torment assaulted me again, and I fell onto my hands and knees. Searing white agony exploded behind my eyes. It felt like someone was carving my heart out. I gasped, clutching my chest, terrified.

She was trying to get away. It was the only answer. She was trying to fly so far away that she would break the bond.

Another roar drifted over the quiet city. The pain receded, and I panted, staring into the night. I told her to go away, but I hadn't expected her to listen. She must have been just as eager to be rid of the bond. She didn't know it wasn't possible. Magic allowed bonded to travel a short distance, and nothing more. She couldn't break the bond, no matter how hard she tried.

I curled into myself and tucked the blanket under my chin as another wave consumed me. She could try all night—it would never break until one of us was dead.

She simply wanted to be free.

I lay stiff on the cold floor, as I had been since Tizmet first tested the distance of the bond. She gave up almost a chime ago, but with my head pounding and my heart aching, sleep was unattainable.

She hadn't come back after pushing the boundaries, and I didn't know where she was. Under normal circumstances, I'd have a vague idea of her whereabouts, but I wasn't opening the bond without fear of death. Pain awaited me on the other side, and I wanted no part of it.

I'd let her roam. I didn't care.

A knock sounded on my door, and I blinked, staring at it. "Come in," I croaked.

The Dragon Lord entered, dressed in his red and black leathers. The crest depicting a dragon wearing a crown emblazoned his chest. He squinted and glanced around the empty room as a servant shut the door.

I watched with puffy, dry eyes as he sat on the end of my bed. His face was stern and hard. The carefree Dragon Lord I had grown to know and detest was gone. In his place was a leader—one whose duty was to care for the King and his realm. And dispose of threats.

He sighed, running a hand through his dark hair. "You look awful."

I blinked in response. I was tired and exhausted—empty of all emotion and feeling. There was nothing else for me to give.

"Ge'org has been monitoring her... from a respectful distance. I can imagine what you've been through last night," he murmured. After glancing at the balcony, he turned to me. "You cannot control her."

"No," I rasped, licking my dry lips.

He crossed his arms and frowned. "Let me be clear—you're a hazard. To the King, to the kingdom, to the other Riders, to civilians. That dragon is wild."

"How is the squire?" I breathed.

"He'll live." His blue eyes pinned me. "He'll live a maimed life. By the grace of the King, he will still be able to provide for his family."

I nodded and stared at my blanket. She caused irreparable damage. In most cases, cuts and stabs were easily mended. But a severed limb?? Arms couldn't grow back.

"I'm minded to send you to the Sands."

My gaze snapped to his, brows furrowing. He would banish me?

"The King, however, opposes that idea. 'Never before has a Rider been banished,' he told me. Yet, never before has a dragon taken someone's arm off. Not since the Treaty. She deserves to be exiled."

"The only way you could banish her is to banish me as well. The chain to the beast."

"Aye, and you've made an impression on our dear King. He's not so eager to be rid of you. He argues you need another chance." Ruveel sighed. "Rafe claims you need to be isolated with her. I'm not so foolish as to ignore the fact that you had a modicum of control after you were alone with her for a length of time.

"I will not, however, release you to the public to roam where you will. Nor will I have you near any of my Riders. Ge'org is one of the few that could take down that beast, and I'll not have her flying recklessly on the frontlines."

My door cracked open as someone called through it. "I could take the beast down."

I knew that voice.

Ruveel leaned back and scoffed. "Took you long enough."

Darrak entered, and my heart gave a thump of excitement. I knew this man. He looked out for me, once. He was safe—like Rafe. With him here, I didn't feel so alone.

"Avyanna." Darrak greeted. He shut the door, then leaned against it.

"Darrak—"

"I think you should ride with him," the Dragon Lord said, cutting off my greeting.

I figured he would be far more reluctant, since it was Rafe's idea. "Why?"

"The battle of Tigath En'or," Darrak said, his gray eyes distant.

"Aside from Rafe, who, for personal reasons, I will not relinquish you willingly," he smirked as if he knew more than he should have, "Darrak is the only one with experience bringing down a dragon."

"You've killed a dragon?" Shock would have played over my face, but I was far too tired to convey my emotions.

"Aye. Before I was the King's bounty hunter, I was a soldier." Darrak shifted uncomfortably against the wall. "In the battle of Tigath En'or, we faced a team of Shamen who controlled a dragon who had lost his Rider." He glared, pain and anger rolling off him. "It was my team who felled the mindless beast."

"It was you who felled it. Don't be modest now," Ruveel said with a twist of his lips. "Ge'org and I were too far away to respond. We have downed our fair share, but few humans have accomplished such a feat."

My mouth formed a hard line. "So you would put me and Tizmet with a dragon killer?"

Rafe had said something similar. It was the main reason he wanted me with Darrak—he could bring her down. Yet, if it came to that, my life would be forfeited, too. Riders rarely survived the loss of their bonded.

"Yes." Ruveel leaned forward, authority consuming his demeanor. "You've done irreparable damage to our image as Dragon Riders. I want you as far away from the palace or any city as possible.

"Lucky for you, Darrak has been assigned a bounty in the mountains of E'or. This will provide you space from densely populated areas and a bit of freedom for your dragon with an anger issue." He folded his hands neatly in his lap, never taking his eyes off me. "Let me be clear, if your dragon harms a single hair on a human's head—Darrak is to dispose of her."

I swallowed. He wasn't the jesting playboy I knew, but the Dragon Lord in full commanding force.

"Darrak is to return when the task is complete," he continued. "You are to return with him to report. If you bring that mad dragon here with the same lack of control, I will press for your banishment. Or slay her myself."

I packed quickly, with no sense of luxury. The servants eyed my balcony with nervous glances, wondering where Tizmet was, fearing another attack. I scrubbed my face with water, but that was the only bathing permitted. After readying myself in a practical dress and oiled cloak, I secured my crossbow over my shoulder and strapped my spear to my back. As a runner escorted me to the stables, I rushed along, my pack hitting my thigh with each step.

Tizmet flew high, gliding through the clouds. I only knew it was her because the scales were not glinting like rubies against the sunlight. I refused to open the door to the bond, partly because I was afraid of the pain, and I wanted nothing to do with her.

That I knew Darrak was a minor consolation, even if we met by chance. Back then, he hid under the guise of a soldier, yet he looked out for me. I felt as if I knew *him*, despite the slight deception of his false identity.

At the palace stables, the runner left me with a young woman. I tried not to stare, but she openly assessed me.

"You're the failure of a Rider, eh?" Her voice had an odd lilt to it, one I couldn't place.

Sighing, I turned to face her head-on. Her eyes were the clearest shade of gray, almost unworldly. She was tall, perhaps six paces, maybe more. The blood-red hue of her hair reminded me of Niehm's. Though where Niehm's was wild and curly, hers was tucked into tiny braids pulled together at the nape of her neck. Threaded through the strands were colorful beads and bits of what appeared to be teeth and bones. Her skin was pale, as if it had never known summer sun. It was clear, without a single blemish.

She wore black trousers and a sleeveless fur vest. Dark tattoos banded her left arm, with vines wrapped around her right, disappearing into her vest. She looked barbaric—like she could take on five men without batting an eye.

"Aye. Who might you be?" I meant to tone it as gruffly as her question, but I was too depleted. The words came out dead and emotionless.

"Mikhala." She offered me her right hand.

At the center of her palm, a strange exotic flower stained her skin, blooming from the end of her vine tattoo. I frowned, but accepted the gesture. She chuckled and slid her hold to my elbow, yanking me in for a rough embrace. She slapped my back, and I coughed weakly. Releasing me, she laughed, giving me a shove. I staggered back a step.

Who was this woman?

"I'm Darrak's companion," she said with an amiable smile.

I squinted, thinking of his attraction toward Niehm. Surely he wasn't like Ruveel—a man who took his pleasure from whatever woman struck his fancy.

Her features pinched with disgust. "Oi, don't tell me you're after him."

"No." I drew out my answer.

"Good. I can't imagine traveling with someone making googly eyes at that buffoon." She pushed my shoulder and headed down the stable aisle.

I hesitated, watching this... wild woman before following. "But you're his companion?"

"Companion, as in, I travel with him. The idea of bedding the man–"

She stopped and faked a gag.

I cracked a smile and stepped beside her with a shrug. "Some might think he's attractive."

"They would be a fool to get involved with him. Arrogant pig."

We peered into the nearest stall. Inside was a tall, dark horse. His coat was mostly black, but graying around his nostrils and eyes, revealing his age. Mikhala rested her arms on the gate, making kissing sounds at the beast. He snorted and walked over, nuzzling her hands.

I leaned my shoulder against the stall. "Why do you travel with him then, if you have such a low opinion of him?"

She scratched the horse under his chin, then reached up to his ears. "Darrak saved me once. That's a story for another day." She winked. "He told me he would show me his world. So, I lend my help with his bounties and he takes me with him."

"Does he travel with anyone else?"

The stable was fairly empty aside from a few stableboys drifting here and there. No sign of Darrak.

"Nah, just me. A couple easily goes unnoticed—any more, and we might blow our cover."

"Begging your pardon, but I doubt you would go unnoticed anywhere."

She flashed a confident grin, then lowered her voice to a conspiratorial whisper. "I'm the distraction."

"Ah... What will I be?"

"Dunno yet." She jerked her chin upward. "Can you ride that beast?"

"Not a snowflake's chance in a plume of dragon fire."

She let out a breathless laugh, then returned her attention to the horse. "Then I haven't a clue. I'm telling you now though, I'm not playing nursemaid. Neither will he. There's too much work to be done. You'll be expected to care for your own."

"I am a trained soldier," I said. A defiant glare graced my features as I pushed off the wall. "I can care for myself."

"Feisty little thing. Good to see you got some fire."

I sighed. "Plenty."

"Such conviction." Mikhala laughed, clearly amused by our exchange. "This will be your faithful steed." She scratched the horse's peppered chin again.

"Looks like a pain to mount."

"What do ya mean? He's a doll."

"I'm tiny." I threw out an arm, gesturing to myself, then him. "He's a giant."

"Ah, well, get a running start, girl. Gotta learn how to mount the big boys. What did they have you riding in the army? A pony?"

"A pigou."

"A—a what? One of those long-eared rabbit horses?"

"Well, that's one way to describe them."

She threw her head back, her laughter deep and throaty—one she didn't hold back at all. I smiled, giving a breathless chuckle along with her. Thunderbolt *was* a rather funny-looking creature, and I suppose her description fit him pretty well.

"I can't believe you rode one!" She slapped her thigh.

The big black horse snorted and went to eat, disenchanted with her mirth.

"He had a waltz. It was great for shooting." I shrugged.

Her ghostly eyes sparkled. "Shooting, eh?"

"Aye, I'm a fair shot with a crossbow," I said, turning to reveal the weapon.

"I'd like to see that."

"Someday." I shrugged again, then turned to the horse.

If my companions were Darrak and this... Mikhala, traveling might not be so bad.

A dragon's screech rent the air high above the stables and I looked up with a frown. Then again, this might be a terrible idea.

The gelding's name was Boulder—or at least, that's what Mikhala told me. She claimed if his rider dropped the reins, he stopped like a boulder and plopped in place. She said Tizmet could probably start eating him and he would sit there patiently, waiting for her to finish before raising an alarmed whinny.

I had to climb a fence to pack my things and strap my weapons onto the giant. Then used the same fence to mount. I hoped wherever we camped there would be a convenient log or stump for me to use. I couldn't imagine asking Darrak for a leg up, and Mikhala seemed the type to tease me about it for the rest of my days.

Darrak appeared as we readied. He greeted Mikhala with a tilt of his head and a pleasant grin. He was obviously fond of the woman. I had yet to determine if it was a friendly gesture or something more significant. I had never seen him interact with a woman other than Niehm and didn't know what to expect. It wasn't as if he went around flirting with all the soldiers.

He took the reins of a bay—an average gelding, with nothing to set him apart from any other. He was stocky enough to plow, but light enough that he could pass as an inn's riding horse.

Mikhala's horse, however, was beyond flashy. It had a rare two-colored coat—white in some areas, with a fiery red in others. They matched, complimenting one another as if the beast was merely a four-legged reflection of her. Its eyes were the palest blue I had ever seen, and they demanded attention. If she was truly the 'distraction,' her horse definitely helped that cause.

Darrak ran a hand through his sandy hair and glanced at the sky. I followed his gaze, as Tizmet circled lower.

"She going to be a problem, Avyanna?" he asked as he mounted.

"Perhaps."

To be honest, I had no idea. Maybe she had given up on me—I was content with that if that's what she chose. I tried and tried to prove myself to her. She brushed my attempts aside. I gave our relationship everything I could, and always came second to her own feelings. I felt like a pawn in the game of life. As if I had no choice over the situations I was placed in.

Darrak made a thoughtful noise, then started us down the path. "Mikhala, I assume you made polite introductions?" he called over his shoulder.

The woman offered me a bright grin. "We have traded blood and are now soul sisters."

Blinking, my brows furrowed at her words.

Darrak threw a resigned look her way before staring ahead. "Well enough. She should be aware of your barbaric tendencies."

She dropped the reins and threw her hands in the air. "Tendencies? Truth be told, Rider, I *embrace* my inner barbarian." She fell back, laying flat against her stallion's rump, and smiled at the sky.

"Is she always like this?" I asked.

Darrak's mouth twisted. "You haven't seen anything yet."

I scoffed through my smirk. Mikhala didn't seem that much older than me. I wouldn't put her over a proper lady's age of twenty-winters. Something in her eyes told me she was younger, though it could have been her playful spirit.

A shadow moved from under a tree in the courtyard, drawing my gaze. My smile faltered, and my heart skipped a beat. Rafe crossed his arms over his chest, watching me follow Darrak. I bit my lip as tears welled in my eyes. We didn't even have a chance to say a proper goodbye. Last night, he was ready to use whatever dark magic to keep me safe—he held me, comforted me. Now I was leaving without a word.

Pulling on the reins to slow my horse, I started to turn toward him.

"Don't do it."

I hesitated at Mikhala's words. Her face was still turned toward the sky, a smile still lighting her lips, but her ghostly eyes were on mine.

"He's my General." I glanced at Darrak, who spoke with the guards at the gate.

"From that look in your eyes, he's more than that." She tsked. "Don't."

Irritation and heartache sharpened my tone. "Why?"

She couldn't comprehend what I had gone through, what I was going through. She didn't understand our relationship. There was nothing wrong with me saying farewell to my old General.

"Some things are better left unspoken," she said.

Darrak moved through the gate, the guards waving us on. Mikhala sat up, following him out. I twisted in my saddle to look at the one man who protected me for over two years. The one man I meant something to. As a person. As Avyanna. Not a Rider or a soldier, but as a woman.

My teeth sank into my lip so hard I tasted blood. Leather bit into my palms as I clenched the reins. Rafe nodded once. My heart stuttered in my chest. The corner of his mouth lifted in a sad smile.

"Coming, molasses?"

I turned away, urging Boulder on. A single rebellious tear trailed down my cheek, and I set my jaw, sitting tall in the saddle—strong and capable. Rafe would see me ride out a woman. He would see me ride out the same way I would ride back.

I would see him again.

CHAPTER 18

Tizmet ignored me.

Despite her awareness of my presence, she disregarded my existence. She flew high, drifting in and out of clouds, centering her lazy circles on me. I couldn't help but wonder what the world looked like from such heights.

I used to have vivid dreams about riding so high—the endless fields mimicked patches of a quilt some farmer made. I dreamed of exploring new areas, and seeing the Sky Trees in person.

Now I had a dragon who thought the idea of bearing a human on its back was insulting.

A dragon who ate people.

I sighed, rolling my neck to work out the kinks of my poor sleeping position the night before. In all fairness, she hadn't eaten someone entirely. She only bit off his arm. Still, she maimed a man. Because of her, he could no longer serve his King. She robbed him and his family of their livelihood.

I blinked against the bright sun. We had been riding all morning. The day was well past its zenith, and our course continued eastward.

"Already bored, eh?" Mikhala called, taking a drink from her waterskin.

"Frustrated." I huffed, glaring at Darrak's back.

He was whistling a merry tune, and it grated on my nerves. We were just on the outskirts of King's Wall, venturing into the eastern farmlands. The mountains of E'or were beyond my view, the distance too vast.

"Does it have to do with big, broad, and brooding?"

I frowned as she fastened her canteen to her saddle. I hadn't seen her use the reins once.

"Is your horse a mind reader or something?"

"Changing the subject. Must mean it's still sensitive." She flashed me a knowing smile. She patted the stallion's thick neck and leaned forward, pressing her chest against his mane. "We've been together a long time. I've worked with him since he was a foal."

"What's his name?"

"Girls and naming their animals." Darrak moaned.

"Shut it! We're not all as cruel and uncaring as you!" she snapped, braiding her horse's mane. "Moon."

"Moon?" I repeated, squinting at the stallion.

"Well, Blood Moon specifically, but I call him Moony. He doesn't mind."

I grinned as the beast flicked his ears, listening to every word she spoke.

"Thunderbolt was my pigou. He taught me not to fear riding."

"I still can't believe they let a pigou in the ranks! Can you imagine the enemy seeing you coming on a bunny horse?!" She closed her eyes and laughed, falling against her horse's neck.

"Well, it was my General who chose him for me."

"Oh! Was that who ol' one-eye was?"

I pressed my lips together, staring straight ahead.

"Oh, I know that look, girly. You're going to tell me everything!"

"Mikhala, really," Darrak called over his shoulder. "Let the girl be."

Woman. I was a woman, not a girl.

I closed my eyes as a grimace lifted my lips. There was only one person who I accepted the term 'girl' as a form of endearment. The taunting praise when he said, 'good girl' made my toes curl in my boots.

I blinked back the emotion and cursed myself. I would not cry. After all, I was a woman. Women didn't cry over—I choked on a laugh. I *had* actually witnessed numerous women in tears over their departed life mate.

Not that he was my life mate.

"Oi, don't get hysterical on me."

I offered her a bitter smile. My heart was shredded and torn to bits. Between my dragon who resented me, and my General who let me go, I thought I deserved every right to be hysterical.

"I'm fine."

"Liar."

"Mikhala!"

"Yes, Daddy?"

I laughed outright at their exchange.

Darrak turned in his saddle and glared. "I swear, it's like having two children now," he muttered, gaze bouncing between us.

"You always said you wanted kids." She shrugged.

"Let them start out as babes first! I didn't expect to be thrown into having two girls at once!" He turned back toward the road, still grumbling. "By the stars, I better end up with boys someday."

We shared a lighthearted laugh. This wouldn't be that bad.

We rode through the farmlands as the sun set behind us. On this side of Regent, safety seemed to be taken for granted. These fields had no walls built around them, whereas, to the west of the palace, property had, at the least, a simple fence of sharpened sticks.

The Shadows never breached Regent in the west, but the locals were aware of their looming threat. The people to the east of King's Wall were nestled between the great protective barrier of the E'or mountains and the palace itself.

Far to the south was a bit more perilous. Several refugees came in from Sandower attacks—nomads who traveled the desert. Shadow Men raids only displaced a few, but it was enough to promise a hard life for anyone who dared settle there.

"Not dining with the farmer's family tonight, eh?" Mikhala asked, eyes darting skyward.

"No. We'll find a barn to bed down in." Darrak turned to me. "Providing your dragon won't burn the barn down?"

I gave him a toothy smile and glared up at the sky. Tizmet had been flying all day and most of the night. I had to imagine she was tired, though I was a poor judge of her character at the moment.

We rode on until sunset, when the dark amber glow dimmed our path.

"If possible, keep the beast quiet," Darrak murmured as we approached a farmhouse. "I'd rather not announce we have a Rider in our midst."

"Well enough," I replied, though I doubted I had any influence over Tizmet's noise level.

Mikhala stopped short and motioned for me to do the same as Darrak pulled his cloak over his chest piece. I pursed my lips. He appeared indifferent while wearing it on the road. Why conceal it when approaching people?

He dismounted and knocked at the door. In a display of patience, he stood alongside his horse as an older man answered, holding a flickering candle. I doubted the stranger could see him in the weak light, let alone me or Mikhala.

Darrak spoke low, and a sense of relief washed over me as the old man nodded and Darrak passed him something. Bowing away from the stranger, he made his way around the small house. Mikhala followed without a word, her horse walking silently.

We rounded the corner to a large barn. After we led our horses inside, Darrak lit a lantern. We dismounted as he secured it to the beam, taking in the space.

"At least it's clean," Mikhala said, stretching.

My mouth fell open in horror as several pops and cracks sounded with the gesture. She beamed at me and cared for her horse.

The heavy flap of large wings preceded the weighted thud of the ground taking Tizmet's weight. I cringed and held my breath, expecting her to roar or scream at me.

Nothing came.

She curled up near the doors, blocking the entrance.

"Well, drafts won't be a concern," Mikhala offered cheerfully.

"And now we have a guard," Darrak added.

I kept my mouth shut against all the comments I could make about moody, temperamental, over-sized, fire-breathing lizards. Instead, I loosened the girth on Boulder's tack.

We bedded down with a quick meal of dried meat and fruit.

Mikhala rested against Moon's saddle, positioned between Darrak and me. "I bet Lady Farmer had a nice stew." She moaned.

"Full of venison and spring greens." Darrak sighed, settling onto his bedroll.

They acted as if they were old friends. My earlier assumption that they were bed mates felt inaccurate now. I climbed into my blankets.

Mikhala rolled her head. "Oi, last one up puts out the light, lazybones."

Groaning, I rose to stifle the lantern, glancing at the weak fire reflected in Tizmet's eyes. I had no reaction, no flare of appreciation, no spike of fear, nothing.

I was simply empty.

Returning to my blankets, I settled in to sleep.

"It seems rather put-out," Mikhala murmured.

I didn't reply. No one needed to know my internal struggles with my dragon. I couldn't even figure out how to work with her, let alone explain to someone what was going on with us.

An obnoxious yawn sounded beside me, too loud in the quiet space.

"Sleep, Mik," Darrak ordered.

"Yesh, shir," she slurred.

After a moment of stillness, the sound of her light snoring broke the silence. I grinned into the darkness.

I would tease her about it tomorrow.

Darrak's fingers clenched fistfuls of his hair. "No! She can't!"

Mikhala bent over in laughter.

I stood immobile in helpless horror.

Tizmet had half of the farmer's prized milk cow in her maw. She glared down at me, daring me to make a move. I frowned as Darrak let loose with curses. The farmer was wailing about the weight of cheese and something about compensation.

With one snap of her massive jaws, Tizmet swallowed the rest of the cow, hissing at me. I shook my head in resignation. I couldn't do anything. Just like with the squire's hand—I was helpless.

Darrak flashed me an irritated look and stalked over to the enraged farmer.

"That was great!" Mikhala beamed at Tizmet with mirthful, tear-laden eyes, then threw her arm over my shoulder. "She swallowed it in two goes! She's a *beast*!"

"Literally," I mumbled.

"She's a dragon!" With a playful snort, she pushed off me and started for the barn. "Don't expect her to act like a human."

I frowned at Tizmet, who sat back on her haunches, glaring at me. "If you're hungry, tell me. Eat *anything* other than the prized cow." I dared not open the door to the bond, but I felt obligated to rebuke her in some way.

Quick as a flash, she snapped her bloody teeth in my face. Warm blood splattered my cheeks and dress. I cursed, turning my back on her, and stomped into the barn.

Mikhala erupted into more laughter, seeing my blood-splattered self. I swiped at the stains, smearing it all over myself, but I didn't care. Frustrated, I snatched my saddle and heaved it at Boulder. I threw it too hard, and it slid over, hitting the ground on the other side. Boulder eyed me patiently, as if I was a dumb child. I clenched my fists and closed my eyes, counting to ten.

"Today is going to be a *day!*" Mikhala roared beside me, slapping my back.

I had very little doubt that today would be anything shy of awful.

Sure enough, a few chimes into our ride, clouds crowded the sky. By midday, the rain fell in sheets, and even Mikhala's bright spirits were dampened.

Tizmet refused to fly, plodding along behind us like a wet, whipped puppy.

A giant, scaled, fire-breathing puppy.

We made slow progress, reaching the edge of the farmlands by the time daylight faded. Darrak bargained with another farmer for a barn to bed in, and we were silent as we shook out our soaked belongings.

The rain was cold, and Tizmet growled, trying to crowd inside. We shuffled our horses and belongings further into the structure, though I was worried. If she threw her head up in a fit of rage, she would burst through the roof. Its meager wood was no match for her strength.

I set out my soggy blanket. This would be a miserable night, even out of the rain.

"Will we have to worry about the prized cow?" Mikhala teased.

"Not tonight. Dragons don't eat that often."

"Thank the sun." Darrak groaned, settling in.

I took a deep breath and plunged under my damp blanket. Tizmet shifted, pulling further away from me as if I would roll in my sleep and accidentally touch her.

She was the queen of grudges.

The landscape gave way from farmlands to woodlands. Mikhala said once we reached the forests, it would be a three-day journey to the base of the E'or mountains. That was reassuring, though the thick canopy left me uneasy. It blocked my view of Tizmet.

"So, how does Avyanna fit into our scheme?" Mikhala asked, sitting backward on her stallion. She leaned against his neck, gazing up into the trees.

How she managed to be so comfortable and trusting on his back—I had no idea.

"Rafe said she was a sharpshooter."

"Oh, yes! You were supposed to show me!"

I refused to act childish and ask what else Rafe told them about me. "So I'll be covering you?"

"Aye. The hardest part will be keeping that dragon grounded."

I frowned. There was no way I could keep her contained against her will. "What exactly is your bounty?" I asked, changing the subject.

"A real meathead." Mikhala sighed. "What's his name, Darrak?"

"Quint."

"He'll need a splint when I'm done with him." She pursed her lips. "He's taken to robbing farmers, leaving a trail of terror in his wake."

"Terror—and babes," he added, his tone hushed.

"Aye, so we end his reign of terror and put a stop to the bastard children." She closed her eyes and relaxed against her stallion. "Perhaps with a few body modifications on the way back to the palace."

I shivered, remembering Victyr. Despite the passage of time, the memory remained etched in my mind.

"Oi! I know!" Mikhala bolted upright, staring me down. "We could have your dragon eat him!"

"No." Darrak snapped.

"Why not? I mean, I could live without the bounty bonus." She pouted.

"He's been ordered to slay Tizmet if she harms another human." I frowned, thinking of the squire—how his stump of an arm sprayed blood all over the balcony, his cries of pain.

"Oh. That's a downer. I am rather fond of big, bad, and scary." She winked. "She doesn't have to eat anyone... yet."

I mustered up a smile that was clearly forced and carried on riding. If it came to that, I would attempt to regain control of her. I didn't relish the thought.

We set up camp a day's ride from the small village of Edgeguard, where the bounty, Quint, was rumored to be staying. From Mikhala, I gleaned the price on his head was five-hundred gold. That money could feed an average family for a year, even longer if they were frugal. It was an exorbitant amount. Although it entailed a certain level of risk—one would have to capture the man and deliver him to King's Wall to claim it.

Darrak had a steady set income in place of the somewhat erratic bounties. Though they gave Mikhala a bonus for her contribution. Not the full bounty—fifteen percent. She wasn't sore over it. After all, Darrak did most of the work.

Tomorrow, he planned to enter the village as a humble farmer seeking employment. He grew out his beard and looked rather unkempt. It was well-known that Quint ran a farm where stolen livestock roamed and barns housed plundered crops. Darrak would offer his help, gaining his trust.

Mikhala would arrive the following day, distracting the villagers, and hopefully, a beauty-addled Quint. I smiled, thinking of it. She hoped to get him alone. Then Darrak would assist in the capture. When I asked if the plan ever failed, they admitted it had a time or two, though he never left her in a bind. Even if he had to reveal his identity and lose the bounty, he refused to abandon her in a compromising situation.

My duty was to stay behind.

I begrudgingly accepted the task. It would be too hard to hide Tizmet if she flew above. Dragons didn't come this way, other than the Dragon Fleet, while patrolling the homeland. Since they worked on a schedule, Tizmet would be out of place.

So, we camped at the base of a set of hills, far off the road. The small fire crackled, spilling embers into the night while we ate a simple stew of boiled meat and greens. Along with foraging, I gathered the firewood, trying to find some basic tasks to make my presence worthwhile.

"So he burst through the doors yelling 'In the name of the King!' and I lost it!" Mikhala laughed, retelling the story of their first bounties together. She set to her job of seduction, and Darrak deemed her in mortal peril, rushing in and announcing himself.

"In my defense, you were shouting." Darrak's bright smile cut through his beard.

"Aye, I had to be convincing!"

His eyes twinkled with mirth as they teased each other. "I want to know where you learned such things."

"Oi, my people are quite open. Not as reserved and modest as your lot."

"Where is your home country?" I asked, setting my bowl to the side.

"Far to the north. Caulden. Have you heard of it?"

"I'm afraid not. What's it like?" I was genuinely curious. I'd never researched what lay beyond Regent's northern borders.

"Cold. Blasted cold." She feigned a shiver. "Your winters mimic our summers. The land is divided into three clans. Hare, Whale and Wolf. I hail from the Wolf. My people are warriors from birth."

It wasn't hard to believe she hailed from a warrior clan. She looked like one. She had an easy friendliness about her, but she didn't strike me as childish.

"The Whale clan are excellent fishers and shipmen," she continued. "I traded with them to purchase passage to your country. Hare are quick and cunning. They control Coldbreach, our port city. And Falsecairn, our trade city. They're the only ones allowed permanent residence inside the cities. Cowards." She cursed with tenderness.

She might not appreciate their ways, but they were still her people.

"Do all your people look like you?"

"This kind of beauty is rare." She tossed her hair over her shoulder with a teasing grin. "Honestly, I'm pretty average. You seem different, though. I haven't seen many with white hair."

"It's from my father," I explained. "He hails from the northern region of the E'or mountains. It's quite prevalent there."

"Tell me about them. Are your parents still living?"

"My mother, yes. My father died in the war when I was four."

"Such is life." She nodded soberly. "Your mother raised a strong woman."

"I grew up in the King's school, Northwing," I muttered, looking down at my hands. "She was unable to support me as a widow."

"You never saw her?"

"Twice a year on the Solstices—until recently."

"And why's that?"

"I joined the ranks at seventeen. I didn't want her to be ashamed, so I asked her not to come."

"Why would she be ashamed?" She pulled back in surprise. "Any mother in my country would be proud to have a daughter that fought."

"It's not like that here." I shrugged.

"People here are different, Mik," Darrak reminded. "Avyanna was the first woman to try to join."

"Try?" Disgust scrunched her face. "You mean they didn't even let you?"

"They did." I nodded.

Darrak shot a pleased smirk my way. "Despite them trying to convince her otherwise."

She slapped her thigh. "Good for you!"

"Anyway, my mother didn't find out until this past Winter Solstice."

"What prompted you to tell her and not simply avoid the confrontation?"

I smiled at her question. She might be from Caulden, but she read my people well. We weren't like her. We avoided conflict where we could.

"She's my mother. She deserved to hear it from me before I ran off to get myself killed. I owed her that, at least."

"Aye, you owe her a great deal more, but that's a good place to start." She winked.

"What about your parents?" I asked, settling against my blankets with a yawn.

Darrak rolled out his blanket on the far side of the fire.

"Both are living. My father is a grumpy old bear, angry that I left. I'll return with tales to tell around the fire for years to come, though. My mother is a traditionalist. She was proud that I strove to be a warrior but wanted me to be a Kailfi. She and my grandmother nagged me about it so much—I needed to escape. Don't tell my father that—he didn't raise a coward." She cut off with a yawn and settled into her furs.

"What's a Kailfi?"

"Shh. I'll tell you tomorrow."

Darrak left early the next morning, wanting to make it to the village with plenty of daylight. He wore rough clothes—patched trousers and a ratty tunic that hung from his frame. With his hat and his bay, he passed as an average farmer.

"Ah, we're free to be women!" Mikhala cried after he left.

"Were we not before?"

"Not at all!" She doubled over, jerking her vest over her head.

I turned away, shocked at her nudity.

"Last one there smells like rotten cheese!" She darted for the small creek that carved through the forest floor.

I stared at Tizmet as if the dragon would offer some sage advice for dealing with Mikhala. She ignored me, resting her head on her paws, gazing into the distance.

Shrugging, I grabbed a spare set of clothes and followed.

Mikhala was already waist-deep. She flung her wet hair and beamed at me as I approached. "Bout time, molasses."

"I was struck dumb by your boldness." I smirked, setting my clothes on a dry log.

My fingers gripped the hem of my dress, and I yanked the fabric over my head.

"Dear moon and stars above!" Water sloshed as she waded closer. "What in all of Rinmoth is that?" she asked, eyes glued to my side.

"A scar." I shrugged, then tossed my clothes aside, rushing into the cool current.

"Is it some kind of ritual? That's..." She trailed off, at a loss for words.

"Happened when I first met Tizmet." I plunged my head into the cold water, gasping as I pulled up and scrubbed at my face. "When she grabbed me, her talon sliced through. Long story short—she healed it and it scarred like this." I peered down at the white scar, its swirling design wide at my side, narrowing to a point at my navel.

"It's beautiful," Mikhala breathed.

Beautiful? It evoked memories of pain. It served as a reminder of my failures.

"What about your tattoos?" I gestured to her arms.

A quick glance showed me the vine ended over her heart, and other than the bands that marked her left arm, nothing else stained her skin.

"This one," she said, pointing to the vine, "represents my family. Each leaf signifies a member, going back three generations."

"That's a lot of family."

"Aye, we're a prolific lot," she teased. Opening her palm, she revealed the detailed flower. "My grandmother always called me her 'Gaudlin.' It's native to my homeland. I've never seen it here."

"Seems awfully soft for a woman like you."

"You don't know the Gaudlin." She laughed. "It's a lovely red flower in all respects. It has the sweetest fragrance, and its petals are softer than a newborn's skin."

I plunged into the creek and stood, letting the water run over me.

"Yet, one drop of sap from its stem can poison an entire well for generations."

"There it is." I nodded. "I see the correlation now."

"Aye, beautiful, but dangerous."

"What about the bands?" I followed her out of the creek to dress.

"Oh, these?" She held out her left arm. "They're men I've killed."

Reaching for my clothes, I froze, then straightened as I scrutinized her. "They're what?"

She threw her head back and laughed. Pulling her trousers up, she put her hands on her hips, her pale, ghost-eyes flashing. "See, that's the fun part. Not only for you, but for my own people. You never know if the bands represent self-defense... or if I'm a rabid murderer."

I blinked and reached for my clothes again. "I'm willing to go with rabid murderer."

"Good guess!"

"I'm right?" I cried, gaping up at her.

She cackled, pulling her vest over her shoulders. "I'm never required to tell."

"Really?"

"Aye. When you take a life, you're expected to take the Band of Death. Yet, we're never obligated to speak of how we took that life. So maybe I was attacked, then killed my assailants. Maybe," she crept toward me, her features melting into a frightful sneer, "I snuck into a house, murdered the three women living there, and ate all their food."

"I'd wager the latter."

Her demeanor blinked into her regular, carefree mirth. "Think what you will," she sang, then started back to camp.

Tizmet was exactly where I left her. The only difference was she actually looked at me as I approached. I took a seat on a log and started to braid my hair at the nape of my neck.

Mikhala knelt behind me. "Let me," she said, then slid her fingers into the strands.

"Tell me about the Kailfi."

"Ah, the destiny that my mother and grandmother chose for me. Well, I rather think it's a bit like your dragons."

"You have dragons?" I asked, trying to face her.

"Sit still." She slapped the top of my head. "No. Seems like dragons belong to your kingdom and yours alone. We have Dire Wolves. They make your wolves look like harmless puppies. They're the largest predator of Caulden, and like your dragons, they can be bonded.

"So, your people have magic?" I glanced at Tizmet, who was once again ignoring me.

"Eh, not exactly. We have a power but few wield it. It's frowned upon. Only someone too weak to survive without it would use it. The Kailfi are bonded to the Dire Wolves as pups. They live their lives roaming Caulden, settling disputes and bringing balance."

"That doesn't sound too awful."

"Well, see our people view the bond as a great honor. If you manage it, you've set yourself for life. Everyone looks up to you."

I thought about the rigorous training I went through to be selected as First Chosen. "How do you do it?"

"You must plunge deep into their territory where only the Kailfi are welcome. If you fail, they eat you."

"Oh."

"Which is an honorable end, by all accounts."

I snorted. Her people were harsh.

"So you were scared?"

My head jerked to the side, and I cursed, holding my stinging scalp. She had a wicked slap.

"No, I wasn't scared," she snapped. "I'm just logical. Why throw my life away on the chance that I could live as a Kailfi? I want to explore the world before I make that kind of commitment!"

I laughed as she finished up my braids.

"There. Now you're a proper savage."

She wove the short strands into braids, tight against my scalp, keeping them neatly squared away. I twisted to flash her a smile.

I think I made a new friend.

CHAPTER 19

"She's a bit lazier after she eats, eh?" Mikhala relaxed in the warm daylight, her head tilted, assessing Tizmet.

I lay back on my blankets with my dress pulled to my knees, letting my shins get some sun. "Aye, it's part of their metabolism. They eat large meals, then rest to digest them."

"Why not hunt with her? The Kailfi do with their wolves."

"She won't let me ride her."

"They don't ride their wolves in the hunt. Normally, they're the bait—luring in testy creatures. But I don't think you have big enough predators here for that."

"There are bears at the base of the mountains," I murmured.

"That's too far. You need something here. How could you help her hunt? Think about it. It would be good for you both."

So I thought about it. All day and night.

When Mikhala headed out the next morning in an obscenely tight and low-cut dress, I had a plan. My only order was to keep Tizmet away from the village. She could fly, as long as she remained unseen.

"Come." I hefted my crossbow and climbed into Boulder's saddle. "We're going hunting."

Nothing.

Well, that was expected. She didn't even bat an eye.

We hadn't explored the thick terrain to the south, and I hoped there weren't many roads. This land might have been unfamiliar, but I'd find my way back to camp easy enough. I headed southwest, plunging into the dark forest. I eased Boulder into a quiet walk and rode as silently as possible. We made it a few hundred paces before Tizmet took to the air. Smiling, I pressed on. She was taking the bait.

Riding in a rough half-circle, I stopped deep in the thicket. We'd traveled quite far, and I hoped my calculations were correct. With a deep breath, I readied myself.

"For Regent!!"

I urged Boulder on, charging like a madwoman, howling at the top of my lungs. Branches slapped at my face and tore my dress, but I prodded him on, shouting louder. Tizmet roared above the treetops and I broke into a laugh. She likely assumed I'd gone mad. Little did she know—she helped my cause.

I crowed and hollered, riding Boulder as fast as he could through the dense trees. Stopping for a breath, I heard twigs snapping ahead.

"Run! Run for your life!" I screamed, cutting off with a wild cackle.

We burst through the treeline and I whooped my delight upon seeing a small herd of deer darting through the clearing. There was a single buck and four doe, but it was enough.

"Tizmet! For you!" I shouted, raising my hand to the sky.

One blazing eye studied me for a breath before she dove and took a doe. She clutched it in her claws and bit off its head before it could even cry out, then pulled up into the air. I beamed as the others dashed into the forest.

Well, that was successful.

Humming to myself, I followed Tizmet to camp, urging Boulder to keep up. She collapsed with her kill and clutched it close.

I slipped from Boulder's back and put my hands on my hips. "I'm just saying some gratitude wouldn't be unwelcome."

She squinted as if puzzling out my words. Bowing her head, she tore off a front leg and tossed it.

I narrowly dodged it and scowled. "A simple 'thank you' would've sufficed," I muttered.

She huffed and opened her mouth, allowing me a split second to maneuver myself out of harm's way. Dragon fire lit the area, heating my side. It was a quick burst, but enough to frighten me.

"Oi!"

I rolled onto my back and propped myself up. My jaw fell in shock, and she snorted, tearing into the deer. She roasted the leg for me.

"Why, thank you," I said with a self-satisfied smirk.

She locked her bright orange eyes on me and tore into the deer's stomach, blood dripping from her muzzle.

The day dragged on. I tidied up camp, foraged fresh greens for dinner, and cleaned all my tack. I nibbled on a bit of hard cheese and venison for my meals. It wouldn't be edible in the morning, and I would give it back to Tizmet, but I was determined to make the most of her offering.

She devoured the deer and watched me as I went through my day. Mikhala warned me this bounty might not be a quick grab. It could take a few days to get settled. It would, however, be far quicker than Darrak's stint at the barracks.

The King sent him on special missions. He was loyal and willing. Wherever he was needed, he would go. Most bounties he took on were long-standing, or the dangerous ones others refused, such as this.

As I settled in for the night, I noticed Tizmet watching me again.

"Shall I tell you a bedtime story?"

She didn't even lift her head, but bared her teeth in response.

"Figured."

The next day, I was getting bored. I hated having nothing to do. By midday, I was sure I was going mad. I started talking to Boulder. It was one thing to talk to Tizmet. We were bonded, and she understood me to an extent. But talking to a horse?

I pushed myself up and grabbed my crossbow. Tizmet lifted her head, watching me. I stalked to the edge of the woods and picked up a small log, then dragged it across the clearing, counting my steps.

With a huff, I threw the thing down and hurried back to camp.

"Eighty paces." I settled along the ground. "Below the twig waving the leaf," I murmured, then loaded a bolt and cocked the string.

I sighted down the bow, formed my lips into a firm line, and squeezed the trigger. I held my position, following it through. The log jostled, so I knew I struck it, but I couldn't see where.

"Well, where did I hit it, sharp-eyes?" I called, squinting.

Not like Tizmet would actually tell me.

Sighing, I stood and jogged closer. My aim was off, below and to the right.

"Again!" I skipped back to my bow and sank to the ground.

I practiced all afternoon. Given my lack of experience in lowlight conditions, I was hesitant to risk losing my bolts. As the sky darkened too much to see, I gave up and settled in for the night.

Perhaps tomorrow I would practice with my spear.

The following day, I was far too motivated to attempt more distance-shooting rather than practice with my spear. I hit an excellent mark two hundred paces out and was eager to try further. I set up my logs and dropped into position. Tizmet roused herself and I glanced up as she sat next to me. I frowned. Did she simply want a better view? Shrugging to myself, I readied the crossbow and sighted down its length.

The bolt thudded into my target nearly two hundred and fifty paces away. It might not be accurate, but I was pleased it hit at all. Smiling, I loaded another and aimed for the log three hundred paces out. I bit my lip, focusing. It would be a hard shot. All things considered.

After a calming breath, I loosed.

Thunk!

"Yes!" I pumped my fist in the air. "What do you have to say about that?" I taunted Tizmet, not expecting a reply.

She, however, deemed I needed one.

Fire shot from her maw. I cursed, rolling away. In a fell swoop of flame, she incinerated both logs... and set the field ablaze.

"Oi! Ever heard of wildfires?!" I ran for my cloak, soaking it with what little water I had in my canteen, then rushed to slap it against the flames.

Tizmet watched, head tilted, as if amused.

Dragon fire could melt steel. Once the oil was cut from fueling it, however, the flames burned at a normal temperature.

It was spring, and we had that downpour a few days ago. Otherwise, we would have sent smoke signals to all the villages around. Scouts would come, then assess the fire's direction to warn villages in its path.

Luckily, I put out the fire before we started such an incident.

Hands on my hips, filthy with sweat, dirt and ash, I glared up at Tizmet. "You simply wanted to prove you were a better shot than me, didn't you?"

She snorted and went back to her place at camp, where she kneaded the ground to a soft bed. Settling herself, she gave a mighty yawn and blinked at me lazily.

Chuckling to myself, I settled on practicing with my spear. That, at least, seemed like a safe bet.

The days blurred together, and I enjoyed my time alone. At first, I had been uncomfortable with nothing to do, but when I searched, there was always something.

I worked on my distance-shooting from every angle. My attempt to hang upside down from a tree resulted in a nasty bruise on my shoulder. Hours passed while I practiced with my spear. I foraged and explored the forest and creek behind the camp. When that wouldn't hold my attention, I pursued the exercises I'd seen Jamlin do, and wondered how, in all of Rinmoth, a man of his size pulled himself up like that. I did about ten pull-ups before my arms gave out, and I clung to the branch like a stranded kitten.

Bit by bit, Tizmet and I re-established our tolerance for one another. I dared not reach through the bond, and she didn't venture to try either, but we no longer ignored each other. I talked to her as much as I talked to Boulder. Though I doubted she understood my words, I had a feeling my emotions trickled over.

I leaned against her massive paw, carving a fishing hook from a twig when the thud of hooves drew my attention. Jumping to my feet, I ran to my crossbow. The bolt slid into place, and I knelt toward the sound's source. What was I doing? Even if it wasn't my companions, greeting a fellow traveler with a loaded weapon wasn't appropriate. I'd been alone too long.

A horse crested the hill, and I scoffed, seeing the bright-colored Moony carrying Mikhala on his back. She shouted and galloped toward us at full speed, arms flung wide as if she was flying. I smiled and rose, easing the string on my bow. Behind her, Darrak led a chestnut horse with a body slung over the saddle, hands and feet tied together.

"Avy-anna!!" Mikhala drew out my name.

Moony settled on his haunches, skidding to a stop, depositing her to the ground. She didn't miss a beat and ran at me as her stallion straightened with a snort. I grunted as she wrapped me in a bear hug. She pulled me into the air, laughing, then dropped me to pull away and hold my face.

"My, how you've grown!" she teased.

Darrak droned as he dismounted. "We've been gone six days, Mik."

The body shifted, and he stomped over, grabbing a fistful of the man's lengthy, unkempt hair.

"Is that the bounty?" I muttered.

Darrak slammed his fist into the man's face and dropped him.

"Aye." Mikhala laughed. "Darrak is quite angry with him."

"It was uncomfortable." He groaned, eyeing the swath of dead grass between my target logs. "All's well?"

"Aye. Tizmet was showing off. Thought she could out shoot me." I turned a teasing smile on the gray dragon.

She huffed and fastened her eyes on the man draped over the chestnut.

"Pack up, then," Darrak said, gathering his belongings from where I stored them.

I glanced at the sky. "It's a few hours shy of nightfall."

"We'll be riding through the night."

"Quint here has a loyal few." Mikhala shrugged, packing her things. "Darrak will send the Home Guard to deal with them, but there are too many for us to handle."

I hurried about, clearing our camp. It was amusing that I transformed the space into a cozy haven within days. I dug out a fire pit, organized a cooking station, cleared everyone's bed of stones. It was the little things that made a camp homey.

Packing up took longer than Darrak wanted, but we managed and set out.

We rode hard. Though I was nodding off, Tizmet's excitement spilled over. She wanted to fly. It made me wonder if she sensed my reservations while we camped, if she humored me by staying put. Perhaps she wanted to be lazy, but by the joy I felt from her soaring through the night sky, I doubted it.

As the sun rose, we took a brief break, allowing the horses to rest. Darrak offered water to Quint, but otherwise didn't speak to him.

"Was it difficult?" I asked around a mouthful of tough dried meat.

"For me? Not at all. For Darrak... oh, it was a fun one." Mikhala snickered as he approached.

"Why?"

"Let's just say there was a sort of initiation with this bounty," a sly smile tugged at her lips, "and Darrak had to play his role."

"Mik, enough."

"He had to–"

"Mik!" Darrak glared.

I flinched, and my eyes widened at his outburst.

"Don't be so sore about it. I've seen you in worse situations." She tsked, wagging her finger. "He had to wallow with the pigs."

"Begging your pardon?" I blinked, confused.

"Avyanna," his tone burned with warning, "I will never take you out again if you repeat that."

"You see, Quint here has the idea that he's better than everyone. So, before you can work for him, he humiliates you to see just how far you will go. After all, no one with any amount of pride or self-worth would work for such a pig. Therefore, our dear bounty hunter had to prove he was naught but an animal—in several ways."

Darrak cursed, sat beside her, and snatched the dried meat from her hand.

I smirked as the two bickered. Looking back at Quint, I asked, "And did your strategy work, Mik?"

She choked.

Darrak smiled wickedly. "Aye, tell her about that."

"No, really–"

"I insist. No, actually—I'll tell you for her." He leaned around Mikhala to grin at me.

She shoved him off, blocking his view with a grimace. "He's a man of odd taste, that one. To seduce him... there were–"

"Feathers."

"Ugh!"

She spun on him, and he danced away, laughing.

"She looked like a chicken, Avyanna! You should have seen her!"

"I'll skewer *you* like a chicken!" She snarled.

"Bock bock!"

I burst into laughter, watching as they darted around each other, wrestling. Resting my back against a tree, I sipped my water. These were friends—they didn't keep secrets from each other. They were open and cared for one another.

Just like the Tennan.

My smile faltered as memories nipped at my heartstrings. The hours Collins and I spent having snowball fights, planning our attack on the others. Jamlin and I sparring, pulling no punches while I 'fought like a girl,' as he would say. I thought of Korzak and how he was always so kind and clumsy, but fought like a bear.

Rafe. My vision blurred. The one person who truly knew me, who knew my struggles and supported me through my journey. I thought of the secrets he entrusted me with—we trusted each other.

My eyes welled with tears, and I rushed over to Boulder. I hid my face in the pretense of adjusting his tack.

I would see them again.

Tizmet's tongue flicked out as she craned her head. I took a deep breath and reined in my emotions. She didn't need to feel my struggles. She had enough of her own. When we arrived at the palace, we would have even more.

I would simply endure. I had to. Because I *would* see my friends again.

CHAPTER 20

W e arrived at King's Wall with Tizmet circling high in the sky. Darrak warned me to keep my hood up, hiding my face. At first, I was puzzled, but as we led our horses to the bounty house, a grim comprehension settled in.

"The man-eater is in the sky!" Someone pointed toward the clouds, shielding an eye from the sun.

"It's the Wild One!" another cried. "They say it tore down an entire room in the castle trying to eat a servant!"

"Stay under cover! It will see you!"

I scoffed, drawing a frown from Darrak. Shaking my head, I kept my hood low as we pressed on.

He and Mikhala yanked Quint off his horse and dragged him into what looked like a storefront. I leaned against the wall outside, peering through the dingy window. I could make out shapes inside, but it was no palace glass.

They shoved Quint forward, and he crumpled. A mountain of a man, as wide as Jamlin and tall as Korzak, leaned over the counter, peering down at the bounty curled on the floor. Mikhala kicked, and he rolled onto his back, revealing his face.

A laugh boomed out of the building, vibrating through the walls. I couldn't help the smile that tugged at my lips with the sound. He nodded and spoke with a cheeky grin as he counted out coins from under the counter. Slipping them into a pouch, he slid it to Mikhala. She threw her head back, laughing at something he said, then danced a jig with herself. Beaming, she skipped out of the building, almost colliding with me.

"Fair Avyanna, it's going to be a glorious day!"

With a breathy sigh, she crashed against the wall, her eyes drifting shut. She looked like a love-struck puppy. Clutching her pouch of gold to her chest, she beamed as if consumed by love.

Is that what I resembled when I thought of Rafe?

Surely not.

Slay me dead and bury me if I ever acted like that in public.

When Darrak joined us, he gave her a once-over. He forced a sigh and pressed his wrist to her forehead. Worry lined his brow. "How long has she been like this?"

"Since she walked out," I muttered, glancing between them.

"It's terrible. I think she's doomed."

"Pardon?"

Her lashes fluttered, slow and heavy. "It's love."

"Definitely." Darrak spoke with grim conviction. "And your father will kill both you and him."

"I'm going to dance with him." She pushed off the wall and staggered to Moony.

"You're not dancing with him." He deadpanned, then turned to me to explain. "Her people have a mating dance. She's not dancing with him."

I snorted, walking to Boulder.

"He asked me to!" She flung herself to her stallion's rump, gazing at the clear blue sky as if her future was written in the clouds.

"You know he didn't realize what he was asking. Drop it, Mik. I'll lock you in your room if I have to."

I mounted after Darrak and watched with wonder as she somehow turned Moony with her legs to follow him. He muttered under his breath, shaking his head, then led us down the roads. He didn't bother with the signs—he probably knew them by heart.

We reached the tall iron gate that separated King's Wall from the palace and Darrak spoke with the guards. They jested about his scruffy beard and laughed at Mikhala lying on Moony. When they spotted me, all mirth left their eyes, and one squinted into my hood. I pulled it back, and their amiable smiles melted.

I pressed my lips together. Of course, I was the downer in the party. Darrak and Mikhala were clearly loved and adored. I was an outcast bonded to a wild animal with the strength and size to tear apart the palace.

They waved us through—a guard pulling Darrak aside, jerking a chin at me. He nodded, and we followed as he rode to the stables. We cared for our horses and I lugged my things into the aisle. Mikhala clutched her coins like they were her most precious belongings. Darrak hefted his pack, gave her a playful shove, and we headed out.

"Avyanna, your orders are to stay in your quarters."

"Yes, sir."

"Oh, so formal," Mikhala jeered, snapping out of her daze.

I shrugged. "It's only proper."

"What we are out there," she gestured toward King's Wall with an exaggerated wave, "we are everywhere."

My lips pressed tight as my brows dipped in a frown.

"You don't ever have to call me 'ma'am,'" she added and threw an arm around me.

Snorting, I shrugged off her embrace. She giggled and skipped beside Darrak.

Servants led me to my room without incident. Tizmet still circled above. I dropped my pack and walked to the bed, ready to collapse. A knock sounded before I could reach it.

"Come in," I called, exhaustion lining my voice.

A servant peeked her head in and glanced around.

"Don't worry, she's flying right now," I sighed.

"Begging your pardon, miss. You know what they say." Her tone was apologetic, and she slipped in with two steaming buckets.

I could forgive her comment for that hot water.

I bathed quickly, washing off the dirt and grime from the road. We rushed here not only to outrun Quint's men, but to send the Home Guard after them that much sooner. Darrak couldn't capture them all, but he didn't want them roaming, either. Bagging Quint meant nothing if someone took his place.

I changed into clean clothes and collapsed on the bed. The servant girl was emptying my bath water when I heard the heavy flap of dragon wings.

"Incoming." I groaned.

A muffled cry sounded as Tizmet landed on the balcony. They repaired it from her last visit, but it was still not properly set. She shuffled her wings along her back and crept into the room.

The door slammed, and I smiled at her. She arched her neck and snorted, eyes blazing.

"Have a pleasant flight?"

She huffed and glanced around before settling on the furs spread over the floor. She was as tired as I was.

Together, we slept.

Tizmet's growl woke me. Rolling over, I realized with horror it was evening. I missed the entire day.

"I'm not going to hurt her, silly thing."

"Mik?" I groaned, sitting up.

Mikhala perched on the balcony railing, giving the dragon a reassuring smile. Tizmet, however, was not buying it and bared her teeth. Mik's braids hung loose, no longer tied at the nape of her neck. She wore her travel clothes—a fur vest, black trousers, and fur-wrapped boots.

"Oi, sleepy head! I need a favor!" She turned her bright smile on me and slid her feet to the balcony, waving her fingers at Tizmet.

"What is it?"

"I need you to cover for me."

"Cover for—by the sun, Mik. How old are you?" I moaned, collapsing onto my blankets. I was no longer a teenager. To engage in such childish games seemed absurd.

"Twenty-one winters, not that it matters. Come on, it's not much. You just need to sleep in my bed."

"How long are you staying out?" I rubbed at my tired eyes and thought of all the reasons not to push her off the balcony.

"Only a chime or two. I just want to dance."

"You mean you want to join that man in bed?"

She flashed me an easy smile and cocked her hip, placing her hand on it. "Aye, I do. Yet, I'm not so foolish as to think I can." She reached up and flipped her hair. "I just want to have some fun!"

My heart stuttered, thinking of the night I slipped away with Rafe. The simple joys we shared, and the memories we had. We hadn't done anything either... Yet, that memory meant everything to me.

Curling up next to him. His ease with the people, and not hiding me or his feelings for me.

"I've been ordered to stay in my quarters. Tizmet won't let me leave." I sighed.

"My room is across the passage! If she sensed any danger, she could hop right out and poof to your side!"

"Poof?" I repeated, pushing myself upright.

She squealed and rushed over to pull me into an embrace. "You're the best!"

"I'm not promising it will fool anyone," I muttered, her arm muffling my response.

"Darrak peeks in on me from time to time, but only through a crack in the door," she said, leading me toward the balcony. "Tonight would be one of those nights."

"What happens to me if I'm caught?"

"Oh nothing, I'm sure. You're a Rider." She waved off my concern with a flick of her wrist. "To be honest, I'm a free person. Darrak will simply be disappointed, and I'll have to deal with his whining for the next five bounties."

"I suddenly think I have far more to lose than you." I sighed, climbing over the railing with her.

"I'll pay you back, I promise." She whipped her red braids behind her. "Now, have you ever scaled a stone wall?"

"Yes."

"Well, the first thing—wait, yes?" A bemused grin slipped across her features.

I returned the look, thinking of all the times Collins and I raced up the fortress. It wasn't the same, but the premise was familiar enough.

"Aye, a fellow soldier taught me."

"I'd like to meet them," she whispered.

I climbed behind her as she picked her way across the stones, then over the passageway. Tizmet craned over the balcony. Her bright eyes followed me, tongue flicking with curiosity. I wanted to assure her I was simply going to the next room, but I was terrified she would lash out.

If she spooked, I would call it off. For now, she seemed alright. With how she acted last time we were here, she would have lashed out already.

Focusing back on my hands and feet, I carefully picked my way across. Mikhala jumped down to a tiny balcony, and I landed beside her. A sleepy haze plagued my senses, and I hadn't thought to check for guards. I trusted she had the mind to check, since she was the one wanting to sneak out.

I glanced up at Tizmet, who huffed a sigh and laid with her massive head resting on the banister. She watched me with glowing eyes but was content to let me go... for now.

Heading into the room, I immediately noticed how cramped it was compared to my own. Mine housed an adult dragon and a human. Mikhala's was simple and small, providing basic amenities and nothing more.

I flopped on her bed, wiggling my toes in the sheets.

"Just go back to sleep. I'll be back soon." She tucked me in and pulled the blanket over my head.

I batted it away and rolled to my side to face the balcony opposite the door. "I'm a lot smaller than you. If Darrak comes and spends more than a blink of an eye studying, he'll notice something's off."

"He's not a creeper. He just peeks to make sure I'm in bed."

"Like a good girl."

"Exactly. Which I'm definitely not." She danced toward the balcony and looked me over once more. "I'll be back soon!"

She beamed at me before she threw her legs over the railing and climbed out of sight.

In Northwing, I'd never been close to any of the girls in the dorms, never formed friendships with them. Though childish, it was amusing to have another woman to cover for. It only took me twenty years to gain this kind of relationship.

Chuckling to myself, I burrowed into her blankets and settled in to sleep.

Mikhala returned before the sun rose—far longer than 'a chime or two.' She crawled into bed with me, writhing in excitement, before throwing her hands over her face with a sigh.

"How long have you known him?" I asked, the blanket pulled up to my chin.

"Gaius? Almost as long as I've known Darrak." She stared at the ceiling with a smile. "Have you ever been in love, Avyanna?" She rolled, propping her chin. Her pale eyes sparkled with joy.

I bit my lip and shook my head. She didn't need to know about my struggles, and I didn't need someone condemning my relationships.

"I know that look, though! You've been smitten!" She smirked. "My money is on ol' one-eye."

I sighed, then shoved off the blankets to stand.

"Wait, Vy."

The shortened name jerked me to a stop, as if an iron grip clenched my heart. My chest grew far too tight—I couldn't breathe.

"Don't call me that," I whispered, glaring at the floor.

"Oi, look at me."

I pulled myself together and faced her.

She sat up, frowning. "If it bothers you, I won't. I didn't mean to bring up a sore topic."

"I—it's complicated."

"It always is." She offered a crisp nod in agreement. "In my country, Gaius would be killed, and I'd be shunned as an outcast. It can be complicated."

"Why?" Curiosity had me settling back on the blankets.

"He's already had a mate."

"Did she die?"

"She left him." She flopped backward, lifting her arm to cover her face. "In Caulden, that's the greatest insult. If your mate willingly walks away from you—you failed them. My father would duel Gaius for my honor. To our people, he's already marked by failure, and in their eyes, I would be doomed to misery."

"That's harsh." I didn't understand Caulden's culture, but they seemed passionate about everything.

"Aye." She laughed. "Good thing we're not acting on our feelings." After a moment's pause, she eyed me. "Have you?"

I bit my lip. "No."

I yearned to confide in someone who might understand my feelings. Elenor and Niehm wouldn't. I couldn't talk to Jamlin about it, or even Darrak. There'd been no one for me to confide in who would have even a semblance of understanding.

Besides Mikhala.

"He's my General," I said, letting myself fall on the bed beside her.

"It's not one-eye? I suppose the Dragon Lord is handsome in his own way–"

"No," I cut her off with a bitter laugh, "definitely not Ruveel. General Rafe Shadowslayer."

"Ah, that's a romance I can get behind."

"Why's that?" I chuckled.

"He's a *man*. The Dragon Lord is an overgrown boy. He toys with too many things, indecisive about what he wants."

"Rafe takes what he wants," I muttered, smiling at the ceiling.

"So, has he taken you?"

"Oi!"

I shoved her, and she giggled. We were acting like girls in the dorms. I scoffed and stared at the wooden rafters. "We're not so free with our affection here," I said. "To give yourself to someone—it's a commitment. You're promising your forever to that person."

"My people might be freer with their feelings, but our bodies are sacred. We don't share them like wild animals." She made a dramatic gesture with her hand.

"Well, what Rafe and I want isn't permitted. I was his soldier, and soldiers are not allowed to share a bed."

"And now that you're a Rider?"

"I'm not exactly a Rider." I rubbed my face in frustration. "It's not like we're stationed together, or will be. Dragons above, I'll fight for it when I'm at the front, but what more could we promise each other?"

Saying the words out loud felt like admitting defeat.

"The war isn't going anywhere. Even if Tizmet and I bonded enough to fight on the front, we'll be in different branches. We'll never see each other. He won't leave the ranks unless he's forced. It's not like he'd retire…" I trailed off, sudden realization pressing on my heart like a dead weight.

"One day at a time, girl."

My nose burned, and my vision blurred with tears. I flung my legs over the side of the bed and lurched to my feet. I rubbed my eyes as I walked over to the balcony.

"Thank you," she called, her voice softer than before. A sorrowful but understanding look graced her features.

My smile wavered. "You owe me."

"Aye, quickly now. Guard changes in less than a quarter of a chime."

Tizmet slept all night with her head on the rail of our balcony, waiting for my return. She flicked out her tongue as I scaled the wall, making my way back. When I reached the top, I peered over the courtyard below. Not seeing a single guard in the early morning light, I stepped inside. I stopped in the middle of my room and pressed the heels of my hands into my eyes.

Why had I believed Rafe and I had a chance? I fought against the tears and threaded my fingers through my hair, yanking on it. Before I was bonded, I entertained the idea of us sneaking around. Where there was a will, there was a way. After I had bonded Tizmet, I thought if we were both stationed at the front, we would find a way.

Just how plausible was that, though? How could a Rider maintain a relationship with a General who crossed behind enemy lines? If by some miracle they reassigned me to his Tennan, Tizmet couldn't sneak anywhere if she tried.

The idea was absurd.

"I've been such a fool." Emotions squeezed my throat, and I stumbled to my knees.

I'd been so in love with the idea of being in love—that someone might actually care for me. The repercussions were obvious—how had I not seen it?

I thought back to our fight right before I met Tizmet. He'd been pushing me away because he *understood*. He knew what I was asking, what I was demanding of our relationship, and knew he couldn't give it.

Then he fought for me, no doubt blinded by his own emotions.

Tears spilled over my cheeks, leaving blazing hot trails of betrayal.

This was why he wanted distance. He needed me to think with my brain and not my heart. He knew what was right, and what made sense—and that wasn't us.

I sobbed, covering my face with my hands. My heart felt like it was being torn out of me, crushed into tiny pieces. Had he known I would come to my senses? Every move he made was calculated. Was this some new lesson from him, to rouse me from my childish love?

Tizmet crooned, and a fresh wave of sobs wracked my body. I didn't even have a proper dragon to support me. I had no one in this—no one who would understand this pain.

Pulling myself up, I staggered to the bed and fell onto it. Curling into a ball, I cried as the sun came up, bringing with it a new day. A new day I wanted nothing to do with.

CHAPTER 21

I stared at the wall as a knock sounded, interrupting my grief. I was a mess, with tears staining my red, puffy cheeks. Tizmet rested her head near my bed, sensing my sorrow, but made no move to get closer.

"Come in."

The revelations I had were mine alone, and no one else needed to know about them.

When the way cracked open, Darrak peered inside, giving me a harsh frown. He entered, quill and parchment in hand, then shut the door in the servant's face.

"I would say it's a fine morn, but you look like you've had a rough night." He chose his words with care.

Not trusting myself to speak, I shrugged and squinted at the writing tools, posing my unvoiced question.

"I'm to fill out a report on you and your dragon. I thought I'd get your thoughts before I sent it off to Dragon Lord Ruveel." He set his things on the table near my bed. Turning to me with a glare, he crossed his arms. "Though, more importantly, I'd like to know where you snuck off to last night."

I scoffed and ran a hand through my short hair. When Mikhala mentioned he checked in on her, I hadn't considered he'd do the same for me.

"Here I was thinking Mik would be the one to keep an eye on. Turns out it was you." He glanced at Tizmet. "You've at least gotten closer to her if you can order her to stay like a dog while you go traipsing about."

"She's not a dog."

"I never said she was. I insinuated you treated her as such." His brow arched in challenge. "To be honest, I don't have a care in all of Rinmoth where you sneak off to. I do, however, care that if someone else checked in on you, they might note that you defied direct orders to remain in your quarters."

Sighing, I dropped my gaze, knowing that Darrak wasn't attacking me. He was looking out for me, and there was no reason to lash out at him. The emptiness inside me resulted from my cry this morning. It had nothing to do with him.

"Don't let me, or anyone else, catch you out," he said with a resigned sigh. "Ruveel will not be so forgiving."

Pulling the lone stool to the small table, he sat and took the quill in his hand. "Now tell me of you and your dragon on this past trip."

After Darrak left, a servant brought in a late first meal, or perhaps my midday meal. I wasn't sure. I was finishing up the soup and bread when Mikhala barged in.

"Knock much?" I asked, shaking my head.

"We're sisters now. Sisters don't knock." She plopped on the bed. Her eyes bounced between my food and me, and she practically danced in her seat.

"What is it?"

She beamed, reaching into her vest to hand me a small piece of paper. I took it and flipped it over.

"It's blank."

"Aye! Free for you to write whatever you wish." She wrapped her arms about herself, hugging tight.

"I don't understand," I said slowly.

"I've secured passage for a note to be delivered for you." She grinned and leaned forward, lowering her voice in a conspiratorial whisper. "In a secret manner, of course."

Suspicion curled deep in my belly. "Who would I want to write a secret note to?" I drew out, studying her face.

"Who? Your General!" She threw her hands in the air like I was the dumbest person she ever met.

"No." I set the paper on the table and returned to my soup.

"No? Wait—what?"

"I said no. I don't need to write him." I took a large bite of bread so I wouldn't have to say more.

"Oh—oh, she's conflicted. Ugh." She stood and snatched the parchment. "I told you. One step at a time. Don't give up on this simply because of what makes sense in your mind. Love makes a way."

"No," I snapped around my mouthful, "I've tried to make my way too many times."

"You're giving up now? You realize what that means? You're giving up on *him*. Don't think a General comes out to secretly watch every soldier leave. I saw that look you gave him. You thought of something last night and are acting on it without giving him a chance."

"He wanted to send me away." I clenched my fists on my lap. "He said we needed space, and now I know why."

"He watched you leave, Avyanna! I might not know him like you do, but I would guarantee it was as hard for him as it was for you. I'm aware of the Shadow Slayer's reputation. People could drop dead around him and he wouldn't bat an eye. But when you left with Darrak and I, he *watched*. He wasn't pushing you away."

I averted my stare, refusing to meet her gaze. We didn't have a chance. There was no way it would ever work out between us. I had to accept it.

"Oi, listen to me."

She waved the paper in my face, and I scowled at her persistence.

"Write a note, a simple question. From what I know of him, he won't reply. But you're different, and I'm curious to see if he'll break the habit... aren't you? If you get no response, well then, you have your answer. You're his soldier, nothing more. If he does, though..." She trailed off, wagging her eyebrows suggestively.

I growled and snatched the paper, glaring at it.

She was right. If he didn't write back, either he was too busy or too worried about being caught. In that case, I could rest easy with my decision to give up on us. If he replied... that proved he would take risks for me as well. It would mean he wasn't really pushing me away, but as he said, giving me space to think on my own.

"Do you have a quill?"

As we rode out the next day, I looked up to the bright cloudless sky and cursed myself.

Remember the Winter Solstice?

I heaved a sigh. Could I have been any more unoriginal? Why couldn't I think of anything else to say? Something dramatic, something dark and alluring. No, I had to ask a nonsensical question. It might have been silly, but that night in Hamsforth still made me flush with warmth. It was the first time I realized what power I had over Rafe, what kind of response my flirting elicited. A smile crept over my face as I remembered his cursing when I stepped out of my trousers and huddled in his cloak.

Mikhala was humming to herself, dancing in her saddle. Moony had one ear cocked back, listening. She told me not to sign it. No names were better in case it was intercepted, but she was confident it wouldn't be.

I wrote something that required a reply—a push to get him to respond. I was nervous it would leave me with nothing but heartache. Still, I wrote it because deep in my heart I wanted to hope. I needed to believe he cared enough about me—that we could make it work.

In all reality, I couldn't see it. With the war, and our responsibilities, there was no logical outcome where we ended up together.

We rode southeast. The E'or mountain chain broke into two ridges at its tail in the south. The locals near there called it the Teeth of E'or. A fitting name, really, due to the horrors that plagued them. It was not a kind place to live.

Our destination was just north of the Teeth, to a hamlet where a woman stayed. Jevelyn of Tikal. The reason behind her five-hundred gold bounty was her notorious anger issues—and murderous tendencies.

Darrak told me she left a trail of blood and bodies in her wake. Her sketch made her seem a slip of a girl, but the artist captured a malicious gleam in her eyes. I was curious to see if she lived up to the depiction. Mikhala said the woman had seven murders to account for, but there were bound to be unknowns.

Tracking the bounties with Darrak and Mikhala was interesting. Not only were they great people, easy to talk to, and eager to have fun—they were genuine. I opened up, and we talked about everything.

Of course, I never spoke of my feelings for Rafe out loud. That was a topic I shied away from.

Darrak had been angry, but resigned when I relayed the attacks at the barracks. He knew Victyr would come for me eventually and warned the Corporals of it before he left. I told him General Rafe rescued me, and he nodded his understanding.

I learned he served under Rafe for a few years when he was stationed at the front. He made it longer than most under his command because he was adaptable. Darrak was a flexible soldier, one who would do what was asked of him no matter the order. He learned to hone his ability to blend in and perfect his stealth.

He spoke highly of Rafe and recalled stories of the absurd things he would do. How Rafe would take his branch of soldiers to rescue others captured behind enemy lines. With infiltration, Rafe's cunning was unmatched by the other Generals. Rafe never simply fought on the front—he attacked the enemy from behind.

We made the four-day journey to the hamlet, Crooktree. Tizmet grew more and more at ease with me, and when Mikhala and Darrak left, I determined to attempt reaching through our bond again.

I rested against her, seeking warmth. Unseasonable cold and wet chilled the day. The rain created puddles everywhere, evidence of its continuous presence for the past two days. Tizmet was irritable, and I blamed it on the weather.

I pulled my oiled cloak tighter about me as a deluge poured down on us, nearly obscuring Boulder, who stood against the treeline, miserable. I took a deep breath and closed my eyes.

With cautious, slow care, I cracked open the door to our bond.

'Tizmet,' I whispered.

No pain greeted me, no shocking retaliation. I sensed her presence, as if she waited on the other side.

'Avyanna.' Her deep, raspy voice replied just as quietly.

I released a breath of relief and let my head fall against her scales.

'I'm sorry.'

There was a chance she wouldn't understand what those words meant, so I pushed the feeling of remorse after it.

I opened my eyes as she made a clicking sound deep in her throat. She curled her body so that her massive head settled on the wet ground, facing me. A breath of hot air rushed over me.

'Tizmet sorry.' Her words were hushed and soft—as soft as a dragon's internal voice could sound.

I gave her a small smile and reached out to stroke her muzzle. *'We're both pretty messed up, aren't we?'* I asked, leaning back. *'We make a great pair, Avyanna the Outcast, and Tizmet the Wild.'*

'Tizmet wild,' she agreed.

I chuckled and shivered against the chill. It really was a miserable day. She blinked and shifted her side, pushing me away. I gave her space. No anger came from her. Perhaps I had made her uncomfortable.

She shuffled behind me, then used her tail to tuck me back against her side. I quickly complied, eager to please, and quite cold. She blinked lazily, and I glanced up, realizing I was no longer being rained on.

Tizmet rested her wing away from her body—above me. She protected me from the rain and tucked me against her warm side as a mother hen would do.

Happiness pricked my heart, and I let out a breathless laugh.

We were going to be fine.

CHAPTER 22

The weather broke and Tizmet and I continued to get along. She communicated as best she could. If words failed her, she pushed emotions or images at me, conveying her message. It was the most relaxing three days I spent with her. There was no fear of another Rider or crowd, or anything else to make her tick. It was simply me and her.

And Boulder, who was content to graze and give us bored looks when we talked about him.

'Tizmet hungry. Horse good.'

I laughed and patted her side as she studied him.

'You can't eat him. Who would I ride back?' I squinted at her with a sly smile. *'You?'*

'Tizmet not carry... things?' She looked down at me in question.

Although she used more words, the proper usage still had room for improvement. If I kept talking with her, she would pick up through my verbiage. She couldn't exactly go to school to learn the common tongue.

'Aye, you don't carry things.' I conceded. *'Other dragons carry their Riders, though.'*

'Other dragons are horses.' She snorted, giving Boulder a pointed look.

I laughed and shoved at her. I was pretty sure that was an insult.

'Do you want me to hunt with you?' I gestured to the thick forest southwest of us.

After lifting her head, she stretched out her neck and pulled her lips past her teeth. With a flick of her tongue, she sampled the air. She pushed her senses through the bond, and I wrinkled my nose in confusion and disgust.

The scent of earth mingled with the fragrance of stone and the greenness of plants. The essence lingered on my palate—a mix of musty dirt and dust.

'*Food.*'

In the image she sent, a herd of plant-eating animals roamed together. They were plump beasts with a set of stubby horns on their heads. Despite their short legs, they moved with surprising agility. Their backs rose to meet the sky covered in thick layers of fur.

'*Cows?*' I asked. The creatures were unfamiliar—something between a cow and a deer.

'*Food.*' She stretched her wings.

I snorted and stepped from her side. '*Go then, have fun,*' I replied, walking over to my crossbow. I'd at least get some shooting in while she was away.

I checked my bolts and string. While looking around for the best spot to shoot, I hesitated. Tizmet was studying me with a strange look in her eyes. I sensed her emotions—she wasn't scared, but she was nervous. Her claws kneaded the ground.

'*Avyanna... stay?*'

'*Do you want me to come?*' I asked, lowering the crossbow.

She raised her lip and bared her fangs, frustrated. Flicking out her tongue, she tried again. '*Avyanna... no leave.*'

I smiled and relaxed. '*No. I won't leave.*'

She snorted and shook out her large wings. Near one hundred paces from tip to tip, if not more, they engulfed the camp in shadow. She crouched low before throwing herself into the air. Her wings pumped down hard, lifting her giant body higher. She pulled herself into the sky, not wasting time hovering about.

She shrank into the horizon, flying north. I hoped whatever herd she was after wasn't too far. We'd been down that road before, and I crossed my fingers, hoping she knew the limitations of our bond.

I rode Boulder at a canter, trying my best to brave distance-shooting from horseback. It was hard enough getting the brute to keep moving when I dropped the reins. As Mikhala mentioned, 'Boulder' was a fitting name for the beast. Fear clenched my heart tight and my hands were clammy as I lifted my crossbow. He stepped into a dip, causing my feet to rattle. I gasped and clutched the reins again.

'*Why ride horse and shoot?*' Tizmet asked, watching me from camp as she gnawed on a large bone.

'*Because I won't always be shooting in ideal situations,*' I said, trying to keep my frustration from slipping across the bond. '*Sometimes, I'll need to shoot from horseback—or another back.*'

I gritted my teeth together and fumbled for the reins. Pulling the crossbow up, I timed my shot with Boulder's gait and let loose.

'*That was terrible.*' I groaned. '*I miss Thunderbolt.*'

'*What is... Thunderbolt?*' she asked.

'*My old horse—a pigou. The one I had when we met.*' I sent her an image of him, and her batting him through the air.

'*Get another,*' she replied without remorse.

I sighed and dismounted, pulling my bolt from the dirt. Using the target as a mounting block, I jumped onto Boulder's back. At one hundred paces out, I tried again.

'*I can't just say I need a special horse.*'

A fraction of my irritation slipped over the bond. I loosed, missing by two paces. Growling, I steered Boulder toward the log.

'*Why?*'

'*Because I'm not special!*' I snapped, without thinking.

My frustration grew stronger with each failed attempt. I could shoot in any other situation—rain, wind, upside down. Put me on a horse and I was worse than a child with a toy bow.

'*Avyanna special.*'

'*No, I'm not!*' I pushed my anger across the bond, letting her know I was upset.

I dropped from Boulder's back and snatched the bolt from the dirt. A shadow loomed over me and I turned to gaze up at Tizmet.

'*Avyanna special.*' Her voice was iron—firm and unyielding.

I huffed, heading for my horse. '*No, I'm not. I'm a human, just like anyone else.*'

She growled and nosed him. He stumbled away from us, looking at her as though she were an addle-brained mare.

'*Tizmet did not fly here for human.*' She bared her teeth, lowering her large flaming eye to my face. '*Tizmet left Sky Trees for Avyanna. Avyanna special.*'

'*How?*' My knuckles popped as I gripped my crossbow and bolt in a painful grasp. '*What makes me special?*'

'*Avyanna is.*'

'*But why? Why me?!*'

I was acting out of turn, and I tried to calm myself. We'd been doing so well. I didn't want to ruin it now.

'*Come,*' she ordered, plodding back to camp.

I twisted my lips and heaved a sigh. Grabbing the reins, I followed.

I removed Boulder's tack as Tizmet settled on the ground, studying me intently. I put away my weapons, then headed over to her. She shifted as I approached, revealing her side. I sighed and pressed my back against her, sliding to sit. She wrapped her tail around me, then peered down.

'*Tizmet live in Sky Trees,*' she started.

She sent images of soaring through trees bigger than even the palace. They were behemoths—the smallest branches were almost as thick as she was. She showed me the blue dragon she mated with, and different clutches of eggs.

'*Tizmet lost much.*'

I glanced up as the sense of doom and sorrow filled her. She craned her head toward the sky and bared her teeth as loss spilled over the bond.

She sent images of creatures with skull heads climbing the trees. The monsters had two arms and legs and moved like humans, but their eyes...

They were like Rafe's.

They reflected light like an animal's. Swirling silver and gray sparkled from the depths beneath their masks. She screamed a warning as they approached her nest.

'*Bad magic. Rotten,*' she said, flicking her tongue out as if she tasted something sour. '*Tizmet scared. Tizmet try to fight.*'

She darted through the branches, lashing at them. After she dropped three, more climbed into their place. She perched on her nest, above her brood, and panted. I felt her hesitation to use her fire. It would burn the tree down and she couldn't save all her eggs.

A Shadow separated itself from the others, walking along the branch, coming closer. She snarled and spit at him. He fashioned his mask to resemble a dragon skull—cut and molded from several smaller bones.

Rafe's words came back to me. Shadows wore the skull of their greatest kill. The Shamans who controlled a dragon wore their bones.

The Shaman strode along the wide branch. She roared, and he held his hands up, gloved palms toward her. Her gaze snagged on his silver eyes. At that moment, she couldn't move—couldn't breathe. Inside, she raged and fought against it. She pulled something in her memory, as if tugging on a string that bound her to the earth. An energy blazed through her mind. Her only intent was to look away from the Shaman's eyes.

Beneath the mask, a smile split his dark face.

Her limbs moved of their own accord, putting distance between her and her clutch. She shook with the effort of fighting against each motion. She struggled to keep her legs in place, to defend her unborn.

'*Rotten dead took Tizmet's eggs.*'

She bowed her head. Both shame and sorrow rolled off her in waves. My heart cracked. I pulled her hurt to me, tucking it away, sending her comfort in return.

The pain was so exquisite—the loss of life she brought into the world, the life she was meant to protect—ripped from her as she watched.

They took her eggs one by one, until all twenty-three were in packs, carried down the tree. Her eyes were locked on the Shaman, but she sensed their evil magic seeping and wrapping around each egg. Fury burned within her. She raged in her mind, demanding her legs move—her mouth to open so she could engulf them all in flame.

The Shaman stumbled back, losing his footing. He barked something and Tizmet felt his control snap. She shook her head and roared, lunging at him.

Pain radiated through her as she collided with an invisible barrier. With fangs bared, she tried again. She opened her maw and slid her forked tongue over her stones, but her oil stayed inside her vent. She snapped her jaw shut with a clack and tried again, but no fire came.

The Shaman laughed as she threw her head into the air and wailed. Foul magic bound her, preventing her from hurting him. Snarling, she dropped off the branch into a steep dive, heading for her eggs. Whatever protected the Shaman also protected the others. In a frenzy, she swarmed them, trying to attack each one, to no avail.

The Shadows laughed and jeered as she flew, snapping her teeth above their heads. Rage burned within her. She was a dragon. None could rival her strength or outwit her cunning. She was the greatest predator.

And they mocked her.

Beside me, she keened, bearing the pain of it all. Dragons were proud. It wasn't only the loss of her eggs—the ridicule was too much.

In her memory, she tore herself from the Shadows, pulling high in the sky. She flew until her muscles burned, until her wings gave out and she crashed to the hot sand. Her rage and her anger erupted in a deafening roar. She whimpered and shook her head as if to rid herself of the dark magic that rooted itself there.

'Tizmet lost eggs. Tizmet lost many.'

Memories flitted through my mind of all the clutches she laid. Some were stolen by the Shadows, and some she crushed in terror when she sensed their presence. She moved her nests countless times, tried hiding different places, but they always found her.

Buried deep within her was the small sliver of hope that one day she would lay a clutch and they would hatch. As long as that blue dragon lived, and she mated with him, there was a chance her young would survive.

That spark died when she found the Shadows pulling organs from his carcass.

As Tizmet pushed the memory, a sense of despair gripped her heart. He was a large beast, bigger than her. Black blood marred his glittering navy-indigo scales.

His turquoise eyes had been removed. They were lying on an oiled blanket. Piece by piece, they carved up his body like a butchered pig.

Tears trickled down my face as Tizmet's total and complete loss of hope rolled through me. Desperate, she swooped down on the Shadows but could not hurt them—just as before. She wailed and screamed as they took him apart.

She shivered. *'Tizmet alone.'*

I blinked through the haze of tears and settled against her. *'I'm here.'*

She arched her neck, bringing her head above me and peering down.

'Tizmet flew far.'

She sent her desperation, her terror and fear. I shrank away from the strength of the emotions. She pushed the memory of opening that door in her mind again, not the bond, but something else. She grabbed onto that intangible thread that tied her to the earth, the thin strand of energy that connected all beings—then yanked on it.

With all her mental strength, with all her anguish, with all her rage, she hauled on that thread. It seemed to shift. It moved, pulling her northeast. A sense of purpose overrode her sorrow, and she roared her victory.

She flew day and night, stopping only to eat or when her body demanded rest. She traveled over land and water, following that thread of energy. It brought her to a cold forest, and there it remained, grounded. Tizmet dug at the earth, trying to get to the end. She yanked on the thread again, but it remained rooted in place.

She raised her head to the sky and roared.

It was the place she would eventually find me and Rafe. The place she bonded me.

'Magic led you to me,' I mused.

'Avyanna special. Tizmet... need Avyanna.'

For the first time, I felt like I *truly* understood her. I brushed the tears from my cheeks and peeked up. She suffered so much. I often thought of her as an animal, controlled by her instincts, yet she *felt*. She felt so much. Every emotion I had was amplified ten times in her. What would make me mad would enrage her.

Tizmet lowered her head to lip at my hair, sorrow and love spilling over the bond. She was as confused as I was. This was as new to her as it was to me. She didn't know what she was doing, or understand my actions, or what motivated me. She simply wanted *me*.

In her despair, she drew on magic, and it answered. It brought her to me.

I reached up and held her rough-scaled jaw. Resting my temple against her lips, I slipped through the bond to comfort her.

'I'm here.'

CHAPTER 23

The following day, I was determined to figure out how to aim accurately on horseback. There were a couple of factors as to why I struggled. The most notable—my unease being so far from the ground.

Riding Thunderbolt was simpler. He was shorter. If I fell, I might not break a bone. He had a smoother gait as well, allowing me to shoot with greater accuracy. He also anticipated my movements in a way no other horse had.

Boulder was a good mount. Steady and loyal—but average. I began to think I needed a pigou or I would never be able to shoot from horseback.

While struggling to aim through Boulder's canter, Tizmet announced Mikhala's return.

'The one with braided fire returns.' She lifted her head and flicked out her tongue.

Following her gaze, I saw Mikhala riding toward us like a wild cat was on her tail. Nerves prickled along my skin. Was she in danger? I kicked Boulder into a gallop, rushing to meet her. Moony ran with his legs stretched out in a ground-eating gallop. Mikhala pressed against him, riding his withers, making herself as small as possible. Her braids flew behind her, whipping like fire.

'Pleasure—she runs for pleasure.' Tizmet hummed the words in the same tone she used while she spoke of flying.

I smiled and pulled up on the reins, letting Moony close the distance to us.

"Avyanna!" She threw her hands up. "I've missed you!"

Moony skidded to a walk, bouncing her on his shoulders. She beamed as if I was a long-lost friend.

"Hail, Mikhala." I chuckled.

They sidled up beside Boulder, and she reached over, pulling me into a hug. I shoved her back.

"Where's Darrak?"

"Oi, already asking about him? I feel like you haven't missed me at all." She pouted, then smiled, twisting in the saddle.

Darrak rode into view, leading a donkey behind him. I squinted at the bounty slung over it and laughed.

"Could he not find a horse?"

"The only horse for sale spooked every time we plopped the body over it. The donkey doesn't care. We were in a hamlet, Avyanna," she said, rolling her eyes. "There weren't many options."

I studied the motionless form as unease pinched at my stomach. "The... body?" I repeated.

"Aye. When she realized she was done for, she took her own life."

Something dark twisted in my gut. I couldn't imagine taking a life, but for someone to feel so cornered, they took their own? I shuddered.

"No worries. I still get the bounty bonus. We're on a streak!" She pumped her fist in the air.

"Hail, Avyanna." Darrak greeted as his bay trotted close.

"Hail." I couldn't pry my eyes from the limp body draped across the donkey's back.

"Let's pack up quickly. I'd like to leave before it starts to stink."

My gaze snapped to his. They treated this woman with such coldness—as if she wasn't a living being with feelings and emotions just hours ago. They treated her like a prize.

"Oi. Wipe that look off your face." Mikhala gave me a fierce glare. "We didn't kill her, and had we known what she was doing, we would have stopped her. This is our way of life. Dead or alive, we bring in the bounties."

"Do you disapprove, Avyanna?" Darrak asked, tilting his head.

"I—you're treating her like nothing more than a trophy," I murmured, gaze trailing to the limp form.

"She's not," Mikhala snapped. "If you want me to relay the stories of those whose lives she stole, of the futures she robbed, I'll be happy to. She was a human, but she was the lowest kind. She'll get a burial, but she doesn't deserve an inkling of my respect."

"Or yours," Darrak added.

I frowned but nodded, returning to camp to clean up.

The ride back was uneventful. Darrak kept the body wrapped in the blanket to keep the flies off. I pulled my hood up and Tizmet flew high as we entered King's Wall.

Spring was giving way to summer, and all the citizens seemed to enjoy the warmth. They bustled about in sun hats and sandals. The vendors sold fresh produce, which people clamored for. Little boys tore around, chasing a ball of rags. I had to pull Boulder to a stop more than once to let one pass.

I gritted my teeth and ignored the whispers about the dragon looming above. Tizmet reached out curiously, sensing my irritation.

'They'll never forget you ate the squire's arm,' I told her with resignation.

'Bad taste,' she replied, pushing a sense of repulsion.

I scoffed, a smile tugging at my lips under the shadow of my hood. She lost her temper and took a man's arm, and all she had to say was he tasted bad.

We approached the bounty house, and I dismounted to stand near the entrance. Darrak and Mikhala carried the body in as I held the door open. Citizens didn't even bat an eye at the corpse being hauled inside.

I peered through the murky glass to watch as Gaius leaned over the edge of his counter. Mikhala rested against it, propping a hip out as Darrak removed the blanket from Jevelyn's face. Gaius spoke as he brought out a stack of papers. Sorting through them, he mentioned something to Mikhala that had her studying her fur-wrapped boots as if they were the most interesting things. He snuck a glance at her and a smile spread over his features.

They were smitten.

I shook my head at their antics, turning to rest my back on the wood siding. They were full-grown adults, acting like children. It was adorable and embarrassing. Rafe would never act that way—at least not in front of others. He was excessively cautious in revealing any vulnerabilities to others. Not that I would ever allow myself to be his weakness, but if anyone knew about us, they could use me to exploit him.

I would not serve as a liability to him. Whatever happened with us, I would not make him regret his feelings toward me—if he still felt for me.

Sagging against the wall, I watched Boulder. His placid gaze shifted around, disinterested in the monotony of life.

"Oi!"

Mikhala skipped out with a bright smile, and I squinted, wondering if she would ask me to cover for her again. She laughed at my expression and jumped on Moony. Darrak shook his head at her antics and mounted his bay. We followed as he led the way to the palace.

The staff completely repaired the balcony's railing. It looked as if it had never crumbled under the rage of a dragon. Tizmet landed in the room and settled herself as a servant girl readied my bath. After disrobing, I tossed my soiled clothes aside, then sank into the glorious hot water.

I barely got out and pulled the dress over my head when someone burst into my room. I yanked the fabric down, ready to tear into whoever dared enter without knocking.

Mikhala smirked.

Tizmet flicked her tongue out, curious. I waved my hand at the servant girl, who stood in silence, mutely horrified by Tizmet's presence. With my dismissal, she ran out of the room.

"Yes?" I prompted, crossing my arms.

"Consider this full payment for covering for me." She whipped out a small envelope from her vest.

I stared at it, frozen in shock.

"I can't." My heart revived, then took off at a breakneck pace as I gawked at her.

She bounced on the tip of her toes. "Open it!"

My hands trembled as I took it from her. It was sealed, but unmarked. "How do you know it's from him?" I breathed, running my thumb over the seal.

"Do you doubt me?" She tilted her head. "I have my ways. Now open it!"

I held my breath and slipped a finger under the seal to break it.

It was a single sentence. Just one, but it spoke to my poor, battered heart more than any book could have.

I remember the floor.

I closed my eyes and smiled so big it hurt.

"Is it good? Let me see!"

Before I could stop her, Mikhala ripped the parchment out of my grasp. I growled, and she danced away, jumping over the bed. I chased her, but she opened it, then halted with a frown.

"He remembers the floor? What exactly did you ask? How is this a testament of his undying love?"

I huffed, holding my palm out. "Give it to me."

"Touchy! You can have it." She sighed dramatically and handed it over. "I expected something juicier."

I folded it with care and tucked it in my dress, over my heart.

She scoffed. "It means that much to you?"

"Maybe I'll tell you someday," I said with a teasing smile.

I traveled with Darrak and Mikhala as summer wore on. Tizmet's usage of words became more extensive and her level of comfort in my presence continued to increase.

She had a dry sense of humor but, for the most part, listened when I asked something of her. If she refused, and I pressured her, she closed off. She balked at being commanded. She enjoyed pushing me around, though. But when I pushed back, she didn't care for it.

I made a deal with Mikhala to cover for her for two chimes every night while we stayed at the palace. In return, she secured the notes between Rafe and I. Tizmet let me know well in advance if Darrak was coming, giving me time to make it to my room. He tried to be sporadic and not keep a schedule, but he was no match for Tizmet's senses.

Rafe and I sent a single sentence each time. No names, places or dates. Nothing that could trace back to us, but one-liners that we knew were from each other.

Remember our first fight?

Remember the lake?

I remember the ogling.

I remember getting the better of you.

We were so far apart, and I missed him terribly, but those simple notes kept coming, assuring me he cared.

The Summer Solstice came, and with it Hatching Day. We were conveniently in the palace, awaiting Darrak's next task. There were still whispers of Tizmet's violence, but they quieted throughout our frequent visits. The servants were less terrified of her and always respected her space.

"Come with me!" Mikhala jumped up and down in my room. "Let's go exploring!"

I laughed, shaking my head. "Why?"

"Because we're sisters. It's what sisters do. They go out and have fun on festival nights!" She twirled in a circle, dancing with herself.

I scoffed, sitting on my stool. "Braid my hair, and I'll go with you."

"Yes!"

"Does Darrak know?"

"Aye, he's freed us for the night, under the condition that you keep Tizzy under control." She spun on her heel, facing the dragon. "Hear that?"

'I am not deaf,' Tizmet said.

I smiled at her resting form. It didn't matter if she was sleeping, part of her was always present and aware.

'No eating people,' I teased.

'I shall be a silent shadow.'

'Tell me you'll fly. You're a rather obvious shadow, no matter how silent you are.'

She snorted and shifted to a more comfortable position.

Mikhala plaited the strands tightly against my scalp in the style her people wore. They were similar to Jamlin's, though woven with four sections, not three. It had grown to a less-masculine length. It was terrible—not long, but not short. Part of me thought about trimming it, simply because it was easier to care for.

My hair had been the one thing I found beautiful about myself, and I wanted that sense of self-confidence back. When I looked in the mirror, I saw a petite woman with no remarkable features. My skin was pale, my eyes a vivid green, but my white hair set me apart. My appearance was—mediocre.

Mikhala was a woman of exceptional beauty. She was striking with her red hair, full lips and high cheekbones. Her smile was bright and contagious, and her bust and hips had most men staring.

"Done!" She stepped back, admiring her work with a grin.

I examined my reflection. Four braids ran down my head from my temple to the nape of my neck, tucking all my white hair in neat rows.

Tizmet roused herself, stretching like a cat. I grabbed my coin purse and fastened the strap, letting it settle at the front of my dress alongside my push dagger. I pulled on a belt with my bandit breaker, strapping it in place.

Mikhala nodded her approval. "You can never be too careful."

"Aye."

We left the room with the midday sun at its brightest. Tizmet took to the air, soaring so high she was naught but the size of a bird. She drifted in and out of the clouds, and I sensed the comfort and pleasure flying brought her. She wouldn't be bored, at least.

'Go. Have fun,' she urged. 'Eat good food.'

That was always at the top of her priority list.

We spent the afternoon walking through King's Wall, enjoying the street food and each other's company. We laughed at the jesters and watched a few dramatic plays. Musicians performed and swordsmen sparred. Mikhala took part in a duel with wooden swords and won a sweetloaf, which she shared with me. I would have participated as well, but they had no wooden spears.

She tried her luck at breaking a wild stallion from the Sands and was thrown like everyone else. Seeing her fly through the air with her red hair waving like a banner behind her was something I would remember for ages to come.

We perused the vendor's goods, most of them having a connection with either Hatching Day or Summer Solstice. Leather bags were crafted with dragons or bright suns engraved on them. Pastries were made to look like dragon eggs or wildflowers. Fresh fruit was cut into beautiful bouquets.

I enjoyed my time with her. This was something I didn't get to do when I was young. I'd been too focused on becoming First Chosen. Forming relationships didn't feel necessary. Yet, as I laughed with Mikhala at a talented dog balancing four bones on his nose, I realized my heart needed this. Being with her was like being with—well, a sister. We were open and honest and never hid anything.

She accepted me for who I was. Even my complicated relationship with Rafe. She had her own drama to deal with—she didn't need to judge mine.

The sun dipped low, but the festivities went on. Mikhala tugged me through the crowd as the tenth chime rang, darting through people.

"Pardon me! Excuse me! Begging your pardon!" I called as she pulled me along.

She laughed as we burst into a small alley. Musicians played on stringed instruments, and the space was alive with dancing. A cart in the corner served drinks, and crates were littered about for people to sit. A quick scan of the crowd told me exactly why we were here.

Gaius loomed above them all, his gaze planted on Mikhala. I couldn't help but scoff and shake my head, though a smile lingered on my lips. I let go of her hand and shoved her off. She spun to face me, giving me a wide grin, dancing backward toward him. She swayed her hips, eyes laughing, and pretended to run in place. I laughed and sat on a vacant crate to rub my sore feet.

She twirled carelessly through the crowd, spinning with her arms thrown wide. She matched the music's quick pace, bringing her closer to Gaius. His big hands caught her around the waist, and he lifted her with ease. He threw her once, muscles bulging with the action as he spun her to face him. She gazed at him with breathless joy, and he smiled up at her. She kicked, and he lowered her to the ground.

The giant danced with her, moving his bulk as fast as she did. From what I'd seen of him, he was playful, just like Mikhala. They were good for each other.

'He's a strong warrior.' Tizmet approved.

I felt her presence glide over us, her wings barely a whisper among the festival's clamor.

'It takes more than strength to make a decent partner,' I replied. *'Mik cares about her family. They won't accept him.'*

'So she will find another suitable mate,' Tizmet said with a mental shrug. To her, it was that simple.

A sad smile spread over my face as Gaius playfully danced with her between two buildings—out of sight of most onlookers. He spun her one last time, and she settled her back against the wall. She reached for his jaw and pulled him to her. His body moved against her, protecting her from anyone's view.

'She's doomed.' I rubbed at my sore feet. My sandals weren't meant for all this running around. I was used to riding on horseback for most of the day.

'Doomed?' Tizmet asked.

'Aye. She's trapped herself. She cares for him too much. If she tries to let him go and find another, her heart will hurt. If she accepts him and takes him as a mate, she would have to reject her family. She's trapped between two painful choices.'

'Then she can make a new family with him.'

'It's not always that easy.'

A heavy sense of sorrow weighed on my heart for her. *'Here, families are everything. It's common for several generations to reside in one household. In Caulden, family is even more important. They live or die by each other's choices. She'd be separating herself from her home, her culture and her people.'*

I felt Tizmet's confusion and laughed. Trying to explain human dynamics to her was always a chore.

Someone approached my left—a man with dark hair and sparkling blue eyes. He was beautiful in the way that young men could sometimes be. The kind that knew how handsome they were and perfected their smiles in mirrors.

His mouth lifted in a crooked grin, and he held out his palm. I stared at it as the music played, thinking of the last time I danced. I glanced back at Gaius, who had Mikhala's arms wrapped around him, slipping under his tunic. Shaking my head, I took the boy's hand and stood.

There was no harm in a dance.

I moved wildly, keeping tempo with the song. Someone brought a drum and beat along with the music. I giggled and twirled alongside him, breaking away and clapping. We snapped our hands to our hips and beat a frantic rhythm with our feet. I beamed as he picked up the pace, and I stumbled, trying to keep up.

He laughed and caught me, righting me so I could continue. His eyes sparkled with mirth. I wanted to enjoy this moment, and not think of anything else. My body swayed, carried with the melody, and I let my mind go silent.

When the music stopped, we broke away, panting.

His gaze landed on me, and he laughed, shaking his head. "You dance better than anyone I've met!"

I gasped for breath and leaned against the building. "Do you flatter all women with such words?" I scoffed with a playful smirk.

"Only the pretty ones." His tone softened.

He wore a smile that said he was interested, but I was only interested in a dance, nothing more.

"Thank you for the dance." I kept my features kind, but my dismissal clear. "I bid you goodnight."

"You didn't come with a man."

"Who's to say I need one?"

"Could be a dangerous place." He leaned against the wall beside me. "A girl like you, all alone."

I glanced at where Gaius and Mikhala had been, and sure enough, they were gone.

"Is that a threat?" I asked, facing him. I was here for dancing—for myself, not for anyone else.

"No, no." He rubbed the nape of his neck, peering at me from under his lashes. "I was simply making an observation."

My grin turned bitter. "Thank you for pointing that out to me. I should head back to the palace now."

Inside, I berated myself for speaking so harshly. I was here to have fun, not let my prickly soldier-side out.

"Palace?" He choked the word out.

"Aye, it's where the Dragon Riders stay." I pinned him with a dark look. "Even the man-eating dragons."

He went as white as a sheet and took a small step away. I turned on my heel and left.

Tizmet flew over the buildings, just low enough that one could feel the wind from her wings. *'Do you toy with him?'* Mirth laced her voice.

'Aye. It would be good for him to learn not to say such silly things.'

I pressed through the crowds, taking my time, enjoying the sights. I trusted Mikhala to be safe. If she was with Gaius, no harm would befall her. If she made a mistake, that was on her conscience, not mine. She was an adult.

'Should I make myself known?' she asked as she flew lazy circles above.

'No, I don't want to damage your reputation any more.'

Gems glittered from the jeweler's stall as I passed. My gaze snagged on the bones carved with delicate details.

'I hardly think that removing a limb damaged my reputation. I am to be feared. People should bow before me.'

'You're looking for the word 'respect.' I laughed across the bond. *'People should respect you.'*

I felt her grimace at the common tongue and all its words.

For the next chime, I wandered through the thinning crowds, making my way back. As I entered the courtyard, Tizmet landed and flicked her tongue out, sniffing at me.

'I've not changed since I left with Mik.'

'Such small beings as you often misplace limbs.' She arched her neck.

I smiled and shook my head, walking to my room.

CHAPTER 24

S ummer gave way to autumn, and I only received one note from Rafe after Recruitment Day. My heart hurt to know he was on the frontline—that I wasn't there with him. When I asked Mikhala, she shrugged, saying it was near impossible, even for her, to get letters to the front.

His last note read, *Remember the night I stayed with you?* I held onto those words for almost a month. Tizmet sensed my sadness and wanted to remedy it, but didn't know how. She proposed we storm the frontlines so that I could mate with him, then return.

Needless to say, I shot down that idea.

Darrak made it clear the Dragon Lord controlled my placement. Until I could ride Tizmet, chances were I would have no place at the front.

We made substantial progress. Most of the time, she listened to what I'd tell her concerning people, and I learned to trust her instincts as well. Once, she suggested we stop for a day while we traveled near a small hamlet. That evening a storm hit with freezing rain. Had we been out, we could have lost a horse—if not one of our lives.

We reached a level of trust that allowed us to maintain some distance now and then. I provided cover-fire for Darrak when he made a quick grab at someone. I even joined Mikhala on a hunt to bring in a pair of brothers.

Gaius had been pleased, and I earned a bit of coin for that one.

Under Mikhala's careful eye, she instructed me how to ride properly, and my accuracy shooting from Boulder improved. He was a fantastic horse—calm and collected every time I rode him. She taught me to ride bareback, though I was not as brave as her to go without a bridle.

After turning in another bounty, we were resting before the next job when Tizmet alerted me that Ruveel was approaching.

'How do you know?' I asked, running to the balcony.

The autumn sky was alight with the fading rays of the setting sun. Still, I found no trace of them on the horizon.

Tizmet arched her neck and snapped her teeth at the sky. *'I smell dung.'*

I chuckled at that. She was adopting my use of language a little too well.

'I'm going to speak with Mikhala,' I said.

I darted out of my room, through the hall, then down the stairs that led to the level below. Without knocking, I threw open her door. She was sitting in the tub, humming and braiding her hair.

"I need a favor."

"Ask it," she replied, without hesitation.

I sat on her bed and nervously tapped my feet. "The Dragon Lord is here."

"And?"

"I want to know how Rafe is."

I hugged myself as her eyes flicked to mine before settling on her reflection in the mirror.

"It will cost you."

"So you can find out?"

"Do you doubt me? It's the palace, girl. I could find out what the King whispers in his sleep," she mocked.

I smiled and bit my lip. Just to know he and the Tennan were safe would be enough for me.

"What will it cost?"

"A full night." She spoke without hesitation.

"A full night?"

"Aye. Tonight."

I frowned and hugged my knees to my chest. "You know the risk?"

"Of getting caught? For you, it's high." She smirked. "After all, we have a Dragon Lord here."

"For you."

Her smile slipped from her face. She looked down at the tub, deep in thought. "I'm tired of playing, Avyanna." She let her braid drop and mimicked my pose. "I love the back and forth, but it's getting old. I want more."

An entire night with Gaius. She was playing with fire as I once had. She wanted it so much that she was willing to be burned. I wasn't so naïve as to wonder why.

I rested my chin on my knees. "What if you get with child?"

She bit her lip and gave me a guilty look—as if she was a child caught with their hand in the cookie jar. "I took the purging tea on the way back."

"So..."

"So my last bleed was yesterday. It's not my season." She smiled down at the water.

"You knew." I accused.

She looked up at me with an evil grin.

"You knew the Dragon Lord was coming—that I'd ask you for this." I snorted and dropped my legs to the floor, leaning toward her.

"Aye. I did."

"And you planned it so you could have your night with Gaius!"

"Aye."

"Dragons' dung, you're good!" I laughed.

"I am." She flashed a sly smile. "So you'll cover for me?"

I shook my head in disbelief. How she knew these things, I had no idea. She was sneakier than Darrak in some ways. It's possible that she had been his riding partner for so long that she became attuned to even the smallest details.

"Aye. You find out where my Rafe is, and I'll cover you for one night spent with your Gaius."

Mikhala said goodbye from the balcony before she slipped out just after dark. The plan was that I would stay in my room unless Tizmet smelled Darrak, then I'd rush to Mikhala's.

Tizmet was on edge with Ge'org near. She loathed him. I tried to keep her as calm as possible, which was fine while she was close. She wanted to fly though, and was used to owning the skies here.

'I'm not saying you can't fly,' I told her calmly. *'You just might have a friend if you choose to.'*

'I need no friend,' she snapped across the bond.

A smirk turned my lip. *'I'm sure that's his only intention.'*

'I pick my mates. Males do not choose females.' She seemed disgusted by the very concept of men having a say in which women they mated.

'Remember, he's influenced by his Rider.'

'Which means he'd try to mate a cow if he had the chance.' Her bright eyes flashed in the dark.

I snickered and burrowed into my blankets. I refused to close the curtains against the chill tonight. If I needed to scale the wall, I didn't want to fight with the heavy fabric. Tizmet preferred it open, as well. It made it easier for her to come and go without the hassle.

We rested through the night, and at the morning's third chime, Tizmet lifted her head. *'They come,'* she said.

"They' who?" I shot upright, fully dressed, aside from my bare feet.

'The hunter and the red's Rider.'

'Both?!'

'Yes. From the north and the south.' She flicked out her tongue in the moonlight, studying me.

My mind raced. I couldn't be in two places at once. But why, in all of Rinmoth, would Ruveel need to visit my chambers in the dead of night? I jumped up and shoved my pillows and blankets together in a heap. Throwing another blanket over the pile, I ran toward the balcony.

'Please don't let him in.' I peered over the railing, searching for any sign of patrolling soldiers or guards, then scaled the wall to Mikhala's room.

'If he tries to enter my den, I'll eat him.'

My foot slipped, my toes losing their grip. I caught myself and sent a panicked look up at the balcony. 'Please don't eat him!'

'Fine. I'll roast him.'

I cringed, but kept climbing. If he dared open my door without knocking, I would not blame her for toasting his arse. If I got caught, Ruveel would find a way to punish me. Yet, if I didn't cover for Mikhala, or at least try, she'd hold it against me and withhold the information I wanted concerning Rafe. She was kind, but tough. To her, a trade was a trade. If I didn't uphold my end of the bargain, she wouldn't feel obligated to uphold hers, either.

Dropping onto her balcony, I dove into the bed. I yanked the blankets over me and threw a pillow over my head, then focused on calming my frantic breaths.

'The red's Rider is here,' Tizmet growled.

'Where is Darrak?'

'Nearing the door.' She paused. 'He lingers.'

I bit my lip and reached over the bond to feel what she felt. She sensed Darrak a distance away, appropriate for Mikhala's room. The Dragon Lord seemed closer, the scent of Ge'org wreathing him. So far, he made no attempt to enter. He simply stood there, making no sound.

Darrak's protective tendencies prompted him to check in, and the way to Mikhala's room cracked, sending a sliver of light into the space. The door stayed open for a moment before closing gently.

I sighed and reached out to Tizmet. 'Is Ruveel still there?'

She pushed her irritation at me. 'He has not moved.' She detested having him this close.

'Do you know where Ge'org is?' Perhaps the beast was nearby, and Ruveel used him the same way I was using Tizmet.

'Two caves down. Sleeping like the dead.'

I cringed and sat up, checking that I was alone. After scouring for guards below, I climbed the wall. My toes and fingers deftly found holds in between the stones as I picked my way back to my room.

'He wakes.'

'Who?!' I hurried at Tizmet's warning.

'The red.'

I sped along. If he was two rooms down, he would only have to poke his head outside, look up, and see me.

'To the balcony!'

I took larger steps, moving as fast as I possibly could. I launched myself at the railing at the same time Tizmet stepped out. Her big body shielded mine, and she faced Ge'org, blocking his view, then hissed.

He snorted as I scrambled over the railing. My arms smarted where I hit the stone, but I ignored it, speeding for my bed. Tizmet snarled and snapped her jaws as Ge'org huffed. I dove into the blankets as Tizmet backed inside, hissing and lashing her tail.

'Thank you!' I said as I settled beneath the thick covers.

She faced me and snorted. Laying her massive head at my feet, she gazed at me with her bright red-orange eyes.

'Silly humans.'

The next morning, Mikhala slipped into my room as I ate my first meal. She wore the same clothes as last night, her hair tied in the same braids, but her face was different. She leaned against the entrance and gave me a small secret smile.

"I take it everything went as planned?" I asked dryly, taking a bite of soft bread.

"Aye. It was—"

"Spare me the details," I scoffed.

Her smile grew to a grin, and she walked over to steal my grapes. "I've news of your General, too."

I set the bread down and gave her my full attention.

"According to my sources, the Dragon Lord turned in a report stating that General Rafe Shadowslayer took his Tennan behind enemy lines. They're on a mission to capture a Shaman."

"Capture?" I frowned. "Not kill?"

"Aye. At least that's what I heard. Which also means no letters would make it to him. No one else would be so foolish as to travel behind enemy lines."

I flinched as if someone punched me. "I would be there if I hadn't bonded Tizmet."

"And it's a good thing you did. They've been gone longer than anticipated."

A shiver ran through me. "By how long?"

"The report said two days. That's all I know."

I scowled at my food. Rafe would take it as it came. Priorities shifted. Adaption was critical to survival. Yet, my heart screamed something was wrong.

'He is a warrior,' Tizmet rumbled across the bond.

I sighed and gazed at her sleeping form. She was right. Rafe was a General. He didn't need me fussing over him. If I had been in his Tennan, he would have punished me for worrying. He would have ordered me to dig the latrine pit or something of the sort.

"I'm sure he's fine," Mikhala assured me, drinking my glass of milk.

I forced a smile. "Aye. I'm sure he is."

However, my heart was not so sure.

CHAPTER 25

The days were short, and the air had a biting chill—signs that winter was settling in. I was about to be twenty—the age designated for women to acquire the title of a Lady. Most my age had chosen a life mate before now—any later and women were considered spinsters.

We traveled in the cold, north of the E'or mountains. We were tracking a bounty on the run, a thief who called himself Robert the Sly.

I bit my lip as I rode, deep in thought.

'Just go. Ask permission and they can deny you,' Tizmet said, annoyance lining her raspy mental voice. She was weary of my internal arguments.

'I can't just leave. If I do, Ruveel will place us somewhere else.'

'Then ask. You've done enough for them. Let them do this for you.' She flew low over our heads with a growl.

'Then I'd be asking for a favor.'

Far above, she roared, fed up with my indecision. *'Then don't go!'*

"Oi, mind sharing?"

Mikhala's voice brought my gaze to her. She frowned, and Darrak studied Tizmet, brow furrowed.

I blinked, tearing myself from my thoughts. My unvoiced confusion was evident.

She waved a hand between me and the sky. "Whatever you and your dragon are bickering about."

"Oh, we're not fighting." I blew a strand of hair out of my face, diverting my focus on the path ahead.

"See, *you* can fool us, but Tizzy is anything but subtle. Something is bothering her."

Tizmet lashed her tail in aggravation. She dipped low enough for me to see the impatience burning in her stare.

I offered a half-hearted shrug. "She's upset with me."

"You're upset with yourself, too," Mik droned, giving me a bored look.

I scowled. How did she know that?

She continued, "You've been quiet and sullen for the past two days."

"It's the snow."

We were trudging through frigid slush more than a pace deep. It made for miserable camping and slow pacing with the horses.

"Liar."

I stuck my tongue out at her.

"Fess up, Avyanna." Darrak turned in his saddle, winter cloak tied about him securely. He eyed me the way a parent might glower at a stubborn child.

"It's nothing–"

"Spit it out, or I'll make you walk the next mile."

Sighing, I glared up at Tizmet. *This is your fault.*

'Stop hiding your feelings,' she shot back.

"We're passing my mother's village." I stared at my gloved fingers, clutching the reins, and refused to meet Darrak's gaze.

Mikhala didn't hesitate with her response. "Would you like to visit?"

I frowned and dared a glance at Darrak. "We have a job." The words held more conviction than I felt.

He shook his head, and a smile tugged at his lip. "It would be nice to stop for the Solstice and have a hot meal."

"Well, you see... I haven't written my mother in almost a year." I spoke slowly, hope sparking in my heart.

Mikhala gawked. "She doesn't know you're a Rider?"

"I'm not a Rider... but I've sent her no updates since meeting her last Winter Solstice."

"Then she thinks you're on the front? With Rafe?" Darrak's grin spread wide over his cheeks. "We have to stop now. What's the name of the village?"

"Stonesmead. Though I honestly don't think–"

"It's settled! We'll break for the Solstice and enjoy a warm meal and a roof over our heads!" Mikhala urged Moony into a run. She threw her arms out as he galloped along, tossing snow in the air.

She thrived in this weather. Though she complained about the winters in her home country, she loved the snow and the cold. She wore a simple black tunic beneath her fur vest and a light traveling cloak. Darrak and I were both bundled up in multiple layers to ward off the elements.

"Stonesmead lies east of our path. We could have reached it today had I known." Darrak's tone was gentle, but a rebuke nonetheless.

"I didn't want to be a bother," I mumbled.

"You're part of our team—hardly a bother."

My heart clenched at his words, remembering the Tennan. My eyes pressed shut against the pain. I didn't know where they were now—if they were in danger or alive. What if something happened to them? To Korzak with his kind, childlike demeanor? What if Jamlin was hurt? What if Dane or Blain had been killed?

'Stop worrying about the unknown.' Tizmet sighed.

I took a deep breath and opened my eyes.

I'd spend the Solstice with my mother for the first time in years—in my family home. In a house, not a school dorm. I smiled to myself. Everything would be fine.

We arrived in Stonesmead with Tizmet flying among the clouds. Hopefully, she would pass as a bird until I had a chance to explain things to my mother. Darrak was relaxed, and Mikhala was eager to meet my only living family.

Whenever my mother visited, she wanted to know about me and what was going on in my life. I knew she was a baker, but barely made enough to make ends meet. I didn't even know where our home was—I couldn't remember. When I left for Northwing, I was only four winters, still it bothered me how little I remembered.

Darrak took it in stride and stopped at the tavern that doubled as an inn. A humble, waist-high fence surrounded the perimeter of the village center. Along with the inn, there was a general store, a stable, a tavern, and a few other oddity storefronts. Outside the wooden fence, homes littered about, each with their own plots of farmland.

We tied our horses and stepped inside, shaking snow from our feet, then shut the door against the cold.

A woman behind the bar shouted a warm greeting. The tavern was empty save for two grizzled men, who squinted at us as we entered.

"Greetings," Darrak called back. He put on his charm, slipping into his role of charismatic traveler.

She held up three glasses. "Drinks?"

"Aye, two mead, one water."

Her eyes sparkled as she took us in. Her gaze landed on mine, and she tilted her head, squinting for a moment before resuming her task.

"What brings you to Stonesmead, fair travelers?"

She set the beverages before us. Mikhala straddled a stool and sipped her mead eagerly. Darrak pushed the water in my direction, and I grasped it while taking a seat.

"Business further north," he replied with ease. "We're looking for someone. Heard they might be about here."

"Have a name?" She leaned against the counter with a smile.

"Annabelle of Visoth," I said quietly.

She shifted to study me. Her gaze lingered on my short hair as if trying to place it. "Annabelle, eh?"

"Aye. Do you know her?" Darrak asked, bringing the woman's attention back to him. He offered a dazzling smile and slid a gold coin across the bar. "I'm eager to make her acquaintance."

Suspicion sparked in her eyes, but her kind smirk held fast. She slipped her hand out to finger the coin. "And why would a group like you be after her?"

"Do you sell to the gossipmongers too?" Darrak lowered his lashes with a knowing smile. "She can sell the nature of our call to them after we leave. We'll not be harming her."

"Isn't that what all the rogues say?" She snickered, then pulled away from the bar, taking the coin with her. "You'd find her at the smithy. She runs a lovely bakery there. Try her sweetloaves. They're to die for."

"I'll be sure to." Darrak winked.

He sipped his mead and bartered for a room. The small inn only had four available to rent. He purchased one for two nights. If my mother didn't have space for a man, he'd retire here while Mikhala and I slept on her floor.

We finished our drinks and headed out the door. The two men from before were long gone, probably off to warn my mother visitors were here to see her.

"Oh, and Avyanna?"

I froze at the sound of my name. Mikhala turned to me with a frown and glanced back at the barkeep.

"You look just like your father."

My heart skipped a beat, and I offered her a smile. "Thank you."

We left the inn, and I mounted Boulder in a haze. The reason for her steady scrutiny was she remembered my father. My mother always said I looked like him, save for my short stature. I trailed behind Darrak as he led the way, following the barkeep's directions.

We arrived at the smithy's in mere moments. It was a small home with few luxuries. There was an open forge where a beast of a man worked. He wore a loose, stained tunic with the sleeves ripped off, reminding me painfully of Rafe. He wiped the sweat from his brow and tossed a scythe blade back into the fire. Turning to us, he squinted and frowned.

We all dismounted, and I followed Darrak's lead, glancing around.

"Greetings," Darrak called, nodding to the man.

The place smelled of smoke and iron, of dirt and sweat. Nothing here reminded me of my mother.

The stranger growled. "Hail."

Perhaps the depth of his voice came with his towering size.

"We were told we might find Annabelle here."

His heated glare could've melted the snow at our feet. "Who are ye to be lookin' for her?"

"Friends. Nothing more." Darrak's easy demeanor didn't falter.

"She dun have no friends like ye."

This wasn't going well. I just wanted to see my mother. My heart raced in anticipation. If this smith only told us where she was, we could be on our way.

"Clearly, you're mistaken. She's quite fond of us." Darrak was relaxed, his smile pleasant. He was trying to placate the irritable smith, but it wasn't working.

"And I ain't fond of liars," he grumbled, picking up a hammer.

My heart halted in my chest. Tizmet dipped lower with the hint of danger.

"Easy—easy there." Darrak laughed, putting his hands up.

I glanced between them, frowning. Who was this smith to get between me and my mother? Why was he hiding her? Was she ill? Did she live in the smith's house?

He stomped closer, clutching his hammer. "I'm warning ye to get back on them horses and–"

"Oi!" I growled and stepped forward to confront him.

He turned his angry gaze on me, and a small chime of fear thrummed through me. Tizmet dove in response.

"We're here for my–"

The door to the house opened.

"Nath dear, dinner is—oh."

My mouth dropped open at the same time Tizmet hit the ground behind us, tossing snow about with her rough landing.

"Mother?"

"Avyanna? What are you–"

She looked over my shoulder as I felt Tizmet lower her head to the smith's level. She let out a fierce snarl and snapped her jaws. My mother pulled a hand to her chest and her eyes went wide in shock.

And she fainted.

We all crowded into the small house. My mother lay on the bed—pale as the snow outside. Her gray-streaked brown hair had come loose from her bun. It trailed off the blankets, the length pooling on the floor.

Mikhala's gaze darted between Darrak and the blacksmith, Ragnath, as if she expected a fight. Darrak leaned against a small table, resting his hand on his sword's pommel.

"How are you here?" My mother gasped.

"It's a long story," I said with a nervous smile.

Tension was thick in the air, and Tizmet snarled outside. Her bright eye lit up the doorway—she refused to let us shut it.

"There's a dragon."

"Aye, that's also a long story. She won't hurt you, though." My laugh was high with nerves.

The squire's missing arm popped into my mind and my laughter cut short as I cleared my throat.

My mother gestured toward my companions. "Who are you?"

"Darrak, at your service, milady." He gave a slight bow of his head.

Mik flashed a toothy grin. "I'm Mikhala. Avyanna's soul-sister."

"Her what?"

I sighed. "Oi, could I have a moment?"

This was my mother, but it wasn't easy to speak with her with them listening to every word. The smith, who couldn't keep his glare to himself, didn't help things, either.

"Absolutely."

"No."

Darrak and Ragnath spoke at the same time. The smith took an imposing step toward him, and Darrak raised an eyebrow in question.

"Nath, please–"

"No! I dunno who these people be, and they come here spewin' lies. I dun trust 'em!"

"Ragnath!" My mother straightened and jabbed a finger his way. "This is my daughter, for love of the sun! Take your hulking arse out of this house or I'll not be making you meals for the next week!"

He looked stricken. Going up against Darrak didn't phase him in the slightest, but threatened with the loss of my mother's cooking—that shook him. He glanced to where Tizmet's bright eye flashed between us all and crossed his arms.

'Let them leave, please.'

'Shall I repay him for frightening you?' she growled across the bond.

'No, just watch him. He doesn't like Darrak.'

She snorted and retreated from the doorway. Mikhala skipped out, and Darrak followed. Ragnath glanced between me and my mother with a scowl.

"A week!" She reminded him.

He muttered under his breath and shuffled his large frame outside, slamming the door shut behind him.

'Open door,' Tizmet urged.

'It's only my mother.'

She huffed. *'Some mothers eat their young.'*

I choked and covered my face.

"Are you well, Avyanna?" Concern laced my mother's voice.

How could I explain my dragon just insinuated she might dice me up and cook me for dinner?

"I am," I said, holding back my smile. My assurance crossed over the bond. *'I'm fine.'*

She snarled her disapproval, but didn't burn the house down.

"Tell me the truth. Are you safe?" My mother held her cheek and looked toward the door nervously.

"Aye, Mom," I snickered, "I am perfectly safe."

"So... Darrak?"

"Ragnath?" I shot back, arching a single skeptical eyebrow.

She blushed and turned away with a sheepish grin. "It's not what you think," she muttered.

I snorted, openly examining the space. There was a single bed. The small kitchen area was filled with resting dough and mixing bowls littered about with various utensils. There were barrels of ingredients and large sacks of flour and wheat on the floor.

Across the little room was a table with cast iron tools laid out. Gears and pins, latches and hinges, and scrap pieces of metalwork were scattered all over. Hanging on a line near the hearth were men's trousers and under-breeches—about the size of the blacksmith. Pinned right next to them was a dress that would fit my mother.

"It looks quite damning, mother."

"Watch your mouth, young lady. You're not too old to eat soap!"

I scoffed and settled on the bed. "I'm always telling you about me. How about you tell me about you and *Sir Ragnath?*"

With a sigh, she threw my words from earlier back at me. "It's a long story."

"I'm not going anywhere."

She was trying to get out of this, and I would have none of it. I needed to know the tale of my mother falling for another man. At least... it better be that she fell for him, and not that he forced her.

She shifted her weight to get more comfortable and started her story. It had been a lengthy process over many years. Ragnath was a widower himself and lived alone many years before really noticing her. He wooed her for three years before she even formally considered him.

Two years later, they were life mates.

"This was a year ago?!" I sat back in disbelief. "Why didn't you tell me?"

"I had only been claimed for a few months when you asked me to come to Hamsforth. I meant to tell you then. First, the giant—your General, I believe, terrified me. Then you told me you were marching off to your death. Pardon me for not telling you of my recent happiness!" Her eyes danced with mirth.

"I simply cannot believe you didn't mention it." I shook my head. "Tell me he's good to you."

"Aye, he's good to me, girl." She spoke with such tenderness, there was little doubt they cared for one another.

"Now, what happened to your General?"

My attention dropped to my hands. "He's on the frontlines," I murmured.

"Without you."

"Because I'm a Rider now."

"I see you don't wear the spaulder."

"Mother, since when are you an expert on these things?" I huffed.

"I think there's more between you."

My gaze shot to hers, and she pursed her lips and nodded.

"I knew it."

"Knew what? There's nothing between us," I blurted.

"Dear, one day when you're a mother, you'll understand. There are some things mothers just know." She tapped a finger on her chin. "Also, children are never good at lying to their parents. Now tell me everything."

"There's nothing to tell."

I loved my mother, truly. These times when I got to sit with her and share our lives—these moments meant everything to me. Yet her love for Ragnath was simple and straightforward. What Rafe and I had was tangled and messy. I didn't want to bring her into it.

"What of that Darrak?"

"Darrak?"

"Aye, the handsome one with the eyes of a gambler."

I snorted. "The eyes of a gambler?"

"He's cunning. I've lived a few years. I know his sort. Is he after you as well?"

"Firstly, no one is 'after me.'" I laughed. "Secondly, Darrak is like a father to me. He's a good man." My smile faltered as sorrow filled her eyes. "I didn't mean that. He cannot take my father's place."

"No, no. You barely knew your father when he fell." She blinked off into the distance as memories clouded her eyes. "You wouldn't remember him. He was a good man, though."

"Darrak is the King's bounty hunter. He's smart, and cunning as you said, but he also has a sense of morality. He's not like other men."

"Tell me of you." She pulled herself back to the present. "Why is there a dragon out there, and why are you riding with a bounty hunter, of all people?"

I smiled and leaned against the bed.

We talked well into nightfall. Mikhala came in at some point and sat next to me, listening and poking around curiously. She explained that Darrak returned to the inn for the night. Ragnath stayed at his forge, hammering away on something, and Tizmet crowded around him, seeking its heat.

'We should build one of these in our cave.' Tizmet interrupted.

'We don't have our own cave,' I replied while explaining to my mother the reason we were this far north.

'One day we will. We must have one of these.' She sent me the feeling of heat and comfort. Like a blanket warmed by the fire on a cold night.

I smiled, but kept our conversation to myself. My mother was intrigued by Tizmet. She didn't understand that she differed from other dragons, though. Few people did. Everyone viewed the beasts with the same level of respect and reverence. They were our protectors, our strongest warriors.

Tizmet was not. She was her own.

"I was surprised Darrak let me come," I said, resting my chin on my knees.

Mikhala shifted on the bed to get a better look at my face. "Why?"

"It seemed inappropriate to ask a favor." I shrugged. "He works for the King. He has a job, and I'm interfering."

"We've traveled together for months now, and you act as if you just met the man. You're more than that to him." She threw her hands in the air. "You're not a child he's playing nursemaid for. You're his friend, Avyanna. If you were in trouble, he would move the moon and stars for you."

My mother leaned around me to frown at her. "Just friends?" she asked.

"Just friends!"

Mikhala and I spoke in unison. We looked at each other and broke into laughter.

A heavy knock startled us, and we turned to the door wide-eyed.

"Yes?" my mother called out, casting a side eye at me.

The door opened, and Ragnath's head emerged from the crack. "Are ye all done gossiping? I'm tired."

He huffed, glaring at me and Mikhala. As his eyes landed on my mother, they softened, and the corner of my mouth lifted in a smile. I didn't know this man—I hadn't even known *of* him until a few hours ago, but the way he looked at my mother made my shoulders relax. He loved her.

"Yes, yes. Come in. I'll warm your meal." My mother stood from the bed and bustled into the kitchen area, lighting another lantern.

Ragnath sat in a chair, taking off his boots. He leveled a glare at me and I beamed in response.

"So does she call you father now?" Mikhala mused.

My elbow landed in her gut. She let out a choked laugh, and I grinned with a helpless shrug.

"Yer dragon is curled 'round the forge," he bit out, crossing his arms over his chest.

"Aye, it's warm."

"She do that at the school? Get all cuddly with dem forges?"

I frowned and shook my head. "At Northwing, she rarely leaves the cave. If it doesn't involve the hot springs or basking, she's not interested."

"How do ye get her to all yer classes, then?"

"Well... she's a Wild One, so we attended none till recently."

"Ah, aye. You were a soldier before, eh?"

"Yes. A member of General Shadowslayer's Tennan." A painful smile lifted my lips.

"Get in a lot of fights?"

I shrugged. "I can hold my own."

"Good girl."

I sucked in a breath, thinking of the man who so often called me that. Frowning, I wondered where he was. Here, I was warm, about to be fed a hot meal. I was in a home surrounded and protected by people who loved me and cared for me.

Was Rafe?

'We will find out,' Tizmet murmured. She sounded more lethargic than I had ever heard her. *'When this fire goes out,'* she added.

'Forges never go out.'

'Truly?!' She stirred from her haze in excitement.

'Aye, it's too much work to build the fire daily. Blacksmiths keep it going all day, every day.'

'Wonders...' She sighed dreamily and curled tighter around the forge.

"Tizmet, the dragon, really loves your forge." I cleared my throat. "I have a feeling she won't want to leave in the morning."

"Leave in the morning?" Mikhala questioned.

"When we... head out?"

"Nah, we're staying until the day after the Solstice. Darrak said we turned in enough bounties this year. We deserve a break."

"But what about Robert the Sly?" I asked, referring to the thief we tracked.

"Do you have such little faith in us?" She laughed, flopping on the bed. "We'll pick up the trail, easy."

I turned back to my mother near the hearth, slipping a pie into a pan. Glancing at Ragnath, I asked, "Would you mind if we stayed two nights?"

"Ye'r her lass. 'Course ye can stay," he replied with a shrug.

"Thank you for your kindness."

He harrumphed and averted his eyes. Gruff on the outside but as sweet as honey on the inside.

Shortly after we ate, we washed up and readied for sleep. Me and Mikhala sprawled on a blanket near the hearth while Ragnath and my mother shared the bed. It didn't take long for me to learn the uncomfortable lesson of what children went through when they lived at home—my mother's smothered giggles and the sound of a slap followed by a playful growl.

I covered my face as more giggling ensued. Peeking between my fingers, I found Mikhala watching me. Firelight danced over her features as she wrinkled her nose. There was a hurt cry from the bed and I grimaced. Mikhala shook her head and laughed with her hands over her mouth as hushed apologies followed.

Tizmet pushed an image of mating dragons to me.

I choked and went into a coughing fit. *'I don't need your help, either!'*

"Oi, keep it down." Mikhala shushed me with a grin. "I'm trying to sleep here!"

My elbow rammed into her ribs, and she kicked me back. I tackled her, snickering as she shoved me off.

"Oi, we're trying to sleep here!" Ragnath bellowed.

We froze and glanced toward the shadow of the bed. She snorted, then burst into laughter beneath me.

"*Trying to sleep!*" I mocked, falling to my side of the blanket.

Amusement colored my mother's tone. "Hush now!"

"Youngsters," Ragnath muttered.

I fell asleep with a smile on my face, feeling like I was finally home.

CHAPTER 26

We spent the Solstice together. Darrak and Ragnath managed to get along. My mother cooked an enormous amount of food, and several of the villagers stopped by for last-minute sweetloaves.

Ragnath was quite jovial once you broke through his icy exterior. We shared stories, and he told terrible jokes. We laughed—though not from the poor comedy, but rather his great booming chuckle, and the way he slapped his thigh at his own humor.

It was cramped inside the small house with us all, but it was warm. Full of good food and better company.

As night fell, my mother insisted we abide by the old traditions, as she did when she visited Northwing during the Solstice. A few observed them at the dorms, but it was the exception, not the standard. We all pulled on our cloaks, and my mother fetched a small bag of seeds. Mikhala glanced between us as if it was foreign to her.

"You've never seen the New Year traditions?" I asked, tying my cloak tighter about me.

"Aye, I've seen them... I've never participated." She shrugged.

Darrak offered my mother an apologetic smile. "I'm not superstitious."

"Well, I am—more than enough for the lot of you. You will all participate," she said with a nod. "Fetch more candles, Nath?"

Ragnath did as she asked, shaking his head with a grin.

The Winter Solstice, or New Year traditions, were believed to close out the old year and bring blessings for the new year. In the dorms, some partook, while others deemed it foolishness and went on their way.

Rafe would have deemed it foolish.

I frowned as a small stab of pain pricked in my heart. I knew him. He would have seen how much it meant to my mother and would at least come along. I wondered if I could ever bring him home to share in these silly traditions.

'Enough.' Tizmet cut through my wallowing. *'Live in the present.'*

Straightening my shoulders, I pulled myself together. She was right. I wouldn't tear myself down by dwelling on the what-if's.

That would be my resolution. To live my life to the fullest and take every day as it came.

"Ready?" my mother asked.

Mikhala's head bobbed in eagerness.

"Yes," I replied.

We headed out the door, a comically large group filing out of such a small house. Tizmet regarded us and lowered an eye that reflected the fire of the forge.

'We won't go far. Just to the woods.'

'Fine. Be safe.' She bared her teeth. *'If I have to leave this warmth, I will be angry.'*

'Stay.'

I laughed and patted her muzzle. She snorted before opening her mouth and firing the forge hotter.

Ragnath studied her in wonder, and a smile lit his face. "I'm not too keen about what be proper," he said, glancing at me, "but ye think she could do that a bit while I work in it?"

"Of course."

If she got to stay around the forge for just a moment longer, she would gladly empty herself of oil.

My mother hurried us along, pressing into the thicket behind her home. The moon was high, reflecting off the layer of white smothering the ground. It wasn't full tonight, but its silver sheen was bright enough to cast shadows. The forest lay silent, save for the crunch of our steps. The trees loomed above us, quietly judging our approach. No breeze stirred their heavy, snow-laden branches.

We stopped at a small clearing, barely big enough for us to circle around. Ragnath handed out the candles, then lit them one by one.

"Mikhala, are you aware of the significance behind blowing out the candles?" my mother asked, her tone reverent.

"Aye, it's like saying goodbye to the old year?"

"It's more than that, dear. When you extinguish the flame, you release all the stress, all the toil and struggles of the year before. Your breath is like the wind pushing away decaying leaves to make room for new spring growth. You surrender anything that holds you back. Your fears, your excuses, all of it, dismissed."

The candlelight reflected against Mikhala's thoughtful face. She frowned, peering into the flickering flame. "So, anything you're unhappy with?"

"In a way. Consequences of actions will still follow you, but you're wiping the slate clean. You recognize mistakes, wrongs or choices that have not brought you joy, and cast them behind you." My mother smiled patiently as she explained.

Mikhala squinted at the light but nodded in understanding.

Once everyone was ready, my mother lifted her candle. Her gaze flitted to mine, then darted back to her tiny flame. Her eyes fluttered closed. "Farewell to times now past," she whispered, then blew out her candle.

Ragnath, to her right, raised his and smiled at her. "Farewell to times now past." He blew it out with a puff of foggy breath.

Darrak lifted his and repeated the same. He held his eyes closed, and for one not so superstitious—he seemed to take it quite seriously.

Mikhala took a deep breath and scrunched up her face. She glared at the flickering flame and yelled with all her might, "Farewell to times now past!"

We all laughed, and Darrak shoved her shoulder. "Your mother would be proud."

Everyone looked at me and my sad little light. It burned small but steady. This had been a terrible year. I was torn away from Rafe and plucked from the Tennan. I was accused of being a harlot, and Tizmet ate a human limb. Irreparable damage had been done to the Dragon Rider Corps.

However, in the same year, I got close to Darrak. I met Mikhala, who I would cherish until the end of my days, and I saw my mother again. And what's more, I saw her *happy*. Then there was Tizmet, who was a dear friend to me now. These past months granted me knowledge and experiences beyond measure.

I would adhere to tradition and dispose of the old year—toss the stress and baggage that held me down. I would stop worrying so much about what people thought and follow the path destiny laid out for me.

"Farewell to times now past."

My candlelight vanished with a puff of breath. A great weight lifted from my chest. I knew the traditions were nothing more than symbols and wishes… but the act of blowing out the candle felt as if it committed me to the choice I made.

My mother nodded, then walked around our small circle, placing a handful of seeds into each offered palm. "These symbolize hope. Our future is an empty field awaiting action. Your first choices will plant the seeds, and you will reap the crop of those decisions." She sprinkled a few in my hand. "Some crops will already exist, buried deep, with roots strong and unyielding. They will spring up unbidden. We have to work with what is under the soil as well as what we plant."

She took her place next to Ragnath and closed her eyes once again. Silently, she made her resolutions, deciding what she hoped the new year would bring.

"Welcome, the year anew," she muttered while lifting her palms with the seeds. She drew in a deep breath and blew, scattering them in the center of our circle.

The others repeated the motion, with Mikhala shouting it like a war-cry. I snickered at her. She was a warrior at all times, even in quiet, somber moments.

I lifted my palm, studying the small seeds. What would this new year hold for me? I was determined to make my own choices and follow my destiny, whatever that may be. My days of following others were done. I wanted to be my own person.

I wanted to be with Rafe.

And I *would* be with him.

Lifting my palm, I closed my eyes. Taking a deep breath, I focused my intentions and blew the seeds to scatter them.

Something shattered deep across the bond.

I screamed, dropping to my knees.

Tizmet roared in the distance, and I braced myself against the snow, gasping as a white-hot pain wound its way through me. My vision faded. The worried clamor of the others milled about me, but I couldn't see them. Soon, their noise muffled to nothing.

It was dark. Pain shot through my side and into my chest. I ground my teeth against the agony, refusing to let them know how badly they injured me. I couldn't open my left eye. They dragged me along the frigid ground, each step starting a fresh wave of torture. My legs wouldn't work, refusing to answer my demand to take my weight. Sharp spasms shot to my shoulders where they wrenched my arms, yanking my weight by the joint–

'To me!'

I cried out and collapsed into the cold snow. The pain melted away, but the horror remained, leaving me trembling.

'Avyanna! To me!' Tizmet roared in outrage across the bond.

A tremor ran through me as trees were uprooted around us. Sound returned to my ears and everyone's shouts assailed me at once.

"Was there magic in the ritual?!" Mikhala demanded.

"No! Leave her," Darrak shouted. "Tizmet is coming for her!"

My mother screamed. "She's my *daughter!* I won't leave her like that!"

"If her dragon harms you, it's my duty to slay it. Don't make me."

Limbs shaking, I tried to push myself back to my knees as Tizmet flattened the trees nearby. She curled her body around mine, forcing everyone away. I shuddered and crawled against her warm scales.

'Why did you leave me?!' Her sense of betrayal slipped over the bond.

'I didn't!'

The vision was so vivid, so real—the anguish so fresh. I flinched, recalling the pain in my side and chest. The darkness. I fumbled under my tunic, feeling my ribs to be sure there was no gaping wound.

'*You used the thread that binds us,*' Tizmet rasped, sensing my discomfort. She curled in tighter, bringing her wing above me to block the glare of the moon.

'*Magic?*' I'd never used it—had no idea that I could. It was taught in the Rider classes, but we never made it that far.

'*Yes. You pulled it. It obeyed your call.*'

She purred deep in her throat. Her comfort soaked into my bones, and I pressed myself against her scales. I was greedy for her warmth to chase away the cold harshness of what I just experienced.

'*I didn't mean to. What did I do?*'

'*You followed the thread to the one you thought of.*'

Panic rushed through my veins. "Rafe," I whispered in horror. '*Tell me it wasn't true. Tell me what I felt was a lie.*'

My terror rang out across the bond, and Tizmet snarled against the feeling. '*Magic does not lie.*'

'*That can't be true.*' Did I witness the past—or something to come? Did I see him as he is? I wrapped my arms around myself and stared into the darkness. All the warmth Tizmet could provide wasn't enough to ward off the chill of dread.

'*I know not,*' she said. '*Calm. I am here.*'

"No. *No*. It can't be real."

It had to have happened in the past. Shadows damaged his eye, and somehow I relived that moment. That was the only explanation.

'*It was a memory.*'

'*Perhaps.*'

'*It was an old memory from when they damaged his eye,*' I said more forcefully.

'*Perhaps,*' she repeated. '*Magic is fickle. It brought me to you, but not when you were there. It made me wait for you. Perhaps you have seen your mate but, in a different time.*'

I shivered against her side. It was just an old memory. That was all.

Rafe was behind enemy lines.

He was late to return.

He was safe.

I felt no assurance in those words.

CHAPTER 27

The next morning, I was eager to leave. Whatever happened last night left me uneasy. Getting back to the palace was my only hope of finding any answers.

I needed the Dragon Lord.

'Can you speed it along?' I complained.

Mikhala scarfed down everything my mother baked while I sat on a rough-hewn chair, sulking by the small window. Outside, Tizmet lay beside Ragnath, squinting into the scorching flames with pure delight. Periodically he grunted or nodded and she would send another blast of fire straight into the forge. He was engrossed in his work on a solid steel bar. What he was crafting it into was still incomprehensible. I ventured into the cold, crossing my arms tight across my chest.

'Patience. He is working,' she scolded, without turning to me.

'You're just enjoying the heat.'

She offered me a snort. *'I am.'*

Everyone pestered me to find out what happened last night, Mikhala most of all. I refused to tell anyone.

The art of using magic was taught to Riders with great caution. It was a slow and purposeful process, never exceeding the Rider's abilities. My vision was only a result of me being thrown into a bond with a mature dragon, having no schooling for it. It was an embarrassment. A sign of being untrained—uncontrolled. It was a failure, one that might result in my death. I had to learn how to control it.

And I needed to find Rafe.

All night, I tried to convince myself it had to be a memory, that it was an event in the past I somehow relived. Yet, in my heart, something about that rang false. My gut told me he was in trouble. And I needed to help him.

I needed to get back to the palace.

'Are you done?' I tapped the toe of my boot against the snow.

'You're behaving like a hatchling,' Tizmet growled without looking at me. *'Go for a walk. Leave me with the Man of Fire and Steel.'*

'Glorified blacksmith,' I grumbled.

Ragnath ignored my presence, enveloped in whatever he worked on. I stormed into the house and grabbed my spear. Mikhala and my mother glanced up at my abrupt entrance. Mik frowned, narrowing her eyes at me, her mouth full of baked goodness.

"I'm practicing," I snapped, stomping out the door.

My crass attitude was unnecessary, but I couldn't shake the cloud looming over me. I was helpless right now, at the mercy of others, including my dragon, who thought a forge was more important than my clumsiness with magic.

'It's not as if you'll kill yourself accidentally,' she said, feeling my thoughts.

'Last night was an accident. Who's to say it won't happen again?' I bit back, stepping into the clearing behind the house. I shrugged off my cloak and unsheathed my spear's blade.

'You reached for it. You grasped at the threads, the magic.'

Fighting against invisible enemies, I worked through my poses. *'I didn't consciously do it!'* I huffed and stabbed at the air, stepping back and defending myself.

'You did. You simply were not thinking of it.' She sighed as if I was the one not making sense.

I slashed and stabbed, working out my frustration. Before long, Mikhala joined me. She drew her shortswords from her hips and attacked.

She helped me work out my anger and my frustration. Her strikes were vicious, leaving no room to think of anything else, save how to parry her next blow. We danced and slid through the snow, each gaining and retreating in turn. She was a warrior through and through.

We broke apart sweating and panting for breath. She doubled over and lifted her head to peer at me through her braids. Her eyes were wild with delight, as if her soul yearned for more despite her body's exhaustion.

'He is finished.' Tizmet's remorse slipped over the bond. She was reluctant to leave the forge.

My knees trembled, and my fingers were like iron bands forged around the shaft of my spear. We fought with such ferocity, I couldn't loosen my grip. "Tizmet—is finished," I said between heaving breaths.

"Good! I can't imagine you could take much more," she taunted.

"Me?" I raised a brow at the sweat dripping from her temple. "Looks like someone's been eating too many sweet cakes."

Her smile brightened. "One can never have too many."

My mother apparently thought so, too. She trudged through the snow with a basket on her hip, packed with at least a dozen mini pastries.

"She's eaten you out of house and home." I sighed, shaking my head with a grin.

My mother scoffed and held my face, her smile faltering. Her gaze locked with mine as tears brimmed the edges of her eyes. "You take care." She choked the words out.

I swallowed past the lump in my throat. "I'll be back."

It was a promise both of us knew I couldn't make. I had no idea where I would end up next, or if I could send word to her.

"Ye better," Ragnath growled as he moved beside her. He threw a heavy arm over her shoulders, smirking at Tizmet. "And bring the dragon with ye."

Tizmet trilled and lowered her head. She flicked her tongue out, tasting the air. '*Tell him I will lend my fire again.*'

"She said she would be happy to let you use her fire again." I looked between the two. Perhaps Tizmet made a human friend beyond me.

He slid his hand from my mother and bowed deeply. "It is an honor."

'*I'm not sure you deserve that,*' I commented dryly.

She snorted. '*I deserve far more.*'

Shaking my head, I hefted my belongings. Boulder and Moony were stabled at the inn where we'd meet up with Darrak.

"We're off, then. Farewell," I called, turning my back on my mother and her home.

Their farewells followed behind me as I stepped away. When would I see them again? *Would* I see them again?

I wondered what seeds I'd grow this year, and the crop it would yield by next Winter Solstice.

The smell of clean and warm stables was comforting to my frayed nerves as I lay against the rooftop. We spent nearly a week tracking down the thief, Robert the Sly.

Word got around that a dragon was always spotted near the King's bounty hunter, as well as the homeland guard. Rumors claimed the fallen Rider rode with the hunter. And while the common folk only gossiped for entertainment, bounties fled like cockroaches.

We tracked down Robert on the run with three other men. Darrak didn't expect much of a fight, but gave me the task of covering him. He seemed to know I needed to keep busy. If I were left to myself, I couldn't guarantee that I would have stayed at camp and not made my way back to the palace.

I frowned down the stock of my crossbow, watching the tavern door. Mikhala was supposed to lead them out, with Darrak following behind. As far as we knew, the others were not bounties, at least not commissioned by the King, and therefore of no interest to us. We only wanted Robert, so if I had to take them out, I would.

Or at least maim them.

'And you say I am a beast,' Tizmet commented on my thoughts.

I shifted quietly on top of the thatched roof. On the Solstice, a weight settled on my chest, and it grew heavier by the day. I tried to keep a tight leash on my emotions. Darrak and Mikhala had done nothing to deserve my irritation. I didn't even understand where it came from. I had never been so ill-tempered in my life.

'You should ask the Woman. She might have a different opinion.' Tizmet pushed memories of me talking back to Elenor, lashing out in anger when I joined the ranks.

It both pleased and irritated me that she was so in tune with my emotions. She read my thoughts well and perceived what I was about to do before I acted. I, however, only got bits and pieces of her feelings. If it was a strong emotion, it often spilled over the bond, but for everyday things, I had to reach over to her side to feel it.

'I simply want to be back.'

The tavern door opened. The fading light would make for a poor shot. I hoped I didn't have to take anyone out.

'You were so bloodthirsty before.'

'Enough!'

She tsked. *'Someone is in season. Perhaps you should mate with Darrak. He would make fine babes.'*

'Tizmet! Enough!' I pushed my anger and irritation, but felt her amusement in answer.

Mikhala spilled through the door with two men. I squinted down the stock as she laughed and drew them to the side of the tavern. No doubt they wondered why she pulled them outside when the place doubled as an inn. Clearly, they were smitten by her odd beauty, like every other poor sot.

'Definitely in season.'

I ground my teeth together and slammed the door on the bond. She could force it open if she wished, but I didn't need her taunting comments distracting me from my job.

I kept my eye on Mik as two more followed them out, far more stealthily than the others. I glared at them as they slunk after their friends like a pack of dirty dogs.

The tavern door opened once more and Darrak came out, waving at someone inside. He glanced in my direction as it shut behind him. My cloak was bundled around me, hood pulled over my white hair. He saluted my way and followed the rowdy group. The two latecomers moved in on the three, Mikhala teasing, playing hard to get. They cornered her against the side wall.

One looked up as Darrak approached and called out to him, spitting on the ground. Darrak shrugged, resting a hand on his pommel, and pointed with the other. Mikhala moved quickly, wrapping herself around their target, pinning his arms to his side.

Two turned on her and pulled their knives while the one facing Darrak drew his weapon. I focused on the one advancing on Mikhala and lowered my aim on his thigh. Chances were my shot would get something important—without killing him.

Darrak reached up to his shoulder and released the cloak draped over his chest, revealing the crest of the King's bounty hunter. The man in front of him stepped back, but the two near Mikhala both shouted, striding toward her.

Darrak drew his sword and threw his fist in the air. I loosed my bolt at the signal, immediately loading another. When I had it loaded and drawn, I looked down my stock and sighed.

It was over.

My shot had flown true, even in the fading light. My target curled on the ground, clutching his thigh. The snow beneath his leg grew dark with his blood. Darrak dispatched the other two, and Mikhala was tying the hands of the one she held.

I pushed myself upright and removed the bolt from my crossbow, releasing the draw. Carefully, I scrambled from my perch. My part was done, and I would receive a portion of the bounty bonus.

At least I was making some coin.

I winced as my boots hit the hard-packed snow. My joints were stiff from lying on the roof since midday, and I was frozen. It hadn't started out bad, with the sun warming me, but as it set, the temperature dropped—resulting in the slower speed of my loading. I needed to work on that.

A small gasp brought my attention to a young stableboy. He gazed up at me from a pile of hay, pieces tucked into his wild hair. He blinked and rubbed at his eyes, clearly having been woken.

I smiled and winked before crossing the road on stiff legs.

"–and therefore, the wrath of King Vasili Aldred falls upon you, and you will be served justice at his hands." Darrak wrapped up his formal speech, as was his custom, while securing a bounty.

"You filthy dog! You hunt for that bastard! He took–" Robert's words were cut short as Mikhala stuffed a gag in his mouth.

"You're the dog." She grimaced, kicking him into the snow.

I curled my lip and lifted my crossbow, resting it on my shoulder. Tilting my head, we all faced the man leaning against the building.

"Are you... are you going to kill me too?" He gasped, wild eyes darting between us in terror.

"I think we should." Mik snarled.

I scoffed at her antics. I hadn't been the bait, but she did this as a job. She acted as if it was different. Perhaps being with Gaius changed her somehow.

"You're not the King's bounty." Darrak spoke with cold detachment. "I don't care for your life one way or the other."

"So... I'll live?" he asked in shock.

"Aye," Mikhala scrunched up her face, "at least until you bleed out."

I blinked, glancing down at the wound. I had aimed to maim—had I hit a blood vein? Would he die? Would he be the first life I took of my own accord? I frowned and turned to Darrak. He simply shook his head. I sighed and cracked my neck in relief.

We left him in the snow with his fallen comrades and headed for the stables. The stableboy looked between us all in horror and ran to fetch our horses. Darrak seized Robert's sturdy gray, tying it to his own horse.

They rarely lingered in the village after taking a bounty. Too many folks could benefit from the profit, and might attempt an attack to claim it for themselves. Usually, they rode out to camp where I stayed, but on a night like this, we would ride till dawn.

Saddled and mounted, we set off into the dark. I opened the bond and felt a small wave of comfort roll over me. She was close. Out of sight, but we would meet her within a chime.

We rode well into the next day. As mere humans, we were exhausted, but Tizmet soared high, enjoying the warmth of the sun's rays. We camped early and were in our blankets as the sun touched the horizon. We were still days out from King's Wall, but we distanced ourselves enough from the village that the risk of anyone attempting to steal the bounty was low.

Tizmet watched while we slept, the one perk about traveling with a dragon. She woke us twice as Robert tried to escape. Once when she batted at him with her tail to knock him flat on his back, and the other when she roared loud enough to wake the dead— which sent him diving to his blanket, shaking in fear.

'Last night was a bit dramatic,' I said the next morning as we readied ourselves for the day.

'Better he know what he's up against.' She snorted, watching him with lazy eyes. He probably thought she looked at him like he was first meal.

The rumors of the fallen Rider and her man-eating dragon had definitely done their rounds. People were terrified of her once they realized I was not a proper Rider. They all heard the story of how she ate a human arm. Though in most of the tales, she swallowed him whole. It really depended on who told the tale.

'Are you bringing in bounties too, then? In it for the coin?' I teased as I mounted Boulder. I watched as Darrak helped the bounty onto his horse.

'Glittering metal means nothing to me,' she said, dipping low to swoop over our heads.

Robert's horse neighed nervously and danced to the side. He hadn't been raised near dragons and saw himself as mere prey.

'You helped out of the kindness of your heart?' I asked.

Normally, she mentioned if a bounty made a move to escape but didn't care to assist in any way.

'You needed rest.' She banked as I glanced up at her. Her bright eye reflected the yellow blaze of the sun. *'You have been sleeping poorly.'*

I recoiled from her words. Everyone was quiet and sluggish after only a single night's rest. I hadn't had a good night's sleep since the Solstice. My palm rubbed against my chest, as if I could relieve myself of the weight there. A small part of my mind wondered if I lost control of the magic at some point and it damaged my body. I had no other explanation for the crushing strain.

'The red's Rider will help?' she asked as we set out.

'I hope. He can at least explain the magic to me.'

'Will he find your mate?'

I bit my lip as we rode. My spear bumped against my knee, strapped to the saddle. The thin braid of my white hair hung near the sheathed head. My heart tensed against a sudden pressure.

'I'm hoping he already has.'

We arrived at King's Wall five days later, making good time. Together, we turned Robert in to the bounty house, and I ignored Mikhala's antics as she acted like a shy kitten.

We rode to the palace as Tizmet circled lower.

'Ruveel is not here?' I asked, feeling let down.

'No.' Tizmet informed me as she landed on the balcony to our room.

I knew the chances were slim. The winter respite allowed him frequent travel to and from the palace, but it was still unwise. Dragons were not meant to be active during these frigid months. The cold took too much out of them, and even Tizmet grew sluggish and lethargic at times. Ge'org needed to be in fighting shape at all times.

I frowned as I cared for Boulder, putting extra straw down for him. It was a cold day, and he worked hard. He snorted, nosing my shoulder. I smiled and pushed back at him. He was the most placid, boring horse I'd ever met. He acted like a rock most of the time. Still, he was a faithful steed. One I would miss if Tizmet ever let me ride her.

She scoffed, offended. *'Comparing me to a horse?'*

'A faithful and loyal companion,' I countered, slipping out of the stall.

I faltered at the scene before me. Darrak had his arms crossed and stood in front of Mikhala. She had her back against a stall door, kicking at the ground. Her hands were balled into fists and she glared at her boots. Darrak muttered something, and she spun without a word. She shoved past him, pushing against his shoulder as she tore down the aisle. I frowned and tilted my head. I'd witnessed the two bicker like an old married couple, argue like a father and daughter, and torture each other like best friends. Yet I had never seen them truly fight.

He turned to me with a scowl and jerked his head, motioning me to go with him. I squinted but fell into step beside him. We walked in silence, and I tried not to pry. It wasn't my place to question where they were concerned. They had been friends long before I came along.

We reached my room, and I opened the door out of habit. It had become like the dorms in the school—I just knew this space was mine. Tizmet already nosed the curtain aside and curled on the thick rugs laying about the floor.

I went to close the door, but Darrak held it ajar.

"A word, if you please."

I swallowed nervously. If this was about Mik, I wanted nothing to do with it. However, I did need to talk to him about getting word to Ruveel about my use of magic and request a teacher to explain it.

I nodded and motioned him inside. I sat on the bed and pried off my boots as he shut the door and pulled a chair up to the bed. He took a seat and steepled his hands in thought, touching them against his lips.

"I want to know how long you've been covering for Mik."

My heart dropped and my skin went clammy.

He knew.

It wasn't that I feared him, or any punishment that came from sneaking out of my room. Darrak was more than fair. I might not like whatever was in store, but he wouldn't be cruel.

No, it wasn't fear that tightened my throat. It was the disappointment in his voice.

"How long?" He brought his gray eyes up to meet mine, and his brows furrowed.

I pressed my lips together and frowned, debating how much to tell him. "A while."

"Define, 'a while.'" His voice was rough with emotion.

My gaze dropped to my hands folded in my lap. "Almost a year."

I hated this feeling. Guilt and remorse filled my heart. Shame and regret. I felt like a daughter who just let her father down and betrayed his trust.

Darrak bit off a curse and ran a hand through his hair. He gave it a harsh tug and leaned back in the chair, crossing his arms. "Why?"

"What she does isn't my–"

"What's in it for you?"

Tizmet lifted her head, flicking her tongue out. She tasted the emotions in the air before she settled again.

"Nothing."

"You're not dumb, Avyanna," he scoffed, tipping his chair back on two legs. Anger sparked in his gaze. "What did you bargain for?"

"Darrak, she's an adult. She can do what she wants. She's not bound by you or–"

"You know what she's bound by?" he snapped, righting the chair with a crash. "Her people. She's not as free as you or she likes to think." He bit out another curse. "I'm going to kill Gaius," he muttered, gazing at the ceiling.

"There's nothing wrong with them being together." I held up my hand when he opened his mouth to interrupt again. "No! Hear me out. I don't care that we think they're not well-suited. They make each other happy. Let them have that much, Darrak. Let them have their little piece of happiness."

A pleading sensation pierced my heart. If I could get Darrak to accept them, perhaps people would accept me and Rafe. I wasn't just fighting for Mikhala's happily ever after—I was fighting for my own.

"You don't know anything." He moaned, shaking his head. "I love you both, truly I do, but you can be so immature."

The pleading in my heart turned to fire. I was younger than him, but I was the age of a Lady. I was not so immature.

"Good sun and dragons above. Do you know what will happen if she mates? If she's already bedded Gaius?" he bit out. "Her people will come for her. The risk is not simply if Gaius tries to accompany her to Caulden, it's if they find out they're together.

"Her clan is her family. They will come find her—the lost pup to their pack. After they kill Gaius, they'll take everything she has, burn her belongings, rob her of coin, and steal away her home. They are a hard people, Avyanna, they are not to be crossed. Their family is their life, and they protect it at all costs."

"How could they?" I whispered, horrified. No loving family would do such a thing.

"You've never seen them, never met them. I have. They are cold and hard, but they love with a fierce passion. It's not just Mikhala and others like her that they're concerned for. They're worried for their little ones that would know she left. They would realize she went against her family's teachings and beliefs. To their young and impressionable minds, that road would not seem so bad. The pleasure would outweigh the punishment."

I grimaced. "That's barbaric."

"It is their way." He leaned back once again. "I care too much for her, and for that fool, Gaius. I've let it go unchecked for far too long."

"You're not her father."

I regretted the words at the same moment hurt flashed across his face.

"Her father would have gutted Gaius and shipped her wild arse back to Caulden. I'm just the man who found the scared, little red-headed warrior from a foreign land, wandering a shipyard. I'm just a simple man who saw fear in her eyes, but passion in her heart. And I'm just the man that will be in her clan's path of destruction."

"They can't hurt you."

"No, you're right. I'm protected by the King. She's not. I'll have to face her father. He will look at me, knowing I let his girl go against everything he ever taught her. I'll have to watch as he takes his revenge and carries out the punishment."

"I didn't know." My words formed slowly. "I—what can we do?"

"Nothing." He grunted, holding his head. "There's nothing to be done now. I'm surprised she's not with child."

"She's not that foolish."

He peeked through the crack of his fingers. "I don't even want to know how you know about that."

"How would her people ever find out? They let her go this far. They didn't care that she left to begin with. Why not leave her alone now?" I asked.

"You think they let her go?" He laughed, rubbing his brow. "Her people followed me for a year before I persuaded them to allow her some freedom. I was convinced she was a warrior at heart and would grow weary of this easy life. I told them she would return to them one day."

My hope plummeted. "Does she know?"

"I've never hidden it from her. Though she is apparently immature enough to have not guessed as much."

With a deep breath, I hugged myself. Guilt and shame soured my stomach. I had a part in how this would play out.

"I will deal with it as it comes." He sighed, pushing himself to his feet.

I spoke up before he could leave. "Wait."

He arched his brow and waited. The anger once burning in his eyes fizzled out, leaving disappointment in its wake.

"I have something else to tell you."

He took a deep breath and held it for a moment before he met my gaze. "If you tell me she's with child, I'm going to lose it."

"No, it's about me."

"If you tell me you're with child–"

My jaw dropped. "No!" I choked.

He chuckled wearily and dropped back into the chair. "I didn't fear that of you."

I tilted my head. "What do you fear of me?"

Darkness flashed in his eyes, but his smile stayed fast. "Other things that are better left unspoken."

As I told the story, I left out Rafe and what Tizmet said. I was vague on how I pulled on the magic and hoped because Darrak was not a Rider, he would not be familiar with its ways. Even I, who studied to be First Chosen, hadn't known the details of how magic worked, and I still didn't.

While I spoke, Darrak cycled through positions on his chair. He started with his arms crossed, listening intently. Then he leaned forward, frowning. Then he ended up holding his head, elbows propped on his knees.

"How is it that both girls under my care have managed to get into such a mess?"

I had to be thankful he at least wasn't angry with me.

"You want me to tell the Dragon Lord that the Rider he assigned to me has unconsciously used magic? With no training, no control, no guidance at all?" He dragged his palms down his cheeks. "Why me?"

"I'm glad it's you." My assurance didn't seem to reach him.

"I'm not! Do you know what my last report said? 'She managed to befriend the dragon, though they fought over whether she could eat the horses. I am uncertain if this is progress. Also, the dragon lit a barn on fire during our return.' How will it make any sense at all if my next report reads something like, 'Ruveel, she used magic unknowingly. Please send help.'"

"She sneezed! It was accidental! The straw was dusty!" I laughed, remembering the barn fire.

Tizmet lifted her head and bared her teeth, flicking out her tongue.

Darrak threw his hands in the air. "Sneezing dragons. Who would have thought?"

"So will you send word?" I asked, smiling at his drama.

"Yes." He leveled his gaze. "I'll do better. I'll send my reports and we will head for Northwing. Chances are, he'll want to see you in training again, with discretion. On the off chance that he'll want to see you in person, Northwing is closer to the front. The respite will end soon and he'll be hard-pressed to find time to leave after that."

My heart sped with excitement at the proposal of seeing Niehm and Elenor again. "When will we head out?"

"First thing in the morning." He braced his hands on his thighs. "Now, is there anything else you wish to confess?"

I flinched, thinking of Rafe, then shook my head and smiled sweetly.

"I'm going to pretend I didn't see that," he muttered, squinting at me. He heaved a heavy sigh as he stood. "I have more than my share of reports to fill out. Get some rest."

With that, he walked out of my room without a second glance. Probably eager to be rid of me and the problems that came with me.

'I wonder what will come of Mikhala and Gaius?' I stood and rang for a servant, then headed for the tub.

Tizmet yawned, curling more tightly on the rugs and furs. *'It is their fight. Not yours.'*

'I helped her get into this mess.'

'She is not a hatchling. She needs no assistance from you. Whatever battle she faces, she must be... big enough to fight on her own.'

I frowned, hoping that both of us were strong enough to fight our own battles.

CHAPTER 28

The journey to Northwing seemed short compared to our other travels of late. Three days passed quickly, and though Mikhala and Darrak argued in King's Wall, they were back to their normal happy selves. I remained silent concerning what he shared with me, and Tizmet was firm in her stance to leave Mikhala and her problems alone. Which I did—for now.

When we reached sight of the outlying villages, my heart soared. Tizmet trumpeted and flew low over us, feeling my excitement. I had so much to tell Elenor and Niehm, and was dying to show Willhelm everything I learned.

Traveling with Darrak, I was free. I was not bound by the rules and laws that governed Riders. Because of the oath I took when I enlisted, I still belonged to the King for another two years, but I was as free as I could be.

Mikhala cast a sidelong glance at me, and I caught her grin. We both took off at a gallop, racing for the closest village. Moony would beat Boulder every time, but it felt good to have the wind tugging at my hair. Just beyond this hamlet were the school grounds and barracks—the only home I'd ever really known... and my friends.

A flash of green darted up from the direction of the Dragon Canyon, and Tizmet altered her flight to greet Flinor.

'He has grown.' Her satisfaction flowed across the bond.

'My, my. Are you smitten?' I teased, chasing after the red and white tail that waved in front of Boulder.

'Perhaps I will take a mate soon,' she said, distracted by Flinor's aerial acrobatics.

I let loose a wild whoop, which caused Mikhala to turn around and beam at me. If Tizmet was calm enough to consider mating, she felt at peace, at home.

Safe.

We closed in on the village, slowing our panting horses to a walk. Laughing breathlessly, we took in each other's appearance. I wondered what Niehm would make of Mikhala. They'd make an interesting pair.

"You have friends here?" she asked, glancing around.

"Aye, inside the school grounds."

From this distance, I could only see the outline of Northwing's stone wall, and the travelers that crowded on the road through the gate.

"Tell me more of them."

So I did. I droned on as we neared the entrance, Darrak catching up with us. He rolled his eyes at our conversation and rode ahead. The eastern gate was most commonly traveled by vendors and hired help, and the guards were busy checking the passes that the common folk carried. One held a hand up, and we pulled to a stop.

"Hail!" the guard called. "Papers?" His eyes flicked over each of us, then settled on the crest on Darrak's chest.

Darrak nodded his greeting. "We come with the King's goodwill," he said, passing a parchment over.

He skimmed it, then his gaze scanned over Mikhala, and lingered on me. "Shall we make it known that her dragon is here?"

A pang of hurt resounded in my chest, and Tizmet roared, amused. The guard lifted his eyes to the overcast sky, searching for her among the clouds.

"She won't be eating anyone." I flashed a bright smile when he gawked at me. "She ate yesterday."

I shouldn't antagonize the locals, but both me and Tizmet were fed up with their fear.

She swore humans didn't even taste good.

He squinted as if figuring out if I was serious or not. With a grunt, he handed over Darrak's papers and motioned us through.

Relief settled over me as I took in the familiar sights. Not much changed over the year I'd been gone. People still milled about, and children were underfoot everywhere. Masters tried to wrangle the hordes of tiny humans into classes—some fared better than others.

Darrak nodded to me, then to the road that led to the canyon before he spoke to Mikhala. "Mik, you'll be staying in the women's dorms."

"How big are these caves you stay in?" She wrinkled her nose.

"Large enough for both us and Tizmet."

"Aye, well then I'll be staying with her," she arched a brow at Darrak, "if you don't mind."

Darrak's gray eyes bounced between us, and he pulled his horse to a halt. He twisted his lips to the side, assessing us. "If I hear a word about you two–"

"Only good things!" She laughed. "Now, show me these caves!"

We left our horses at the stables and hiked up the cliffs to the cave Tizmet settled in. It was spacious, with room for her to stand on her hind legs without reaching the ceiling, and wide enough for her to stretch without touching the walls.

Mikhala peered down the steep path with wide eyes. "You make that trek every day?" she asked as she gasped for breath.

"Aye. Normally, dragons are kind enough to carry their Riders." I cast a sidelong glance at Tizmet.

'Like pack mules. Beasts of burden.' She sniffed, licking at her talons.

Mikhala hefted her pack. "Ah, that explains it."

I caught a glimpse of green rounding the bend as we entered the cave and settled our packs. I removed my spear from its sling and lowered my crossbow to the floor. It was quite a pain dragging everything up here, but I didn't dare leave it with the stableboys.

Tizmet tilted her head, and I noticed her anticipation. I smiled and turned to the cave entrance, where Flinor landed nimbly with Dareth peeking from behind his dragon's neck.

"Hail!" he shouted with a wave.

"Greetings Dareth!"

I made my way to him as he slipped from Flinor's back. His beast snorted and tilted his head, meeting Tizmet's intent stare.

Dareth raised his eyebrows, glancing between them. "I see she's handling the travels well."

"She is. A bit thinner than I'd like, though."

She was slim for a dragon her size. She should have been more filled out, but being active during the cold took its toll.

"Happens to the ones that stay awake," he said with an unconcerned shrug. "Flinor could use more rest, but he hates missing out on anything exciting." He flashed a knowing smile at Tizmet. "Like a lady dragon mysteriously arriving."

Mikhala barked a laugh, admiring the two dragons with her hands on her hips. Flinor was still smaller than Tizmet, though not by much. He was a mighty beast, one that would make a worthy mate if she ever chose him.

'Perhaps.' She agreed with my musings and clicked at him before curling into a tight ball in the center of the room to rest.

"Dareth, this is Mikhala. Mikhala, Dareth."

His locks fell over his shoulders as he dipped into a bow. "Pleased to meet you."

"You as well. You remind me of home." She smiled, then reached out to touch his fine hair as he straightened.

"Oh?" He glanced at her hand, then back to her face in good humor.

Her smile turned thoughtful. "The men in my home country grow it out. They don't cut it all off like they do here."

"It's a terribly tedious thing to keep it short." His gaze danced over to mine. "I see you're growing yours out."

I ran my fingers through the strands. It was just long enough to pester me by falling in my eyes, but not so much to tie at the nape of my neck. Mikhala taught me how to braid the front and fasten it to the side so that it stayed put during our practice bouts.

"Cutting my hair was my General's way of teaching me a lesson—and I learned it."

"What lesson might that be?"

"To get what I wanted, I had to sacrifice everything."

A dark, twisted sensation clenched my heart. With it came the familiar nagging worry whenever I thought of Rafe.

I lost everything. When I strove to fight on the front, I had to let it all go—my pride, my honor, my dignity. I had to prove my commitment as a soldier, that I'd go to any lengths to excel.

It was through Rafe's actions that I learned the value of the things I'd lost. My self-worth, my femininity—I cherished both now more than ever. I valued my privacy, my freedom to think and act as I willed. It took time, but I learned to respect myself through my trials. I was a woman now, complete and whole. I could make my own decisions and abide by my oath to the King. If anyone thought poorly of me because of it, I wouldn't care in the slightest.

"That's a hard lesson to teach. Even harder to learn." Dareth's eyes sparkled as he studied me. "You don't resent General Rafe for it?"

I shook my head and bit down on the turmoil that swirled inside, causing my fingers to fidget. "He was helping me, though I didn't know it at the time."

Mikhala moved to Flinor, drawing our attention. I swallowed as Dareth looked away, hoping he hadn't sensed my nerves. I needed to shake off this unease and figure out the magic I used on the Solstice.

"What has brought you back?" he asked, as Mikhala walked around Flinor, trailing her hand along his scales.

"I have questions."

"What kind?"

"The kind the Dragon Rider Masters can answer."

I rubbed my arms. For whatever reason, I wanted to keep my use of magic secret. I didn't want to share with anyone that I connected to Rafe. How could I explain what I did, how I tapped into magic, and avoid that detail?

"Ah, so you will attend classes again? Think she will handle it better?"

My arms crossed tight to my chest. "We're not here to play games like hatchlings."

Tizmet's bright eyes were on me, sensing my agitation. She never assured me what I witnessed was the past and not something to come. She couldn't. There was only so much she understood about magic. She knew it caused me distress, and we were both aware that there was little I could do about it.

My helplessness made it worse.

"Ah, so you have grown!" He smiled at me with fresh eyes.

"She's not a hatchling. It's insulting to treat her as one," I said with a firm nod. "I have questions and will take tutoring, but I refuse to suffer through classes where I'm expected to be peers with new Riders."

"That's understandable. Which Masters are you seeking? Perhaps I can help."

"I'm not sure. I'll wait on the Dragon Lord for guidance."

A sly smile spread over his face. He saw straight through me, and thankfully, wasn't offended by my avoidance of the topic. I wouldn't put it past him to know exactly why I came back. He was a jester, but far more intuitive than people gave him credit for.

"We'll wait on his word, then." He conceded.

Me and Mikhala made our way down to the hot springs where I showed her the glory that was earth-heated water. I missed the soothing warmth, and we stayed in the pools till we wrinkled like prunes. Tizmet stayed behind, opting to linger in the cave to rest. She wouldn't have wanted to leave the warmth of the springs once she had a taste. Brumation was a hard temptation to resist. She wouldn't risk it.

As the sun dipped lower, I showed Mikhala around. We caught a few looks from other Riders whose dragons were too young to join the front or were in brumation. I ignored them and walked toward the dorms. We were checking on Darrak, but I hoped to run into Niehm or Elenor.

The next day, I would take Mik to see the barracks and planned to 'accidentally' cross paths with Willhelm.

We made our way across the quiet yard. Most of the children and workers already turned in for the night. There were plenty of odd tasks to be completed inside—laundry, cleaning and cooking. The outside was silent, however, and Mikhala skipped next to me.

We entered the large stone dorm, and I bristled at the guards at the doors. Their strong presence was something I took for granted when I lived here. They were vigilant in their task—watching and protecting the civilians that lived and worked here. Now they felt stifling. I could almost feel their eyes following me as I made my way to the secretary.

Mikhala leaned against the desk and peered over at the papers laid about. The secretary was new, one I wasn't familiar with—a firm reminder that I hadn't visited the dorms in almost three years.

"Greetings." I plastered on a polite grin. "We're here to see the King's bounty hunter."

The woman's dark brow arched as she took us in. She batted Mik's hand away as she reached to touch a feathered quill. "It's too late to be paying male guests a visit."

"It's naught but the seventh chime." I frowned. "Send for him."

"Are you so entitled you would order me about?" she snapped, leaning forward on her desk. "Do you not remember your place, Avyanna of Gareth?"

I recoiled as if I'd been struck. Who was this woman to be so offended by my presence? Why was she treating me as if I insulted her by asking a simple question?

My tone iced over as I straightened to my full, but unfortunately short, height. "My *place* is to meet with the bounty hunter." I gestured to the runner boy, who sat beside her. On her other side sat a girl, for the same purpose. "If you would be so kind..."

"As I have already stated, it's too late for appropriate visits," she said, her voice positively frigid.

My lip lifted in a silent snarl, and I leaned forward to bring my face a whisper away from hers. "Fetch him, or you will answer to your King." I didn't blink as I stared her down.

A menacing smile spread across my cheeks as Mikhala shifted next to me. The secretary's glare flitted her way, and I knew she held out her bounty hunter patch for all to see.

I really loved Mikhala.

The secretary sat back with an irritated huff and leveled her fiercest glare at us—which wasn't too frightening. I had faced down an enraged dragon the size of the dorms. She was nothing.

"Send for him," she snapped.

The boy shot to his feet and ran past the twin guards into the hallway that led to the men's dorms. I pushed off the desk and took a step back, Mikhala following. I caught the young girl staring at me with her mouth hanging ajar, and I wagged my eyebrows at her. She blushed and ducked her head. Mikhala snorted, and we moved to one of the few benches in the lobby.

We waited, bouncing our knees like immature children. This new year gave me confidence and freedom to act as I wanted. I remembered the days I would have never acted so playful in public, too concerned for my reputation as a serious student or soldier.

Mik was a terrible influence.

Two sets of feet padded down the men's hallway and we peered down the hall. Darrak emerged, freshly bathed if his damp hair was any indication. His stare settled on us, and he tossed the boy a copper as we rose.

He smirked at Mikhala. "You decide to stay in a room instead of a cave?"

"Actually, we were wondering what you had in store for tomorrow?" I asked, before she came up with a snarky reply.

"I have some business for the King that I can wrap up." His gaze turned watchful, and he studied us as if we were wily teens. "Did you need something?"

"We hoped to get a pass to access the barracks." I was proud my voice didn't break with my nerves.

His eyes narrowed on me, and he shifted, crossing his arms over his chest. "See now, I think you could handle yourselves there... but I fear for the soldiers."

Mikhala laughed, and I flashed him my brightest smile.

"We won't cause trouble. I wish to see Willhelm."

"That was the Commander that looked after you, correct?"

"Sergeant, but yes. He took care of me the best he could."

Something dark crossed his features. "Petty little after I left."

The memory of Victyr's attack flashed in my mind. I'd been weak and vulnerable—naïve. Not anymore. I was stronger, more aware now. I could fight and care for myself. No one would lure me away. No one would get the better of me.

"I'd like to see him." I shrugged.

Darrak ran a hand through his short beard and glanced at Mikhala, who stood as primly as a schoolgirl awaiting a passing grade.

He heaved a sigh. "Fine."

She whirled on me with a smile, about to speak, but he cut her off.

"Conditions!" he barked.

I snapped to attention. "Yes, sir!"

He groaned and dragged a hand down his face before pinning us with a stern glare. "There will be no instigating or antagonizing. You leave the soldiers to their duties, and you will not interrupt their training. You will see your friend and get out of there. Your pass will end at midday."

At that, I deflated. I hoped for at least a day there. I wanted to show Mikhala everything our barracks had to offer—where I trained and slept... the pits.

"Those are my conditions." He lifted his chin. "Understood?"

"Aye," we answered in unison.

The secretary drafted up our pass, and Darrak returned to the men's dorms. I wondered at what business he had here. Perhaps the King's bounty hunter could find work anywhere.

I led Mikhala through the women's dorm, looking for Niehm or Elenor, with no luck. The glares and open malice I received were discouraging.

"You've shaken up their lives," Mikhala offered as we returned to the Dragon Canyon.

Tizmet woke and lazily stretched across the bond to feel out my emotions. She retreated and dozed again, deeming my mental state sound enough to handle on my own.

"I didn't do anything to them." I kicked at the icy path and almost slipped.

"You say that, but you changed everything."

She stooped down to ball a bit of snow in her bare hand. The action had me shivering despite my warm cloak.

"You showed them that a woman's place might not always be hiding behind the men. You've paved the way for future women. I wonder how many girls heard your story and tried to join the ranks."

"I haven't heard of any."

My face scrunched as she tossed the snowball at a tree and hit it dead center.

"Maybe not, but I would wager some parents have heard of nothing less. You've started something, Avyanna. It will be in the record books for as long as Regent stands. You've shaken the very foundation of their lives."

"I hardly think it was that significant."

"I *know* it was. You just wait and see. They will talk about you long after you're dead and have passed the Veil. They're angry because you've changed things. People don't like change." She balled up another bit of snow and eyed me.

"Don't even—"

I ducked as she chucked the ball at me, then scrambled to keep from slipping. She threw her head back at the bright moon and laughed.

When she calmed, she continued, "Then, in addition, you would have never met Tizmet if you hadn't joined the ranks. The common folk here regard that as a blessing, do they not?"

"Not a blessing, but a respected position." I watched her carefully, making sure she didn't pick up more snow.

"Well then, there you have it. Not only did you rebel, with no consequences to your actions, you were granted a boon for your effort. Now every young girl will beg their parents to let them enlist."

"There were consequences." I endured far too many.

"Aye, but they don't know that. They look at you with resentful eyes because they do not know your story, they only know *of* your story."

She stooped down to scoop up some snow, and I sidestepped, shoving her with all my might. She laughed and stumbled, but didn't fall. The icy ball in her fist glinted in the moonlight as she grinned.

"Better run."

I prided myself on being able to fight my way out of gnarly situations. I was an adult, fully responsible for myself and my well being.

And I knew when to run.

CHAPTER 29

T he next morning found me warm and comfortable. I bedded down along Tizmet—the dragon was like a furnace. The tip of her tail was ever so slightly twitching against my calf, half of her mind lost to a dream. I stretched and burrowed deeper against her side. It was frigid despite the tapestry that Flinor and Dareth had hung yesterday.

Last night, I returned to the cave, wet and shivering. Mikhala was brutal when it came to playing in the snow, and its chilling bite had no effect on her northern skin. I, however, had been painfully numb. I sniffed at the memory and pulled my blanket to my chin.

'Cold?'

Tizmet's voice was sluggish. She was exhausted from all the winter traveling. She would do well with a few day's rest tucked in a quiet, safe cave.

'Sleeping next to you?' I teased. *'I slept as snugly as if it was a warm summer night.'*

She rumbled at my compliment and slipped the tip of her tail around my leg.

'I have to get up, though,' I said, remorseful. I didn't want to brave the cold.

'Why?' Clearly, she thought sleeping the day away was the wiser choice.

'I have friends I wish to see.'

Her drowsy mind snapped to full awareness, and I twisted, finding her bright eye studying me.

'Should I come?'

I sensed the wariness she tried to hide. We made so much progress in our relationship, but sometimes the smallest things triggered her.

'All is well. They are old friends. You've seen Elenor and Niehm.' I pushed their images at her. *'Then there's Willhelm. I wish to see him as well—you haven't met him.'*

'I should meet him.' She spoke with conviction, as if he might dare an attempt to steal me away, and she had to prove he was no match for her might.

I laughed and shoved at her shoulder. *'Sleep. If you wish to meet him, I'm sure he would be delighted. I'll be back this evening,'* I assured her.

She blinked, keeping her wide pupil trained on me, and gave my calf a squeeze. *'I will rest, but will come if you need me.'*

'I never doubted you.' Smiling, I rubbed a hand over her scaled side.

I rushed to get dressed because it was so blasted cold. Hearths were tucked in the corners of most caves, with chimneys carved out of the stone. They were a pain to clean, and without prior notice of our arrival, no one had bothered to ready it.

"Mik!" I hissed at her sleeping form.

She placed her bedroll as close as Tizmet would allow, which in all honesty was far closer than any other person would get to her. She was a mere pace from Tizmet's right side, curled with her back toward the dragon.

Her groan answered me, and I crouched next to her pack to rummage through it. "Rise and shine. We're going to the barracks today," I called in a sing-song voice.

'Is that a normal greeting for the morning?' Tizmet asked, amused. She hadn't moved a muscle since freeing my leg, retaining all her energy for warmth.

'For her, it's as good a greeting as any. There will be fighting.'

Tizmet rumbled in understanding.

"Will there be food?" Mikhala moaned.

I yanked what I was looking for from her pack. "We have to go to the women's dorm, but yes. Up!"

"What are you doing?" she asked, watching me with sleepy eyes.

"I have a treat for you, and I'll need these." I grinned, holding up her black trousers.

They fit fairly well with my belt, but I had to roll up the bottoms several times to get them short enough for me to wear. I worried they would come unrolled, so I secured them tightly.

My baiting worked, and she was up and moving behind me. I cast a longing look at my spear, but it wasn't practical to wear on a trek around the barracks or the dorms. Mikhala wore her shortswords at her waist, and I settled with my bandit breaker and push dagger.

A chill seeped into my heart as I hesitated, staring at the bandit breaker as I threaded it onto my belt.

Rafe.

Rafe taught me how to use it.

I rubbed a thumb over the sheath's soft leather, and detachment blurred the edges of my awareness. The world around me dissipated as if I drifted away, lost in my memory of him.

'To me!'

I spun to face Tizmet, who now stood with teeth bared. Her tail thrashed wildly, sending my blanket flying.

'What?!'

'Don't pull the threads!' She snapped at the air and took one step toward me, bringing her muzzle to my cheek. Her breath teased my short hair. *'Not without me,'* she added, voice softening.

I finished fastening my belt and reached out to cup as much of her chin as I could. *'I wasn't.'*

'You were. I felt it.'

How had I pulled at magic without knowing? I was so caught up in my thoughts about Rafe—my gut telling me something was wrong. Perhaps I blindly reached for it again.

This was dangerous. I needed to figure out how to use magic, or I would end up killing myself.

'I'm sorry.'

My emotions burned through my chest, and I sent them to her. Where my fear and anxiety met her, she pressed warmth and contentment. With her, I felt loved, safe and secure. She cared for me and would protect me, even against myself.

She gave my temple a soft nudge. *'Should we find him?'*

'I doubt we could.'

I closed my eyes, holding her tight. Her comfort wrapped around me like armor. *'He's probably back safe and sound, anyway.'* I clung to those words, hoping they would provide the reassurance I needed.

They didn't.

"Are you all done?"

I sighed at Mikhala's question and bent to retrieve my winter cloak.

"Aye, coming."

'Perhaps I should come.' Tizmet gazed at the mouth of the cave and thrashed her tail again.

'I'm fine. Really,' I insisted. *'Get some rest. I promise everything will be fine.'*

We headed to the dorms to grab a bite for breakfast. I was hoping to run across Niehm or Elenor and wanted to avoid first meal with the soldiers.

Inside, we hung our cloaks in the lobby. I stood straight and tall as the secretary from the night before glowered at us. People were already milling about this early. Men funneled from their side of the dorm, and a few women joined them, pressing out into the cold.

I led Mikhala up the stairs to the old common room where I used to take my first meal. When we arrived, I stopped in my tracks. It had been turned into a nursery.

Children littered the beds—too many for a quick count. Nursemaids bustled here and there, tending to the young ones. Some were being changed, others dressed, and a wet nurse fed two babes in a chair tucked in the corner.

The smile fell off my face. All those little souls without family... If a mother and child sought sanctuary at the school, they were roomed together. These children didn't have mothers. The wet nurse's eyes caught mine and her smile faltered.

I stumbled a step as a familiar pang ran through me. This was why I joined the army—so I could fight for these little ones. I remembered little Ran, the boy who tipped me over the edge. Where was he now? How was he taking to his life here?

"Oi, Avyanna?"

Mikhala's concern snapped me out of my thoughts, and I shook my head, trying to clear them.

"Avyanna?" A familiar voice called.

I spun to see a pair of icy blue eyes. "Elenor!"

I snatched her in a fierce hug. She endured it stiffly, giving me a motherly pat on the back.

"Dear, what are you doing here? At a nursery, no less?" she asked.

"I was looking for some food." My excitement at seeing her faded into apprehension. "Where did all these babes come from?"

Elenor heaved a weary sigh and waved a hand at the nursemaids, who had stopped to watch us. "This way," she said, turning down the hall.

I nodded to Mikhala, and we followed her imposing figure.

"There have been more raids to the south and west," she stated in hushed tones. "More and more refugees are spilling in and we've no place to put them. We've had to start filling the outlying villages."

I frowned as she flattened her lips, the only evident sign of frustration on her face. The Elenor I knew wouldn't refuse anyone a bed, even if she had to sleep people in the stables. It had to crush her to delegate refugees outside the safety of Northwing's walls.

"What about the homeland guard?" I asked.

"They're far too busy patrolling the borders. The enemy slips in, ravages, and leaves. Few escape, and those that do have nothing to return to." She frowned, a wrinkle working its way between her brows.

She stopped at the threshold of a modest room, and I peered in. Three women stood in front of tables bearing sparse loaves of bread.

"We're on rations. I'm afraid there's no preserved fruit left," she said, almost mournfully. She remembered how I loved any bit of fruit or vegetable.

"We will take no more than the others." I stepped up to the thin elderly woman.

She took us in and glanced at Elenor.

"Give them each a ration."

The older lady handed each of us a loaf, giving a small bow. "May your day be well and bring bounties."

"Thank you."

"Bounties." Mikhala chuckled to herself as we walked further along the hall.

"Ah, Elenor, this is Mikhala." I bit into my bread, motioning to her.

Elenor looked her up and down. "I see."

I choked, forgetting what Mikhala looked like to others. Covered in furs, red hair braided, hanging wildly about her. Tall and broad, two swords swinging at her hips. To me, she was just Mikhala. To others, she was a wild woman.

She gave Elenor a sly smile and savagely ripped a bite out of her bread.

"She travels with Darrak and I," I explained as we stopped in front of one of the few windows.

"The bounty hunter?"

"Aye."

"Is he on orders here?" she asked thoughtfully.

A stray silver hair fell from her immaculate bun and it struck me how much more silver there was than black now. The refugees were weighing on her.

"No, I'm here for me," I said, gazing out at the people milling about below us. "I've questions for the Dragon Rider Masters."

"Seeking classes again?"

"No. Answers."

"I see."

Below, a group of men piled into a wagon, heading down the road to the school gate.

"Where is Niehm?" I asked.

"In the Masters' quarters, handling a meeting. She will be occupied till at least midday."

"I'll be in the barracks till then."

"Looking after Willhelm, I presume?"

"Aye."

A faint smile teased her cold eyes. "He will be pleased to see you. I think he misses you."

My laughter bubbled up, and I ducked my head. I missed him, too. I missed his comfort, his company and the way he listened without judgment.

"We can chat later tonight?" I pressed.

She peered down the way at the sounds of scuffling women. "Perhaps. Though it is unlikely." Her eyes traveled back to mine, more weary than I'd ever witnessed. "I've been terribly busy of late. I will try to find time."

"Thank you."

I gave her hand a squeeze. She had a job to do, and it was no easy task. I couldn't fathom how she managed to carve out hours for me while I stayed in the barracks.

She nodded with a parting smile before heading down the hall, her mouth pressed into a stern line.

"Bit cold, isn't she?" Mikhala murmured, watching her go.

"She appears that way." I took a deep breath and started toward the staircase that would take us to the yard. "Yet, she was there for me when no one else was."

She was a mother to me when mine was away. For that, I would always be grateful.

"That counts for something." She bounced down the stairs beside me.

"Aye, it certainly does."

We entered the barracks, and the first spot I took Mikhala to was the obstacle course. She grinned like a child in a bakery, drooling over sweetloaves. Dancing in place, she challenged me to a race. I agreed, not because I thought I could beat her, but because I needed something to lift my spirits after seeing the overcrowded dorms.

Despite my familiarity with the course, the snow and our differing heights nullified any advantage I had. The first lap, I almost beat her, but the second and third I trailed behind miserably.

Our competition drew a crowd. We laughed, enjoying ourselves as we threw curses and taunts at each other. The soldiers cheered, far more taken with Mik than me. I dropped out, leaning against the small fence surrounding the course. A soldier eagerly took my place to run against her.

She leapt over the hurdles like some graceful mountain cat and scaled the net faster than anyone I had ever seen. She climbed almost as fast as Collins.

Collins.

My head fell forward. I nudged the dirty snow with my boot. Where was he? What was he doing? A familiar ache in my chest flared up. I should be with them—not here enjoying myself.

"I see you made a friend."

That voice had me whirling. I flung my arms out, ready to throw them around him. A subtle sense of panic widened his gaze, and I stopped myself with a shy shrug. I forgot how proper he was, and it would be unseemly for me to embrace him. His company wouldn't let him live it down.

"I missed you."

"Likewise." He released a breath of relief and leaned on the post beside me. "You've been well?"

"Aye, better than I expected."

"I've heard stories about your dragon."

I flashed him a mischievous grin. "The man-eating variety?"

"Something of the sort." He nodded, but watched Mikhala as she took on another soldier.

"She snapped and ate his arm. Hardly his entirety."

'It was terrible,' she commented drowsily across the bond.

"Without a limb, most men would say they're as good as dead," he said, raising an eyebrow.

"He's being cared for."

"Must we watch our limbs around it? Lest we look appetizing?"

I threw my head back and laughed. His tone was jesting and his eyes danced with mirth. He didn't believe she was a man-eater, after all.

"I think one should always keep a close eye on their limbs." I grinned.

"So you've done well with her while you've been gone?"

"Aye. We've worked out all the nasty man-eating bits."

We talked the time away. Mikhala finally dropped to the snow, panting like a dog. I smirked in amazement. She somehow managed to get in the good graces of these soldiers within moments—while I tried for over a year to become one of them.

"I want to show you what I've learned," I said, turning to Willhelm.

He brushed his dark hair back from his brow. "And what's that?"

"Get me a training room and a spear—and I'll show you."

"Sparring?" Mikhala called.

I pushed off the fence. "Aye!"

Willhelm shook his head at our antics, but led us to an empty training center. The crowd followed us and my heart raced with nervous excitement. It would be a show with an audience. I wasn't used to anything more than Darrak or the occasional bounty we took in.

I snagged a short spear from the weapons rack and eyed Mikhala.

She crossed her arms, kicking out her hip. "Oh, no. I'm all tuckered out. You'd best me in minutes. Pick someone else."

My excitement faltered, glancing at the soldiers. They watched me warily, having heard of me, or at least recognized me from before I joined the Tennan. To them, I was nothing more than a weak, poor excuse of a warrior.

"I'm up."

I turned to Willhelm with narrowed eyes. In all my time in the barracks, I never once saw him fight. He remained too dignified to come to blows. He was a leader, a teacher, not a fighter. My gaze traveled up and down his build. He was dressed immaculately in his uniform, as always. It fit snug and professional on his lean, solid frame.

He removed his cloak and draped it over the weapons rack, then selected a shortsword and shield. Seeing him with the weapons, I nodded in satisfaction. They suited him well.

"I've never seen you fight," I mused, draping my cloak near his.

His eyes glinted as he rolled his shoulders and bent his knees. "It's your lucky day."

A slow smile spread over my face. Even though Mikhala and Darrak beat me more often than not, I was familiar with their style. Willhelm was different. With no knowledge of his combat capabilities, it would be similar to how I'd fight the Shadows. I had to learn quickly.

Dropping my gaze to his neck, I refused to look him in the eye. If I was going to approach this like fighting the Shadows, I would give my complete commitment.

Raising my weapon, I shrugged my shoulder. Willhelm struck fast, moving quicker than expected. I spun the shaft, batting his sword away, then striking with the blade. He deflected easily with the shield and let my blow roll off him. We shuffled apart, and I grinned like a mad woman watching his feet.

This would be fun.

We danced around each other, striking and parrying. I took a hit off my thigh and I landed one on his shoulder. We thrusted and slashed and attacked and dodged.

His pristine uniform became disheveled and moisture beaded on his damp forehead. Sweat dripped down my back, and I brushed my hair out of my face for the hundredth time. We panted for breath, and I shook with exertion. He proved a more worthy opponent than I thought possible.

Gasping for air and rolling under a blow, I spun around to his back as he turned, leading with the shield. I made a mad slash at his feet with the shaft. He moved a fraction too slow, and the wood thumped against his ankle. His mouth opened, baring his teeth as he jerked out of the way. I pressed my advantage and used every ounce of willpower I had, attacking him relentlessly.

Finally! I made contact under his armpit, and he stumbled back. Snarling, I charged, thrusting the wooden spearhead at his chest. He batted it away, and I let him, whipping the spear fast.

'Pull up.'

I jerked my arms, pulling the strike before it landed with full force. We froze, staring at each other. I grinned, tapping the spearhead against his temple.

"Got you." I panted. *'Thank you.'*

I was so exhausted and caught up in the fight—if Tizmet hadn't butted in, I could have severely injured him.

'You care for him,' she said in way of explanation.

"Well fought." He straightened with a matching grin. Sweat dampened his tunic and plastered his hair to his forehead. He wiped at it with his arm and gave me a tired salute.

I returned the gesture. "Well fought."

I faced the crowd as he replaced his sword and shield on the rack. Mikhala was collecting coins from grumbling men, and I choked on a laugh.

"Wagering on me?" I called hopefully.

"Aye. It was looking a little rough there."

She held out her palm toward a soldier. He cursed and threw a copper in her hand, storming off.

Willhelm sank into a chair against the wall.

"You fight better than I expected," I said with a timid shrug.

He squinted at me, amused. "I'm not sure that's a compliment."

I laughed and put the spear on the rack, then grabbed my cloak. "Honestly, I never knew you could fight."

"Just because I don't go around starting fights, doesn't mean I don't know how." He stretched his legs out in front of him and closed his eyes. "A wise man knows how to avoid fighting."

"A wiser man knows when something is worth fighting for," I replied, sinking into the chair next to him.

He peeked through heavy eyes, studying my face. "What are you fighting for?"

Rafe.

I bit my lip and wrapped my arms around myself.

He chuckled and leaned back. "Keep your secrets."

We passed the time, talking about the barracks and my adventures throughout the last year. Mikhala often commented when she thought I left out important, amusing details. I enjoyed speaking with him. Willhelm was the type of man that no matter how long we were apart, or whatever changed in our lives, he would treat me like an old friend.

As we neared the midday chime, I said my goodbyes. Willhelm had to see to his company, having left them to their own devices for too long. I desperately wanted to hug him, to hold him, and let him know how much I'd grown to care for him. He was too proper for that. So, I settled for a salute. His eyes sparkled with appreciation as he saluted me and we took off in different directions.

"He was nice," Mikhala commented as we left. "He can *fight*."

"Aye, I really didn't know he could. At least not that well." I laughed. My muscles shook and complained with every movement. I'd feel worse on the morrow.

"I'm glad you sparred with him." She tossed a small purse in the air with a jangle. "I made a decent amount of coin."

"I'm pleased you bet on me."

"Didn't doubt you for a minute." She grinned, throwing her arm over my shoulders.

We met with Darrak for the midday meal, which was a piece of cheese and a bowl of broth. We ate at a table in the formal dining hall, one of the few spaces men and women occupied at the same time.

"I received word from the Dragon Lord," Darrak said around a mouthful of cheese.

"Oh?"

I stirred my broth. It was unappetizing, but it was all they rationed to the workers. I felt guilty, knowing the tables in King's Wall were overflowing with food, while so many here begged for seconds.

"He arrives tomorrow."

My eyes shot to his. "So soon?"

It was still the winter respite, but he was a busy man. To break away from the front so quickly at word of my request was unseemly.

"I wager he's interested in this development." He glanced at someone behind me, and a sly smile lifted his lips.

"Is it Niehm?"

"Who?" Mikhala swiveled to search for who snared his notice. "Oi! Red hair!"

"Perhaps it's Commander Rory," I mused, watching Darrak's eyes dance. "Though I doubt you'd be so excited to see him."

He straightened to his full height. Putting on his most charming smile, he called, "Lady Niehm."

"That's Master to you."

Her familiar snappy tone lifted my spirits. I turned with a smirk to take in the fiery-haired woman with dark green eyes. I met her fierce glare right before she knocked my head to the side.

"Oi!" I rolled with the blow, ducking under her hand. "What's that for?!"

"Not writing!"

"Now I know what Darrak means," Mikhala said with a note of understanding.

"I barely had a moment to myself!" I showed my palms in a placating manner.

"What about all those times we left you at camp, and you had *days* to yourself?"

I smacked Mikhala's arm to get her to shut up. "Friends are supposed to cover for each other!" I hissed.

"Oh, no. I know that look." She jerked her chin at Niehm. "It's the same my mother gave before she sentenced me to a week's worth of latrine duty."

"I can think of a few duties for you." Niehm glared. "If you are actually sticking around for any length of time."

With a glance at Darrak, I offered a helpless shrug. "I'm not sure."

He tilted his head, still grinning like a fool. "We will be here for a few weeks, at the very least."

"Fantastic! I've heard the Dragon Masters are looking for more strapping young folk to carry the dung from the canyon." Niehm crossed her arms over her chest, not taking her eyes off me.

"Oi, now, now, now," I started with a nervous laugh, "I'm here to *learn*, Niehm."

"Oh? What classes? Any on how to communicate? To let those who care for you know you're not dead or dying? That the dragon you bonded hasn't eaten you?" She edged in, slapping her hand on the table, forcing me to lean backward. "Or have you resigned your friends to hear news of you from hearsay and rumors?"

My nervous smile wavered, wondering if she was done.

"I really like her," Mikhala whispered.

"Likewise."

Darrak's comment drew her attention. I stared up at her chin as she glared him down.

"You again," she growled, pushing back to stand with her arms crossed.

"Aye, me again." His voice practically dripped with charm.

Mikhala's eyes bounced between the two. Her gaze found mine, and she raised a single eyebrow in question. I gave a nervous, one-armed shrug.

Niehm broke her glower from Darrak to land on Mikhala. Her scowl softened, and a bit of her wild, angry, mama-bear look faded. "A word, Avyanna?"

"These are my friends, Niehm. Sit." I motioned to the empty spot at the table.

"Friends," she murmured. "I warn you, what I have to say is not for their ears."

I heaved a heavy sigh. There was no getting around it. She was going to tell me off in no certain words.

"Aye, they've probably seen me at my worst."

Niehm cleared her throat and sat beside me. Taking a deep breath, she launched into a grand lecture on how I failed my friends by not writing them. Her remarks were sharp, but her tone was soft. It might've been a rebuke, but that she sought me out to berate me spoke volumes. She cared for me. She missed me.

Fighting the smile lifting the corner of my lips, I sipped my broth to keep my mouth busy.

I missed her, too.

CHAPTER 30

T he next morning, Tizmet roused me, announcing Ge'org and Ruveel's arrival. I hurried to ready myself, though I doubted I was first on the Dragon Lord's list. I wore a simple green dress and braided my hair as Mikhala slowly woke.

Tizmet shifted from foot to foot, eyeing the cave entrance. I rarely felt unease from her anymore. Even concerning Ge'org—she was always confident and self-assured.

'Is all well?' I asked.

She tilted her head and flicked her forked tongue out. The muscles along her back trembled.

'Something is amiss.' She spoke with deliberate hesitance.

I reached through the bond to test her emotions. She was nervous, anxious—almost fearful.

'Is it Ge'org?' I joined her and pressed my hand on her shoulder.

She snapped at the air and narrowed her glare. *'I do not fear the red one.'*

She grappled with her nerves, attempting to stifle them. Frowning, I pulled the tapestry further open. Frost covered the stone walls, and my breath fogged in front of me. The weak morning sunlight reached its cold rays over the canyon's edge, dropping to its depths.

Across the way, Ge'org stood at the ledge of his cavern. His black and red eyes flashed as he tested the air. His strong talons kneaded the stone, crushing it beneath him as he shifted nervously.

Something riled them.

'I will come with you today.' Tizmet stepped beside me, snorting at Ge'org.

"Oi, what are we doing today?" Mikhala danced foot to foot, trying to get some warmth in her body. She stopped to admire Ge'org. "Oh, he's a pretty one."

He tilted his head and took a long sniff, flicking out his tongue.

"Tizmet doesn't care for him."

She raised her lip and growled. His eyes left Mikhala and darted back to her.

"Pity, those would be some cute hatchlings."

Tizmet turned to peer down the canyon, *accidentally* knocking Mikhala to the side in the process. *'Hatchlings are not worth that headache,'* she snipped.

I scoffed as Ruveel walked out to lean against Ge'org. He gave me a casual salute, which I returned. He tilted his head at Mikhala and hooked a thumb through his belt, cocking his hip to the side. She waved gaily back.

"Never been a fan of his, to be honest." She spoke through the fake smile plastered on her face.

Ruveel held up a finger, then disappeared into his cave.

"No? Why not?" I asked.

"Don't get me wrong, he does his job well. There's something about men like him I can't stand."

"The slippery, sly, whoremongering type?"

"He's not terribly sly." She scrunched up her face. "Just too full of fake charm. As if he's putting on an act, hiding the man beneath."

"I agree." I sighed. "We best get on to first meal. Who knows what's in store for us today."

We headed down the steep path, taking care with our steps as the frost and melting snow made it slick. Winter was thawing, and I was eager for the heat of summer. Warm balmy days, and the bright hot sun.

'Warmth would do me good,' Tizmet muttered.

She glided to the canyon floor to wait for us. I watched her as I descended, noting how her stare kept pulling southward. There was nothing there besides empty training grounds. As I pondered what drew her attention, a sharp wind had me clutching the rock wall for purchase.

Ge'org, a great wall of crimson, flew past to land next to Tizmet. Ruveel sat astride him, glancing back at us before focusing on his mount. He rode without a saddle, something I had seen few Riders do. Perhaps Ge'org was tired of wearing it. I couldn't imagine being saddled all the time would do his scales any good.

'And you wonder why I do not wish to be ridden,' Tizmet grumbled. She bared her teeth as he landed.

'I could ride you without a saddle.' Hope drenched my thoughts.

'Then my scales would not be irritated, only my pride in anguish.'

We wound our way to the main path at the base of the cliffs.

"I've never seen his dragon up close," Mikhala breathed, taking in his hulking figure.

Ge'org was massive—larger than Tizmet in both height and bulk. He was layered with muscles. If he stretched his neck, he towered over her by ten paces, at least. His scales shone a deep blood-red in the weak light, and his eyes matched the darkness.

The Dragon Lord was a small figure compared to his mass, sliding down his shoulder. When Ruveel met stone, he gazed up at Tizmet, craning his head to take her in from her maw to the tip of her tail.

"She's thin." An edge of judgment sharpened his tone.

"She eats as often as she would." I frowned. I didn't feed her. What she wanted, she took. It wasn't as if I starved her.

He peered under her belly. "When did she last eat?"

"The day before last." I crossed my arms. Was the first thing I heard from him really going to be that I wasn't caring for her correctly? I was not tending to a hatchling. She was a full-grown dragon, able to meet her own needs.

"Have her eat a hog every other day. She should have been in brumation this winter." His blue eyes were sharp with disapproval.

"Begging your pardon, but I was assigned to the bounty hunter," I snapped. "Our jobs hardly allowed time for brumation."

"Had I been informed your dragon needed it, I would have assigned her to brumation."

"You think she would take your orders?"

"*You* would take my orders," he growled, crowding me.

I had to tilt my head back to see his face, and mentally shushed Tizmet when she snarled. "I've been the perfect example of one of the King's Owned," I said with a bitter grin.

"No more eating people?"

"None that I would tell you about." Part of me recoiled that I dared to talk to the Dragon Lord this way. This was inappropriate. He was my superior, and here I was taunting him.

He glared at me for a moment. Just when my smile began to shake, he snorted and took a step back.

"My, how she's grown. Our little kitten has fangs." A cheeky smirk overtook his face as he ran a hand through his hair and rolled his eyes.

"I'm not your kitten."

"I trust you've had a grand time with her, Mik?" He ignored my comment and glanced at her.

She tossed him an easy smile. "Aye, it's been fun."

"Great. Go find Darrak. Avyanna and I have issues to discuss."

She shrugged. "Perhaps he has better food." She stalked off with a wave.

A thrum of nervous energy skittered across my skin, and I fought to keep control of my expression. He didn't need to know about the tight knot of anxiety that twisted in my stomach. I hoped he would simply assign me a tutor. There was no way to explain how I used magic without mentioning Rafe.

"Let's talk over first meal." He started down the path that led to the Rider's grounds.

I lingered in place. I really didn't want to discuss this in public.

He stopped with a sigh, peering over his shoulder. "Coming?"

"Could we," I cleared my throat, "speak in private?"

In unison, Tizmet and Ge'org both snapped their heads to the south. I frowned at her, puzzled by her actions. Ruveel studied Ge'org with the same quizzical expression.

Dread spiraled through me, trickling over from the bond.

'What is it?'

I pressed my palm to her leg. Her muscles were pulled taut and trembled beneath my touch.

'I know not.' She flicked out her tongue. *'I cannot place it.'*

Whatever it was, it disturbed both of them. Ge'org huffed and snaked his head above the ground, nudging Ruveel. The Dragon Lord rubbed his muzzle affectionately.

"If you wish to speak in private, we shall take first meal in my quarters."

The last place I wanted to be was trapped in a room with this man.

"Perhaps the top of the canyon?"

He leered at me. "Afraid to be alone with me?"

"I simply think it would be inappropriate."

He heaved another sigh and pressed his lips together. "I'm ravenous. Let's grab a bite to eat and head up."

We headed to the Riders' dining hall, which felt far more luxurious than I thought it should be. Despite its humble stone exterior, the building boasted beautiful details that outshone anything in the dorms. It was far better than the barracks, which was little more than wooden walls with benches and tables scattered about.

Vivid, intricate tapestries and paintings hung in neat rows, depicting legendary dragons and Riders. Fires roared and crackled in the many hearths, lending to the coziness.

Food was laden on tables, and people milled about, sampling it. A twinge of irritation twisted in my chest when I noted the dried fruit. The common folk had nothing more than broth and bread. I doubted those in the barracks had much better. But Riders were permitted such luxury?

I followed Ruveel as we filled our cloth napkins. I selected a small loaf and a tiny wedge of cheese. The dried grapes made my mouth water, but I passed them up. It didn't feel right.

Ruveel was pulled to a stop many times by Riders who came to greet him. He was polite and took the time to speak with each of them. To my surprise, he didn't act haughty or gloat. He treated them with kindness and efficiency, as if they would one day fight under his leadership—which they would.

I ignored his shameless flirtation with two women who approached. They eyed me warily, and I brushed them off. They had nothing to worry about with me.

I was destined for another.

That dreadfully familiar pull returned, as if my chest caved in on itself, collapsing under some unseen pressure. I bit my lip and fought to breathe, to appear normal. My heart spasmed. An invisible thread wound its way around it and tugged. I flinched.

Ruveel froze mid-conversation with a young Rider. Turning slowly on his heel, he glared at me. I stood up straight and smiled. He frowned, studying my face. With narrowed eyes, he resumed his conversation with the man to excuse us.

We made it out of the hall with no other interruptions.

"Care to tell me what that was about?" he asked.

The cold air nipped at my skin, sneaking under my winter cloak. I pressed my lips together. "I'm not sure what you're talking about."

His hand snapped out. I spun—but not quickly enough. He gripped my arm and jerked me to face him.

"Magic is not to be toyed with."

I felt more than saw Tizmet lift her head from her boar to watch us. She was eating outside the hall, a safe distance away from Ge'org. They had been fed their choice of meat, as was the custom, while their Riders ate.

"I'm not toying," I growled through gritted teeth and yanked out of his grasp.

"You were First Chosen. You should know the consequences." He bit the words out. "You've studied enough of the records to know what happens when untrained fools play with magic."

"I'm not playing with anything! I didn't even use it!"

He thought I was little more than a child poking at a snake. I wasn't. I understood the dangers, even if I couldn't control my grasp on it.

He studied me, a muscle working in his jaw. Tizmet swallowed the rest of her boar and approached, growling low in her throat.

"It seems we have much to discuss," he said.

He turned down the path, leaving me with no choice but to follow him like a schooled child.

Tizmet tested the wind, flicking out her tongue. I peered up at her and reached across the bond to sense what she tasted.

Humans. Animals. Wet. Cold.

'What are you looking for?' I asked, nibbling my bread.

'Not sure.' Something tugged at her attention, but she couldn't see it or smell it. It was there all the same—demanding her focus. She snorted and turned a fiery eye on me, licking her lips for any remnants of the boar. She settled on the ground and cast a baleful eye at the overcast sky. *'It would be better if the sun were out.'*

At the top of the canyon, the wind tore at us. The melting snow lent a wet chill that saturated my clothes and wicked away all warmth.

Ruveel tossed a grape at me, and I caught it with ease, popping it into my mouth. Apparently, he noted my yearning when I passed up the fruit.

"Tell me how long you've been doing this," he said.

"I haven't been 'doing it' as much as *experiencing* it." My response was sour, and I schooled my temper. "It started on the Winter Solstice."

"Magic is often easier to summon on the Solstices."

"Why?"

The wind teased his tousled hair, tossing it about. His blue eyes danced over my face but wouldn't meet my gaze.

"Some believe it's the magic itself, that it's eager to be drawn on, easier to grasp, if you will. However, I doubt that. Emotions run high on the Solstice, making the door to magic more accessible."

"Emotions play a role?" I asked. That explained a lot.

He shifted on his moss-covered rock, watching Ge'org. "They are not the key that turns the lock, but they are an important ingredient in the recipe. If you only have high emotions, but no dragon, you'll never use magic." He sighed, his stare pulling back to mine. "You should be learning this from a teacher."

"I would accept a tutor, but classes are no place for Tizmet."

"I see you've at least grown closer."

"She's quite docile now, I assure you," I said, layering on the sarcasm.

Tizmet turned her head to him and bared her teeth into a dragon-like smile and snarled.

"With your relationship deepening, it would be easier for you to reach across the bond and use magic." He studied me closely. "That is what you did, correct?"

"I–" My gaze dropped with my frown. "I don't know."

He bit out a soft curse and ran a hand through his hair. "We cannot access magic without our dragons for a reason. They are there to protect us. With the bond comes the ability to use it, as well as protection from it.

"Dragons are magic, but they are beasts of flesh and bone, just the same." Ge'org shifted closer to him. "They have the focus of a predator. They can single out one thought and not let anything in this world shake them from it. Without that focus, we, as humans, are prone to distraction. With distraction comes–"

"Loss of control," I finished.

He nodded. "Correct. At least you were listening in *some* of your classes," he scoffed. "Those who have tried to handle magic on their own have failed and suffered dire consequences. Women especially are prone to loss of control."

"Why?"

I tilted my head. That didn't seem fair, but could explain why few females ever passed the test of aptitude.

"Your minds." He offered a light smile. "Your minds are like a ball of river eels—everything touching and constantly in motion. Like a wildfire, all-consuming." He laughed. "Men are more—base creatures."

"Simpletons?"

"I never said that." He grinned. "We possess a greater capacity to separate our thoughts. We have a heavy hand and determination. It's why female Riders are usually assigned to guard the borders instead of the front. The less they draw on their gifts, the less chance they have of failing, and therefore the chances of magic being loosed to wreak its chaos are lessened."

"Are there not any women who've mastered it?"

"Agatha would have your head for insinuating she couldn't manage it," he said, referring to a well-known Rider on the front. "That being said, they are few. What I want to know, however," mirth died in his eyes, smothered by a blanket of seriousness, "is why you're using it without proper training."

I glared. "I told you I'm not consciously doing anything."

"To be fair, I didn't sense you summon it. It swelled to you as if it knew you would use it. Tell me about the Solstice."

It was my turn to shift uncomfortably on my stone seat. Tizmet sensed my anxiety and curled her tail around me to lay the tip across my boots.

"It was during the tradition of greeting the new year," I started. A glance told me he was nodding along, fully aware of the tradition. "I blew out the candle, and when I scattered the seeds—Tizmet said I left her."

"Where did you go?" he asked, frowning.

The question caught me off guard, and I stared at my boots. "I'm not sure. I thought I was somewhere else, in some other time. Tizmet pulled me back, and I woke in the snow."

"What did you see?"

"It was dark. I–"

"Were you thinking about any one person?"

"I was thinking about my intentions for the new year."

"Which were?"

"To follow my own destiny, to be my own person," I snapped, jerking my gaze up to him. He pried more than a nosy old woman.

"You belong to the King." He laughed. Shaking his head, he sighed and gave me a softer look. "It's been known that a few can use magic to see through another's eyes—share their body, if you will. Perhaps you connected to someone, and your dragon pulled you back. Did you feel any of the magic loose around you?"

"I don't think so."

"Think of magic as if it were an underground river. It's roaring and flowing, just waiting to be tapped into. When someone digs a well, it could spill above the ground. When you reach for it, never pull too much. If you do, it sloshes around, making a mess of everything.

"Magic does not have intent. It is chaos—a wild vine growing where it will. If you pulled too much and couldn't control it, or return it, you would feel it raging around you."

"I didn't feel anything after I woke."

"Then I'd wager you didn't pull too much."

"But what I saw, *if* I saw someone else, could it have been another time?" I asked carefully.

"I've never heard of that. Are you thinking you saw the future?" He stared as if he saw straight through me. "What did you see?"

"I don't exactly remember. It's been a long time."

Tizmet's head shot into the air.

"You're a terrible liar. Tell me what you—"

His voice caught as Tizmet scrambled to her feet and towered over me. I jumped to my feet, looking up at her underbelly.

"To arms!" he shouted.

I ran around Tizmet's leg, watching him climb up his snarling beast. "What is it?!"

She used her paw to push me back underneath her. '*Hide!*'

"Rally to the south!" he called.

Ge'org reared on his hind legs just as Ruveel found his seat. The great red dragon was in the air in a single lunge, careening over the cliff edge.

"*AWAKE DRAGONS!*"

Magic carried his command. It echoed over stone and snow, demanding obedience. Ge'org's deafening roar followed.

'*What in all of Rinmoth is going on?*' I shoved against Tizmet as she once again tried to tuck me under her like some wayward hatchling.

Her horror carried across the bond. '*They're here.*'

The Shadows.

CHAPTER 31

Air left my lungs as Tizmet snagged me up in one giant paw. She launched off the cliffside and scrambled into our cave. She retreated to the back with me clutched tight.

'*Put me down!*' I pushed at her talons to emphasize my words.

She opened her mouth to hiss. '*Mine!*'

Reluctantly, she complied and set me on the stone floor, but as I stepped away from her, she tucked me against her side and wrapped her tail around me.

'*Tizmet! Let me go! I can fight!*'

I shoved at her gray scales. She pressed against me, wedging me to her flank.

'*I cannot!*' She snarled, turning a bright eye on me. '*You can fight them, but I cannot protect you!*'

A shiver ran through her as she thrust her memories at me. When she was helpless to protect her young, unable to defend her nest. When she found her mate dead, knowing loss with no hope of revenge.

'*I am not helpless!*' I screamed, slapping her side.

She snapped her jaws in my face. '*Neither was he!*'

'*There are little ones out there!*'

She recoiled as I pushed my anger at her. There were children in that dorm—the nursery. Just how far would the Shadows reach? How much damage would the school take? They launched their attack on the least fortified side of the grounds. To the south, the school lay in front of the barracks and canyon. The refugees were trapped between the Shadows and the only defense Northwing had. I needed to be out there.

'*Let the red care for them.*' She spoke without conviction.

'*You're one of the largest dragons here!*' I pleaded frantically. '*Just seeing you would have them rethinking their attack!*'

'If they see me, it will only motivate them!' She snarled. *'Why do you think they come? They are after dragons, Avyanna. If you show them there are more of us, they will come in larger numbers.'*

Growling, I pushed against her, but she closed off the bond. Her reluctance was warranted, but I was not her hatchling. I knew how to fight. I could help protect them.

Deep, resonating roars answered from the depths of the caverns. Flinor would have been the one to rouse the dragons in brumation, though Ruveel's summons would have started it.

'Please. Let me go.'

My people were under attack. This was *my* fight. This was why I chose to be a soldier. I was prepared to meet the Shadows head-on, knowing that when they looked at me, they faced a fearless warrior, not little Ran or other vulnerable children. The enemy would see *my* spear, and I would stand my ground, protect my home and the defenseless. I would not hide away while my people suffered.

She shuddered under my pressure, and I pushed harder.

'I am not a hatchling. I was trained for this. Let me go.'

With her head tipped toward the ceiling, her deafening roar shook the cave walls. She dug her claws deep into the stone floor. *'Your bow,'* she growled as she released me. *'You will stay on the rooftops.'*

I ran to my belongings and snatched my crossbow with the quiver of bolts.

'Please, this once would you—'

She snarled and snatched me, barreling out of the cave. Air ripped from my lungs, knocked from the impact of her claws wrapping my middle. I clutched my weapons tighter. Wind slashed at my eyes, dragging tears across my skin. Dragons, one by one, emerged from the springs below, launching skyward. They were groggy, but adrenaline roused them quickly. A gold beast, half the size of Tizmet, but an adult in every right, watched as we flew above it. It blasted a war-cry and took to the air behind us.

'There are many,' Tizmet said, voice thick with worry.

'We are many.' I pushed back at her. *'This is our home. They're in for a lesson.'*

'But who is teaching?' she asked.

I frowned as we sped through the sky. She was right. They should have never gotten this close. Who could have predicted that we would be attacked on our own soil?

My stomach lurched with her wing beats, and I forced deep breaths into my lungs, staring into the distance to steady myself. Thick plumes of smoke billowed ahead. I hoped it was Ge'org's fire and not buildings. His red scales gleamed as he dove toward the ground, obscured from my view. Flinor's bright green shone as he lunged behind, crossing the patch with a burst of flames.

Tizmet's flight faltered. Her apprehension thrummed through the bond.

'He will be fine.' I tried to assure her.

She wanted to see him prove himself. She would take no less than a warrior as her mate, yet part of her still ached over her last mate's death.

'He will fight well.' She picked up her pace.

As we neared, she dropped lower, out of sight of the unfolding battle. I wanted to see what was going on, but anxiety buzzed through me as the first screams reached my ears. My knuckles were white against the crossbow. I steeled myself as Tizmet lurched upward, leaving my stomach behind.

Approaching the dorms, she swerved in a steep dive, colliding onto the rooftop with a rough landing. She released me, and I stumbled from her grasp. Her claws sank into the slated shingles, shattering them as she scrambled for purchase. I dropped to my belly—the friction from my clothes allowed a stronger grip. It wasn't too steep, but the slick snowmelt made any traction precarious. Screams, both masculine and feminine, assaulted my ears. The clang of steel beckoned me to the far edge. Tizmet hissed and sunk low, snaking her head along behind me as I crept closer.

My mind refused to make sense of the scene before me.

A mob of skeletons garbed in black danced with blades and spears, facing off guards, soldiers and civilians armed with whatever they had. Hunters tore through everything, blind with rage. The gruesome creatures sent my stomach revolting. One, a bear brutally stitched and spliced with a horse. Its eyes were ebony orbs, dripping dark sludge. Rot festered the seam where the bear's gut met the horse's shoulders. Chunks and strands of loose flesh swung with its movements, and I choked back my gag.

There were so many of them. How could numbers so vast possibly make it this far into Regent?

I fumbled, loading a bolt, then leveled my hold. Shadow Men and Hunters poured over the southern gate, scaling it as if it were no more than a simple staircase. I took aim as my heart beat a frantic tempo. Finding my target, a Shadow draped in black garb who charged at the soldiers, I loosed. After a breath to follow through, the bolt plunged into the Shadow's chest. He staggered, clutching at the wound.

I loaded another. My hands trembled with adrenaline, and I struggled with the winch. I forced my panicked breathing to calm and aimed at the next Shadow who descended the wall.

From my position, I picked off those I could as Ge'org and Flinor rained fire from above. I focused my attention on the Shadows, the black-garbed men with skeletal masks, just as Rafe taught me. The Hunters dropped like stones with their deaths. Soon more soldiers joined the fray and the other dragons finally roused themselves enough to join in.

My hands steadied and my heart lifted—we were well-suited to take on this fight. They attacked not only a barracks—but a Dragon Rider school. What could they have hoped to achieve by striking here? They clearly had no chance.

'He comes!'

Tizmet shook in rage, and I loaded a bolt, but hesitated. Her wrath boiled over the bond, coloring my vision red, and my trembling started anew.

I knew who was coming.

He climbed over the gate, and I took close aim. Flames danced and skittered, a striking contrast to his black robes. They swirled about him, so dark it seemed as if they swallowed the day's feeble light. The scarf, cinched tightly around his throat, gave the illusion of nothingness, his form lost in shadow. Scraps of the frayed, tattered cloth tugged in the wind.

On his head, he wore the bones of a creature, cut and reshaped into the semblance of a skull.

A dragon skull.

"PULL BACK!"

Ruveel's shout was touched by magic, the force of it rattling my teeth.

I lifted my sight from my crossbow and appraised the scene. Shadow Men flanked the Shaman, but the flow over the gate had ebbed. They battled on the grounds—around the dorms. Flames devoured everything in their path, creeping closer to the dorms by the second. Tizmet keened behind me—irate. She was helpless against this. She couldn't attack the Shadows, simply because of this one Shaman.

He was the one who bound her to his will.

"PULL BACK!"

The order repeated, and the dragons obeyed, veering toward the canyon. The Riders did as their Lord commanded.

Yet, I was no Rider.

I took a deep, calming breath and readied my aim as the Shaman stepped forward. Something inside me recoiled. His dark, twisted magic marred the King's grounds, tainted the place where I grew up. His vile presence stained my home.

I judged the distance once, twice, and a third time. I let out my breath and pulled the trigger. Keeping my focus on him, I loaded another bolt and winched the draw back. My shoulders stiffened as I glared down the stock.

The Shaman's head twisted my direction. My bolt jutted from his shoulder. Terror paralyzed my heart.

Don't look them in the eyes. Rafe's words echoed in my thoughts.

My gaze dropped to his neck. It was a smaller target. Harder to hit.

I wanted him dead.

Glaring down the flight track, I took a deep breath. I hauled on a door in my mind. It responded eagerly, and I gave the roaring river behind it one purpose.

Kill him.

My finger pulled the trigger, and I didn't move. The bolt flew straight and true. It didn't waver, didn't shake. The wooden stabilizers aided its flight as it careened forward.

His black gloved hand thrust upward. It should have stopped—or at least slowed my shot.

Instead, it defied all laws of nature and struck. It impaled deep into the Shaman's neck. His hand clutched his throat, and he staggered.

The surrounding Shadows faltered, their movements frantic. I felt his gaze, cold and hollow, but I avoided it, staring at his neck instead. Dark blood oozed past his scarf and dripped between his fingers. He yanked the bolt out of his throat, and my stomach churned.

He pointed it at me.

A wave of fear crashed over me as every Shadow looked up. They found me.

He stumbled, falling to one knee. No one rushed to help or assist. They simply left him to his fate. He fell forward, dying upon the bloodied mud.

Behind me, Tizmet reared on her hind legs and stretched her wings. She bellowed with enough rage to fight the war herself and came crashing down, shaking the rooftop.

'*Up!*' She slid her head close to me.

I blinked, frozen in shock.

'*Up! The battle is ours! Ride with me!*'

Her profound sense of freedom, of anger, crashed into me. I scrambled across the roof, slipping as I rushed to climb her foreleg. The other Riders made it look so easy. Perhaps it was the cold, or the nerves, but getting on dragonback was far harder than it looked. My dress tore as I straddled her, finding my seat. I settled between her shoulders, thighs gripping her neck. It was like riding a barrel. Only a barrel would be easier. I pinned my crossbow and quiver of bolts between our bodies and leaned forward as she steadied herself.

My stomach lurched. My hands sought for purchase in vain, and when she dropped off the dorms, I sunk my nails into her scales. She ducked her head and pumped her wings, jarring me with the movement. I gripped her tight as her body vibrated with her deep growl.

She shifted beneath me and pulled up, hovering in place. She loosed her fire on every Shadow below. I saw nothing of the fight—her massive form blocked my view. All my concentration focused on maintaining what little grip I had as she ducked her neck down and pumped her wings hard, bringing us higher. I felt like a doll strapped to a bucking horse, clinging on for dear life.

'*Today we fight! We kill!*'

She inhaled, sharp and long, then let out a roar that left my ears ringing. My heart raced with a blend of fear and excitement as we ascended toward the low-hanging clouds.

I freed my dragon.

On my hands and knees, I gasped for air. The ground beneath me still bucked and blurred, and I gritted my teeth as another wave of nausea rolled through me. Turning away from my vomit, I tried to keep up some pretense of dignity as I knelt on the bloodied ground.

Tizmet sat next to me, tearing into the body of a Shadow. I made an effort not to think too hard about the crunching of bones or the soft squelching of shredding skin. A quick glance revealed I was not the only one horrified by her eating the bodies.

'Please don't eat them.' The weak request shivered through our bond. My body heaved again, and I spewed the contents of my stomach.

'My kill!' she snapped.

I shuddered and wiped my face with my cloak.

Dragon fire burned several outbuildings and trees. Survivors battled the flames that threatened the dorms as the civilians evacuated. The dorm itself was stone, but there were many additions constructed with wood. One of which was ablaze, as well as two nearby trees.

Once the Shaman fell, the dragons returned, and the battle was over within half a chime. Tizmet took her revenge on the Shadow Men, unleashing fire like I'd never seen. The flames threatening the dorms might have been her fault, but I'd been too busy trying not to vomit on her or myself to steer her away.

Once we landed, she tore through the bodies, unbothered by their foul taste. The soldiers drifted about, checking for survivors while casting horrified glances our way, but I was far too nauseated from the ride on dragonback to give them any heed.

"I gave the command to pull back!"

I closed my eyes at Ruveel's angry tone.

"Are you too simple to understand what that means?!" He drew closer, and Tizmet snarled a warning.

"I am no Rider." My voice felt far too small as I straightened. I gazed up at him from the ground, my legs too weak to support my weight.

"You belong to the King. Therefore, you obey *my* command." He crossed his arms, his glare sharp enough to cut steel.

I couldn't find it within myself to be bothered by his tantrum.

"When I say pull back, you retreat. You don't try to be a blasted hero!"

"I wasn't."

I resisted the urge to lie on the ground. The rush of adrenaline left me trembling and weak. I wanted nothing more than to melt into the cold mud and rest.

"You're worse than Rafe!"

My eyes shot to his.

"The fool goes behind enemy lines, and look how well that worked out! You'll end up the same as him if you don't learn to take orders!"

My heart faltered, and my throat constricted painfully. "The same as him?" I breathed.

"Aye! Blast it all!" he bellowed. "What is your dragon doing? Dragons don't eat humans!"

He stepped closer, and Tizmet paused, leveling her head at him. She let out a low hiss, splattering him with dark blood. He swiped at it, disgusted, as Ge'org landed behind him.

"Where is General Rafe?" I asked. The words sounded so distant, even to my ears.

My body trembled as his blue eyes whipped back to me, his dragon towering at his back.

"Dead."

The ground gave way under me and my vision went black. I braced my hands on the frigid mud and took a shuddering breath.

"You're confined to your cave until further notice—"

"He's not dead." The words slipped out as I struggled to pull myself together.

He wasn't dead. I would know it if he was. I saw him on the Winter Solstice. He was out there, alive. He was hurt.

"I assure you, he is. Up. Get your dragon to your cave. You've done enough damage for a lifetime."

My breaths came in quick bursts and adrenaline returned to my veins, giving me a paltry amount of strength.

'Will you fly with me?'

She turned a flaming eye on me. *'Not to the cave.'*

'No. Not to the cave.'

She snorted and lowered herself, stretching out her leg so I could climb to her back.

"He's alive."

My body moved of its own accord, letting my heart lead. I grabbed my weapons and climbed on. My arms shook, and I slipped multiple times.

"Avyanna of Gareth—don't!"

I settled on Tizmet's withers, leaning forward to pin the crossbow between us, and stared at Ruveel. He mounted Ge'org with far more efficiency than I had, rushing as if he knew what I intended.

'Now!'

She leapt and flapped her wings, hitting Ge'org's head with a wingtip in the process. In three wing beats, we were airborne. She pumped hard, gaining altitude. Ge'org snapped at her below us and let out an angry bellow.

'Hurry!'

I clung to her neck like a tick, sinking my nails into her scaled hide. My cheek pressed against her warm body as I clamped my eyes shut to ward off the nausea and vertigo.

I just had to stay on.

'We are free?' Tizmet questioned as she raced for an updraft.

'We'll be banished for this,' I said, braving to crack an eye and peer behind us.

Ge'org struggled to catch up. Ruveel's anger was a tangible thing—even at this distance. Tizmet banked west. Shocked and curious eyes watched from below.

'Faster.'

'Do you doubt I can outfly him?' she asked—almost teasingly. Clearly, she was still on a high from the battle.

I shuddered against her scales. *'If he catches us, we'll never have another chance.'*

He thought Rafe was dead. He couldn't know—or perhaps he didn't if he lived. I would know if he was gone. I'd feel his absence with every breath. It would settle deep in my bones.

'Then he won't catch us.' She pumped harder, launching us faster. *'I will not be trapped again.'*

A sense of calm and gratitude caressed me like a balm to my anxious, fearful mind.

We flew hard, Ge'org roaring behind. As we stretched out over the edge of the Great Northern Lake, Tizmet caught an updraft and soared higher and faster. Ge'org was a mighty beast, and seeing him in battle gave me a new appreciation for him, but his bulk was no match for her speed. Tizmet was Wild. Everything she did, she learned out of necessity, for survival.

"Avyanna of Gareth!" The Dragon Lord used magic to bolster his command and carry it on the wind. "Turn back, or suffer the consequences!"

I cracked my eyes to glance over my shoulder without breaking my grip. Ge'org's flight careened to a halt—he couldn't catch us.

I refused to heed Ruveel's orders, refused to think of what this would mean for me in the future. I only had one goal now.

Find Rafe.

CHAPTER 32

T izmet crashed to the ground, jarring me. The freezing cold left my limbs rigid and unresponsive. I couldn't move my fingers or release my grip. She snaked her head around to sniff at me and eyed me curiously.

Cursing under my breath, I fought against the stiffness in my fingers, attempting to make them budge. *'I can't move.'*

'Perhaps you were not meant to fly.' She lipped my cloak, tugging me off her back. My arms moved with a sluggishness that betrayed my exhaustion, and I collapsed onto the cold dirt in a heap. The crossbow dug into my ribs and I groaned, rolling to the side.

'Now I know why Riders use saddles.' I moaned.

Failing in my attempt to sit up, I resigned myself to laying on the ground. I blinked up at the dusky sky. We landed near a forest's edge, and even though I had no idea where we were, or where we were going, Tizmet was confident in our survival. I had time to ponder my decision to run—recognize it as an ill-contrived plan, but I made my choice and now had to live with it. I would take life as it came and simply deal with it.

My only purpose was to find Rafe. I had to find him.

'They use saddles to make us look more like horses.' She huffed, using her nose to jostle me.

'I'm pretty sure they're used so that we don't fall off.'

I winced, feeling the strain in my fingers as I worked them, hoping to relieve the tightness. She cooed and curled around me, cutting off the cold, wet air. She settled her head against my back and sighed.

'You freed me.' Awe and gratitude softened her tone. *'I will carry you, but I shall never be saddled as some simple beast.'*

I smiled and curled against her, grateful for her warmth. *'Thank you.'* My chest felt too small for my heart. *'I only ask that you carry me till I reunite with Rafe.'*

A purr rumbled deep in her throat. *'I will help you find your mate. I would never hear the end of it if I refused you.'* A hint of amusement lingered in her words.

'I know he's alive. I just know it.'

Even as I assured her, that familiar tug pressed on my chest.

'He is,' she agreed. *'How will we find him?'*

That was a good question... and one I didn't have the answer to. I didn't know where he was, other than behind enemy lines. Would I even be able to rescue him? If he was so deep that trained forces were incapable of retrieving him, how would I—a single woman armed with only a crossbow—help him? And what of the Tennan? Were they alive? Were they trapped alongside him?

'Do you really think your bow is your only weapon?' Tizmet prodded.

I rolled to meet her gaze. Her eye shimmered like a fiery sunset, with vibrant shades of orange, red and yellow. The narrowed pupil trained on me.

'You would fight for me?'

I hadn't thought of using her. She was an adult dragon, independent of me, and there would be no ordering her about as a tool.

'Avyanna, today you granted me a... boon.' She blinked once before continuing, *'I have been trapped and helpless—robbed of my young and my mate. I sought you out of desperation and loneliness. By slaying the Shaman, you released his spell over me. I can move and do as I wish, without fear of dark magic. This once, use me. Use me as a weapon against them. Help me teach them to fear a dragon.'*

Every inch of me melted at her words. For once, she saw me as a benefit, not a burden. I proved my worth to her, and she was asking me to show her once again. My heart fractured inside my chest—she was seeing me as her equal.

'Fight at my side,' I reached out a stiff hand to stroke her scales, *'fight with me and we will teach them a lesson they will never forget.'*

I thought the discomfort after the flight was bad.

Oh, how naïve I was.

Each breath was a struggle. Each movement pulled the sore muscles along my ribs. Moving was torture. Every limb was stiff, screaming in pain. Who knew simply clinging to a dragon's back would result in so much agony?

I whined as Tizmet stretched out the next morning. She sheltered me all night, giving me a warm place to sleep. The frigid ground leeched all of my warmth, but she was a furnace, keeping me comfortable.

I didn't have a pack—or my spear. I had the dress I wore, my cloak, my two blades, and my crossbow and quiver. Though, after yesterday, my supply of bolts wasn't in the best shape.

'Why did I think it was a grand idea to go charging off without a plan?'

'No plans are the best plans.' Tizmet flicked her tongue, tasting the air.

'I doubt that logic.'

I groaned and inched upright. As I made my way toward the treeline to relieve myself, my steps were stiff and slow, resembling the unsteady gait of an old dog.

'There is a herd of deer nearby. I hunt.'

'You just ate yesterday.'

'I do not need it—you do.'

She launched herself into the air. It was a show of absolute strength and wonder, watching a dragon rise.

'I can't eat a whole deer.'

'Then I shall eat what you do not.' She banked south. *'Start a fire, little one.'*

Grumbling, I managed to collect some wood, cursing and wincing with every movement. Every bit was soaked through, and I had no flint or steel. If Tizmet offered her flame, it would light wet or no.

A frown creased my face as I contemplated the events unfolding at Northwing. Did they put the fire out at the dorms? Where were Darrak and Mikhala? Were Elenor and Niehm alright? Did Willhelm join the fighting, and I missed him?

A pang of remorse rang through my heart. I rushed off so quickly without checking if they were harmed. I doubted I would have had any chance to depart if I attempted to sneak into our cave for provisions. Ruveel would have stationed a dragon to keep watch, and even Tizmet would have been hard-pressed to get out, let alone with me.

Hugging myself, I stared at the wet pile of wood.

I disobeyed a direct order and voided my contract with the King. I was a deserter. Deserters were banished—or executed. I bit my lip. I better adapt to getting around with nothing but the clothes on my back. It would be all I had until I found Rafe.

What would Rafe think?

What would my mother think?

A carcass dropped in front of me, and I jumped with a yelp and a curse.

'Enough of those thoughts. They will get you nowhere.'

Tizmet landed and swiped the deer. She tore off a haunch, tossed it to me, then squinted at my pile of sticks. *'No fire?'*

I gave her a flat look. *'No flint.'*

She snorted and opened her maw, letting out a small stream of fire. It licked at the wood greedily, and I scrambled to remove my push dagger to skin the deer. The flames cracked and popped, devouring the branches.

'I don't have that much wood!'

'Cook faster,' she said with a mental shrug, then tore into her meal.

I hurried to clean the meat and place it over the fire.

'Did you see water?'

'Further west, there is a river.'

I nodded to myself. Traveling would be a pain without a waterskin or flask. I had to locate Rafe as soon as possible, but prepare for the possibility of it taking months. I had no supplies, and that needed to be remedied.

When the meat sizzled over the flames, my stomach grumbled with hunger. Too impatient to allow it to cool, I ate—hissing between bites from the heat. I doubted Ruveel would come after us. It was more likely he'd resign me to my fate, but I wanted to keep moving.

After filling my belly, I kicked wet dirt over the small embers. Tizmet scrunched up her face but ate the rest of my deer, not willing to waste any.

My nervous hands brushed my torn dress as I avoided her gaze. *'I only have one idea.'*

'I will help.' She already knew what I planned, being privy to my thoughts.

Taking a deep breath to calm myself, I bit my lip. If this went wrong, I could die—Tizmet could die. We could unleash a plague, or—

'Calm yourself.' She huffed, blowing in my face.

I coughed and glared at her. *'This isn't easy. I don't even know how to access it properly.'*

'You used magic well enough when you slayed the Shaman,' she shot back. *'I aided your focus then, as I will now. All will be well.'*

She nudged my chest, causing me to stumble against her side. I sighed and sat down, pressing against her scales. My eyes drifted closed, and I drew in a deep breath, filling my lungs. Wrapping my arms around myself, I exhaled and felt for the magic. I rolled through my thoughts, searching. When I reached across the bond, Tizmet gently pushed me back into my own mind.

'Find it within yourself,' she urged. *'Think of him.'*

My lips pulled into a frown. I wanted to find him. Yet, I was reluctant to feel that sense of dread, that impending doom that came with thoughts of Rafe. I squeezed myself tighter and let my thoughts wander to him.

My vision from the Solstice. The misery with each step, unable to move under his own power. The agonizing pain in his side and chest.

Something clicked into place as my heart ached. He was out there—without me. I doubted I could have prevented his injury. Still, I wished I was there for him, as a source of solace throughout his torment.

Shame rushed over me for even thinking that way. He was a *General*. He'd been beaten and hurt, and here I was, assuming things would be different if only I were there. I was a simple, barely trained soldier.

What good could I do?

Still, my longing reached out, and slowly, behind my eyelids, a glowing mass came into view.

'Think of him.' Tizmet reminded me softly.

I furrowed my brow, picturing his face—broad and bullish, with a firm jaw and nose. His shaven head and shadow-touched eye.

'Find him.'

The mass grew brighter and clearer. It was a rat's nest of gleaming strings, threaded here and there, winding around everything—Tizmet and myself included.

She shifted in my mind and pushed an image at me. Air rushed from my lungs. Rafe sat beside me against the cave wall with his legs stretched out. Mischief danced in his eyes as he said something, and he smirked when I frowned.

'Rafe.' I sobbed his name and my heart nearly shattered.

A thread flared, singling itself out from the others. I latched onto it. Everything else faded to black, and I grasped it within myself, following its path as it wound and stretched southwest. It was impossible to judge the distance or note any landmarks, but I held on nonetheless.

A dizzying rush fluttered through me as I zipped along the thread. I could have sworn wind brushed against my cheeks, whipped through my hair.

Everything jerked to a stop, and I gasped. All went black. No more glowing threads.

Wave after wave of searing torment slammed into me, and I opened my mouth to scream. Sharp metal tore at my naked skin, flaying it from my side. My body moved, flinching away from the agony, but cold bands snared my wrists and ankles, pinning me in place.

I tried in vain to pull needed air into my lungs, to breathe past the pain. It was too much.

'To me.'

The distant voice was but a whisper, drowned out by the misery that engulfed me. My head pounded a vicious beat, and my bones screamed in dull torment. My body felt like it had been dipped in acid.

'To me!'

I flinched at the deep command, blinking at the void that consumed my vision. I couldn't breathe, couldn't move—couldn't *think*. It was too much.

My eyes shot open, and I lurched forward, gasping for breath. Trees and an overcast sky greeted my gaze. I sank my hands into the soft wet earth and heaved as the pain faded.

'*Foolish,*' Tizmet muttered, nudging my back as I trembled.

'*I did as you said!*' With a sense of desperation, my fingers dug into the mulch, needing something tangible to hold, to stay grounded. '*We have to get him. Now!*'

I jumped up on unsteady feet. The world swayed beneath me and I threw out a hand to steady myself against Tizmet's side.

She huffed and flicked her tongue out. '*Follow the thread. Do not connect with him.*' She blinked a bright eye, and her concern trickled over the bond. '*You are too weak for it.*'

My fractured heart splintered a bit more. She was right. Whatever he was going through, I couldn't take it. That torture, that agony—I was too weak. Too helpless.

'*Up, ride.*' She nudged me with her foreleg. '*We have a mate to rescue.*'

A wave of dread rolled over me. I couldn't do this—but I had to. If the Dragon Lord wrote him off as dead, there would be no one sent to his aid. I might be weak—insignificant, but I refused to abandon him. He wouldn't have given up on me.

Clenching my jaw, I snatched my crossbow and bolts. Climbing up, and slipping multiple times, I settled myself on Tizmet's back. I wrapped my arms and legs around her neck and pressed my cheek against her warm scales.

I would rescue him.

Or die trying.

CHAPTER 33

T he next few days passed in a sore, tired, cold blur. With the weather warming, the last of the snow melted, eliminating my only reliable water source. Every movement was painful, my muscles failing me. Riding Tizmet was no easy task. Humans simply weren't meant to ride dragons without saddles.

We rose with the sun and flew well into the night. Tizmet hunted, and I ate once a day. Her full stomach made her slow, and though she enjoyed the daily food, it wasn't worth the delay.

I grimaced and pressed my cheek against her as we soared through the cold sky. My cloak was tucked around me and my crossbow, but the chill bit right through it. The daily use of magic took its toll, and my head pounded a terrible beat. My mind wasn't accustomed to its demands. Tizmet intervened often, stepping in to redirect my focus on Rafe.

A shudder ran through me as he crossed my thoughts. I hadn't slipped into his awareness since the first morning after we left—which both comforted and worried me. I didn't sense that he was further away. Perhaps it was Tizmet who kept me from connecting with his consciousness. That or–

'One day at a time.' Her motherly tone cut through my thoughts before they spiraled.

I braved a peek, cracking my eyes a sliver to see. *'Are we near the front?'*

We soared above the trees, as high as possible without me freezing to death. The higher we went, the colder it became, and as much as I hated it, my grip would begin to falter. We were flying in plain sight, and that unnerved me.

In the distance, I saw a treeline. It appeared as any other forest, the same as the woodlands below... but proportionally *wrong*.

'You call them Sky Trees.'

I cracked open my eyes a bit more, taking in the sight. They were too far away to make out any details, but knowing what they were, the proportions made sense. Their immensity blocked all daylight, encompassing everything below in a shadowy, oppressive aura. Had I been on horseback and approached such a dark forest, I would have thought twice about entering.

'Your mate lies a day's flight past the tree line.'

'You can sense that?' I shivered against the cold and tucked myself against her scales. *'You're a far better judge of distance.'*

'I flew many days to find you.' She craned her neck to eye me, and blinked once before straightening.

I smiled to myself. For all that I loathed being bonded in the beginning, I wouldn't have been able to attempt any of this without her.

The afternoon passed in a cold blur, and I struggled to reserve what little strength I had. Tizmet reached over the bond to check on me several times. It always seemed like an easy thing to ride a dragon—at least to me, but now I understood the cost.

I was barely conscious when we entered the Sky Trees. I wouldn't have noticed a difference if it hadn't been for Tizmet dodging the massive trunks and branches.

With the sun dipping below the horizon, combined with the thick, endless canopy, the darkness was stifling. It pressed against me, squeezing me from all sides. Glancing around, I could barely make out the trees' faint silhouettes.

It was deep into the night when Tizmet grew weary enough to land. She dropped, and I roused myself to peer down. She shifted beneath me, attempting to stretch out her exhausted muscles, and I bit the inside of my cheek to keep from crying out. We were suspended hundreds of paces above the ground, perched on a branch that seemed as wide as a house where it connected to the trunk.

I clung to her tighter. *'Ground! Why can't we sleep on the ground?!'*

'Prey sleep on the ground.' Amusement colored her voice.

'What in here is big enough to prey on you?'

'It's the principle.' She sank her claws into the thick branch, then craned her head back to snort and flick her tongue out, studying me.

'Don't you dare.'

'If you act like a hatchling,' she bared her teeth, *'I shall have to treat you like one.'*

I scrunched my eyes closed, but couldn't bring myself to move as she nipped at my cloak. A whine escaped as she tugged at me, lifting me from her back.

'Don't drop me!'

Silent laughter rumbled through her as she set me down on the branch.

I had no pride.

I dropped to my hands and knees, shaking like a leaf. It was a tree, but one that grew a hundred times too large. The bark was rough and grooved as any other. If I moved along its surface in this stifling dark, I'd trip and fall to my death.

It was plenty wide for me to walk down the center and stayed level for about ten paces before it sloped downward. As I surveyed the landscape from our lofty position, a chill ran down my spine, reminding me of the immense distance that separated me from solid ground. The slightest misstep—

Tizmet huffed and nudged my backside. With a string of curses, I sank my nails into the bark. I scrambled toward the base of the branch, the widest point, and therefore, in my mind, the safest. My back pressed against the uncomfortable grooves as I faced her. She stretched out in front of me, talons sinking in, anchoring her.

'I wouldn't let you fall, wingless one.'

'Start poking fun at my lack of wings and I'll start making fun of your size,' I grumbled, trying to find a comfortable spot.

'My size is intimidating—unlike your small stature.' She settled her head near my feet.

I rolled my eyes and pulled my cloak around me. It was terribly uncomfortable, but it would have to do for tonight.

Throughout the depthless dark, an itch tortured the space between my shoulders—as if we were being watched. Several times throughout the night, I woke to a crash in the distance. Tizmet would lift her head and taste the air. This was her world, where she grew up. Here, she was the leader.

'It is a dark wing.'

She pushed image of a bird—one more immense than anything I'd seen. Larger than the great northern eagles. Those beasts were as tall as I was when standing, and their wingspan, double that.

The creature had large yellow eyes, reflecting the weak, filtered moonlight that trickled through the trees. The name was well-suited, as I couldn't tell if the bird was simply dark gray or brown, or solid black.

Every little sound woke me, despite Tizmet's presence. Here, I was not at the top of the food chain. Among the Sky Trees, I was prey.

And I felt it.

The sun rose the next morning, and though no clouds impeded it, we still had to wait well past dawn for enough light to travel by.

I grimaced and climbed up Tizmet's foreleg, trying not to look down. I settled into my uncomfortable seat on her withers. She craned her head back to flash me a mischievous look.

'Don't–'

I bit my tongue as she lurched off the branch, diving toward the ground. I held on, gripping her scales for all I was worth. My stomach flew to my throat, and I had the distinct feeling that if I'd eaten breakfast, it would've made an unpleasant return.

She lowered her head, giving me a clear view of us rushing to meet the ground. I immediately tucked my forehead against her scales and hissed through my teeth. She rumbled and snapped out her wings. Pulling up, she flitted among the tree trunks, while my stomach felt like it continued its journey to the forest floor.

We flew for chimes before I had to take a break. My limbs shook with exhaustion, and I needed to relieve myself. We landed, and Tizmet brought me the largest rabbit I had ever seen. With her help cooking the flesh, I ate it quickly, and she showed me strange, large moss that held moisture to drink from.

Resting my back against a rock, I closed my eyes. My head throbbed, but accessing magic was getting easier. I wasn't sure if that was good. The ease made me nervous. I didn't want to reach for it blind and unprepared.

The door to magic, the great mess of glowing strands, opened to me as I tugged on it. Tizmet stretched across the bond and curled around my consciousness.

I thought of Rafe and the time we spent on the beach at Northwing. Not our conversation—just being together. I focused on him and seized the glowing thread that flared. Grasping it tight, I tugged—then frowned when it ended just west of us. I released it and closed off the door before I let my mind ponder that.

'If we were that close, wouldn't we see more Shadow Men?' I rubbed the bridge of my nose, then my temples as the pain swelled.

'We are near the Shadows,' Tizmet said, lifting her head to the west.

I pushed myself to my feet despite the desire to lie down and sleep. My body screamed at me to rest, and my mind was fuzzy. Scrunching my eyes shut, I rubbed at them furiously, then brushed my hair out of my face and stifled our small fire.

Tizmet's concern flowed over me, but I let it roll off and climbed on her once again.

'We have no other option,' I said with resignation. I sensed her silent agreement as she crouched down low. Launching herself into the air, she beat her wings to gain altitude.

The sun dipped toward the horizon, and daylight faded below the canopy. Tizmet landed as light as a butterfly, anchoring herself on the branch.

I peered around her, eying the group of men far below. *'It can't be.'*

'The ones from our bonding.' With a confident nod, she affirmed her statement.

I squinted through the fading light. Five shapes moved about the small camp, tucked against the base of a tree. The site bore the marks of a long-term stay, with worn paths leading to and from makeshift shelters. I couldn't see enough to identify who was down there, but it didn't make sense.

Why weren't they with Rafe?

Tizmet lifted her head and flicked out her tongue, looking at the branch high above us. She rumbled a warning growl, and I tried to peer around her.

'The silent one comes.'

'The silent one?' I asked, squirming in my seat.

Without a sound, a man slid down, riding a coil of rope. I squinted at his silhouette as he hung just above Tizmet's bared teeth. He had the thin but strong build of the twins, and his face sported the black heavy beard they grew when they couldn't trim it to a decent shape.

The man swung his weight to the side and dropped to the branch. Tizmet flicked her tongue out, testing the air as he shook the rope and glanced up. He gave it a harsh tug, and it came loose, falling toward him. A small grappling hook fell, clanging against the bark. He must have used it to get around.

"Dane?" I leaned as far as I dared without dismounting.

"The others are there." He jerked his chin at the camp. His voice was quiet and raspy as always, rough from disuse.

My gaze roved over his dirty clothes, and the shortsword dangling at his side. "What happened?"

"You better hear it from Jam," he replied, avoiding my eyes.

Unease wound through me at his words. "Should I wait for you?"

"No."

I nodded and gave him one last forlorn look before Tizmet lurched over the edge. It took us mere seconds to land. The men shouted curses as they scrambled for weapons. I slid off Tizmet's back, grasping my bow. My muscles screamed in protest, and I staggered, almost crumbling in a heap. Tizmet hissed and growled. They drew weapons on her, and she wasn't happy about it.

"Oi, Jam?" I called out, trying to position myself between them.

"Hold!"

Relief rang through me at Jamlin's deep voice. I stumbled around Tizmet, grinning at the five men standing before me. My smile faltered as I noted who was there—and who was not.

Jamlin took up the front, rough and unkempt, with his longsword pointed at Tizmet. To his left, Blain, hand on the pommel of his weapon, with Zephath tucked behind—his sword drawn. To Jamlin's right stood Tegan with his ax, and Xzanth with his bow nocked.

They were all tired and worn. They wore dirt like camouflage, and I frowned at the way their clothes hung off them.

"Jam?" My voice was unsteady, my confidence gone. The smiling eyes I had once known were sober and wary.

"Avyanna? What are you doing here?" Shock and anger laced his words.

"It's a long story." I shirked. "Where's Rafe?"

The line of men shifted and cast glances at each other. Zephath shot Jamlin a vicious glare.

He ignored him. "Did you see Dane?" he asked.

"He's checking if they were tailed," Blain offered.

My eyes didn't leave Jamlin. "He said you would tell me what happened."

"Whose orders are you under? What is your mission?" he barked.

His harsh tone made me flinch—this wasn't the greeting I expected. "I'm under no one's orders." I formed my words with care, frowning as I eyed them. They gaped at me with a mix of hope and horror.

"Do you want to repeat that?" Jamlin's gaze darkened, as if he understood exactly what I meant.

An edge crept into my voice. "What happened to Rafe? Where is he?" Tizmet bared her teeth, making us seem more imposing.

"That's none of your business as a Rider."

"But as a deserter," Blain tilted his head, blue eyes flashing, "it might be."

"It's my business as his friend." I bristled.

"You didn't deny being a deserter." Zephath accused.

"No." I leveled him with a glare, and Tizmet rumbled, sensing the tension in the air.

The men stilled and stared at me in shock.

"Oi, lass," Tegan whispered, his jaw slack.

They stilled, their shock palpable. Their horror only made me feel more adamant about my decision.

"I've made my choices." I lifted my chin. "Where is Rafe?"

Heaving a sigh, Jamlin lowered his sword. "You'll want to sit, little one."

My stomach twisted in knots as I listened. I sat around the meager campfire—my back pressed against Tizmet. She laid her head beside me, keeping an eye on the men. Zephath retreated under a lean-to shelter. He pulled his knees up to his chest, gazing into the distance with haunted eyes. Jamlin told the terrible tale, pain lacing every word while Xzanth and Tegan stared at the ground. Blain rested his chin on his hand and didn't take his eyes off us.

"We were doing well. We were behind the Shadows, scouting out their camp. As we continued our mission, we made substantial headway, armed with a report that offered crucial context of their numbers. We decided we would stay another two days, then take a Shadow and hightail it back to the war camp.

"We were on our last day when a Dragon Fleet attacked." Jam shook his head and glared at the ground. "We were watching a Shaman, and the Legion was supposed to be further north. The dragon and company attacked—without the rest of the army. Whether they were under orders or acting on their own is unclear. Though I know the Dragon Lord wouldn't sanction such a reckless attack."

"It was a young dragon—a gold with a Rider just as inexperienced." Blain interjected.

"Young and foolish," Jamlin spat. "The Shaman had control of the beast in mere breaths. We weren't going to intervene—that wasn't our task. Yet, Rafe couldn't let a Shaman have a dragon."

"It's too dangerous," I breathed, running a palm over Tizmet's cheek. She clicked under my touch, drawing their eyes.

"Perhaps he couldn't let it be—because it reminded him too much of someone." Blain arched a brow.

"I'd like to think he'd be above that." Jam cut him a hard look before turning back to me. "Regardless, he took Korzak and Garion with him. Collins must have snuck after as well." He tugged at his braids. "It was horrible. Shadows killed the Rider and massacred the troop. Rafe brought the mad dragon down, but at the expense of Garion and Korzak."

An oppressive silence fell, and my eyes burned. I couldn't breathe. The faces in front of me blurred with unshed tears. Korzak was gone? Garion? I thought of Korzak's childlike innocence, despite his hulking frame. They had always been kind to me, and I felt the sharpness of their loss.

"And Collins?" I tried to swallow the lump in my throat.

"We don't know." Jam let out a curse at the pain of reliving the memory. "They took Rafe, and we know Collins was stalking them. We followed his trail as they retreated west for the respite." His grimace conveyed his remorse. "Don't look at me like that, Avyanna. Do you know how many Hunters there were? How many Shadows? If I led us after him—we would all be dead."

I dropped my heated glare to my boots. I *did* understand. He made the logical choice. He saved what men he could.

My angry, tear-filled gaze slid to his. "Collins never returned?"

"No. When we pulled back after the first snow, he never followed us." Jam shifted in his seat, pinching the bridge of his nose. "I know you don't want to hear this, but Rafe is—"

"Alive." I took a deep breath and lifted my chin. It was time to tell them *my* story. "He is alive. I can use magic to track him, though I don't know what state he is in. I am no Rider—but Tizmet is with me." She swelled in pleasure across the bond at my inclusion of her. "With her, I'm going to find General Rafe and bring him back."

Jam regarded me with thoughtful eyes. "You disobeyed Ruveel, didn't you?"

"I'm finding my General."

He squinted as if he could read me more clearly that way. Barking out a bitter laugh, he sat back, crossing his arms over his chest. "And how exactly do you plan to do this? Using magic? Last I heard, you weren't riding, and she was a man-eater."

Tizmet bared her teeth, and I grinned. "She does like to eat her kill." I snickered at the concern that danced over Tegan's face. "Yes, as I said, I'll use magic to track him. Tizmet will lend her fire."

"That changes nothing." Blain's mouth formed a thoughtful line. "A Shaman took Rafe. Your dragon isn't safe from them."

Tizmet raised her head, towering over us. Her bright eyes glimmered against the dark canopy above. '*I have fought a... Shaman before. This time I am wiser.*' She pulled her lips back in a snarl.

"She has experience fighting Shamen," I said, avoiding the detail that she fell under their control. "And I've killed one."

"You killed one?" Tegan blurted, disbelief coloring his tone.

I gave him a sly grin and patted my crossbow. "Aye, shot it right through the neck."

Xzanth inclined his head in congratulations. "Impressive. How did you manage that?"

I told them about the attack at Northwing. Their faces grew somber, then angry. That's why we had soldiers at the front—to protect our lands. That such a large group made their way through our defenses, unscathed enough to attack a school—was appalling.

Tegan groaned. "We're spread too thin."

"They are as well," Blain countered.

"We're not on their soil," Jamlin stated. "We have more to lose—"

"Will you come with me?" I cut in. The men gave me curious looks, and I frowned. "Will you come with me to rescue Rafe?"

They stared with furrowed brows, conveying their confusion as if I'd grown a third eye.

"Will we come with you?" Tegan echoed.

"Aye. I can fight, and I can find him, but it would be nice to have someone watching my back."

There was a pause, and I took a deep breath, glancing from face to face, wondering what they were on about.

"Don't tell Rafe it was a rescue," Jam snickered, "poor man would die from embarrassment."

CHAPTER 34

We spent the next few days discussing tactics. According to the latest report from the Tennan, Rafe was entrenched in the distant west, surrounded by hostile forces. Before everything fell apart, they were headed to a small outskirt village, one they mapped but hadn't approached.

The Shadow villages remained unscathed by any attack, as no troops ever made it that far into occupied lands. It wasn't as if the forest crawled with Shadows. As Blain pointed out, their presence was as scarce as our troops, yet stumbling upon one was always a possibility.

The Tennan practically worshiped Tizmet. Not because she was a fearsome beast to demand respect... She mothered them.

I smirked as she dropped her second elk in the four days we'd been at their campsite. She preened and licked her talons as the men praised her and offered thanks for the food. These past months, they refused to abandon Rafe and Collins, yet were unable to press forward. Without knowing the land, they were starving. Despite their best efforts to survive, they were far from thriving.

Tizmet watched over us at night, forcing me to sleep on the lowest branch of a Sky Tree with her. She would wake and let out a rumble now and then to scare off the dark wings that plagued the camp. The sheer enormity of their size suggested that dropping Jamlin and flying away with Zephath was well within their capabilities.

Zephath was still cold and sullen. He refused to talk to me unless it was to insinuate I was less of a soldier because I deserted my post. He ate Tizmet's kill readily enough, though. His stomach didn't care that a deserter brought him food.

After a few days of precious sleep and meat, their overall morale improved. They spoke of returning to the warfront with Rafe with renewed vigor and eyed me and Tizmet with hope.

On the sixth day, my headache was barely noticeable. The break from using magic did me good. We broke camp, taking down the makeshift shelters the men constructed from giant leaves, vines and sticks.

We set out on foot. The men's horses were long gone. They'd eaten one—and with no way to feed or water the others, they ran them off. Tizmet soared ahead, keeping watch from the trees.

As I looked up at the colossal timbers, a sensation of vertigo overcame me, yet their splendor evoked a profound reaction inside. It was so odd to walk among such massive growth. I had to climb their roots as if they were small hills. It didn't take long for me to grasp the significance of the barracks' obstacle course. One used muscles they never would have thought of as they navigated the forest floor. Wading through dense knee-deep moss, climbing over steep roots, pushing our way through thick walls of vine—the training paid off.

We kept as silent as possible as we went, making camp at night but not setting a fire. At Tizmet's insistence, we all slept on low branches. It was uncomfortable, but she insisted it was safer than the ground.

We made steady progress, albeit very slow. Every time I thought of Rafe, that familiar pang of despair tore at my heart. If only I set out earlier. A fortnight passed since I left the school, and at this rate, it would take another two weeks before we were anywhere near the village.

Despite my dread and anxiety, I pushed on. There were times when I needed help, yet everyone did. I struggled to climb a ledge. Jamlin got caught in the vines. Tegan slipped in the boggy moss, and Zephath couldn't pull himself up to the lower branches to sleep.

The days blended into one another. Only once, Tizmet had to direct us away from a horde of Shadow Men. We avoided them and made our way to our destination.

I would not be distracted. I was too close.

The night came when Tizmet was adamant that we settle in the higher branches. She sensed Shadows, and the village was near. We struggled to climb, using sharpened bones to dig into the rough bark. Tizmet buzzed with excitement, eager to have her revenge on the people who took her mate and young.

I curled up beside her side in the least uncomfortable spot. To keep her anticipation from keeping me awake, I had to close off the bond, just enough to sleep. My body was exhausted, but I was excited too.

I would see Rafe soon.

I jerked awake. Xzanth slept closest, and I scrambled over to his side. His eyes fluttered open as I pressed my lips to his ear.

"Below us. Two." I barely breathed.

We were high enough that they shouldn't have caught wind of my voice, but I wasn't taking chances. Throughout our travels, the forest's stillness was palpable, making me hyper-aware of every sound I made, no matter how small.

In complete silence, Xzanth rolled, nudging Blain. His eyes shot open, and he stared as Xzanth held up two fingers, then pointed below us. Blain looked across three sleeping bodies to Dane. The twin sat up, nodded once, and retrieved his bow and grapple.

I watched in amazement as he moved without a sound, working his way down the tree. He was so careful, and quiet, that it brought to mind Tizmet's reference to him as the 'silent one.'

'If they are alerted, I shall eat them.'

Tizmet's enthusiastic hum reverberated through our bond. She lay against the branch, making herself as flat as possible. For the first time, I saw the value in her coloring. When I realized I bonded to a gray-mottled dragon, I was marginally disappointed. After all, every Rider wanted a beast the color of precious gems or gold—one that stood out.

Tizmet blended in.

Which was quite advantageous for us in this situation.

'I thought you didn't like the taste of humans,' I replied as I crept back to her side.

'The blood of my enemy is satiating.'

'So it's different because they're Shadow Men?'

'They are my enemies. Devouring them is pleasurable.'

I smiled, but bit the inside of my cheek. I couldn't wait to tell the Tennan that she was developing a taste for man-flesh.

The others woke and waited in silence. Dane disappeared long ago, and all eyes were on Blain, who sat picking dirt from under his nails with a knife, ignoring us.

Tizmet flicked her tongue out, and I stretched across our bond to connect with her senses. She marked the thick odor of two men with the overlying flavor of something tepid and rotting. Their essence hung heavy in the air, telling her they were close—and not moving.

My heart raced as I recalled last night's climb up the tree. Had we left tracks? Had they spotted them in the weak pre-dawn light? They were more at home here than we were, and I was willing to wager they'd see signs of us if they knew where to look.

'Now!'

Tizmet slid off the branch like a serpent. At the same moment, a sharp crack sounded from below, followed by something fleeing through the underbrush. I grabbed my crossbow and loaded a bolt.

"Dane got one!" Blain called.

Tizmet tore into the other. The men made a clumsy descent as I laid out as close to the edge as I dared. Both Shadows were down, but I was concerned with what sped off when Tizmet dropped. My gaze swept across the woodland, struggling to make out any details amidst the murky undergrowth and dense roots.

Xzanth crouched beside me. "Ahead, to the right."

I followed his direction, searching for anything out of the ordinary—out of the ordinary for an overgrown forest.

A curtain of vines trembled and swayed. There was no breeze.

I sighted down the flight track and aimed at the center mass of the dark shadow. Judging the distance once more, I loosed the bolt. A shriek rent the air and sent chills up my arms.

"Got it."

My panic swallowed Xzanth's confirmation when the creature tore itself from the vines. It streaked over a root and out of sight.

'Tizmet!' I pushed to my knees as she snarled.

'It's too fast.' She scrambled up a tree and hung off the side, launching her pursuit.

Whatever I hit was faster than her. In here, with the crowded trees and overgrown forest floor, she didn't have a chance at catching it.

I cursed. Xzanth frowned at Tizmet's tail as she flitted through the thick branches.

"How close is the village?"

"Within a day's walk," he replied, hurrying over to grab his pack.

"If Tizmet doesn't—"

"Climb down," he said in a gentle but firm voice. His brown eyes found mine, and I took strength from his steady calm. "Today is the day."

Tizmet returned, frustrated. I shuddered when she sent me the image of it darting beneath her.

It was a rotting patchwork of an animal. It had the back feet of a giant rabbit, the front of a cat, and the head of a dog. Pieced together with a new hide, thick dark fur hung off its frame. I retched when she pushed its scent of decay at me.

It was *wrong*.

It outpaced Tizmet, and she had to pull up before she announced her presence to the village. We hurried along after her, running where we could while she perched in a tree waiting for us.

The Shadows knew we were coming—and knew we had a dragon.

I panted, throwing my weight over another root as if I took on a hurdle at the barracks. Sweating and shaking, I ran on, taking my place behind Tegan. The man's red hair was easy to follow in the forest.

That the Shadows expected a dragon's arrival could be a fortunate turn of events. It would distract them and rile their greed—bring the Shaman out where I could see him. Tizmet was well-versed in combating them, aware that meeting their eyes would be a grave mistake. I had to trust that she wouldn't trip up and would watch my back.

We ran on till I spied Tizmet's tail hanging from a tree. She clicked deep in her throat. *'Faster, they are gathering.'*

"They're getting ready for us," I called out between gasping breaths.

Jamlin held out his fist. "Halt!"

The group gathered under Tizmet as she thrashed her tail from side to side.

"We are not here to take them all on," he said. "We're here to rescue our General."

I panted, my legs knocking together as I met his dark eyes.

"Avyanna, you and Tizmet are our distraction. They're after her, so stay as high as you can and wreak havoc. Tegan, Dane and Zan, you flank to the north and circle in. Zeph, Blain and I will circle to the south and enter the village. Once Rafe is found, pull back. Blain, Dane, don't you dare get killed."

Jam eyed the twins. Dane gave a single solemn nod, and Blain shook his head with a smirk.

"Don't just stand there! Move out! Avyanna, get on that dragon!"

I shoved my crossbow at Zeph before he tore off. He glared at me, but took it anyway. I wanted my hands free while I rode. I couldn't risk worrying about my bow falling to the ground.

Tizmet landed as the men cleared, and I scrambled up her back. I didn't care that I was clumsy or that I slipped. They were too busy rushing off, and I was too eager to get to Rafe.

'Give them a reason to be afraid.' I grinned and latched on.

She reared up and stretched with a deafening roar. Her neck shook with the force and the sound vibrated under me. She launched into the air and flew straight to the sky.

I clung to her scales as she climbed higher and higher, flitting to the top of the trees where the branches grew small and crowded together. She altered her course, banking west toward the village. My heart raced with the anticipation we shared across the bond. She was ready for her revenge and I was ready to get Rafe out of there.

I peered over her shoulder and spotted the first group of Shadows, scaling the lower branches. They moved like ants, working orderly and following their leaders, all clothed in black. They climbed with ease, as if this was an everyday occurrence.

Tizmet flew over them without a care.

I smiled as she ducked under a branch and weaved around a tree. For the first time, I felt the thrill of flying. We had a purpose—to strike terror in their hearts. And we *would* give them something to fear.

We passed over another group, perhaps twenty. Hunters moved along with them, scrambling up the bark, leaping from tree to tree as if the gaps were mere skips. A pulse of unease rang through me with their presence, but Rafe always told us we would see more of them than Shadows.

Tizmet passed the group and flew a couple more breaths. She let out another roar that left my ears ringing, then careened in a steep dive. I tucked in close against her neck and shivered. Wind tore at my eyes, pulling tears past the side of my face. Her body shifted beneath me and as the ground neared, she threw out her wings. She glided over the village and a cacophony of screams followed her hiss of dragon fire.

'Wait! Rafe could be in a building!' I tried to peer over her shoulder as she pulled up and gained altitude to make another pass.

'Find him! I will burn their nests to the ground!' Her voice dripped with rage.

I gritted my teeth together and closed my eyes, resting my forehead against her warm scales. If I reached out with the magic, she wouldn't be there to help me. I couldn't risk it mid-flight, not while I tried to stay on her back.

'Tear off the roofs!'

'Gladly.' She banked for another pass.

I could barely see anything past her shoulder, but I could feel her power. She rained fire and swooped low to lock her claws around a thatched roof, hauling it up. It scattered like kindling. A few Shadow Men took to their bows, taking shots at her. An arrow pierced her wing, and she screamed in defiance, then set them ablaze.

We decimated the center of the village, knowing the two teams scoured from the north and south. Working west to east, we did exactly as Jamlin ordered.

We brought chaos.

The surrounding screams were rendered insignificant, my mind consumed with finding my General. The source of those cries didn't matter to me. I had no time to consider whether they were masculine or not. I couldn't bring myself to recognize the fact that children might live here.

We had a job to do.

They were my enemy.

'Our enemy.'

Tizmet roared in victory as she tore the thatching off a structure far to the east. She scattered the pieces and landed roughly, jarring me. With a mad swipe of her tail, she sent two walls crumbling—the others wavered before tumbling in half.

She trumpeted across the bond. *'Found him!'*

I trembled with nerves as I slid down her shoulder. She whirled and spun around me, setting fire to every building and Shadow she spotted. While she took care of the destruction, I turned to Rafe.

His prone frame lay on a rough-hewn table.

"No—no, no, no, no, no!" My frantic words squeezed from my tight throat as I rushed to his side—as if my denial could undo all the wrong.

What lay before me was a weak imitation that paled compared to my Rafe. The body was mere skin and bones, his hair thick and black, matted with gore. His left eye was missing. Dried blood and puss encrusted the wound.

The scent of waste and decay hung heavy in the air. My gaze traveled from his bruised and bloodied face to his chest, where his skin was flayed apart, secured with metal pins. His intestines and organs draped on the wood.

The table was a gruesome sight, with blood and chunks of flesh pooling and spilling over like water. Bruises and deep cuts marred every surface. His right leg was bent in several places at unnatural angles. Two of his toes were missing.

I quaked in horror as my gaze traveled back to his face. My mind echoed with aching, gut-wrenching realization. No human could endure such torment.

Strength fled me. I fell to my knees as tears spilled down my cheeks. How could I be too late? How?

I spent too much time obeying rules. Sobs choked my lungs, and I took his swollen blue hand in mine. It was too cold. I wasted days enjoying my life, while Rafe wasted away—tortured and mutilated. I enjoyed food and friends while he remained here, enduring the terrors of the Shadow Men.

My lips brushed against his knuckles, and I shuddered as another sob decimated my body. Why would the magic bring me here, to see him like this? How long had he been dead? Who killed him?

I would rip out their heart and crush it before their eyes.

His hand twitched.

I rocked back, dropping it, staring in horror. I swiped at my eyes as it swung limply off the table. Tizmet's roars and snarls seemed worlds away as I watched his thumb twitch again.

It was the smallest of movements.

A dead body wouldn't move.

I lurched forward and pulled myself over him. The door to my magic opened eagerly. I gave it a single purpose as I unleashed its power.

Tell me he's alive.

Power welled and pulsed around us. I drew more, seeing through the eyes of a Rider. Magic flowed and ebbed, flaring brightly within Rafe. I choked on a relieved sob and deflated against the table.

Magic slid out of my grasp.

Tizmet screamed, and white-hot pain laced through my chest. My breath caught, and I looked down, expecting to see a gush of blood. It felt as if my rib cage exploded. A fierce ache swelled beneath my breastbone. I choked on a gasp, struggling to breathe as I clutched at my stomach. My free hand trembled as I shoved Rafe's organs into the gaping cavity.

My right knee gave out as the pressure inside bulged. I growled through bared teeth, working faster. I tore his flesh free from the nails holding it open and folded it over him the best I could.

"Tizmet!" I screamed.

She spewed an arc of bright flame around us, eyes flashing.

'Help me!'

She opened her maw and roared her defiance. A thrum of her fear plunged deep into my gut. She seethed with anger, and not all of that fury was directed at the Shadows.

'My fire is failing!' She snapped her jaws at me.

'He can't be moved! I have to close up the wounds!'

I would not leave him. Even if I had to stay here and die with him, I would not leave him.

Tizmet snarled and rushed to me. She lifted her head and released a jet of flame, encircling us within a raging wall of heat. She crowded in, wrapping her massive form around me and the table. Spreading a wing over us, she pressed her nose to my side and let out a hot hiss.

'Close his wound. That's all.'

Magic swelled to my call again, and with it, the pain in my chest faded. I grasped it, not bothering to worry about the consequences of my actions—and pushed it at Rafe.

I melded it along his flesh, trying to seal it. My fingers lost their grip on the bloody skin, and the flap fell from my grasp. I cursed and clutched it again, sinking my nails in. Tizmet snatched control of the magic, and as I held his body together, we worked to close him up.

My hands shook, and my knees gave way long ago. I rested my weight against her. She supported me as I poured magic into Rafe, closing his wounds, pushing everything into him, my sole intent to heal.

I drew back, terrified that I hadn't done enough, but not knowing what else to do. He didn't stir. I couldn't feel the beating of his heart. Tears burned and defeat flooded me as Tizmet lurched upright. I collapsed with the motion, one bloodied hand still grasping Rafe's.

I squinted through the smoke and carnage. In front of us, a Shaman stood. On his head, he wore the bones of a dragon, fashioned to resemble their skull. His gloved hands bore no weapons, but power emanated from him with every breath. Behind him stood four Hunters—misshapen, gruesome creatures. They were large and fierce, bearing talons and predatory teeth.

"You," I rasped, blinking to clear the haze.

The Shaman spoke something in a foreign tongue and pointed at Tizmet. She snarled and backed away, leaving me to stand between him and Rafe.

'Mine!' I growled and pushed to my feet. I swayed, my legs unsure of my weight.

There were small knives littered about the shack's debris. I dared not ponder how many had marred Rafe's body. I stooped to grab the largest and eyed the Shaman's neck. He repeated those garbled words, pointing to Tizmet as she took to the sky.

"You don't know what you've done."

I swiped at my hot, angry tears and clutched the weapon tighter. My legs trembled as I stepped toward him. He laughed and pointed from my blade to Rafe again, saying something I couldn't understand.

"You tried to take him from me," I whispered.

The Hunters tensed and snarled.

I took another step. "You tried to take Tizmet from me."

His hand lowered, and a Hunter crouched, ready to pounce.

"Not even your army can protect you!" I screamed, then threw myself at him.

The bear-creature leapt. At the same moment, Tizmet dropped from the sky, crushing two, then ripping her talons through the third. I snared my magic and melded it with one purpose.

To kill.

I moved in ways I had never been trained—fluid and dynamic, as if guided by an unseen force. Ducking under the creature's lunge, I jerked my blade up, splitting its fur. It lashed out with its snake-like tail and I leapt high, power filling my veins.

As I came down, my knife plunged into the Hunter's back, dragging, splitting through its rancid flesh. It spun and staggered. Black fetid blood dripped from its maw with its guttural growl.

"Die."

Whether by magic or succumbing to its wounds, it collapsed to the side.

The Shaman raised his hands, stretched out to the dying creatures. If he sought to bring them back, he would fail.

"You're mine." I snarled.

The hilt of my blade felt sticky and warm with gore as I stepped up to him. He said something as I angled my knife. Part of my mind still wondered why he hadn't raised a weapon to me.

Tizmet's muzzle came down. I blinked, staring into her flaming gaze. She closed her jaws. Bones crunched within her maw, and I relented the flow of magic.

'Ours.'

CHAPTER 35

I turned to Rafe, content to share the kill with Tizmet. She consumed the Shaman while I hurried to the demolished shack. In the corner, debris from the crumbled walls covered a pair of legs.

My heart fractured as I knelt near the pile, throwing chunks of stone and rubble.

No. Please—not him.

"Avyanna?" Tegan's voice rang over the roar of flames and distant screams. "Oh, sun, moon, and all the stars." He cursed as he neared.

I took a quick look behind me and saw him gaping at Rafe.

"Tegan, here!"

His green eyes shot to mine and darted to the pile I sifted through.

Tizmet walked close and sniffed at the motionless limbs. *'He is dead.'* She rumbled, whipping her head away to glance at the sound of shouts.

'I don't care. I'm not leaving him.'

Tegan helped me pull wooden planks off the body. Tizmet snarled and nosed us aside. She grabbed most of the wood and tossed it. I fell to my knees as my heart shattered a little more.

Collins lay thin and crumpled—skeletal. He wasted away long ago, but I knew that face. My hand shook as I reached out to his dust and grime-smudged cheeks, brushing sandy hair from his sunken eyes. With the motion, clumps fell from his head, and I recoiled in horror.

Tegan removed his cloak to cover the young man, and I returned to Rafe. I tried to wrangle my emotions as I stared down at his broken body. I was too late for either of them. Rafe would never make it back. Tears blurred the raised white line where I joined his skin with magic—a petty attempt to keep him alive.

The last bit of my heart gave way.

'Carry us? Please?' I begged.

Tizmet blinked at me. Her orange eyes swirled as she stormed across the bond to test my heart, or what was left of it.

'I will do my best.'

"Tegan," I faced the fierce warrior, "the warfront is north?"

"Aye, you're seeking a Healer?"

"Yes."

"Head northeast. Your dragon should sense the other Riders. They'll be rousing now. You should hit it within a few day's flight." He frowned at Rafe. "We'll meet you there. Think he'll make it?"

"He will if I have anything to do with it."

I climbed on the table beside him and nestled my head on his bony shoulder. It frightened me to see him so thin. The Rafe I knew was solid—a mountain.

Tizmet grasped us as gently as possible in her front claws. I tucked my arms around him, keeping his back safe from the sharp edge of her talons. She stumbled a step on her hind legs before she took a running leap to launch into the air.

I reached for magic again as she flew. My head pounded, demanding I stop, but I pulled harder. I had no idea what I was doing, but I twined the threads of our magic and wound them about us.

I had to keep him alive.

Tizmet traveled all night and well into the morning. Exhausted, she slumbered on a high branch, curled around us. She breathed deeply, her mind barely aware, as I cried against his shoulder.

My energy was completely drained, and every muscle throbbed. I needed rest, but it wouldn't come. Sleep was out of the question as long as Rafe remained in harm's way.

Sobs tore through me until I had no more tears to cry. The weight of Collins' death rested heavy on my soul. I whispered my regrets—how sorry I was for not coming sooner, for being too weak to head out on my own. I apologized for every chime he was subjected to torture.

My fists clenched against him, encrusted with blood and dirt. I could never atone for the anguish he endured due to my failure to heed the magic.

Tizmet woke before dawn and flew slowly among the branches until daylight. With the sun, her pace increased, able to see further. I rested my head against Rafe. His breathing was too shallow. His heart thrummed so lightly I had to press my hand hard against his chest for its meager beat to reach me.

I clung to consciousness but drifted in and out as I maintained the magic between us. The relentless ache in my head was so overpowering that it blurred the line between reality and dreams. Everything was cloudy and confusing. The only thing I knew—I had to keep him alive.

I was conscious enough to hear Tizmet's growl and snarls. She landed and laid us on the ground. Voices seemed leagues away and Tizmet stayed close, but my eyes refused to open. My mouth felt as if it was coated with sand, and my arms fastened around Rafe, frozen in place.

A warm touch pressed against my throat, then ran down my body. They tried to tear me from him, and I groaned, gripping him tighter. I couldn't leave him. I wouldn't.

Tizmet snarled, and the hands that tried to separate us halted.

The pounding in my head became too much, and I retreated within myself again, allowing only one thought.

I would keep him alive.

"Avyanna, please. Come to us."

The voices pulled me out of the haze. Panic and pain combatted within the deep recesses of my mind. Had I fallen asleep? Where was–

My arms clutched a body against me. He was here. I still had him. I reached out, checking the magic. It enveloped us, twining together. I pushed more power inside him and tightened our threads. The strands flared brighter, the view almost blinding.

A woman spoke somewhere nearby. "She's trying to heal him."

"No, she can't! Things aren't right! If she heals him that way, he'll still die!"

Part of my awareness recoiled. I was hurting—by healing him? I placed my trust in magic to fix him, without considering the consequences.

"Avyanna, are you with us?" The feminine voice was closer.

I didn't want to listen—it was too loud against the rushing in my ears. The pain in my head intensified with every sound. I withdrew and nestled into Rafe.

"You need to let him go. You need to release him."

Anger seeped beneath my skin. Let him go? I walked away. He went to the front without me. I abandoned him, and this happened. This was my fault, and now she wanted me to let him die?

"Never." I choked the word through cracked lips.

After her heavy sigh, she spoke again. "She needs to be treated at Northwing. This doesn't happen here. Riders know how to control their magic—she obviously doesn't. A half-baked Rider attacking a village of Shadow Men. Absurd!"

As long as I had Rafe, I didn't have to listen to them. I reached across the bond. Tizmet was resting, belly full. She sensed my touch and sent her comfort. She was nearby, and that was enough. Her worry trickled through. I was using too much magic, draining every bit I leached into, and she didn't know how to stop it.

I reached out to reassure her. It would be fine.

Pain in my chest swelled, and I winced. Moaning, I burrowed deeper under the blanket. With each beat of my heart, the agony increased. The pressure built, and I gritted my teeth against the torment until it ebbed.

This was my price to pay for losing control of magic.

"Blast it all!"

The curse startled me, and through hazy vision I saw thick black hair and Rafe's face—his left eye socket was a dark crusted hole. I let my eyelids flutter shut, and dropped my head back to his shoulder.

"No! No ma'am. Wake up!"

My shaky vision darted about the room. Too fatigued to be controlled, it roved where it would. My gaze passed over Rashel, then lowered under the weight of exhaustion.

"Flaming son of a dungheap!"

Tizmet growled behind her. *'Wake,'* she urged.

I pushed back—my refusal apparent. I wanted to sink into the pain and let everything else disappear. Keeping Rafe alive was all I needed. Nothing more.

'Come to me.'

I cracked my eyes and glanced at worried faces. Rashel was bent over us, with Ruveel beside her. Elenor and Darrak stood behind them. Several Healers lingered in the background.

"Avyanna, you listen to me. You need to let him go." Rashel pressed her hand to my cheek.

"No." My lips split with the movement, but no sound came out of my mouth.

Ruveel crossed his arms over his chest, but looked at me with tenderness. "He is gone."

Too bad I didn't want his sympathy.

"He's mine." My voice cracked, and I licked at my bleeding lip. I didn't care who knew or who thought ill of it. He was mine.

Rashel sighed and arched a brow at Ruveel.

He shook his head. "You want someone to experiment with? She's all yours." He shrugged. "I have no use for her."

"What of General Shadowslayer?" someone asked.

Ruveel's gaze met mine when he spoke. "He's dead anyway." With that, he turned and stormed off.

My breaths grew shallow as my eyes slid shut. I couldn't be bothered to keep them open. It took too much strength I didn't have.

"Avyanna, I know you're tired, but now is not the time to rest," Rashel said. "You got him to us, but he's all wrong. He's been healed up with his organs misplaced."

A warm hand covered mine as I gripped Rafe's shoulder. Feeling the bone underneath heightened my protectiveness.

"Avyanna, I'm asking you to help fix him. We have to operate, put everything back together, but he won't make it without you."

She drifted in and out of focus.

She spun, glaring at another Healer. "Hold her. And wet her lips for love of the sun!" Her features softened as she stroked my cheek. "Be strong—for him."

"I won't... let him... die," I rasped.

Someone sat behind me. I shrank away from their touch, still convinced I was his best chance. They hadn't seen him splayed open on that table. They only saw him as he was now—and they already wrote him off as dead.

"I am a Healer, and I took an oath to save as many lives as I can." Rashel squeezed my hand again. "I am asking you to help. We will need you."

Tizmet crooned at my feet, and my grip relaxed. I couldn't do it alone, as much as I wanted to. If something was wrong inside him, I was at a loss on how to fix it. I imbued him with magic and commanded it to heal, but it might wander without purpose—or worse, mend what didn't need fixing.

Rashel nodded to the Healer behind me and strong hands gently pried me off him. I moaned as if they ripped my heart out of my chest. Tizmet growled at my sense of loss, and her nose nudged my feet.

They pulled the blanket from him, and Darrak moved closer to Elenor as she turned away. Whether she averted her gaze out of modesty's sake or horror wasn't clear.

Dirt, blood, waste and sweat smothered every inch of him. His chest barely moved with his faint breaths. I knew his heart still pulsed. It beat alongside mine, entwined with magic.

His belly was distended, not shrunken in like when I found him. That was a bad sign, but I didn't know how to fix it. The cuts along his length were scarred over, and beneath the grime, most of his bruises faded. However, magic couldn't regrow his toes—or replace his eye.

His leg had healed, though at a terrible angle. My stomach turned. A lingering doubt darkened the edges of my thoughts—had pouring magic into him done more harm than good?

Rashel traced the raised white welt that snaked from his chest to his hip, branching off in several directions. "You did this?"

I opened my mouth, but no words formed.

"Get her water!" she snapped at someone behind her, then softened her tone, focusing on Elenor and Darrak. "Leave, please. This will be unpleasant for everyone."

Darrak frowned and worked a muscle in his jaw. He nodded once and led Elenor away.

I glanced up, realizing my surroundings. Northwing. Tizmet brought us to the cave in the Dragon Canyon. I idly wondered how she got everyone up here. *'I roared until they sent someone.'* She nudged my mind, then wrapped comfort and safety around me like a blanket.

A Healer dabbed a wet cloth on my bloody lip, and I stared through heavy eyes as they washed Rafe. With every layer of dirt and grime stripped away, fresh crimson mixed with the black crusted blood. A rancid odor stained the air.

With swift efficiency, they washed him. After cleaning his back, they moved him to a fresh blanket beside me. I fumbled for him, seeking contact. Rashel caught my struggle and gently placed his hand on mine. It was cold. So cold.

"Someone start a fire. I can't feel my fingers, let alone use them."

She fired off a list of orders and set out small, but wickedly sharp, blades. She moved with professionalism that emitted an air of confidence. I would trust her with Rafe.

Not that I had a choice.

The next few chimes were torture. Bile rose in my throat as they cut him open, relieving pressure in his stomach. They worked quickly—cutting out dirt, bits of wood and debris that I healed inside him.

Every time she dragged that knife through his skin, I was ready. When she nodded and removed her blades, I immediately wrapped magic around him to heal what she corrected. It was tedious, painstaking work.

Several times, the Healer at my side placed a cold rag on my neck to bring me back. My head throbbed with relentless abandon, drowning out Rashel's words. I struggled to keep up as she moved along his body.

When she finished with his abdomen, she held the skin as I knitted it together. Then they moved to his leg.

I watched in silent horror as they pounded mallets into his leg to re-fracture his bones. They realigned every spot. At one point, they cut through his calf to be sure it set properly. I fought hard to keep myself conscious enough to heal the last break.

The insistent drumbeat in my head echoed, mirroring the ache in my chest, and I struggled to control the magic. My connection with Tizmet slipped, and the last shred of control dissolved. I fell into a welcoming darkness.

I drifted awake—warm, comfortable. Safe. I smiled to myself, and my lip split open. With a sharp breath, I jerked upright, crying out as every muscle screamed in agony.

Everything from my neck to my feet hurt—even my nails ached.

"Well, that's one way to wake up."

Rashel sat in a chair, nursing a steaming mug. The fire crackling in the hearth cast her in an amber glow as she set the drink down and stood.

I forced the tension in my shoulders to relax as I lowered myself onto the hay-stuffed mattress—with Rafe. My teeth clenched tight as I curled around him.

She knelt on the rug beside me. "He still hasn't woken." Her wrist pressed to my temple, and she held my face, peering into my eyes. "You, however, slept for four days."

The cave's tapestry rustled and Tizmet stormed in, dripping wet. She rushed to my side, ignoring Rashel's curses, then stared down at me with a fiery eye.

Rashel pushed at her head, and Tizmet snapped at her hand, a harmless display of irritation.

"Man-eater or no, I healed your Rider. Mind your manners!" she scolded.

Tizmet huffed. *'You have slept for too long, little one.'*

I smiled weakly, careful of my lip. My anxieties melted away as she mothered me.

'What happened?' I asked.

'Too little. Life is lonely without you.' Tizmet confided, settling down to lie in the puddle of water.

'I wouldn't leave you,' I assured her. *'Did you come from the springs?'*

'Yes. I felt you wake. I needed to see you.'

'Thank you for coming.' My fingertips brushed her muzzle.

"Enough of your silent conversations. Dragon, take your dripping scales out of here. I'll not have this cavern sullied with your puddles," Rashel said, putting her hands on her hips.

Tizmet eyed her, lips pulled back in a snarl.

Rashel raised a brow. "Yes, what mighty teeth you have. Shoo."

The dragon snorted out a puff of black smoke. *'You are well?'* she asked, sniffing at my hair.

I waved her off. *'I am well enough. Weak, hungry—but awake.'*

She nosed the top of my head, then hissed at Rashel before making her way out.

"She's watched over you like a mother hen," Rashel muttered, nearing the pot in the hearth. After spooning its contents into a cup, she came back, eyeing me as she handed it over.

My stomach rumbled as the savory smell of rich herbs and warmth greeted me. I sat up and took a careful sip. The hot broth carved its way down my parched mouth and dry throat, soothing it. I closed my eyes and moaned, relishing the sensation.

After another small drink, I blinked down at Rafe. He was still so thin. Too little muscle clung to his bones. A swath of white gauze concealed the hole where his left eye had been. His black beard covered his face. It was so foreign, almost comical, to see him with hair. The blanket we shared hid the rest of him, though I felt either trousers or under-breeches on his thighs. His thin shoulders were bare, and I peered at the sleep shift someone dressed me in.

"He's made no progress, nor declined." Rashel bent down to check his pulse. "Neither food nor water is sustaining him. We've been wetting his lips and mouth, but that is the most we can do."

By instinct, I reached for the door to my magic and checked the threads that wound around us. They glowed bright and intact, though slack. I left it, refusing to force it again. My head was light. The incessant headache finally abated.

"He's alive." My voice cracked as I spoke, rough with disuse.

"For how long?"

"As long as it takes."

Rashel sighed and sat back in her chair. She took a sip from her cup and eyed me over the rim. "We need to talk about this."

I took a long drink from mine. "There's nothing to talk about."

"You cannot keep him alive forever. No," she cut me off as I opened my mouth, "you will not drag his emaciated body about, keeping him alive by pure willpower and magic."

My lips formed a tight, defiant line.

She continued, "You have shown us a great deal. We never knew Riders and Healers could work so well beside each other. You have no training, none at all. Imagine if a Rider were *trained* as a Healer! On the front, they would be far more valuable than just another fire-breathing beast.

"You've given us knowledge that can save more people, and we as Healers owe you a great deal for that. However," she sat back and eyed me sharply, "what I will not allow is someone to keep a body alive while the soul has passed beyond the Veil. What makes you any different from the Shadows who defy the will of those they control?"

My heart hammered at a painful rate, but she wasn't done.

"Do you think your General would want you lugging him about, just so you can keep his heart pumping?"

I dropped my gaze to my cup—a roughly sculpted clay piece, with a chip missing from the rim. It was gray and brown, finished with a clear glaze. Focusing on that was far safer than what she was telling me.

"Avyanna."

Braving a glance, I met her tender gaze, a lump forming in my throat.

"Yours is not the only life you're playing with," she said. "I want your word that, if the time comes, you'll let him go."

I drank the rest of the broth and set the cup on the stone floor beside the mattress. After pulling the blanket to my chin, I settled against Rafe, wrapping myself around him.

"I can't."

"You'll have to."

I ignored her and closed my eyes. Coarse black hair from Rafe's chest tickled my arm, and I burrowed against his side. He would have protected me. I had to protect him.

I couldn't let him go.

Not yet.

The next few days passed in a sleepy blur. Niehm and Elenor visited with Darrak and Mikhala.

Mikhala was the only one excited for me. She praised my initiative and talked about how she saw me take off after the battle, and wished she'd been there to see me off.

After the attack, the dorms caught fire, destroying the men's wing. They were forced to seek shelter in the outlying villages, many taking over barns.

Darrak constantly eyed me with disappointment. His only words to me were, "You've made your choice, you'll have to suffer the consequences."

I was sure that alluded to my upcoming punishment.

Niehm had far more to say.

I took her verbal beating with a grain of salt. I had just reunited with her, then departed with no explanation. Yes, I could have died and left her regretting her last words to me. Yes, I could have been taken captive and beaten, or worse. When she finally let me speak, I apologized for my failure to give her a proper goodbye before I left.

Elenor watched, letting Niehm scold me. She remained silent unless I asked her something directly. I hurt her—hurt all of them. I didn't realize the damage I'd do by going off on my own. To them, all it did was prove what little trust I had in them.

Why didn't I have the patience to wait, discuss it with them, and ask for their assistance or find a solution? I departed without warning or preparation, following my own path.

As I thought about them, I watched Rafe.

I followed my fate.

Tizmet only left my side to eat or soak in the springs. Flinor and Dareth came to greet me, and I thanked them for everything they'd done. With Tizmet's refusal to be a beast of burden, they were more than helpful in bringing all the supplies up.

Rashel stayed with us, monitoring our health. I was on the mend, my head clear and my muscles regaining their strength.

I tried to practice with my spear, much to Rashel's objection. While training, I had an episode where my heart spasmed, followed by waves of pain, driving me to my knees—like someone hacked away at my breastbone with a dull knife. My left arm lost all feeling.

Upon her inspection, Rashel declared that my poor control of magic resulted in it attacking my heart. Something was wrong, but she couldn't say what. We did several exercises, the more strenuous ones provoked the onslaught.

Tizmet would snarl right before a surge came, as if she sensed it. She was angry at me for pushing myself, but I had to press the limits to find out how much I could do without triggering the pain.

It was dark, the fire low and flickering as shadows danced along the walls and ceiling. My heart ached, both from my exercises and my grief. I rolled to my side and brushed a dark strand of hair from Rafe's face.

'Will he ever wake?' I questioned, not expecting Tizmet to reply.

'I cannot answer that... and neither can you. No one can.' She shuffled closer, her breath warm against my back.

I frowned, tracing his jaw. He was so peaceful, as if he was lost in sleep. I could almost pretend he was just resting, ready to wake up and tease me at any moment—if not for his gaunt cheeks and the hollows under his eye sockets. Tears burned as they blurred my vision. I choked back my whimper as I rested my head on his shoulder.

'Perhaps you are trapping him.'

I scrunched my face at those words, and she sensed my confusion.

'Maybe he is not fighting back. He is safe, wrapped in your magic. There's no need for him to do anything. You're keeping him alive.'

'I can't risk letting go.' My lips pressed together. *'I can't live with that guilt.'*

The only response I got from him was when I first found him. It didn't make sense. How could pulling my magic back help when it was the only thing sustaining him?

'Can you live with knowing you've created a shell of him?' Tizmet pushed over the bond and wrapped herself around me, holding me tight. *'Could you live with yourself, knowing you kept him like this? Give your mate a chance to fight back.'* She keened quietly behind me, pleading with me to let him go.

Tears spilled, leaving hot trails down my cheek. I just wanted him to wake up. Assuming responsibility for his life was not my intention. I couldn't live with myself if I made a mistake and let him die.

'He would have died without you. You can only keep this up for so long.'

I cried against his shoulder, sobs wracking my body. Rashel got up and walked out of the cave, leaving me to my tears.

I wanted to lie to myself, say I could keep him alive forever. That I'd strap him to my back and care for him until he came back to me.

Yet, I couldn't.

He'd been unresponsive for weeks. Without my magic, he would have died long ago. I couldn't let him lay there and gather dust.

I screamed, slamming a fist on his chest. "WAKE UP!"

I didn't care who heard. His body jostled with my strike, but lay there—limp. No response. No flinch or twitch. Nothing. I curled into his side and pulled his hand to my face. The calluses were still there, rough against my cheek.

A long time later, deep in the night, I began the slow and painful process of unwrapping the magic from us. When grief and fear overwhelmed me, Tizmet offered her aid. We worked slowly and carefully, stripping the protective cocoon of glowing thread that kept him alive. It was almost like I freed him from a coffin.

Except, I felt as if I was putting him in one.

We finished in the early hours of the morning. My head throbbed, both from crying and the excessive use of magic. My face was puffy and swollen, stiff with my dried tears. I grasped Rafe's hand and pressed it to my chest as if sensing my heartbeat would bring him back.

"I love you."

Grief pulled me down, and I drifted into a deep sleep, knowing he didn't hear those words.

CHAPTER 36

Something stirred, gently pulling me from sleep. Groggy, I frowned and tucked Rafe's warm hand more firmly against my chest. My eyes burned from crying, and instead of opening them, I drifted off again.

The fire died to smoldering coals. My blanket barely kept the morning chill at bay. I shivered and pressed myself closer to the warm body beside me. Dread knotted in my stomach at the idea of prying my eyes open. I dared not reach out with magic. I didn't want to face the fact that I'd lost him.

Tizmet made a sound deep in her throat, almost a purr. I reached across the bond and took comfort in her presence. Bolstering myself, I braved a look. My vision was clouded, and I rubbed away the crust that formed from my tears. I blinked, seeing Rafe's face. His gaze glittered in the weak morning light.

"Rafe?" I breathed.

The corner of his mouth twitched.

"Rafe!"

I shot up, and my jaw dropped. He was awake? He was really here?! Where was the Healer?!

He turned his head to follow my movement and choked out a garbled sound, trying to speak.

"Water!" My voice sounded strange, still consumed by disbelief. "Water... water!"

I threw off the blanket and ran to the pitcher near Rashel's empty chair. I trembled as I poured a mug, then stumbled back to him, spilling it over my hands. His eye twinkled as he watched me with the smallest hint of a smile. Propping his head, I struggled to hold the cup steady at his lips. He sipped, then erupted in a series of coughs. I cursed and set the cup down, rolling him to his side. Did he wake only for me to drown him?! I grimaced as the coughs shook his weak body.

As he settled, I laid him down again and glared at Tizmet. '*Where is Rashel?*'

'*Giving you space to say your goodbyes, I would think,*' she replied, mildly amused.

'*Goodbyes?*'

'*Last night, she knew you were letting him go. She was prepared for him to pass.*'

'*Please, fetch her. Get someone! I don't know what I'm doing!*'

'*This once, I will be your carrier pigeon,*' Tizmet teased.

Rafe's arm shook. I gripped his hand, and his fingers trembled against mine. His brow furrowed with concentration, as if he wanted to say something but lacked the strength.

"What is it?" I felt so helpless. I didn't know how to make it better.

Tizmet made her way to the cave entrance, nosing the tapestry aside. She sucked in a breath and bellowed the loudest bugle I ever heard. I ducked my head, trying to shelter my ears. After two more great blasts, she returned and loomed over me to peer at Rafe.

'*He is weak.*' She laid down with her nose at our feet, content to rest with us.

'*Aye.*'

His lips moved again, but no intelligible words came out. I squeezed his hand and brushed his hair from his face. "You're safe now. I'm here."

He blinked, and his eyebrow twitched as if he had something to say about that. I grinned as more tears welled in my eyes. I would gladly take his teasing for the rest of my days. His thin fingers tugged at my hand, gently urging me back to the bed. I smiled and shook my head, but climbed in next to him. As I settled against his side, he let out a long sigh.

"Better?"

He struggled with his tongue and mouth again, making choking sounds. I shifted, placing my ear close to his lips. Bracing myself over him, I tried to make sense of what he was saying.

"Clo—clos...er."

I leaned far enough to beam at him. A tear slipped free, falling to his cheek. I wiped it away as happiness bubbled up inside me.

"You asked for it." I laughed. I nestled in, curling over him. My leg draped over his, and I pressed my belly to his hip. Throwing my arm over his chest, I gripped him tight.

"This is as close as you're getting for now," I said, wiggling my nose as the hair on his chest tickled my face.

Rashel returned within a chime, bringing a stretcher and two Healers with her. I couldn't hide my smile as she walked in, somber grief lining her face. She saw us and straightened her shoulders, perhaps preparing to tell me I had to surrender his body.

Rafe's eye was closed, though he wasn't asleep. His fingers jerked and twitched against my palm, assuring me he was still with me.

She stopped ten paces away and frowned, noting my expression. She sighed, waving at the others. "Has he passed?"

He chose that moment to take a shuddering breath and open his eye. I beamed like a fool and trembled against him. Rashel rushed over and fell to her knees. Pressing her fingers against his neck, she barked out a list of orders for the two Healers.

They scrambled to stoke the fire and gather items for her as she pulled the blanket from us. Firmly pushing my arm away, she laid her ear to his chest and listened.

She sat up with wonder splayed across her features. "You let him go, and he came back?"

Tizmet was right. I had to pull my protective magic from him so his body would fight. It was content, allowing me to do all the work. Once I drew away, his heart realized it needed to do its job, and completed the task with vigor. I tried to explain as much to Rashel, the best I could.

The next few moments were a mad rush of Healers checking he was well. I pulled myself from him and they tested his reflexes. They made sure he had sensation in all his limbs and understood us clearly.

They offered him spoonfuls of broth as I supported his head. Rashel assured his voice would return, though his path to recovery would take some time. She wanted to be sure that his intestines and bowels were put back together properly, and she stayed to monitor us as the others left. She busied herself writing in her journal as Rafe slept and I dressed.

"You know you reached him just in time?" she murmured.

I belted my dress. My bandit breaker slid on as I fastened the buckle. "What do you mean?" I felt as though I was late.

"He wouldn't have lasted long like that. They must've split him open as you arrived." She lifted her head thoughtfully. "That was quick thinking, though, closing him up. You at least got all of him to us."

"He was... everywhere."

With a glance his way, I frowned and shuddered, remembering his guts spilled over the table, dangling to the floor.

"I can imagine the horror. I've worked on the front. It's a hard job piecing soldiers back together." She scribbled something down in her journal. "Most don't make it."

I sat in a chair beside the mattress opposite of her. Tizmet lay at the entrance, both guarding and watching.

"He will be well though... right?"

He was so thin. I never imagined he could be so small. His beard hid the gauntness of his cheeks, but his neck and shoulders lacked the muscular strength I was so accustomed to.

"If you're asking for a promise, I cannot give it." Her focus remained on her writing. "This is unprecedented. I do not know what to expect."

Frowning, I busied myself by braiding my hair. I didn't want to get my hopes up simply because he woke up. Just having him awake for the short time we did felt like more than I could ever ask.

"That said, provided we put him back together properly, and he passes his food and drink, I think it's a positive sign that he's conscious." She pushed a stray strand of black hair behind her ear and sketched something.

"Thank you."

"I just said I wasn't promising anything." She gave me a sharp look.

"No—thank you for caring for us." Sincerity brightened my smile. "I'd wager everyone else would have given up."

"I almost did." The corner of her mouth twitched with her mirth. Looking down, she added, "You're quite bullheaded. Worse than your dragon."

Tizmet snorted in reply, glancing back at us before resuming her study of the canyon.

Rafe woke twice more throughout the day, sipping broth both times. Once while I went through my motions with my spear. I wasn't able to exert myself without risking an attack, but I could at least practice the movements. He watched, and I slid through the positions easily. Relief blanketed me when I noticed he fell back asleep.

Rashel settled in her place in her chair as night crept in. She alternated between jotting notes and drinking tea while gazing into the fire. We took our dinner in the cave, refusing to leave him. Tizmet left for an evening flight, then returned under cover of darkness.

A groan alerted us to Rafe as he woke again. Rashel did her tests, and assured me he was well, then we worked together to give him more broth. After he drank, she retired to her chair, and I curled next to him.

I held his hand tight in mine and pressed my chest to his side. Tizmet slept with her head stretched out, touching her nose to my back. I felt safe. Secure.

I was finally content.

Rafe moved his thumb against my wrist, tracing small circles. He croaked something, and I scooted my ear closer to his mouth.

"Think—think we can," he took a deep breath as if it was hard for him to speak, "get her... to leave?"

"Why?" I frowned as I searched his face.

His gaze dropped to my night shift, then to the blankets hiding us. He raised a dark eyebrow. I threw my head back and let out a burst of laughter.

"Quiet, you two," Rashel scolded. "Act like the sick patients you are."

I flashed her a smile and snuggled in closer, resting my head on his shoulder.

"I'm glad you're back," I whispered as he drifted off to sleep.

The next morning found me with my back turned as Rashel helped Rafe relieve himself. I couldn't imagine how humiliating it was to require aid with such a personal task. She assisted me when I suffered the effects of the tinge berry tea, but for some reason it made me uncomfortable that my Rafe needed help.

It was a good sign though—we put everything back correctly. He experienced no pain, and so far, Rashel said his stomach sounded normal. I took it as a small victory.

He was up for longer periods throughout the day. We sat him up and worked his limbs. Rashel explained we needed to help him build muscle so he could walk under his own strength again.

Whenever she questioned his torture, he went silent. He refused to talk about it, and often stared at the wall as if it held all the answers. She stressed that she simply wished to know to help future soldiers. He shut her out and ignored her. I couldn't imagine what he went through, or how he endured for so long. I knew he'd been with the Shadows since the Solstice, though I didn't know if that was when they captured him, or if I witnessed a memory.

Rashel eventually gave up and retreated for a few chimes, leaving us alone. I tidied up the cave, making myself busy as he tracked my every move.

I put my hands on my hips with a teasing smirk. "Don't you have anything better to watch?"

His mouth quirked up, and he lifted a weak hand, beckoning me to him. I sighed, feigning dramatics, and sat beside him. In truth, I wanted to do nothing else.

He pressed close, and I found myself almost in his lap. He wrapped his arms around me and buried his face in my neck.

"Be good." I warned him.

Silent laughter shook his chest, and he cleared his throat. "Thank... you."

"You owe me." My fingers slipped through his beard. "This has to go," I teased.

He smirked and moved my hand to his hair.

I laughed and gave it a tug. "This—I haven't decided," I murmured, then rubbed my chin. "I'm not sure I like it. It reminds me of Willhelm's hair."

He pinched my leg, and I yelped with a laugh. He smiled and pulled me against him. I relaxed in his embrace. Thin or not, hair or not, he was my Rafe. I would take him however he came.

"M—mine," he whispered.

"I'm yours," I breathed, then closed my eyes, letting him hold me.

CHAPTER 37

Rafe glared at me with a damning eye. I laughed as Rashel and another Healer worked with him, trying to get him on his feet. He could move his legs, but he was still too weak to walk under his own power. I smirked, enjoying the few moments he was at the mercy of others—a vast difference from the independent General I knew.

"Come here," he rasped.

I snickered, but obeyed, shaking my head. The Healer shrugged Rafe off. Though, instead of resting his weight over my shoulder, he lowered his arm to my waist. I had a moment of confusion and arched my brow. I couldn't support him like that.

Then he pinched me.

I yelped, darting away with shocked laughter. He fell on Rashel, and she cursed as he collapsed to his knees, still glaring.

'Even weak, he gets the better of you.' Tizmet snorted at the cave entrance. *'I would not let Flinor treat me so.'*

Her fascination with the green beast grew stronger with each passing day. I smiled, knowing she would mate soon. She would make a strong clutch of dragonlings.

'You worry about your mate.' I pushed back with a laugh.

Rafe arched a brow at me. I crossed my arms and gave him a challenging stare.

"Enough, you two!" Rashel rolled her eyes. "Would you take this seriously? Jenneth. Come help me." She jerked her head at the young Healer, who darted to Rafe's side and hauled him up.

"It was his fault."

"How very childish of you to pass the blame," she muttered as Rafe straightened.

I did my exercises as they worked with him. I strained, pushing myself faster through the moves, wondering if today would be the day I'd train without an attack.

"Avyanna, don't push yourself." Rashel warned me as they laid Rafe on the bed.

I panted as I swung the spear, slicing through the air. The thin braid swung in an arc. Spinning into a thrust, I shifted my feet. My pulse pumped a steady rhythm, and I pushed myself faster.

I was calm. My heart was strong.

Blocking an imaginary blow, I moved in an intricate dance. As I worked, a smile spread across my face. Exhilaration of fighting again surged through my veins.

Tizmet snarled. I spun to meet her fiery gaze when it hit.

Pain exploded in my chest. Pressure behind my breastbone pushed out, and I staggered to my knees. The spear clanged against the cave floor. My mouth opened, but I couldn't catch my breath. I threw my hands out to catch my weight, but the strain was too great. They gave out under me, and I collided with stone.

Tremors wracked my body. I heard voices and Tizmet's growls but couldn't process them. I clutched my chest, struggling to fill my lungs for what seemed an eternity.

The pressure snapped, and I gasped for breath. I came to—drenched in sweat and trembling. I was on my side, with Jenneth pinning my arms, and Rashel holding my legs. My head swam as if I'd pass out, and I sucked in lungfuls of air.

"Between the two of you," Rashel said between clenched teeth, "I need three assistants. You're worse than children!"

She released me, and I panted against the floor as Jenneth stood. Rafe was halfway off the mattress, holding himself up by his arms. His sharp glare berated me for my foolishness. He hadn't seen an attack yet, and I imagined the shock I'd feel if the roles were reversed.

My attempt at a reassuring smile shook on my lips. "I'm fine."

"Of course you are." Rashel guided me to my feet. "Jenneth, get that fool back on the bed. Honestly, General, what did you think you were going to do?"

We stumbled to the mattress, and I settled as Jenneth helped Rafe.

He rolled to his side and pulled me close, tucking my face against his neck. "What was that?" His voice was rough and low, barely audible, but clearer than days ago.

I wrapped my arms around him. "Nothing," I whispered.

He pushed me back and gave me a hard look—he didn't believe me.

"It comes with using magic." I gave a weak shrug.

"Is it because you healed me?"

"It's because I don't know what I'm doing. Magic is foreign and–"

He sighed and pulled me to him, crushing me against his thin frame. I smiled at the strength behind his embrace. He was still so weak, but he held me with such determination.

"You shouldn't have," he murmured.

"You shouldn't have gotten captured."

He made a noise of agreement and rested his cheek against my hair.

Rashel had us promise to stay in bed. I agreed, glancing at Rafe, who gave me a wicked smirk and nodded. She sighed and slapped a palm to her face. Muttering curses, she left with her assistant trailing behind.

After the attack, Tizmet ventured out to fly. She grew more restless and anxious by the day. I urged her on, knowing she craved the spring air—and reminded her that Flinor would be watching.

It was just me and Rafe.

He slid his touch down my ribcage to my hip. "Alone at last."

"Be good," I teased, then took his hand in mine to keep it from wandering further.

"I can be good." His voice dropped lower—emphasizing the promise.

As if I doubted it.

"Rafe, talk to me."

"I am."

His thumb traced small circles against my hip and I shivered at the heat pooling low in my belly.

"I refuse to do anything till you're back to normal." I met his gaze.

His touch stilled, and hurt flashed across his features. He turned away, as if to hide the emotion. "The beard needs to go, eh?"

I laughed, leaning enough to watch him, but kept my body pressed close. "The hair as well. It doesn't suit you."

My fingers trailed through the black, silver-streaked strands. I gave it a tug, which drew a low growl from his throat.

"I can do that."

"And you need to gain weight."

His eye found mine and twinkled with mirth. "You don't like your men skinny?"

"Not at all. I like them big and bulky."

"Fat?"

"Muscular." I snickered and slapped his shoulder.

The corner of his mouth curled up. "I've got work to do then."

"You do. I won't settle for a life mate, you know. One would have to prove himself."

I lost him again. His dark gaze settled along the tapestry. I frowned as he built up walls around himself, shutting me out.

"I want to be sure you're alright, Rafe," I murmured.

"Obviously, I have work to do." His tone was teasing, but pain lingered on his features.

"No, I need to know you're alright," I held his head, rubbing my thumb at his temple, "in here."

He shrugged off my touch. "I'm fine."

"Are you?" I bit my lip at the distance the motion created.

He slammed a fist into the blankets and put his back to me. It was the most he could do to deflect. Part of me mourned his confinement.

"You don't need to get inside my head, Vy."

"I just want to know you don't need help."

"Help like that Healer would have? She wants to know what they did to me so she can document it. Write it down like I'm some kind of experiment. You saw me, you know well enough what they did."

Silence hung thick and heavy between us as I gave him a moment to breathe, to collect himself. I pressed my chest against his back and leaned over him. His eye darted to the side, glancing at me before landing on the wall again.

"I remember a General who found a poisoned girl," I whispered. "He healed her, cared for her. And all the while, he took notes. You see, he studied poisons. Rashel studies bodies. She only wants to know what they did, so she can help others. Wasn't that what you were doing?"

He grunted a noncommittal response.

I smiled and settled against him. Pressing my forehead between his shoulder blades, I wrapped my arms around him.

"I'll tell her what they did to my body," he said at last, "but nothing else."

What more was there? Had they tortured his mind as well? I wished he shared it with me so he wouldn't have to suffer alone. The physical abuse he endured was more than anyone should have to bear.

"I'm here," I whispered against his back. If nothing else, he needed to know that.

He took a deep breath and held it. "I'm not normal, Vy. If that's what you want in a man, I'm not it."

Again, I let that comment hang between us. He was hurt—he needed to vent. I couldn't fathom what he'd gone through. It was important for me to be here for him when he voiced his vulnerabilities.

"General Rafe Shadowslayer."

I sat up and rolled him onto his back. He didn't fight me. I braced my arms on either side of him and stared into his eye. Letting him voice his insecurities was one thing, but I wouldn't sit here and let him believe them.

"I disobeyed direct orders. I left my home, my safety, for you." My palm rested over his heart, and I pressed a chaste kiss to his lips. "All I want is you, Rafe of Deomein—no one else. I want you when you're healthy, and when you're weak. I want *you*."

Heat burst through me. My eyes scrunched shut as pleasure coiled deep and hot. I gasped, jerking away from him.

Tizmet's emotions flooded over my own as roars filled the canyon. I gaped at the entrance as my cheeks burned. I shoved her emotions back over the bond and closed her off.

"Your dragon mating?"

My heart pounded in my ears as the sensation ebbed. "Aye"

"Lucky girl." He smirked.

Scoffing, I settled beside him. He wrapped his arm around me and held me close. He was hurting. I was aware that soldiers faced physical and mental challenges after enduring torture... but witnessing Rafe's struggle was heart-wrenching. He had always been so strong and sure. To see him so weak—it broke me.

My body flushed, and I squirmed against him, shoving Tizmet's passion from my mind.

I would support him. Each and every day, I'd help him find himself again. He was mine, and I was his. He would have me on my worst days and I would suffer him when he was bullheaded.

Smiling to myself, I rested.

Tizmet flew with Flinor, too busy to warn me. She had her priorities, and monitoring me was not among them at this time.

"At least you're comfortable."

The harsh words pulled me from my doze. I startled and sat up. Rafe's hand encircled my wrist, keeping me close.

Rashel glanced over her shoulder at the Dragon Lord, who rode Ge'org into our cave.

Tizmet wasn't going to be happy about that.

Ruveel slid from his saddle and eyed the space with disgust. His hair was tousled by the wind and his cheeks were flushed from flying. He settled his cold blue gaze on me as he closed in, and Rafe tightened his grip.

"I heard you'd arrive today." Rashel's voice was positively frigid. "Might I ask that you follow proper etiquette and send word before you storm into my den of healing?"

"Den of healing?" he mocked. "Between the dragons in the sky, and these two, one would wonder if that's all it was." He sneered as he stopped at the edge of our bed and crossed his arms. "It worked then?"

"It appears so." Rashel spoke slowly, as if he were simple.

"Praise the sun. Now, Avyanna of Gareth, I've a word to speak with you." His voice went flat and cold as he crouched beside me.

"Let's list your failures. One, you were the first to be given a second chance at First Chosen, and you failed. Two, you were the first female to join the ranks, and you failed. Three, you were the first Rider to be chosen by a Wild Dragon and join the Dragon Legion, and you failed."

I flinched with each damning sentence, biting my tongue. Each word felt like a slap across my face.

"You disobeyed direct orders from your superior. Your dragon ate human flesh—on multiple occasions." He pushed to his feet and loomed over me, rage rolling off him. "You abandoned your forces and struck out on your own without any leadership or military authority."

He reached into a small leather pouch and tossed a few coins at me. I turned my face away as they landed against my cheek and dress.

"That is your pay from your service to the King, with clothing and care deducted."

I snapped my gaze back to his and glared for all I was worth.

"From this moment forward, you are labeled an Oath Breaker, denouncing your rights as a citizen of this realm. You are hereby banished. By my grace, you have two days to collect your belongings and say your goodbyes—which is more time than I feel necessary. After which, Riders will escort you to the southern border."

Shock had me frozen in place.

"You are to leave Regent and never return. You have no friends, no allies here. Should you cross our borders, you will be treated as an enemy of the King."

He turned and walked around the bed, and my wide eyes fell on Rashel. Her lips were pressed together and her brow furrowed in anger.

I knew banishment was a possibility. However, pondering it and hearing the words were two different things. This was real. My world came crashing down.

"What did you learn?" Ruveel's voice softened as he spoke to Rafe.

The following silence was stifling as I stared at the far wall in horror. What just happened? What was I going to do? I had nothing. I *was* nothing. Banishment was a fraction softer than the death penalty. I blinked at the four gold coins.

They would last me a month—maybe two on my own with no friends, no supplies, no aid...

Shock muted my mind, no longer capable of processing the weight of his words.

"You come here," Rafe's tone was rough but strong, "and banish her—and you want to know what I've learned? You're a coward."

"Rafe, it was–"

"I don't care what it was." He coughed before pressing on. "You've signed her banishment?"

"Aye, you of all people should understand–"

"Prepare to sign my—my resignation papers as well, then."

Silence lapsed so deep you could hear the drip of water outside the cave.

"You can't be serious."

Rafe scoffed. "Dead. You wrote me off as *dead*."

Another pause, broken only by the roars of dragons outside.

"Considering I'm still General, and she's nothing to you," his breaths panted with exertion, "I'm going to ask that you leave a sick man to tend his wounds." When there was no movement, Rafe went on. "Wounds that were received after cleaning up *your* Rider's mistakes."

Angry footfalls came around the mattress as Ruveel marched to Ge'org, who bared his teeth. He mounted his dragon with far more grace than I would ever be capable of. Not sparing us a second glance, Ge'org's tail whipped above our heads, and he dove out of the cave.

Rashel stared. She opened her mouth as if to speak, but clamped it shut, then stormed out after him.

"Come here."

The hand about my wrist tugged, and I turned, my movements stiff and foreign. Rafe struggled to rise, and I frowned, laying beside him.

A quick breath of disbelief rushed from my lungs. "I've been banished."

I'd never heard of anyone being exiled. It was worse than death for some. I had Tizmet—that gave me an edge.

A pitiful edge.

"Rafe, I–"

I choked, trying to swallow past the lump in my throat.

"Hush. I know a woman who lived off dragon-caught meat," he winced, taking a slow breath, "and drank from moss to rescue someone. A woman who could rival me in foraging and get the upper-hand on Jamlin in a fight."

He leaned back and tucked his hand under my chin, lifting my gaze to his.

"You see, I think she can handle banishment. She's made of tougher stuff."

"I'll have to leave my friends—my family." Tears welled in my eyes. I was so sick of crying. "I'll have to leave you."

"Quiet." He wiped away a rogue tear. "By the sun, moon and stars, we're never separated for long. As for your friends, you can write them."

"Niehm would like that." I meant to laugh, but choked on a sob.

"Where's my fierce little kitten? Where are her claws?"

I cracked a small smile and wiped at my cheeks.

"You've tried to force your fate before," he said. "Now you need to follow it. Let it take you."

"I don't want to live in a future without you." I buried my head against his shoulder.

There was a pause before he took a shuddering breath and answered, "If you want me, I'll always be there."

I enjoyed my time alone with Rafe, realizing tomorrow would be my last full day with him. I gathered the four gold pieces and slipped them into my coin purse. It wasn't much, but it was something. With it, I'd survive for a bit outside Regent—on my own.

I hoped I might find a friendly village and make a living there. Doing what? I had no idea. Growing up in the dorms, I had experience with everything but mastered nothing. The idea of becoming a seamstress boiled my blood. My entire life, I dreamed of being important—making a difference. Avenging my father. Subtle pain lingered inside as I added that failure to the extensive list.

Tizmet returned, angry she smelled Ge'org. She felt something happen with me, but was too distracted to pull herself away. She spent the entire day with Flinor, and I tried to be happy that she would have a clutch.

But what did that mean? Did the young belong to Northwing or Regent?

'They will be mine,' Tizmet said in puzzlement as she settled in her corner, pleased but exhausted.

'Will you raise them without Flinor?'

'I would have raised them alone in the Sky Trees if I had them there.'

She flicked out her tongue and cleaned her ruddy claws. The dragons' mating dance was a beautiful, bloody affair. I perched on the edge of the mattress. Rafe tried to stay awake with me, but succumbed to sleep.

'Would you want to return? Raise them there?'

'No. It is too dangerous. My young have always been taken. I will settle where I settle. Stop worrying.' She stopped her cleaning and eyed me, her bright orange iris flashing. *'You will leave your mate?'*

My heart twisted as I gazed out at the dark canyon. *'I wouldn't, were it my choice.'*

'Then he will come with you?'

'He's too weak.'

I blinked at him. He couldn't keep up with a flying dragon. He had to bide his time. And probably fill out paperwork. *'He made it seem like he would find me, if it's possible, outside of the kingdom.'*

'What of your friends? Your family whose blood you share?'

'Letters will have to do. They can come visit.'

A twinge of despair tightened my chest. Visit where? I knew next to nothing of the world beyond Regent, only the limited information I'd gathered about the nomads who traveled the Sands. Could I integrate with them? Not likely.

'Sleep, little one,' she urged. *'A new day will work everything out.'*

I sighed and changed into my night shift. I rifled through my pack, noting the paltry few belongings for one being banished. A blanket, a few dresses, a pair of Mikhala's trousers, and a tunic.

I climbed back on the mattress as the ninth chime sounded. Rafe stirred, pulling me against him. I let him hold me and keep me safe.

Footsteps sounded on the path, bringing a groan from Rafe. He turned his head to the entrance and glared. "One night. One night alone," he growled, voice crackling.

"I heard that—and no." Rashel eyed us with exasperation, then sifted through some papers before she took her seat. "This chair is uncomfortable. If I could trust you two, I would gladly be in my bed right now."

"We're adults. Go." Rafe's tone lacked that note of command he had before.

"You are my patients. As such, I will monitor *all* your activities to be sure you do nothing... strenuous."

"What we do is our business." He tried again.

I pulled the blanket up to hide my smile. It was amusing, listening to him negotiate. The man, who was always in control of any situation, was haggling like a commoner.

And he said he wasn't normal.

"What you do at this time, General Rafe, is my business. Let's be transparent, shall we? You are in no condition to do anything more than cuddle dear Avyanna."

My shoulders rocked with silent laughter, and he pinched my side.

She continued, arching a brow at me, "And I'm sure, given your sentence, you will be in no position to carry a child."

"I couldn't anyway," I said, adding wood to the fire.

I wanted to keep them bickering. It was better than thinking about what the future held. The silence that followed made me rethink my words. I frowned, looking away from her gaze.

"Why would you say that?" She set her journal aside.

"I... well–"

My ears burned, and I curled into myself, embarrassed. This was something I didn't think I would have to discuss for a long time, and even then it would be just me and Rafe.

"Go on," he whispered, rubbing my arm.

"Avyanna, I'm a Healer. I could shed light on matters, clarify things, before they get out of hand." She glared at Rafe.

"Well, you see... since I have been off the tinge berry tea and that last incident."

Rafe stiffened behind me.

"You haven't had a moon cycle," Rashel finished for me.

"Aye."

She sat back in her chair and steepled her fingers, pressing them to her lips. "There are reasons Healers never offer that tea, barren wombs a prime example. This is your doing, Rafe."

I opened my mouth to object, but his voice rumbled before I could speak.

"Aye." That single word carried the weight of his remorse. "It's my doing."

My nose scrunched, and I tried to face him, but he held me tight.

She sighed, studying us. "You may have a moon cycle, Avyanna. Yet, you may not. As such, I would still advise abstinence till you are prepared to bring a child into this world. One never knows what the future may hold."

My happiness deflated.

She was right. I didn't know what my future held.

CHAPTER 38

My friends bombarded me the next morning. Elenor and Darrak stood in the back of the cave, watching with dismay as Niehm and Mikhala fired off their outrage.

At least they had something to bond over.

"I can't believe it! You saved a *General!*" Mikhala roared.

"They should commend her as a hero." Niehm threw her hands up, exasperated. "She led a rescue, for love of the sun! She helped pave the way for new methods of healing!"

"For that, I owe her," Rashel said, bustling inside.

Mikhala bounced on her heels. "Then make the Dragon Lord take it back!"

"No one can make him do anything." Rafe's voice was rough and quiet, but demanded attention.

Everyone turned his way as he pushed himself upright. Earlier, as guests arrived, he combed his unruly hair and changed his tunic. I smiled fondly at him. He wore a scowl like the old Rafe I knew.

"No one but the King," Darrak added from the back. He stood tall and brooding, with his arms crossed over his chest.

"Then file a petition," Niehm snapped.

He shrugged. "The King would have been the one to sign the banishment."

There was a slight pause before Mikhala lifted her chin, jaw set with determination. "Well, we have to stop this."

"There is no stopping it, Mik," Darrak said. "What's done is done."

Elenor's features conveyed her pain despite her even tone. "Avyanna made her choice, and now she has to deal with the consequences, however severe they might be."

There had been enough people yelling in outrage—I didn't need to add to it. I broke my silence. "I'd like to get word to my mother."

Niehm made a strangled noise and scrunched up her face. "You're just going to take this?"

I stared at my hands. All yesterday and last night I thought of it—trying to plot a way out. I came up with nothing. And if Rafe did, he hadn't bothered to share.

"No," I met her heated gaze, "I'm going to own it. I have no regrets. I did what I did, and cannot go back and change it." With a glance at Rafe, he mirrored my resolve. "I don't regret my decision. I disobeyed orders. The Dragon Lord cannot risk having people undermining him. That's what got Rafe in that situation."

He nodded his agreement, and Niehm sighed in defeat.

"I have to be made an example. No matter how noble my intention, even if I saved Ruveel himself, I would still have to face the consequences and be punished. Don't look at me like that, Mik. There's no way out of it. I've accepted it."

Niehm pointed an accusatory finger at Rafe. "And you're just going to let her?"

"I don't *let* her do anything," he said. "She is a woman. She makes her own choices."

Mikhala tilted her head, studying him. "So she saves your bony arse and now just... walks away?" she asked, as if she was genuinely baffled by the idea.

He gave her a bored look in answer.

"I'm going to ask that this meeting resume later." Rashel interrupted.

Tizmet chose that moment to return, huffing at the humans crowded inside her domain.

"I'll bring you stationary so you may write your mother," Niehm said as she squeezed past her.

Elenor gave me a sober nod before following.

"Mik, let's meet up later to say goodbye to Willhelm. One last race through the obstacle course?" I asked with a small smile.

"So you can remember the feeling of me beating you? Aye, I'll be around." She shook her head. Giving me a rueful smile, she left Darrak, who didn't budge.

Tizmet snorted and pushed inside, tasting the air as she walked past the bounty hunter. She sighed happily and settled into the corner.

'Will you be sad to leave Flinor?'

'He has served his purpose as a mate.' She seemed distant, preoccupied with her own thoughts.

My mouth twitched in mild amusement before settling on Darrak, who lingered.

"Leeds," he said.

I squinted in confusion. Leeds?

Rafe growled. "Where?"

"It's the best I have." He rubbed at his jaw. "Beyond the E'or, due north."

"No, she needs something south."

"There's nothing there," Darrak bit out. "Only sand and scorched earth. Her banishment is there for that reason."

"Begging your pardon," I interjected, glancing between them, "what are you going on about?"

Rafe's dark gaze flitted to Rashel, then back to me.

"I'm indebted to her." She held up her hands in defense. "I won't rattle off your secrets."

"Your word," Rafe demanded.

"Really?"

He glared, letting her know he wouldn't budge.

"Fine," she relented, "I give you my word as a Healer. It's the best you'll get."

He nodded once before turning his sharp eye on me. "You need a destination."

"That would be nice," I said, my voice dripping with lighthearted sarcasm.

Darrak dipped his chin. "Leeds is her best bet."

"North of E'or?" Rafe spat. "They're dumping her at the southern edge of the Sky Trees."

"Travel goes faster on dragonback."

"Dragon or no, it will take her over a month—two months to journey that far." Rafe clenched the blanket in his hands and ground his teeth.

"Leeds is a city?" I asked.

"Town at best." Darrak shrugged. "It's comfortable, quiet—the folks are kind. I know the law keeper. An honest man."

My heart pricked at the thought of actually making plans beyond tomorrow morning.

Rafe snarled. "No. Pick something closer."

"There *is* nothing closer!" Darrak raised his voice and took an angry step toward us. "I've crossed the borders more times than I care to recall. South is a wasteland and southeast is worse. The Teeth of E'or split and it's not friendly territory.

"The villages along the E'or range are rickety shambles. They couldn't support another soul without dragging them down. Leeds is the only sound option. Mind you, I'm not even recommending it." He directed his anger toward Rafe with a glare, blaming him for his current predicament.

"What about Gryphon?" Rafe asked through gritted teeth.

Darrak let out a bitter laugh, eyes dark. "She would be ensnared and tucked away in a dungeon. Nice people. Their King treats dragons and mages like a manageable plague."

"What's Gryphon?" I dared to ask.

"A kingdom southeast of here. You don't need to worry about it." Darrak hedged.

"Perhaps I'd like to try for it."

Rafe looked down at the blanket. "No."

"I should have a say in all this." With a scowl, my glare darted between them. "I'll go where I want."

It was true—I had the freedom to wander to any destination that called to me. However, I trusted these two. Darrak experienced the land and people beyond the borders. Rafe was older and wiser.

Rafe lifted his eye to mine, and I pressed my lips together. Anger and uncertainty swirled in his gaze. He was helpless in this and he hated it. The General I knew would never allow himself to be caught in this situation.

Yet, he had no control.

"I'll be fine." I patted his thigh, then turned to Darrak. "Tell me about Leeds."

Rafe grunted and clasped my hand. He gave it a painful squeeze, then tucked it around his back. I smiled and leaned into him.

Darrak told me everything he could. The lawkeeper, Rothfuss, ruled the town with an iron fist. He'd been a King's Marshal, dismissed from service after a falling out with the King himself. Darrak omitted the details of their dispute, but he trusted the man.

Leeds sat on a sunless bog, and a permanent fog blanketed the land. Located at a crossroads between the path to the E'or mountains and the rest of the swampland settlements. Most of the populace was peaceful, though they were on that side of E'or for a reason. He warned me to be cautious.

I tucked as much information into my mind as I could. Tizmet idly listened as she slept, reserving her energy for tomorrow. The idea of being exiled didn't upset her at all. She wasn't bound to these people—this kingdom. She was bound to me and therefore viewed the banishment as freedom. Still, she sensed my unease and anxiety, and tried to be considerate of my feelings.

Darrak left, and I organized my pack for the umpteenth time. Rafe watched with a dark eye and glared at Rashel. She took the hint and made an excuse about some business to attend to and set off.

"Come here."

With a sigh, I peered at him through my lashes and nestled into the bed. He wrapped his arms around me, and I burrowed against him. He might've been thin, sick and wounded, but in that moment I took strength from him. My breaths tightened, jagged and uneven, as I fought off my tears. I was bigger than that—better than that. I was banished, not dying. My eyes fluttered shut as I breathed in his scent.

I could handle this.

"I will come for you," he said. "You won't be alone."

"What of the Tennan?" My voice was muffled against his chest.

"They're not your Tennan. Don't worry about them."

"They were mine."

"They *are* your friends—not your responsibility." He lifted my chin to bring my face to his. "Start worrying about yourself."

"I don't want to leave you." I choked out as rebel tears swam in my eyes.

"If I could ride, I wouldn't let you," he murmured.

His lips met mine, firm, yet gentle. My fingers wound through his hair and held fast. I kissed him back, letting my need take over.

I shifted to his lap, and he growled in response. Something snapped inside me at the primal sound. Power flowed through me, knowing I could elicit such a response from him. He pulled me tight, moving my legs to straddle him. His lips grew rough and needy. He curled his fingers through my hair and tugged. I moaned and arched my back as he nibbled a spot under my ear, then left a blazing trail of hungry kisses down my neck.

"Oh dear!"

Something moved at the edge of my vision, and I gasped, throwing myself off him. Dareth's wide eyes bounced between us. Embarrassment set my cheeks aflame, and I cleared my throat.

"What?!" Rafe barked, his voice thick and husky.

His steady gaze stayed on me as he hauled me back into his lap. My teeth sank into my lip, but I didn't fight it.

"Well... I was just—perhaps later would be a better time." He spun on his heel, sending his blond hair flying, and took a step toward the path.

"You've already interrupted," Rafe bit out.

"If you'd like to resume," he stumbled over his words, "normally, one would close their tapestry."

"I'd like nothing more than to resume," Rafe snapped.

A thrill shivered up my spine hearing his old commanding ways come out.

"Yet, you're here for a reason," he continued. "Why?"

"Erm—I was sent to measure Tizmet." Dareth rubbed the nape of his neck, looking her way.

She slumbered on peacefully.

I frowned. "Measure her for what?"

"I'm not supposed to tell you." He flashed a bright smile. "It's a surprise."

"I'm afraid I haven't liked the past few surprises," I scoffed, but agreed with a nod.

"You'll rather enjoy this one, I should think."

He avoided our gaze as he neared Tizmet. He spoke in a low voice, and I felt her awareness grow, though she didn't deign to open her eyes. She stretched out from her curled position, rested her chin on her forelegs, and dozed.

Rafe glared as Dareth moved around Tizmet, muttering to himself. His hand crept up under the blanket and his thumb rubbed against my calf. I did my best to ignore the heat that flushed my cheeks.

"All is well." His gaze landed on us, and he glanced away, heading toward the mouth of the cave. "Should I close the tapestry?" he asked.

"Yes."

"No." I arched a brow at Rafe, then laughed and shook my head. "There's no need."

"Alright then. I'll be there to see you off tomorrow. Rest well." He marched down the path.

"No need?" Rafe grumbled.

I daresay it was almost a whine.

"No." I grabbed his beard and gave it a light tug. "You heard what Rashel said."

"Excuses."

My eyes darted to his lips, and I licked my own. I craved him, but I needed self-control. This wasn't the time or the place. He knew that as well—he just enjoyed pushing me.

As I wanted to push him.

I growled and tried to detangle myself from him, but he held me fast.

"Let go." I shoved at his chest.

"Why?"

"We can't do anything."

"Can't, or don't want to?" he asked, holding my knees in place.

I struggled against him. "Does it matter?"

"Aye, it does."

He stilled, then gripped my waist. I braced myself against him.

"If you say we can't, we certainly can. I don't give a flaming dungheap about what anyone else thinks." He cleared his throat, trying to ease some of the raspiness out. "If you don't want to, I won't push you."

My heart raced at what he offered. It wasn't hard to read what he wanted. Part of me wanted to give him the fraction of happiness we could have in this stolen moment. At the same time, I knew that I wasn't in a position to settle down and claim a life mate on the eve of my banishment.

And what if I came with child?

My lips pressed to his in a quick kiss, and he didn't push me for more. "I want you. You should know that." A smile tugged at my mouth. "But—this isn't the right time. It's not wise."

He grunted and smirked. "The roles have reversed. I used to be the wise one."

"You're blinded by desire," I teased.

"As you wish."

He chuckled, and my heart swelled at the sound as I slipped off his lap.

I settled against his shoulder and laughed. "You think it will take me a month to reach Leeds?" I asked, changing the subject.

His grin dropped into a vicious frown. "Two moons, if not longer. You don't know the way, and there won't be anyone to guide you."

"It will be an adventure."

"A perilous one." He glanced at the entrance, then back at me, his gaze dark. "Ruveel is all but offering you to the Shadows. Between them and the Sands, your chances of survival are slim."

"I'll make it."

"Has your dragon ever been to the Sands?"

"No. Other than here, she's lived in the west."

"She won't know how to survive there." He cursed and pinched the bridge of his nose. "She'll love the heat, but without knowing where to find and conserve water–"

I braced my palm on his cheek, guiding his gaze to meet mine. "I will make it to Leeds," I whispered.

"It will take me time to sort things out here."

As he searched my face, the torture in his expression broke my heart. What if I hadn't been able to go after him, knowing he was suffering? Anguish didn't come close to the helplessness I'd feel.

"How long?" I asked.

"Months."

"I'll wait for you."

"You'd better." He pulled me against him. "Don't go and find some young fool to run off with."

"When have I ever even looked twice at a man?!" I shrieked, grinning wide.

"I've caught you."

"When?!"

"Collins."

My smile faltered as I thought of his body among the rubble. "He was my friend." A good friend. One who died because I took too long.

"I know." Rafe sighed and stared at the blanket. "I'm just not–" He bit off and ground his teeth together.

"Not what?"

"I sometimes wonder what you want from me—and if I can give it."

"I want you. That's all."

"I'm old, Vy." He ran a hand through his dark, silver-flecked hair. "My past molded me a certain way. I'm not going to change."

Here he was, showing his vulnerabilities again.

"I'm counting on it. And you're not that old," I shot back.

"Older than you."

I laughed. "Why do you always bring that up?"

"Sometimes I think you forget."

My lips twisted into a scowl. "I want you, Rafe. I want *us*."

"Well, you're stuck with me then."

"Good."

We spent the afternoon together. I didn't want to leave him, but I didn't have a choice. He would come. This wouldn't be a forever goodbye, just a temporary parting. We would see each other again.

Rashel returned to do Rafe's exercises, and he shooed me off to go say my goodbyes. I made my way down the path, taking everything in. I would never witness the canyon's beauty again.

My frown deepened as I caught the judgmental looks from other Riders. Despite saving someone's life, I felt like the majority considered me an outcast, a rebel. I heaved a sigh and ignored them, making my way to the dorms.

With a disgusted glance, the guards granted me passage, and I searched for Mikhala. Walking through the hallways, I peeked into common rooms and up and down stairwells. I rounded a corner, and a boy slammed into me, his head bouncing off my belly. I stumbled a step as he flashed a quick, mischievous grin, then darted off. His laughter echoed down the barren halls.

"Ran, come back here!" An older woman bustled after him with a bar of soap and cloth in her hand. "Begging your pardon, miss. He refuses to bathe!" Her cheeks were flushed with exertion as she rushed after him.

A thrum of sorrow echoed in my heart. Ran was the boy who tipped the scale when I joined the ranks. He lost his whole family to a Shadow raid and witnessed the massacre. A sad smile crept over my face as I resumed my search. He obviously recuperated from his trauma. He was my reason for fighting. The thought of leaving him and all the people I vowed to protect weighed heavy on my soul.

What would my father have said? I was so young when he died, but I imagined he'd be horrified, as any father would. My mother might be more understanding, but a father? They would never forgive the man who caused their daughter's reputation to be sullied and, in turn, banished.

Good thing he wasn't here and could withhold his blessing from me and Rafe.

I deflated at that thought, shoulders crumpling in around me.

How selfish was I to think like that? So many children like Ran had no father. They would give anything to have their families back, and here I was, thankful mine wasn't here to disapprove of my choices.

"Well, you look as glum as can be expected."

Niehm's voice snapped me out of my worries. She had one hand on her hip, giving me a resigned stare.

"Just wrapped up in my head." I stood tall, shrugging off my thoughts. "Have you seen Mikhala?"

"She's in the barracks, challenging the men—waiting for you, I presume." Her steady gaze looked me over. "I'll walk with you."

She offered me the crook of her arm, and I chuckled as I linked mine through hers.

"I'll miss you," I said as we walked down the stairs.

"Write me. You're off to have such grand adventures. Tell me about them."

"I'm not sure they're going to be grand, but it will definitely be an adventure," I scoffed. "Trying to survive. 'Tis the stuff stories are made of."

"Only the best." Sorrow lined her small smile.

"You're not wearing your sword." I pointed out as we neared the barracks.

"No, I don't feel the need to defend a young woman any longer. I think she can protect herself."

"Not worried about yourself?" I asked as we passed through the gate.

Niehm was permitted as a Master, and I along with her. They let me through with glaring nods, likely knowing about my banishment tomorrow.

"Why would she be worried?" Darrak pushed off the wall behind us, coming to stand on my other side.

"We're looking for the madwoman," Niehm said shortly.

"Mik? She's challenging some Sergeant. Briggs, I believe."

"To what?" The idea of Mikhala facing the burly man was baffling.

"Hand-to-hand combat."

"Briggs is huge!"

His shoulder rolled in an unconcerned shrug. "You've seen Mik fight."

"Aye, but Briggs? The man is a beast."

"He doesn't fight like a girl, that's for certain."

Niehm scowled. "What's wrong with fighting like a woman?"

"Nothing," we replied in unison. I laughed and Darrak smiled.

"It just means she'll fight dirty. We women get our way," I added.

She nodded, smiling to herself. "That's true."

"Avyanna?"

With a smile on my face, I looked up at the familiar voice. That I'd be able to see him sent a rush of relief through my soul.

"Willhelm." I clamped my hands into fists to keep from grabbing him in a hug.

His shoulders were slumped as if a great weight settled on them. He limped as he approached, and I frowned at the leg he favored.

"What happened to your leg?"

"It's what I get for taking on two Shadows at once." He shrugged. His eyes danced over my face as his smile fell into a frown. "I've heard about tomorrow morning."

Niehm glared at the soldiers murmuring nearby. "I think everyone has."

"I'm sorry to hear it," Willhelm said, his voice gruff.

He wasn't the type to go against his superiors, even if he disagreed. He was a military man, destined to give orders and receive them. The army was his life. He was principled. He accepted and respected authority.

"I'm sorry to be banished, though not for my actions."

"A word?" He glanced at my companions.

They looked at each other before heading off. They spoke in low tones, with Niehm throwing him angry looks.

Willhelm found a bench and sighed as he took a seat. I sat beside him, idly watching the soldiers mill about.

"How is he?" he asked, rubbing at his wounded leg.

"Rough. It appears he's on the mend, but this has never been done before."

"I've heard. The Healers are eager to see the results."

"I won't be here to witness the outcome," I said bitterly, leaning on my elbows.

"If he's on the mend, you'll have to trust he'll continue that trend."

"Trust someone like Ruveel to watch over him?" I scoffed, rolling my eyes.

"He can hold his own against the Dragon Lord."

"But he's just a man," I said, frowning. "If I were here, I could–"

"You won't be." He interrupted in a gentle tone. "You will have to trust us to take care of him physically and that he is mentally able to care for himself."

My heart broke at the truth in his words. His arm stretched out along the back of the bench, and I leaned into it. He gave me a tight smile as he squeezed my shoulder before pulling away. It was as much of a hug as I'd get from him.

"I must be the laughingstock of the barracks," I grumbled, scanning the soldiers.

"Not at all," he replied. "That's what makes you dangerous."

"I don't understand."

"Every soldier wants two things—that their comrades would move the sun and moon for him, and that their Commander would not abandon them." He sighed and gazed out over the men. "General Rafe was written off as dead. In their eyes, he was abandoned—until someone had the guts to go rescue him."

He gave me a knowing smile. "You're dangerous because others want to follow your example. You've shown them that if you disobey, there's a chance you still might get what you want. That's the reason for your banishment. The King cannot execute a Rider, even for desertion. His subjects wouldn't look kindly on it, especially after you saved a General. A successful kingdom cannot have soldiers who do as they wish. You're dangerous because you inspire them to be more than just their orders."

My hands clasped tight in my lap. "I didn't mean to do any of that. I just wanted to save him."

"You followed your heart, not your orders."

"Had I, Rafe would be dead."

"He would."

"I don't regret it."

"I didn't think you would."

"Do you regret that I did?"

He took a deep breath and studied my face. Silence lapsed as he pondered the question. His eyes were warm and caring, as they always had been. Willhelm's honesty never led me astray.

"Pardon my asking, but have you committed to him?"

My eyes narrowed. "I don't see how that's related to the question."

"I cannot answer otherwise."

The man was a portrait of patience no matter how hard I pushed him.

I crossed my arms against the cold and my vulnerabilities. "Aye. We're committed."

"And will he let you go?"

"He can't stop it."

"Let me ask it this way. Will you have a future with him?"

I avoided his intense gaze and bit my lip. "We're going to try."

He hummed, and another silence lapsed. He was almost a father figure. If he didn't approve, it would crush me. Not that it would change anything, but I would be hurt.

"If you can carve out happiness someplace else, then maybe it will all be worth it." He took a breath, pausing as he formulated his next words. "I might disapprove of your actions, but I don't regret them."

A relieved smile tugged at the corners of my mouth, and I nudged my knee against his.

I would miss him.

CHAPTER 39

Parting with Willhelm, he settled for squeezing my shoulder, and tears welled in my eyes. I refused to let them fall and walked away before I blubbered like a fool. Even before I joined the ranks, when I helped the Masters in the barracks, he looked after me—offered me guidance and protection. He was my first friend, the one who made me feel accepted and understood. I would miss his stability and practical advice. His steadfast loyalty was a pillar of strength, always there when I needed it.

Mikhala beat me on our run through the obstacle course, as expected, but only by a margin. Sergeant Briggs had to call it. We laughed and sparred a bit, saying goodbye in our own way. She had a mischievous charm that was impossible to resist. Her fiery spirit and spontaneity would be missed.

I returned to my cave, where Rafe waited. He was finishing his exercises, and Rashel was completing her daily tests. I stared, lost in thought, wondering what the future truly held. We could make plans until we were blue in the face, but it would never be enough to control the outcome.

Destiny, fate—no matter the title—are fickle things. Despite anyone's best efforts, it forges the path when and how it wants. When I joined the ranks, I tried to force my way, change my future to one I thought I needed.

It seemed destiny wanted me to be a Rider, though not the kind everyone imagined. I had to relinquish control and allow fate to determine my course. Every choice made in life brings a consequence. Good acts with poor intention have repercussions that ripple and expand if not addressed.

I would accept my punishment and see where it took me. Still, a strong sense of desertion filled my being. Not just because I was parting ways with my loved ones, but because I swore an oath. I pledged my loyalty to this kingdom, promising to shield its people from the evils they encountered and to never abandon them in the face of those terrors. Until now, I stayed true to my word, protecting them, and that vow was now broken.

"I will watch over him."

Rashel's soft voice pulled me back to reality, and my focus sharpened on Rafe.

I glanced her way with a smile. "Your word as a Healer?"

"My word as a Healer."

Niehm brought me plenty of stationery to write my mother. I wrote and thought and stressed, struggling to find the right words for my concern and apologies. She had to *know* how much I loved and appreciated her, how happy I was that she found love again, and how I'd miss her sweets and her comfort.

I struggled with how to conclude it, not wanting to add a formal farewell. Saying goodbye to my mother forever, while still alive, was a heart-wrenching prospect. The sensation was akin to being locked away in the depths of a dungeon, my freedom withheld.

I ended the message by informing her I was headed to Leeds. I hoped against hope that someday she might brave the trek over the mountains, that I'd see her again before one of us passed beyond the Veil.

Niehm took my sealed letter and left me alone with Rafe once more.

As night fell, Tizmet lifted her head and bared her teeth in a silent hiss as Ge'org landed in the canyon. She resented him as much as I resented Ruveel. Thankfully, they both avoided our cave.

"Does the Dragon Lord see all the banished off?" I murmured against Rafe's chest.

"Generals see soldiers off. The King's Captain sees civilians off. It's only fitting that the flaming heap of Dragon dung would see you off."

"What will it be like?"

"Silent. Oppressive. Stifling." His voice was rough with emotion.

"Why?"

"Because we're sending the banished to their deaths. Few ever make it out there. It's worse than a beheading. More often than not, exile leads to a slow death by starvation."

"I have Tizmet. I won't starve."

"Agreed. In the south, you'll die of thirst before then. Have her dig deep in the old river beds. Fly at night and try to find blasted shade in the day." His voice cracked, and he cut off in a curse.

"What is it?" I asked, propping myself up.

"This whole situation is worse than emptying a chamber pot after spiced pottage was served."

I smiled at his new curse.

"You come and pull me free of–" A tremor moved through his jaw. He glared at the wall for a moment before returning his gaze to me. "I can't help you. I'm in no condition to go with you, and I cannot order anyone to go in my stead. This is worse than being helpless. This is *my* fault. I got you in this mess."

"You did nothing but help," I murmured, then pressed my palm to his cheek. "If you weren't there, the Shadows would have a dragon. Your actions saved countless lives."

Tizmet rumbled in agreement from her corner.

After a moment's pause he said, "Jamlin knows."

"Knows what?"

His gaze wandered to the entrance as if he expected someone to be standing there, listening. "What I can do." With a cruel twist of his lips, he corrected himself. "What I could do."

"He wouldn't tell anyone," I assured.

"I don't like people knowing things they can hold over me."

"Well, there's no proof anymore."

His eye was gone. They ripped it from his skull. I would never see that cold glint of silver again.

"You used it on the gold dragon... That's why they removed it?" I whispered as my thumb brushed the soft skin above his cheekbone.

"Aye. The Shaman killed the Rider and ensnared the beast, but I took over." Bitterness tainted his proud voice. "That's why they kept me alive. Why Collins was–" He cursed, gripping my leg under the blanket.

Pain skittered across his features, and I leaned in to kiss him. The weight of terror he survived was too heavy for me to lift. I couldn't heal the wounds inside his mind, but I could distract him.

And I would have—had Rashel not taken that moment to come in.

"This is why I can't leave you two," she muttered.

I giggled as Rafe groaned in mock anguish. I rolled to his side and settled with my head on his chest. Sighing, I lay there, watching the dim light of the setting sun fade throughout the Dragon Canyon for the last time. The impending banishment filled me with a sense of dread, knowing I would be torn away from everyone I loved. Still, there was a flicker of excitement building within, curious about what the future held. This would be a new chapter of my life. I had to make the most out of it.

There was no going back.

The next morning, I was awakened well before dawn.

Under the careful scrutiny of armed guards, I readied myself and grabbed my pack. Tizmet was alert and snarling when Ruveel entered my cave.

The cave.

It wasn't mine anymore.

"Avyanna of Gareth, do you have your belongings?"

"Yes." I stood as tall as my five paces would allow and lifted my chin. I would face this sentence with my head held high and refuse to show any defeat.

His eyes were cold and hooded as he questioned me. "Have you said your goodbyes to friends and family?"

"Yes."

He glanced around the room, ignoring Tizmet's anger, and nodded to himself. "It is my duty to see you off the grounds. You will then be escorted by a team of Riders to the southernmost border. Are you ready?"

"Stop."

Rafe's voice froze my heart. Seeing him struggle to get up from the mattress made a lump form in my throat. Rashel stepped to his side, supporting his weight as he retrieved my spear from its place against the wall.

"The banished are not supplied with weapons, General," Ruveel spat.

"Curb your tongue, you dog," Rafe growled.

He hobbled over with Rashel's assistance, handing it to me. I gazed at him with longing before my hand wrapped around it.

"It was bought by my own coin, a gift to her. The banished are not furnished with the army's weapons. Their personal belongings they may take, as stated under article four of banishment," Rafe rasped, breathing heavily.

"Thank you." I forced my voice to remain steady. My long white braid hung from the sheathed head. It swayed as I faced Ruveel. I met his glare with confidence.

He relented. "So be it."

I followed as he spun on his heel and marched down the path. The guards stepped in line behind me. Tizmet lashed her tail and stopped at the precipice. Riders idled on their ledges, watching as they led me off the grounds.

Rafe was right. It was silent and oppressive. Their judgment weighed heavy in the air, like a blanket, smothering all sound.

Tizmet sucked in a deep breath and released a deafening roar of defiance. It echoed off the stone walls. No one flinched as they watched with guarded eyes.

'They have not cowed us,' she said, then belted another roar before she took to the sky. *'They are freeing us.'*

She darted through the canyon, letting out a loud screech, a sound I never heard a dragon make.

'Let them watch as their protectors leave them. Let them judge and watch as we fly away to flourish in another land while they wither.'

'They are my people. I want no harm to come their way.'

Ruveel turned his head as Tizmet streaked past, but otherwise kept moving.

'Your people are abandoning you. They have accused you of having courage where they were cowards, and think to punish you for your bravery.'

'They are still mine. I swore to protect them.'

'They released you from that oath.' She made a second pass, her bright orange iris glinting as the sun peeked over the lip of the canyon. *'You are free to defend only yourself and those you wish.'*

The draft from her wings tugged at my cloak, and I frowned, but kept my head high. I shifted the pack on my shoulder and hefted my spear.

We made our way down, then Ruveel led me across the grounds. Those in the barracks were freed from their duties to view the banishment, perhaps to ward off any reckless ideas they might have. A mix of people gathered at the gate—civilians and soldiers, young and old. Some nodded and smiled, while others simply offered an answering look of determination.

I glanced at the deep woods to my right, remembering when I picked prickleberries for a grumpy General. My mouth quirked, recalling how he lashed out, throwing them all over the floor. He was a battered man, physically and mentally. Yet, he let me in. Somehow, I wormed my way under his guard and into his heart.

I cherished that memory.

The flap of wings drew my attention. Flinor slowly descended, landing near the gate, a man in his paw. Dareth rode him. His long blond hair whipped behind him like a banner. Rafe struggled to get his feet under himself, then leaned against Flinor's green scales.

A clap sounded from my right, breaking the silence, and I whipped my head to find the source. Another set of hands joined the first, echoing deeper into the multitude. Nobody searched for the rebels who dared to applaud me as I was banished from Regent. All eyes were on me.

It grew like a crescendo until Ruveel leveled the crowd with a fierce glare. Ge'org dove from the sky, letting out a fierce, silencing roar. The applause died out. He snarled and lashed his tail, towering over as Ruveel continued.

My friends gathered at the edge of the horde, pressed close to Flinor. Rafe was white under his dark beard, the exertion taking a toll on him. I slowed as I walked past. Niehm and Elenor pulled me into hugs. Mikhala gave me a bright smile and a wink as she gripped me tight, nearly crushing my ribs. Darrak offered a sober nod and slipped me a piece of parchment. I placed it in my pack and returned his gesture with a salute.

Willhelm stood near Rafe, ready to pick him up if he fell. I bit the inside of my cheek. His brown eyes glittered with resigned pride. He reached out to me, and I lost it. I threw my arms out, pulling him in for a hug. I wrapped him and squeezed. He stiffened in shock, but slowly melted into my embrace, gingerly hugging me back.

"You've been like a daughter to me," he mumbled into my hair. "Be safe."

I nodded and pulled away as tears trickled down my cheeks, blurring my vision. With my wrist, I wiped at them as I turned to Rafe.

He pushed his thin form off of Flinor and took halting but determined steps toward me. I lifted my chin as he towered over me. His dark hair had transformed him into another person, but I knew that eye.

He lowered, and my eyes fluttered closed as he closed the distance.

He kissed me.

Around us, the crowd erupted into whoops and cheers, and I tried to pull away, shocked.

He didn't let me.

He kissed me fiercely, letting his lips do the talking. I went limp in his embrace, his body crushing against mine. Gripping the nape of my neck, he threaded his fingers through my hair and crushed my body against his.

Breaking off the kiss, his dark eye simmered with unspoken promise. I sucked in a shuddering breath and blinked. My brain scrambled to make sense of everything that was happening.

Keeping me close, he placed his lips to my ear and whispered, "I will come for you."

I trembled against him, fear taking hold of my heart.

"Be a good girl," he muttered, stepping back.

He staggered. Willhelm looped his arm over his shoulder as the cheering and applause died down.

"I will." I choked out, then turned from him. There was nothing I could say to make this easier.

I took a step away from him as my heart ripped in two.

Tizmet landed outside the gate as Rashel approached. I blinked, clearing the haze of tears as I glanced at the cart behind her, pulled by Healers. In it lay a Rider's saddle.

"Avyanna of Gareth, you have shown us wonders. Through your efforts, we have learned more than we could have possibly hoped concerning the ways of magic and its application to Healing. As a token of our thanks, and a symbol of our debt, we wish to provide you a saddle for your dragon."

I looked between her and the two Healers in wide-eyed shock.

"Will you accept this gift, knowing that you may call on us at any time for aid?" she asked.

"Within your oaths." Ruveel's commanding voice bit out behind me.

"Within our oaths," Rashel repeated, leveling a glare at him.

"Well–" I looked up at Tizmet as she sniffed at crafted leather. *'I won't ask you to wear this.'*

'I will for you.' A hint of amusement lingered in her tone. *'We have a long flight ahead of us. It would be nice if you refrained from pulling on my scales the entire way.'*

"I thank the Healers for their gift, and accept," I said, clearing my throat.

Ruveel stayed back, but the two Riders, who were my escorts, came to help secure it. I never put a saddle on a dragon and had only a vague idea of how to fasten it properly.

They remained silent, judging me all the while with their eyes. I ignored them and took the aid they offered. I strapped down my spear and pack, then traced the Healer's sigil embossed into the light brown leather.

Conscious of the quiet crowd, I made my way onto Tizmet as gracefully as possible, slipping only once. As I secured my legs in the straps, I avoided looking at anyone.

Tizmet shifted under me, and I moved with her, reveling in the security a simple seat could provide.

My back straightened as Ruveel climbed onto Ge'org. My gaze wandered to my friends. Niehm clutched Elenor's arm as if it was the only thing keeping her up. Darrak and Willhelm stared on with grim determination, and Mikhala smirked with her arms folded over her chest. Rafe didn't look up. Instead, he glowered at Ruveel with an expression of pure hatred and vengeance.

"Avyanna of Gareth, you have proven yourself a danger to the good people of this land. You have broken your oath of protection and have instead endangered their lives. I remove you from the Kingdom of Regent as a blemish and stain on our history. You are never to return. If you dare cross our borders, you will be viewed as an enemy and treated as such. I hereby banish you from the realm of our good King, Vasili Aldred. Begone."

Ge'org threw himself skyward with a mighty roar, climbing high. My escorts both gestured for me to follow.

Looking down at my friends one last time, I gave them a confident nod, and Tizmet launched. She let loose a bellowing trumpet, and I gritted my teeth, trying to calm my stomach as it objected to the movement.

The Riders took to the air below us. The crowd erupted into cheers, and I smiled as tears streaked my cheeks. Up here, I could tell myself it was from the cold wind. Not because I was leaving everything behind.

Tizmet's wings worked hard to catch Ge'org, and the crowd's ovations faded. After a good distance, he pulled up and hovered. With a nod from the Dragon Lord, my escorts flanked Tizmet, and we pressed on.

Into the unknown.

I closed my eyes against the pain in my heart and settled my forehead against Tizmet's smooth scales, repeating Rafe's words in my head.

I will come for you.

ANOTHER CLIFFHANGER?!

What happens next? Find out in Fulfilling Fate, the thrilling conclusion to the Fate Unraveled Trilogy!

RAFE

The gray dragon launched skyward, carrying the slip of a woman who stole my heart. Rage swelled under my skin. Some foreign emotion crushed my chest as the beast let loose a defiant roar. The cry was so loud it shook the very earth beneath my feet.

Avyanna leaned forward as her dragon beat its wings, carrying them higher. The Riders serving as her escorts mounted with effortless skill. Their dragons inhaled sharply before throwing themselves into the air. They flanked Tizmet, heading south, being led by Ge'org.

I dipped my head and let loose a snarl of frustration as my knees gave out. Curse this weak, pain-ridden body.

Willhelm, Vy's barracks "friend", took my measly weight and helped me shuffle back to Flinor and Dareth. I glanced back up one last time—the dragons naught but specks in the sky. The crowd watched on in silence, none of them ready to move. They stood around and did nothing. I would not. My mind raced with all the tasks that needed my attention.

I made that woman a promise. And I kept my promises.

Eda, the mousy girl that helped me limp about, gasped at my curse. I bared my teeth as I struggled to get my legs to obey my commands. It wasn't even that crude. Vy wouldn't have batted an eye.

Regret squeezed my old heart like a dragon's claw. I took a step a little too forcefully and my feet didn't catch up with my momentum. My body pitched forward, and I grunted. Eda grabbed at my thin shoulders, trying in vain to keep me upright.

"Flaming son of a dungheap!"

I fell to my knees, bracing myself against the floor. At least the Healers' quarters had wood floors, not stone—or dung mixed with dirt like the Shadows.

"Slower, General," Rashel scolded.

"Is this not *slow* enough, you black-haired witch?!" I growled, angry at myself. Angry that I had to seek help to get on my feet.

"Take care with your words," she quipped. "Not all of us are as vulgar as you."

Eda's face was red, her temple beaded with sweat as she slid her hold under my shoulders, hauling me upright. Even her thin arms were stronger than mine. My knees smarted from the fall, and I knew the ache well enough to know I would be sporting more bruises tomorrow. I threw a one-eyed glare at Rashel—the bane of my existence.

She sighed from her rocking chair in the corner. "If you rush this, you won't get stronger—you'll get weaker."

My legs trembled as I stood, lending me no confidence in my balance. I was so weak.

I hated it.

"Give yourself grace," she said. "You went through too much."

I spun, teetering as I leveled another withering glare, which she promptly ignored.

Her bored attention refocused on her journal. "Your body simply needs time. You're pushing yourself too hard." She barely glanced up at the assistant. "Take him to the bed."

"No." I growled.

Still, Eda gently tugged me toward the sun-forsaken white mattress—my prison. My body was so weak. I despised it. It staggered behind her, resigned to rest as well.

"I don't have *time*." I snarled.

"You do, actually."

My legs gave out, muscles collapsing as I crumpled near the bedside. I attempted to catch my weight, but my arms were too weak. They couldn't stop my fall, only soften it.

Rashel jumped up as I crashed to the floor once more. Eda went to help, and I jerked away from her touch. I closed my eye, resting my head against the bedframe.

I *hated* this.

"She will be fine." Rashel's words were soft as she lifted me onto the bed.

My fists gripped the sheets as I flopped onto my side, giving them my back. Emotions roiled, and I fought them off. I tucked them away in a nice neat box in my mind, to be reviewed at a later time. I couldn't deal with them now—the regret and hurt. That nagging ache and worry over Vy's wellbeing... if she was even still alive.

Despite my best efforts, something tore through that little box, and a guttural scream shredded my throat. My fist slammed into my thigh.

I could take *pain*.

I could take *anger*.

Not this flaming weakness. I was as helpless as a babe in a man's body. Humiliated, damaged.

Rashel's voice was hushed as she dismissed her apprentice.

I was broken. Useless. I was a failure and always had been. I was a murderer. No good to anyone. Collins' face shot through my memory. I screamed, the sound tearing my throat even as I clenched the sheets in an attempt to ground myself.

It was no use.

I was suddenly back in that horrible, *horrible* shack.

Collins hung from the ceiling, strung up by his arms. His head lulled forward, taking what little rest he could. He'd been up there for days, his hands a sickly dark shade. My stomach turned at the sight of his flesh peeling away to reveal the bone beneath.

The pounding in my skull was relentless. My fingers throbbed around the nails driven into my palms. The sores on my back stung. I'd been laying in a soup of my piss, waste and blood for... Shadows knew how long.

What worried me the most was my left leg. It was the only part that didn't hurt. It was eerily numb. I definitely felt my right, and my foot ached where the thrice-blasted Shadows severed two of my toes.

How was I going to get Collins free and escape this dungheap of a village if I couldn't walk?

The dim light in the shack flared, and silent horror wound its way around my soul. Two Shadows entered, letting the door close behind them. The lantern glinted off the tools in their gloved hands. Dread awakened in my stomach, turning uneasily—regardless of the lack of sustenance.

The small blades and leather straps had me grinding my weak jaw and glancing at Collins. The young man's eyes fluttered, but lack of food and water, combined with torture and exhaustion, left him lethargic. He groggily caught my notice, and his blue gaze flew open in panic. I glared past my pain.

He could do this.

I could do this.

I would help him get through this. He was my soldier, and I was his General. I would stare him down, let him know I was here for him. I would give him what strength I had.

Cool, gloved hands grasped my head in a gentle but firm grip. My heart raced, realizing those straps were for me. Those blades were for me. I crushed my panic. My fingers twitched as a Shaman leaned over me. The dragon mask concealing his face grinned, teeth shining and white. Silver eyes met mine, daring me to look away. His eerie voice said something in a fast language. It ended with an inflection, as if he asked a question.

"Drink piss," I rasped.

Honestly, I wasn't sure if my words were clear or even audible. The next thing I knew, they fastened the strap across my forehead, pinning it in place. Another Shadow handed the Shaman a knife. My whole body trembled in uncontrolled terror as he brought it to my left eye. I bit down on my tongue so hard that blood filled my mouth, threatening to drown me.

The last thing I saw with that eye was the glint of metal as the blade pressed down.

I surfaced from the memory in a daze. The weight of lethargy turned my limbs into solid iron. My body felt like I had gone days without sleep and couldn't hold my eyes open for another single breath.

Rashel leaned over, tucking the white sheet around me. A weak moan escaped my lips. I should be awake. Training. Exercising. Eating. *Anything*.

She turned to me with a pitiful smile and held up a bottle, upending it on her finger. My brain screamed at me to stop her, to get up and move, but my body was just too tired.

"Sleep, General."

She wiped the oil over my top lip, and the sickly sweet scent overpowered my mind. I drifted into a blissful, dreamless sleep.

Swinging my two shortswords against Jamlin, I pushed myself harder. The man spun, and I cursed myself as I overextended and he slapped me with the flat of his blade. I stumbled and tripped over who knows what—probably my own feet.

"Flaming blast of a dragon's arse!" Colorful curses tumbled out as I regained my balance. I gasped for air like a blasted fish out of water and held my swords up, ready to block.

"No," I said, seeing his expression. "Again."

Jamlin's lips formed a hard line, and he dropped the point of his blade.

"Flames take your mother!" I launched myself at him.

The man simply stepped aside, and I staggered with my momentum. I pulled up short, managing to soften the blow when I ran into the training hall wall.

"Rafe, I–"

"Again!" I roared, charging him.

Jamlin barely got his sword raised in time to block my weak strikes. The worst part was the way he made me feel insignificant, like my efforts were futile. I was no threat. I snarled like a dog, letting loose of my sword in a throw.

Stupid? Yes.

Jam dodged, but not fast enough. The weapon nicked his shoulder, drawing the tiniest bit of blood as it clattered to the dirt.

I *would* get better.

And I *would* find Vy.

My stallion snorted and pranced beneath me, his eagerness evident as we trotted through the war camp. Tents and banners swayed in the light breeze. Smoke drifted on the wind, bringing the scent of roasted dark wing flesh. The soldiers would eat well tonight.

"Rafe, my man!"

I craned to the left, searching the gathered crowd with my good eye.

My only eye.

A small smile lifted the corner of my mouth. Petty few could draw a grin from me, but that hulking form and clear gaze could any day.

"Teak," I called. "What, did Agatha get sick of you?" I arched a brow at the dark bruise marring his cheekbone.

"Nah, she practically worshiped me."

"Don't let her hear that!" Someone jested from deep in the crowd.

He approached my horse and gave me a brotherly slap on the thigh. "Took a Shaman down and earned this for my troubles."

"Didn't take Egoth?" My smile dropped into a frown.

"Would I let a Shaman near a dragon?" He laughed. "You must have hit your pretty head harder than I've heard."

My cheek twitched at the thought. Rashel kept a tight leash on her apprentice, as well as any help she called for. It was unlikely that any rumors or tales came from her mouth, or that of her direct staff.

But a screaming, raging General was hard to hide.

"Rafe? Man?"

I rolled my shoulder, and the movement forced my mind into the present. Looking down at Teak, I offered a stiff nod. His blue eyes reflected my pain. He clenched his jaw and returned the gesture.

"Good to see you, mate," he said.

He stepped back from my stallion, and I spurred the beast on, keeping my head up. I rode through the sprawling camp as soldiers drifted about. There were less of them, most would be on the front, further west.

I ground my teeth together as I headed for Faulkin's tent. In order to be released from my oath, I needed to see him first. He had sent for me, refusing to answer my correspondence like the prick he was, and instead requested that I be present for his review.

The sun peeked from behind the drifting clouds, bringing its hot rays on the sweltering camp. The place was full of familiar scenes and faces. I knew the paths like the back of my hand. It was more my home than my cursed little village in the south had ever been.

My glare cut over the tents, wondering why it didn't *feel* like home.

"You're jesting."

"Do I jest, Rafe?"

I choked in disbelief, staring General Faulkin down. "Do I look like one to take a joke?"

It wasn't possible. There was no feasible way this man would stand between me and my freedom.

He leaned over the map splayed on the table and tapped his old, wrinkled finger against the wood. He shifted a dragon figurine to a new location. "You took an oath," he droned.

My shock gave way to anger. I always knew he was a cruel bastard, but this was unacceptable. "Life oaths can be pardoned." I snarled.

"Daring to teach me the law, boy?" He peered from under his bushy white eyebrows.

I stepped forward, gripping the pommel of my longsword. "I'll teach you—"

A cold, wind-chilled hand gripped mine, squeezing painfully. I growled, whirling on Ruveel, who stood beside me.

"Ah, let them, Ru! It would be fun!" Teak called from behind.

Annoyance flashed over Ruveel's features as he strode over to the table. "He's proven himself unstable in the past. I wouldn't put it beyond him now."

"Regardless of your instability, Rafe, you're valuable. We need you." Faulkin's tone was dry enough that even a child would know he lied.

"I have given my life to this war. I'm *done,* Faulkin."

"Your *life?*" Ruveel snorted. "Don't be so dramatic. We've all made sacrifices."

He moved the small dragon figurine and placed it further east. Faulkin looked up at him with his brow raised in interest.

"Fleet three needs a rest," he said, then picked up another, moving it further southwest.

My lip curled. "You haven't made the sacrifices I have."

Faulkin served longer, but he was the strategist. He rarely, in his many years of service, ever fought on the front.

"Oh, and leaving a love behind. Yes, that's something completely foreign to every soldier." Faulkin sighed, straightening and leveling his icy blue gaze on me. "We've all heard the tales. The great General Rafe and his lowly soldier. To be frank, it's disgusting that you would take advantage of a girl like—"

Red colored my vision and I lunged, avoiding Teak as he leapt to grab my arm. That dodge cost me, however. Faulkin ducked below my swing, and Ruveel caught my fist. My body shook with fractious rage, even as Teak chuckled.

Faulkin made a sound of disgust and walked around me to the other side of the table, studying the black skeletons that represented the Shadows.

"Regardless of your *sacrifices*, Rafe. I deny your request. Clearly," he nodded to my fist, still in Ruveel's hand, "you can fight. Your claim to be unfit for battle is pathetic."

I jerked back, glaring at Teak. The man stood with his hands in his pockets, shrugging with a sheepish grin.

"Without all our voices in unison, your oath still stands," Ruveel stated.

Blood boiled in my veins. "I'll petition Aldred. The King can override you."

"And you think he will?" Faulkin scoffed. "Trusting the word of a weak, love-addled General over all of us?"

"You'll regret this."

"Perhaps." He pointed to the row of Shadow markers across the map. "We need a way to get them to converge. As Ruveel said, we are too spread out. They need to focus on one area. That's where you come in."

I sat on my horse, stomach turning in pure disgust.

"And we just keep riding?" Jam asked in disbelief.

I didn't grace him with a response. This was the stupidest, most childlike idea Faulkin ever had. It was petty, and it was going to get me and my men killed.

And they said *I* was reckless.

"They've never had one get away," Zeph murmured from somewhere behind.

They never made an *effort* to retrieve men lost to the Shadows. I wrestled with the rage that swelled in my chest, grinding my teeth against the growl that built in my throat.

My lip lifted in a silent snarl at the idea of a *rescue,* but it was accurate. Avyanna did not rescue me, so I could march behind enemy lines again and get myself killed.

Who would come after me this time?

No one, that's who.

I would die. Jam would die. Zeph would die, proving his father right for once. Xzanth would join his wife and daughters beyond the Veil. Blain and Dane might make it out. I knew in my soul I was still underestimating the twins. Tegan would die with a smile, daring to laugh in the face of death itself.

I gave my *word*.

I will come for you.

Anger burrowed deep in my bones, and I spurred my stallion faster. Best to get this over with quickly. They wouldn't take me again—I wouldn't let them.

"Now?" Tegan called.

I kicked my heels into my stallion's sides, and he launched into a gallop through the thick underbrush of the Sky Trees. As we flew into a small clearing, I let my rage burst out in a battle cry. Drawing my shortswords, I heard the first shocked calls of alarm.

This village didn't stand a chance.

The rest of the army took their time catching up, letting a few of the Shadows slip past them. Something sick twisted in my gut as Xzanth aimed at a Shadow bearing a mask of dark wing bones.

"Hold!"

That sick feeling festered, wrapping itself around my heart. Teak jogged up to Xzanth, blood splattering his face and tunic. He flashed Zan a smile, then shook his head. The man lowered his bow, glancing at me for verification. I shifted my eye to Teak, the General who had been my closest brother, who grew up alongside me on the warfront.

Pity consumed his expression as he met my stare. "We all have to play the game, Rafe."

I wheeled my stallion from the scene, fighting the nausea that turned my stomach.

This wasn't a game.

I wasn't a pawn.

"General, a letter."

I squashed the hope that bloomed in my chest, stuffing that thrice-cursed emotion in a cage and locking it away. I glared at the messenger, then at the desk.

He bit his lip—the pathetic sap practically shaking in his boots. He ran inside, threw it on the table, then rushed for the exit.

The letter flitted to the dirt floor. I lifted my gaze back to the boy, who grimaced. I threw my arm over the back of the chair, waiting for him to act again. With a gulp, he took the few steps into my tent and picked up the sealed parchment, then laid it on the corner of my desk, trying in vain to keep out of my reach.

He thought I would beat him for his insolence.

Good.

I grunted my approval, then returned my attention to the reports that cluttered the desktop.

"Good day, sir!" He snapped a salute that I ignored, then ran out of the tent, the oiled flap settling behind him.

I eyed the wax seal, and dreaded hope flared, turning my stomach. I swallowed against the bile that snuck up my throat and placed the letter on top of a battle report. So much depended on the words inside. Scoffing at my hesitation—I ripped the seal, scanning the lines in a quick pass.

My eye froze on the King's signature at the bottom. Familiar and comfortable rage surfaced, and a low growl rolled out. I jerked upright, kicking the chair back. The paper crumpled in my fist as I stomped to the stove. Throwing the pathetic scrap of parchment into the flames, I aimed a vicious curse at the King.

I stormed into the sheets of rain. Teak sat on a stump just outside. My lip lifted in disgust as he flashed me a look of pity. Water dripped off his chin as he stood, his clear eyes saying far more than words ever could.

"I'm in need of a sparring partner," he offered roughly.

My anger shuddered through me. The King's dismissal set me off. I craved bloodshed. Giving him a jerk of a nod, I stalked past, heading for the sparring grounds.

"It's working." Ruveel rested his palms on the war table, nodding at the figurines on the map.

It was late autumn. The stove in the tent's corner did little to ward off the cold. I tipped my chair back with my arms crossed over my chest. The damp chill soaked through my trousers and nipped at my skin.

My rage kept me warm.

"Someday, you will learn to listen," Faulkin said with a quiet chuckle. "They are sore over the one that got away. Let them waste their Hunters and troops trying to get him. If we bottle them up, we will thin them out enough to advance in the spring."

"The Fleets have less than a month before I call them back."

"Give me three weeks." Faulkin argued.

"A fortnight is the most I'll offer."

"The dragonlings can handle a week more."

"Telling me how to use my Fleets?" Ruveel laughed, then rested his hip against the table.

I glared at Faulkin. "Seems to have no quarrel with ordering my men about."

"Come now, Rafe. It's working though. You're grand bait," Teak jeered. "Can't say you're a pretty catch, but they're after you, anyway."

Faulkin sneered. "I don't know what that girl ever saw in you."

Avyanna.

Her name was Avyanna.

I leaned forward, slamming the legs of the chair against the hard, packed earth.

"Come now," he puffed out his chest, "what girl has a chance against a ruling General? She obviously sought promotion. There's nothing else for a simple girl like—"

"Article eleven," I spat, then stretched to my full height. I stalked over, crowding him.

He stood his ground, refusing to back up, and I pressed my chest against his. He wasn't shorter than me by much, but it was enough for me to glare down my nose at him.

"We abide by article eleven. What are you getting at?" Ruveel asked.

"I daresay Faulkin is due to see the frontlines."

Teak pushed out a dramatic sigh. "You know he's exempt."

Coward.

"He's not exempt."

A cruel smile spread over my face, watching his anger grow. Ah, yes. There he was. The weak old man hiding behind his status.

His neck reddened. "We made a joint decision."

"I changed my mind."

"Rafe, this is below you." Teak groaned.

Ruveel blew out a hiss. "I won't let you—"

"Oh, but won't you? It's no longer a unanimous decision. Much like signing my release papers."

Ruveel stepped forward. "Faulkin, send a petition to Aldred—"

"You think he'll pardon you, old man?" I scoffed, and my spittle sprayed his face. "If you're too weak to give your men a fighting show, perhaps you belong back in the homelands with the widows and babes."

His cheek twitched, but he refused to wipe the spit away. With his jaw set in a firm line, he grimaced. "I can still lead men better than you ever could, *General*."

Pathetic little man.

"Prove it. Give the lads a good show." Bitterness poisoned my words. "Tomorrow we're heading to the Dread Fall. Your plan, *General*, is a decent one—unless you don't trust your strategy, or can't hold a sword beyond that between your legs. We all know how old age affects *that.*"

"You shame yourself and your men." He seethed. "I would honor mine by leading the charge."

"Lead?" Teak didn't hide his nerves. "Faulkin, really–"

"How bold of you," I droned. "I should be *honored* to have you by my side." Sarcasm dripped from my words.

Faulkin made a sound of disgust and turned back to the table, brushing his shoulder against my chest. I smiled wickedly as he resumed studying the map, drawing his finger along the valley called the Dread Fall.

Yes, I think tomorrow's charge would go well.

Very well.

"What are you doing, General?!" Anger and disbelief filled Faulkin's voice.

With skillful precision, I guided my sword to loop through his reins, drawing them into my grasp. I hauled him along as my stallion sped into a gallop.

His plan was to have the bait—me and my Tennan—charge the center, luring the enemy down the steep cliffs. The rest of the army would press in, surrounding the forces they brought our way. The Dragon Fleets would split, offering cover-fire, and separate the Shadows from their men in the valley.

His horse let out a screaming whinny as my stallion dragged it along. Faulkin himself gripped the mane. "Release us!"

I rode on, studying the landscape. When we were in the middle of the expanse, I dropped the reins and his beast shied away.

He scrambled for purchase. "Curse you, Rafe! You'll pay for this!"

A smile spread over my face.

I was counting on it.

My stallion whirled to the side, eye on the walls of the steep ravine as my Tennan followed me with some of Faulkin's company. I caught Blain's gaze as I examined the undergrowth. His eyes were wide and his mouth hung open in a gaping smile. I paused, taking a moment to raise an eyebrow in challenge. He shook his head and let out a bark of laughter.

High-pitched shrieks assaulted my ears, and I jerked on the reins, wheeling my stallion to face the closest Shadow as they descended. I urged my horse to Faulkin as he fumbled to draw his sword. Throwing myself, I tackled him to the ground before he completed the act. The old man grunted as I crashed into him. Not at all sorry I gained most of my weight back since my torture.

His horse screamed, backing up and tossing its head, uneasy. My stallion spun and charged the way it came. Like a well-trained steed.

Faulkin's darted straight at a Shadow, who reached the bottom of the valley. Two patchwork Hunters flanked him, a mess of claws and teeth, covered in thick, black, matted fur.

A hysterical laugh bubbled up as bloodlust took me. The Shadow wore a bony mask of a human skull.

Perfect.

I hauled Faulkin's head up by his white hair, craning it back so he could watch the Hunter eviscerate his horse at the Shadow's side.

The second creature made a garbled noise that might have been an attempt at a growl, then moved to flank us.

A gleeful chuckle slipped out. I was unable to contain my amusement. Jerking to my feet, I hauled him up. I pressed a knife to the old man's throat and pulled him tight against my chest as the sounds of fighting rang out. He struggled against my hold, but his small stature was no match for the bulk I put on these past months.

The Hunter snarled behind me, and I shook my head with a grin. I had been through enough of these missions as bait to know that the Shadows saw my men as disposable, but they wanted me alive.

A shiver ran up my spine. I didn't think too long about why that was.

The Shadow spoke in its quick, high-pitched language, saying something to me or its beasts, I wasn't sure.

Not like I cared.

Faulkin fumbled for his sword, trying to turn away from the Shadow, whose bright human skull was almost illuminated against its darkened face. I gripped Faulkin's hair and forced him to stay put.

"Watch, *General*." Cruelty wound through my chest. "Isn't this what you wanted?! For me to face them, to fight this close. To be bait, draw them out. You want me to brave their gaze, be a pawn in your games."

He whimpered, and I pressed close to his ear.

"*Join me*," I whispered.

Faulkin scrunched his eyes shut. The din of battle drifted further away as I focused on the older General.

My breathless laugh sounded manic and sour as I kept him between me and the advancing enemy. "Don't you want to know how it feels to have your will stripped bare? To be a puppet in your own body?"

I grappled, reaching over his face for his eyes as he fought against me, shouting his rage. I managed to find his eyelid and pried it open. His blue eye danced in panic.

He looked at the Shadow.

A horrible joy spread through my heart as he froze, gaze locked. A twang of the bowstring was the breath of warning before an arrow sprouted from the Shadow's neck.

I whipped to the side, glaring at Xzanth as he panted. Horror filled his glare. The man's black and silver hair danced around his face. He nocked another arrow, and drew in a flash, leveling it at me.

Offering him a terrible smile, I released Faulkin as the screams finally reached my ears. The General stumbled, drawing his sword in a fluid movement. He spun, blade trembling in the remnants of fear.

I turned my grin on him.

"You are hereby detained until review!" he shouted, eyes darting behind me where I was sure another Shadow or Hunter loomed.

"You there!" He whirled on Xzanth, pointing his sword. "If he risks another soldier, kill him!"

As if he could.

The chain between the frigid iron cuffs on my wrists was taut, pulling my shoulders back at a painful angle. The set around my ankles wasn't much better.

I'd been through worse.

"–you weren't there." Faulkin's tone was dreadfully serious, his cold gaze drifting to me.

I smirked, letting my eyelid droop.

"I'm telling you, he didn't mean it." Teak tried again. "He has an explanation. Right, Rafe?"

"You weren't there." Ruveel echoed, then studied me as he leaned his hip against the table. His glare darkened. "I saw him hold Faulkin."

Faulkin touched the fragile skin torn near his eyelid. "He bared my eye."

Aye, I had done that. And would again in a heartbeat.

He continued, "If he were any other soldier, he would be executed—beheaded without trial."

"He's not just another soldier." Ruveel sighed, pinching the bridge of his nose.

Teak paced, rubbing his scalp through his cropped hair. "He did it out of spite. You all are a bunch of daft old women." He gestured between the two. "You've been using him as bait. What did you expect?"

"Obedience."

"He's not a *soldier*." Teak's voice pitched higher. "He's a General."

"Not anymore." Faulkin growled. "I move that we place him in the stocks."

I grinned at the old man. His words were music to my ears.

Teak groaned and rubbed his face furiously.

Ruveel frowned, shaking his head. "The soldiers look up to him. He's the 'One who Survived' in their eyes."

"Well, he was about to be the 'One That got a General Killed.'" Faulkin grunted. "We can't allow the soldiers to believe they can pull such stunts."

"Honestly, Faulkin." Teak sighed. "How petty do you think our men are? Not a single one of them would have the gall to pull a stunt like that."

"Gall has nothing to do with it. That was insanity," Ruveel whispered.

There it is. Finally, the Shadow-bred dungheaps understood.

Teak turned to me, and I met his puzzled gaze, arching an eyebrow in silent question.

Come on brother, speak for me.

"Mad. His mind is—he's been under considerable stress." Teak's words were hesitant. He didn't want to say such things. He studied me, brows pulled low over his clear eyes. "There's only so much pain a man can go through before he snaps."

"We throw the maddened in the stocks," Faulkin snapped.

"Not Rafe," Teak shot back. "Send him to the homelands. Let him stay at the palace over the respite. If Aldred deems him mad, then he'll dispose of him as he sees fit."

Faulkin slapped his thigh, finally taking his gaze off me for the first time since they dragged me into the blasted tent.

"Will that always be your course of action, Teak? Rafe messes up—oh send him home for a rest."

Teak bristled, ready to speak, but Ruveel beat him to it.

"I agree," he muttered.

Skepticism lined Faulkin's brow. "Pardon?"

Ruveel's steady glare tracked my every breath. "If he's truly mad, King Aldred will keep him tucked out of sight from those loyal to him. If they can't see him, they'll forget about him." He prowled toward me, crouching to my level. "He'll rot in a dark cell, dying a lonely, forgotten death."

The cocky grin fell from my face. So be it.

"Is this really necessary?" Vasili Aldred, King of Regent, sighed.

The guards fumbled my weight between them, dragging me into the throne room, then dropped me to the floor.

"Apparently, I'm a threat to the kingdom," I grumbled, giving him a bored look.

"So I have heard."

The King rubbed his temple for a moment before holding his hand out. A scribe placed a parchment in his waiting palm, and stepped back, granting the illusion that this was simply a conversation between two men.

"This is quite damning, General."

"You denied my resignation."

"You swore a life oath to Regent and her King."

"And the debt's been paid. I've given the War of Shadows my best years. I'll never get those back." My tone stayed calm, steady. I couldn't risk my anger seeping through. Not yet. "I've sacrificed everything for this kingdom—for *you.*"

"Yet, here you kneel."

I ground my teeth together.

"You're not mad." Aldred laughed, then flicked his wrist at the guards. "Unchain him." He reclined, watching me with hooded eyes. "You, General Rafe, are a cunning man. Reckless? Yes. Insane? Some might think so, yet in this report—General Faulkin escaped relatively unscathed... something I doubt he would have managed if you had any other intent."

As he spoke, the guards pulled at the bands about my sore wrists and ankles. The physical pain was nothing compared to the ache building in my heart.

He went on. "After your little trick, you then proceeded to fight the Shadows, per normal. You wouldn't let your actions risk the lives of your men or the soldiers."

Still? Was this *still* not enough?! Worry worked through my chest, and I shoved it away.

"No, I don't believe you're mad." Aldred hummed as a servant brought him a plate laden with apples, sliced into neat rows. "I believe you've played your hand and are where you want to be. Off the frontlines." He gestured to the sweet fruit. "Apples?"

"You're not going to pardon me." I deadpanned.

"Rafe Shadowslayer," he sighed, "you are the one person who has survived trials at the hands of the Shadows. Do not think that I'm ignorant of the role you have played in our recent series of victories. You draw them to you like moths to a flame. You are special, unique—you know this."

I knew of another who was special and unique.

His voice lowered, forming each syllable with care. "I would not willingly part with you for anything."

Yet, he threw her away like a used rag.

"As King, I will do everything in my power to keep Regent safe. Shadows are pressing in, my army falters—and you want me to let one of my Generals go?" He rubbed at his temple. "I cannot. I know you, Shadowslayer. You understand my need."

As if I didn't have needs.

"Please, eat. Rest."

I grunted and pushed myself to my feet, shedding the chains that clanked as they struck the stone floor. Rolling my shoulders, I shook off the soreness.

"They didn't offer me first meal."

Aldred laughed. "I would think not."

He took the plate from the servant, extending it to me. He had known me for too long—and was far too trusting. My steps were small and sure as I approached.

He lowered it so I could grasp an apple. I snatched the plate and threw it as hard as I could manage. It slammed into his face with a satisfying crunch.

The King screamed. Blood ran like a river from his broken nose. The servant and scribe scrambled away in horror, one gasping with a hand clasped over their mouth. Guards shouted and rushed me. Their firm grips yanked me down the stairs.

"I've given you my *LIFE!*" I roared. "You won't use me anymore! I am not a pawn to be placed about on a map!"

I raged as more guards hauled me back, fumbling with the iron cuffs. Buying myself time, I struggled against them.

"You could have kept her here!"

"The girl?! Ruveel's banished?!" Aldred shouted, pressing a cloth to his nose. He leaned low on his throne, his gold crown glinting in the light. "Regent is *no* place for a Wild Rider."

My lips spread in a snarl as I yelled through bared teeth. The guards secured the bands about my ankles and yanked the chain painfully tight.

"Take him to the dungeon!"

MORE COOL THINGS!

Scan the QR code for more details concerning merch, signed copies and even a top-secret, super-secret, not-so-secret club with bonus content!

The Password is: Prickleberry.

THANK YOU

An author is nothing without a reader.

My first thanks is to my readers. You. I wouldn't have made it this far without you. You are the best—truly.

I would be amiss if I didn't thank Jessie, the one who started me on this path. Ali, who saw me through the middle hump I never want to get over. And Nick, the one who pushed me to the finish line.

The Fate Unraveled Trilogy would still be naught but manuscripts if not for Sarah Emmer, who paved the road for me or Erynn Snell who took the time to edit this behemoth. You both have been a godsend.

There are countless others I owe my gratitude to. I cannot begin to express my thanks and appreciation for all the other Indie Authors out there who have helped me along the way. Thank you.

M.A. FRICK

M.A. Frick is a mere peasant.

Once upon a time, she read to escape the world. Now she writes to create worlds.

Not only the mother of worlds, but the mother of three children—she is joined by her husband who supports every adventure, no matter how absurd it may be.

Made in the USA
Monee, IL
05 May 2025

16816129R00215